Camberwell Beauty is the latest addition to the phenomenally successful career of Jenny Eclair, described by the *Daily Mirror* as 'the wildest and wickedest comedian in Britain'. A regular at The Edinburgh Festival, she scooped the prestigious Perrier Award in 1995 for her show *Prozac and Tantrums*, later released as a top ten selling video.

As well as her continuing stand-up success, Jenny has co-written with Julie Balloo the successful Radio 4 comedy series *On Baby Street* and *Just Juliette*. They have written several plays, including *The Inconvenience* and *Mrs Nosey Parker*.

Jenny was the first female to guest edit men's magazine *Loaded*, she made her West End debut in Nell Dunn's *Steaming*, and garnered a string of television credits such as *Pick 'N' Mix*, *Jenny Eclair Squats*, *Edinburgh or Bust*, and *Jenny Eclair's Private Function*.

Camberwell Beauty

A novel by
Jenny Eclair

A *Warner* Book

First published in Great Britain in 2000
by Little, Brown and Company

This edition published in 2001 by Warner Books

Every effort has been made to trace the copyright holders
and to clear reprint permissions for the following songs:
'I Should Be So Lucky'
'Maggie May'
'It's My Party'
If notified, the publisher will be pleased to rectify
any omission in future editions

All characters in this publication are fictitious and any resemblance to real persons, living or dead, is purely coincidental.

A CIP catalogue record for this book
is available from the British Library.

ISBN 0 7515 3099 9

Typeset by Palimpsest Book Production Limited, Polmont, Stirlingshire
Printed and bound in Great Britain by
Clays Ltd, St Ives plc

Warner
A Division of
Little, Brown and Company (UK)
Brettenham House
Lancaster Place
London WC2E 7EN

www.littlebrown.co.uk

For Geof and Phoebe
(the porky pigs)

Thanks to Little, Brown, Julie Balloo, Richard Allen-Turner,
my iMac and the people of Camberwell – cheers.

1

Hello

Welcome to South London, to one of the nicest streets in one of the country's vilest boroughs: Lark Grove, SE5. A determined middle-class oasis of skips and bay trees, where Volvos sniff each other's bumpers, and men called Giles live with women called Samantha. This is a satellite-dish-free zone of tall houses with big front doors, standing shoulder to shoulder, five floors apiece. Come inside, shut the door and smell the coffee. You could almost be in Kensington.

This is where the actors, writers and media-types live, where small children wearing smart uniforms and shoes in the shape of light bulbs get ferried every day to schools that are not local. Round here, ten-year-olds never get to ride their bikes beyond the front gate and nannies carry cans of Mace.

In these houses people laugh, cry, eat, argue, sleep, fret, toss, turn, masturbate, penetrate, yawn and fart.

You can do your shopping here: there is a supermarket round the corner where they sell dented tins of vegetables in syrup and corned beef in brine. But up the hill and half a mile away or so, there is a nice Sainsbury's with a deli counter full of fat herbed olives, cheeses that smell of the Queen's sick, hams as pink as babies' clove-studded buttocks and, of course, shelves and shelves of buttery yellow chardonnay: £3.99 a bottle. Here the carpark is full of mummies' second cars, nippy little hatchbacks: Polos, Pintos and Puntos, with biscuits on the dashboard and dollies on the back seat.

Lark Grove is bang slap between an art school, where young people wander up the steps with bits of birdcage in their hair and cardboard portfolios beneath their arms, and one of London's largest mental hospitals, where inmates jabber and weave baskets that they wear on their heads. Spot the difference if you will.

This is a colourful area, full of girls with dyed purple fringes and savage dogs on strings, where junkies fall down and the drunks trip over them and nobody raises a pierced eyebrow. Here, there is vomit on the pavements, syringes in the gutter and graffiti all over. This is where someone once went to the effort of writing 'Sophie Dahl eats too much Dhal' in six-foot orange paint letters on someone else's wall, and a man bit the head off a pigeon and no one knew whether to call the hospital or Charles Saatchi. Here live the mad, the bad, the arty and the ordinary. You can get a very nice house in these parts for a fraction of what it would cost somewhere else. The architecture is chipped but good, and there are blue plaques littered about where famous music hall comics once lived, drank, ran out of jokes and committed suicide.

At the bottom of Lark Grove, big red buses trundle north towards Piccadilly Circus and John Lewis and then back the other way to deepest South London, where angels, mortals and pit bull terriers fear to tread. After all, not everybody can live in Islington, and at least round here you can park your car – albeit with the crook lock on and the radio removed.

People end up here for all sorts of reasons, even posh types who put holly wreaths on their doors at Christmas and scoop the poop from their pathways. There are just enough of them to have formed their own small tribe, a last bastion of well-educated, flute-playing, council-tax-paying, pasta-eating people, braving it out amongst the great unwashed, the Spam eaters and estate dwellers, with their bad breath and cataracts. Professional people like Anna and Chris and Nigel and Jo, successful middle-class types with everything going for them: jobs, kids, cars, holidays, tennis-rackets, tumble-driers, shoes for every occasion, and no reason to weep or gnash or seethe or spoil it.

Imagine a day when the weather is glorious, and you take a picnic out to the countryside and somehow find a warm (but shady) spot overlooking a lake and lay your tartan rug on grass (that is not damp) and eat sandwiches (that have not gone soggy) and delicious chicken legs – marinated, grilled and crispy – and the lemonade is cold and all is calm and the water is still. Why is it that someone has to come along and chuck a big rock in the lake so that everyone gets splashed, and the sun goes behind a cloud and the day is ruined?

Don't trouble trouble till trouble troubles you.

Some people live accident-free lives: they do not fall into stinging nettles, birds don't shit on their heads, blood clots dissolve in their veins and wasps leave them alone. Others court disaster, ripping new trousers on rusty nails, slicing their fingers on sharp knives, biting into the salmonella sausage and banging their heads wherever they go. Life can be one long banana skin, so look before you leap and for heaven's sake remember: a stitch in time saves nine.

Some people are luckier than others: they have nicer lives with more things. But luck can run out and whose fault is that? Fate has a fickle finger, and when you're least expecting it, she can poke you in the eye.

It was an accident . . . was it really?

Nah nee nah nee nah nee – see, even the sirens sound sarcastic.

2

Introducing Anna Cunningham, née Redfern

July 1999

I really mustn't have a drink; it's not even elevenses. I never used to drink that much but recently I like to be pissed most of the time. I never used to drink spirits but I'll drink anything now. These days I look at nail-varnish remover and I get thirsty.

The other morning I quite fancied watching *Kilroy*, something about 'When Habits Become Unhealthy' – ha – but I just lay on the sofa. Listen, I could see the remote control – I didn't even have to search for it, it was on top of the telly – but I just couldn't be arsed to get up and fetch it. I just lay there till the street lamps came on, eating brandy-snaps, drinking warm lager and remembering what my life used to be like.

Let's go back, shall we? Let's start a long time ago, not right at the beginning, that was forty-one years ago when life was a simple matter of reflexes: hungry, cold, wet, smelly, waagh waagh. We'll begin before the Pink House, before the children, before Christopher, years before. Let's start when I was a little girl . . .

Once upon a time, when I was a little girl, I lived with my mother and father, Sylvia and Brian Redfern, in a very modern house in an oxymoronishly nice part of Birmingham. My name is Anna. I am a born-and-bred Midlander but let me make it quite clear I never had the accent.

My dad had the house designed at great expense, and against even greater judgement: all concrete and glass and built on one level, which I believe was all the rage back then. It had underground central heating, which because of all the glass had to be on all the time. Consequently the windows got steamed up and I'd play noughts and crosses by myself in the condensation. I remember we had a den – people did – just a small room with pine and brick walls and big black-and-white photos of things like 'Pebbles on a Beach'. My mother would sit in the den and play Joan Baez records; my father, on the other hand, had never got over Elvis Presley.

It's all come back into fashion now: long leather sofas, sheepskin rugs, beanbags and girls are wearing halter-necked tops and blue eyeshadow again.

My parents were glamorous I suppose; well, as glamorous as you could be living in Solihull in the seventies. We even had a pop star over the road: that bloke from Slade, the one with the fringe cut too short and sticky out teeth. I used to go round to his house and get his autograph, trace it and sell copies in the playground. Once when I rang the doorbell, he answered with a tin of furniture polish and a duster in his hand, but on the stairs behind him was a platform shoe (female) and a shrivelled pair of tights.

I went to an all-girls school. That's why I ended up boy-mad – apart from my dad I didn't know any! I didn't even have any cousins. I didn't know you were allowed to have boys as friends.

My dad earned a lot of money, back in the days when ten grand a year meant something. He imported Scandinavian furniture; I suppose that's why we had so many peculiar chairs and why I'm so good at mid-twentieth-century design. I can spot an Eames in a skip at a hundred paces, you know.

Every morning when my father had gone to work, my mother went to the bottom of the garden and sat in a shed, which she called her 'studio', and made silver and enamel jewellery, which she sold to women's boutiques. She had long, brown, thin fingers, nimble and precise; I remember she was terribly good at getting knots out of fine, silver chains. When she worked in her 'studio', she wore a navy denim artist's smock and tied her hair up with a Liberty silk scarf. She was terribly elegant, even her feet were lovely. I suppose that's why, when it came to fucking other women, my dad always chose fat blondes with big tits that jiggled when they giggled. My mother wasn't very jiggly or giggly. She wasn't very mumsy either. I had friends at school with mumsy mums: dumpy middle-aged women with bad perms and wide bums in slacks. When you went round to their houses you'd get sliced white toast with tinned baked beans and shop-made cakes. At our house you got gherkins. My mother had North European taste buds; she was a fiend for the smörgåsbord, so we ate Knackerbrot and pumpernickel, Emmenthal and salami. Sylvia didn't believe in chips. I think she was the first person in Solihull to own a fondue set. I remember once we had reindeer meat; rather chewy, as I recall.

They argued a lot, my parents. See, that's the trouble with open-plan houses, you can hear every ashtray that gets hurled at the wall. According to my mother, my father, was 'a drunken sot, full of promises but even fuller of shit', whilst Mum, according to Dad, was 'a tight-arsed, frigid bitch who wouldn't know a good time if it came up and bit her on the bum'. Bang, smash, 'Shh, you'll wake Anna.' But I was already awake, making Lego houses that had staircases, separate floors and doors you could close. Some days my mother wore sunglasses even though it was raining, and once my dad had to go to casualty to have his lip stitched up.

In the summer of '73, my dad had a pink convertible Thunderbird imported from America, but my mother crashed it trying to get it into the garage, which was a stupid thing to do because it was obviously too big.

'Are you completely retarded, woman, or are you just blind?'

Sylvia was on Valium; they used to dole it out like candy in the seventies. There was nothing really wrong with her, she was just 'emotionally fragile' the doctor said. Brian went on a lot of business trips; he was always away, usually in Denmark or Sweden. He was terribly unfaithful, you could almost smell it on him: air hostesses, secretaries, customers; he was a difficult man to resist, with a lot of personality and the money to match. Even when he got older and his sideboards began to look ridiculous, he was a 'lady's man'. It never bothered me, it was something I'd grown up with: Dad's midnight fumblings with the front-door key, 'Sorry I'm late, Sylvia,' and my mother's poisonous response, 'Been playing with your little girlfriend, Brian? Been shagging Treacle, have we?'

These rows would escalate like milk boiling over in a pan. 'You're a laughing stock, Brian, they're laughing at you behind your back.'

'You're a vicious woman, Sylvia, you've got no heart. Is it any wonder I have to go elsewhere for comfort? You've never loved me, you're not capable.'

And they'd be up all night: Dad drinking brandy out of a balloon-shaped glass, Mum smoking long, white menthol cigarettes, her face slippery with Ponds cold cream.

'You're so transparent, Brian, it's so obvious, it's embarrassing. Christ knows why I put up with it.'

'Ditto, cow.'

'Bastard.'

'Bitch.'

Sometimes I'd wake up in the morning and find Dad lying under his big leather coat on the sheepskin rug in front of the fire. My mother would seem revitalised after a fight and would be humming round the breakfast bar making cinnamon toast. 'Dried apricot anyone?'

Other people's relationships are a rule unto themselves. Personally I didn't really blame my father. My mother, despite her social prowess, her charming 'mine hostess trolley' façade, was rather humourless; she found most people and most things vulgar and common, and she was the kind of woman who would never eat a melon without using a knife and fork. On the other hand Dad, despite having a melancholy side, was the life and soul of the party, always the first to arrive and the last to leave, and when he ate melons he ended up with sticky ears. My father liked to do things with gusto: he drank too much, ate too much and farted long and hard. He is dead, my dad. He died overexerting his arteries whilst deflowering a chambermaid in a hotel in Aberdeen.

My mother might have curled up and died of shame but she didn't. She married a Swiss banker and lives in a cuckoo-clock chalet overlooking the shores of Lake Geneva and is, by all accounts, quite happy.

So this is where I lived and how I lived until I became an adult, met my husband, married him and had two children.

Last night I dreamt we were together again and it was all like it used to be. Everything was back to normal, we were all in the Pink House and even Nibbles was still alive.

3

Introducing Josephine Alexandra Metcalf

Anna used to make me feel so hockey-stickish; whenever I was with her I could feel my tights laddering. It was pointless sitting next to her, she was so lovely. By contrast I'd feel fatter and sweatier and as sexy as tapioca: imagine how Elton John must feel when he is sitting next to Elizabeth Hurley – that's how it was with me and Anna Cunningham. Even on the days when I felt good about myself, I would bump into Anna and feel like a laundry-basket on legs. There have always been 'Annas' in my life; I remember girls at school who had the same casual air of superiority, girls whose blazer buttons didn't dangle, girls who knew how to pluck their eyebrows properly and looked fantastic smoking.

Some women are better than others at being female; they wear delicate jewellery and can do things with their hair. I have always been the type to wear a man's watch and I have never in all my years managed to buy a handbag that matched my shoes.

I am not a glamorous woman, I am not exotic, but I am intelligent and I have always been capable. Maybe it's something to do with being tall, maybe it's because I am the daughter of an army officer, or maybe it's because, by comparison, there are so many fools about.

I somehow felt like Anna's big sister, which is silly really because in actual fact she is older than me; in the past you would never have believed that but these days it shows. It's weird the way that women fall apart; she is unravelling like a woollen jumper. I can't believe I was ever jealous of her, she has changed so much. Sometimes I have to think hard to remember her as she was.

Grey-eyed, black-lashed Anna: the only woman over thirty who could get away with wearing a bikini. Dark-skinned Anna, with her ruby-red toenails and tattooed left shoulder blade that she would accidentally-on-purpose show off in company. Beautiful Anna, a modern-day Mona Lisa – smiling or smirking? Lucky Anna, wife and mother, smelling of Penhaligon's Bluebell, sat cross-legged on the floor, bare brown feet in size four suede pumps the colour of butterscotch. Jesus, it just goes to show how fragile it all is . . . that happiness thing.

She must be ten and a half stone now. Okay, I know it's the pot calling the kettle stuff, but she's only about five four and she's got small bones. I'm eleven stone but I'm five ten and I've always been chunky – you can't expect a woman with a size nine shoe to be petite. I am one of those blondes who looks useful on a playing field: beefy of shoulder, powerful of rump. I would have made a wonderful cut of meat. When I was younger, I would have killed to be like Anna. It's always been rather an effort being me, having to make up for not being cute or sexy, for always dropping things and being the type of woman destined to walk with one foot in the gutter because the heel has broken off my shoe again. I realised when I was a teenager that I was in a 'like-it-or-lump-it' situation, so I set about developing a personality. If you are almost six foot and big-boned you don't have much option; you cannot be convincing wearing Angora sweaters and being kittenish, so I became a 'good sport' and I have been ever since. Up until now. Now my patience is as thin as the flesh on a supermodel's backside. I am at breaking point.

I just wish she'd snap out of it. I can't have her lolloping around on my sofa all day, just eating and crying and leaving balls of snotty toilet paper around the place. She's driving Nigel mad. It's not that I don't have any sympathy, I do, but at the risk of sounding like some third-rate therapist, 'You've got to move on.'

I said to her yesterday, 'Come on, Anna, why don't you get dressed? It's a beautiful day, you could go for a walk.' Meaning, 'Will you please get up off your backside and go and get some milk!' She didn't get it, of course; she spends most of her time pretending to be deaf. Basically she does sod-all, won't lift a finger to help, can't put a cereal bowl into the dishwasher; not because she's physically incapable – if she'd had a stroke I might feel a bit more sympathetic – it's just that she won't.

The only thing she does do with any enthusiasm is drink. She's just drinking herself into oblivion. Now I don't mind the occasional drink, but these days I know my limits, I've cut down. I try to stick to the guidelines they suggest in those pamphlets that you pick up from the doctor's, you know the ones, Solvent Abuse Amongst Teenagers – Spotting The Signs, Meningitis – The Facts. I am a mother, it is my job to be vigilant. I reckon three units a day is sensible. Anyway, I've got enough problems with flyaway hair and the beginnings of a double chin without having to contend with a great big boozer's nose.

You don't realise how dull pissed people are till you have to deal with them when you're sober. Anna slurs and repeats herself and starts hiccuping, and truly I'm not mean (I sponsor a little poor kiddie from Africa – as if two of my own weren't enough), but it annoys me when she opens really good bottles of red – you know, £8 jobbies – and spills most of it on the carpet. And if I find one more half-eaten sandwich on the stairs, I promise I'll swing for the bitch.

Shhh, listen to me. I'm not always so nasty, but I have a slight hormonal imbalance and my period is due. My breasts are lumpy, my knickers feel tight and no, oil of bleeding evening primrose doesn't help.

When she first told me everything, my jaw dropped to dislocation point and I literally dribbled. But when she tells it for the umpteenth time and you know the ending, which is basically her, off her face, wallowing in self-pity, dripping fag ash all over my Conran velvet sofa, well it makes me want to scream. It's the way she blames everyone else apart from herself, like she had nothing to do with it! Mind you, it's taught me a few lessons, one of them being that a friend in need is a right pain in the arse.

I wish all this had happened to someone else. I don't want to be involved any more. I want things to go back to how they used to be; I want things to be normal again. I am so bloody tired, sometimes I wish I had never met her, that she'd never moved into the Pink House. But it's too late now. As my mother would say, 'if wishes were wishes then pigs would fly'.

4

Stair Rods and Broken Buddhas

1989

If walls could talk, eh?

Every house has its secrets, so what a relief then that they can't tell tales; that they can't open blabbery mouths and spill beans all over the place like gossip lava. The 'Pink House', so called because it has been pink for as long as anyone can remember, used to belong to a titled lady, who went doolally tap and beat her companion with an ivory cane.

'Myrtle, you're a useless piece of old shit.'

This is not nice language from anyone's lips but when it is hissed by a wispy-haired octogenarian weighing a mere six and a half stone, it sounds more shocking than normal.

'Did you hear what I said, cloth-ears?'

'Yes, Lady Edwina.'

Lady Edwina used to live in the Pink House with her husband, the celebrated game hunter and poker whiz, Sir Elliot Morgan, until he shook to death, all yellow with malaria, and left her alone, mad with grief and box upon box of handmade lingerie. They'd had a son, but he'd died in the Second World War – and what use is a son with his head blown off?

Lady Edwina advertised in *The Lady* for a companion: 'has to be good at cards', she specified, and Myrtle arrived on the doorstep, with only the slightest whiff of the Elephant and Castle about her but otherwise ever so clean.

Myrtle handled Edwina for a good number of years, diligently cutting crusts off cucumber sandwiches and forgoing tea-bags for sink-clogging Assam leaves. She was good with bad-tempered types, having been married to a publican whose face would regularly turn navy blue with rage. Myrtle hadn't got any children because Tommy had once punched her that hard he'd ruptured her bits and pieces and that was that. Myrtle hand-washed Edwina's fancy pants and buttoned her little kid gloves when they went for an occasional stroll and generally put up with all her silly nonsense.

'That Queen Mother, Myrtle, she's a bitch, never returns my calls. I tell you, if I ever come face-to-face with her, I'll scratch her eyes out, fat-arsed cow.'

Myrtle called out the doctor on a number of occasions but Lady Edwina wouldn't see him, 'the nigger houseboy'.

Lady Edwina started cheating at cards; if Myrtle said anything she would get a whack on her head with the cane. 'If I don't keep my trap shut, I'll end up with brain damage and be as nutty as her,' she thought, and obediently played by whatever rules Lady Edwina decided to invent.

'Today we shall play by the Grand Duke of Marmoris rules: threes are sixes until I say "torpedo" and then they become Jacks. Have you got that, you stinky old dunderhead?'

'Yes, dear.'

It could have been worse; Lady Edwina kept her continence right to the end, and she was always very well turned out, with a faceful of Max Factor, complete with pencilled-on eyebrows (she'd lost her original pair in a shaving craze back in the twenties) and a slash of vivid orange lipstick, 'tangerine dream'.

'No wonder your husband pegged out early, Myrtle, you're a boot-faced old trout.'

'Yes, dear – ow!'

Edwina took to hitting Myrtle on the ankles, until she had to resort to elasticated bandages and thick hiking socks.

That last winter, when Lady Edwina got a bad cough that went to her chest, Myrtle decided not to call the doctor. It wasn't as if she was putting a pillow over Edwina's face. At night she had to plug her ears with cotton wool so that she couldn't hear the old lady hawking and raving in the next room. She'd been quite impossible for months now, keeping cheese under the bed because of the Russians, refusing to have her nails filed until they had grown sharp and yellow and left jagged scratches down Myrtle's face. 'I'm a tiger, Myrtle, and I'm going to tear all the flesh off your horrid old bones, you plip plop.' She hid in cupboards and behind doors and giggled when Myrtle tripped over the things she'd left on the stairs. Myrtle was rather near-sighted; one day she fell a full flight and her ladyship laughed until a little bit of wee dribbled into the gusset of her silk camis.

'You're a bad girl, Edwina, I'm going to have to give you a smack.'

That was the last straw really, the fight on the landing: Lady

Edwina clawing Myrtle's face, snatching at her bun, Myrtle stamping on her ladyship's little feet and boxing her ears. In the end they were fencing with brass stair rods and the china Buddha on the windowsill was decapitated in the process.

She didn't last much longer, didn't Edwina; she was never the same after the fight, then she got the cough that turned into pneumonia and then she died. The day that Myrtle found Edwina slightly stiff beneath the counterpane (she didn't hold with duvets, didn't Lady Edwina) she simply pulled the sheet over her friend's head and went downstairs for a cup of hot chocolate before phoning the doctor.

There was a post-mortem because her ladyship had died at home, but it was decided that natural causes were to blame, and as for the broken arm, well little old ladies are forever knocking their brittle little limbs. Whoops, snap.

Lady Edwina left a will. Myrtle got the big mahogany cabinet, all inlaid with mother-of-pearl giraffes and a donkey sanctuary got the rest.

It was spiteful really. Lady Edwina knew that Myrtle was frightened of the cabinet, and neither of them could abide donkeys for that matter, but when the nice man came from Peckham to value it, he offered her five hundred pounds on the spot – cash. Myrtle accepted his very kind offer, went straight to the nearest travel agent and booked herself a two week all-in holiday at a posh hotel in Grand Canary. When she got back, she moved into a nice little sheltered accommodation unit just off the Borough High Street and regularly thrashed all the other old dears at gin rummy.

Several months later, had you happened to glance upon a Sotheby's auction catalogue, you'd have seen the giraffe cabinet with its reserve price of fifteen thousand pounds.

You win some, you lose some.

The Pink House was on the market, 'A superb specimen of late Georgian architecture. Beautifully proportioned five-bedroom house in need of some modernisation. Large mature garden, off-street parking, early viewing recommended. 5 bds, 2 bthrms, ktchn, diner, dble living rm, many orig feats'.

People view houses for all sorts of reasons. Some have no intention of buying, they are just being nosy; occasionally people will thieve small items – an ornament, a silver spoon, maybe a little clock – from behind the estate agent's back. Happens all the time.

Three weeks after the 'For Sale' board went up outside the Pink House, it was sold. A couple called the Cunninghams bought it, pipping a BBC Radio 1 producer to the post.

'Congratulations Mr and Mrs Cunningham, I hope you'll be very happy here.'

'Bet they won't,' whispered the walls, but no one heard.

5

Monkey Keanu and Baked-Potato Bottoms

As soon as Anna set foot in the Pink House, she turned to the estate agent and said, 'I want it, very, very badly.' For a moment, Adrian thought it might be his lucky day. He'd heard rumours of this sort of thing, the housing business was rife with them. After all, estate agents are one up on window cleaners, they haven't got chappy hands. Estate agents have manicured fingers that they can run up and down a twenty-denier tight without leaving a tell-tale snag. Adrian had read about this sort of thing in the magazines he bought from petrol stations. Bored housewives in red bras looking for a little afternoon's distraction; cheaper than mooching round Harvey Nichols and more fun than a stretch-and-tone class at the gym. They were at it like rabbits apparently. Adrian looked at Anna: he wouldn't chuck this one out the bed for farting, mind you, she had to be at least six months pregnant. Still, if she was already up the duff, then . . . He'd have to enter her from behind, doggy style; wouldn't do to get on top and squash that little baby.

'Of course, I'll have to get my husband over.'

Blimey, he was out of his depth with this one. Adrian's erection retracted like one of those old-fashioned tape measures.

'But I'm sure he'll be very interested. He likes me to be happy and I know I could be happy living here.'

'Ah, ah, aha,' stuttered Adrian, the penny dropping almost audibly. Well, that was a relief anyway; he reminded himself he was engaged. Adrian's fiancée was a twenty-five-year-old girl who managed a branch of Russell and Bromley and, let's face it, a twenty-five per cent discount on a decent pair of men's leather brogues is almost worth being faithful for.

The buying and selling of houses is a fraught business. 'I want' doesn't always get, but the Cunninghams were lucky; the man they were up against for the Pink House had the sale of his flat fall through when the prospective buyers realised it was bang slap next door to a needle exchange and decided to move to the Cotswolds instead.

Adrian phoned Anna. 'You've got it, Mrs Cunningham, you've got the Pink House.' Anna laughed for a good ten minutes and the baby inside her did a celebratory lap of honour around her womb. Adrian was pleased, and with some of his commission he had a pair of shoes handmade by Joseph Lobb, which pissed his fiancée off no end.

The Cunninghams moved in on a Tuesday. It was two months since Lady Edwina had been cremated and several days before

Myrtle was due back from the Canaries. It was April, not a bad time to move – or go to the Canaries for that matter.

'Can you watch what you're doing with that box.' Anna's husband Chris tried to sound authoritative but his voice rose to a squeak.

Really, could the man not read? It said on the side, in big permanent marker, CHINA.

Chris Cunningham would have liked to have taken the whole day off work. What with the wife being pregnant, it didn't seem fair.

'Oh, just go, I don't need you under my feet all day. If you don't go you won't have a job and then where will we be? Up shit creek, that's where. Go on, fuck off!'

Chris didn't like it when Anna swore; it didn't seem very nice, especially now, now that the foetus she was carrying was big enough to have ears. He kissed his wife and left a bit of boiled egg in her dark hair. 'Bye bye, Anna, toodleloo, Pandora, be a good girl for Mummy.' Pandora cried when her daddy left, she always did; boring really, three years old and already a creature of habit.

Jo Metcalf (number ninety-five), cardigan buttoned wrongly and dog's lead in hand, watched the Cunninghams move in. She noticed that the woman was very pretty and very pregnant and that the husband was on the corpulent side, whilst the child could only be described as 'chunky'. Jo hovered, the husband kissed the wife – who reacted as if a fly had landed on her neck – and the little girl followed him across the front garden and waved him off as he reversed his BMW out of the drive. Not many houses down the Grove had off-street parking – another perk to living in the Pink House. Jo allowed herself a moment's peevishness, 'not fair'. As the ginger-haired man drove off, Jo caught the woman's eye and she smiled her most welcoming 'I'm a mum, too, I know what it's like' smile, that conspiratorial grimace that women give each other in supermarkets when their kids are having tantrums and are lying on the floor black in the face. But the woman didn't smile back; maybe she was short-sighted, and the thought of her having to wear glasses cheered Jo up.

She tugged at the lead. Time to get home, have some breakfast; Jo was on a diet, the side effect being she was constantly ravenous and headachy. It made her bad-tempered, not eating; she had already snapped at Georgina, but then Georgina at four would try the patience of Mother Teresa. Jo snorted at the thought of the saint of Calcutta. She'd not had kids, had she? No wonder she was so bloody patient, she wasn't covered in stretch marks. For a second, Jo visualised the unworldly one with leaking breasts and itching piles; huh, that'd soon wipe the smile off her smug face.

At that moment Gloria deposited a pooh on the pavement. Good job she was a dog. Jo dragged the Westie off by the throat. Maybe Georgina would make friends with the little plump girl; they were about the same age, that would be nice. Mind you, Georgina wasn't the friendliest of little girls. Jo's head started to thump as she thought about her daughter. The word 'bitch' sprang into her mouth but she swallowed it. You can't accuse a four-year-old of being a bitch. But she was . . . 'difficult'. Not ten minutes ago when she dropped her off at the nursery, Mrs Lomax had requested 'a word'.

'It's about Georgina: she's been nipping.'

'Oh, no.'

'I'm afraid that's not all. Yesterday, she was found with both hands around Avril's neck and the poor little thing's eyes were bulging.'

'Of course I'll apologise to the mother.'

'I wouldn't worry, she's dead.'

'But still . . .'

'Avril is the nursery-school rabbit. You were actually on the rota to have her next half-term but considering recent circumstances I think it's better we don't risk it.'

'Yes, of course. So what shall I do?'

'If you could have a word? Georgina may only be four but she's quite bright. I think she knows she's being nasty.'

Oh, great, fretted Jo, I can just see that on her report. 'Georgina is clever but a vicious, manipulative little cow'.

I've never had anything like this with Henry, thought Jo, whilst Gloria stopped for a wee – it was worse than taking a granny on a motorway, going out with Gloria. Henry's never been cruel . . . too wet, I suppose. Jo didn't like thinking horrible things about her children, but there was an honesty switch in her head that had a habit of going into overdrive.

That's the problem with motherhood, you have to stick up for your kids. Mothers speak in a code: 'she's very artistic' – translation: she can't read. 'She's very imaginative' – she's a lying, two-faced slag. 'He's a kind and gentle lad' – he's a snivelling coward. 'She's a happy child' – she's fat. Mothers may privately think what they like about their children but they must never voice these thoughts; speaking the truth about your kids is the last unbroken social taboo.

Jo was outside her own house now and she looked up at where she lived. It was very big but rather brown compared to the Pink House; it looked like it was wearing a sensible school uniform as opposed to the extravagance of the Pink House's party dress. She fumbled for her keys, which were at the bottom of her bag. As she fished around she found a bag of milk chocolate buttons and before you could say 'low fat, high fibre', she'd emptied them down her neck. Fuck it, might as well have bacon and eggs now.

At that moment, Nigel came stomping down the stairs. 'This house is a bloody tip, Jo. When's that new au pair arriving?'

'Couple of weeks,' his wife replied, hoping her husband wouldn't get close enough to smell the chocolate on her breath.

The Metcalfs had been unlucky with their help; they'd had to let the last one go when they realised that she'd been offering blowjobs for a tenner in the gents toilets of the pub opposite. They'd packed her back off to Liverpool. Anyway Nigel hadn't wanted the children picking up a Scouse accent, 'Verbal equivalent of having head lice,' he'd said. Ta-ra Tamsin, with your dyed-yellow hair and love bites.

Nigel was tucking his shirt into his trousers; he was only a couple of pounds heavier than when they'd first met. Still, he hadn't carted two babies around, had he? Anyway, he was sporty, actually enjoyed it: badminton, squash, swimming – he was naturally competitive and had a collection of silver cups to prove it. Jo had done an exercise video once but had put her neck out so badly that she'd had to spend three hundred quid seeing a chiropractor twice a week for a couple of months. 'And that was just from getting the cellophane off it,' Nigel always joked. Sometimes he could be a bit mean.

'The new people have moved into the Pink House,' Jo grunted. She was picking up the dungarees Georgina had refused to wear for nursery from the floor in the hall. 'Maybe we should invite them over for supper.'

'What the hell for precisely?'

Nigel couldn't see the point in making new friends; he hardly had time for the ones he already had. Nigel's social circle consisted of a small, hand-picked selection of chaps who individually suited his different moods: there was Roger to play tennis with, Bob who was always up for a couple of rounds of golf, Sam with whom he discussed football and cars, and his one, left-over childhood friend, the obligatory blast from the past, Keith. That was quite enough, especially if you considered the amount of people he had to socialise with in the course of his work: agents, producers, writers – boozers one and all. Nigel was quite happy to get pissed with these people but he didn't really want them in his home. Most of them would be rather surprised to find out he was married with kids.

Nigel was expertly applying a Paul Smith tie around his neck. Slightly too short to be really handsome, he was like a pocket-sized matinée idol and always very well dressed. Nigel liked his shirts very white and very starched so he took them to a professional cleaner. Jo was the kind of woman who couldn't be trusted not to hurl a pair of navy knickers into a whites-only wash.

'Listen, Jo, I can't stand here yakking on, some of us have got to get to work. I'll see you tonight. Might be late – I'll call.'

Nigel didn't consider what Jo did for a living as work. As far as he was concerned, she sat on her backside in a second-hand bookshop, waiting for customers to spend fifty pence on an out-of-print Jilly Cooper.

'See you when I see you.'

Nigel wasn't faithful to his wife. It wasn't intentional, these things just happened – and kept on happening. It wasn't something they discussed.

Back up the road, removal men in brown overalls were swarming round the Pink House, up and down the front steps, unloading the van. Anna thought one of them looked a bit like Keanu Reeves, but only a bit and only from a certain angle. In fact, imagine if

Keanu had been born in Deptford and never been to an orthodontist – that's what he looked like. Mind you, viewed from another angle he looked like a roll-up-smoking monkey. As 'Monkey Keanu' brushed past Anna in the hallway, he said, 'Get us a cup of tea, darling.'

'Please,' said Anna, and she wasn't sure but she thought she might have felt the slightest pat on her bottom. 'Cheeky bugger.'

All the furniture from the old house looked too small for the Pink House and some of it Anna would gladly have put an axe through. It was a good job her husband earned a lot of money and that her father had croaked a few years back and left her a decent-sized pile; she had a lot of things she needed to buy. Anna fenced her daughter into a corner of the dining-room with heavy boxes and went to make the blokes a cup of tea. They all took sugar; 'Monkey Keanu' took three. 'You'll get fat,' she said, and he laughed and poked his tongue out at her. There were little shreds of tobacco on the end of it.

At lunchtime, Anna went out and fetched fish and chips; it seemed like a nice thing to do and anyway, she had to feed her daughter. Pandora was starving; she'd already chomped her way through a packet of Jaffa Cakes and then she'd gone and helped herself to one of the old boys' tin-foil-wrapped packed lunch. She was halfway though a cheese-and-onion sandwich when Anna had found her, tears streaming down her face and bits of onion hanging out of her mouth. Worse than a puppy.

Anna unwrapped the fish and chips. All the blokes had settled themselves in the kitchen, there was nowhere left for Anna to sit. Monkey Keanu caught sight of her dithering with a plate of cod and offered her his lap. 'Here, missus, sit on this.' All the men laughed, Anna went pink and Pandora pushed her chips into her face as fast as she possibly could.

After lunch – 'Very nice, Mrs C' – Anna made the blokes sort out Pandora's bedroom, and once she'd found some sheets and a duvet she put the child down for a nap. For a while she sat and stared at her daughter, until Pandora started to dribble and a little bubble of snot billowed out of her left nostril every time she exhaled. Anna hoped she'd be clever, it was her only option having missed out in the looks department. Anna was suddenly rather tired so she sat and read a bit of newspaper that lay on top of one of the umpteen cardboard boxes. That Princess Di was looking ever so scraggy. But then everyone looks skinny when you're eight months pregnant. Anna went out on to the landing; she had to watch her step, some of the stair rods had gone missing and the carpet was lethal.

'Watch yourself, missus,' said Keanu. He was coming up the stairs with a crate marked BATHROOM. Anna squeezed up against the wall; she was standing where the stairs went widest following the curve of the wall down to the ground floor. The next thing she knew, he had put down the crate, narrowly missing her foot, and with one thigh pressed against the case so as not to let it fall, he pushed himself against her and shoved his tongue in her mouth, all fishy and chippy and faggy. Anna hadn't tasted anything so delicious for a long time; it was better than Belgian chocolate, better than tandoori chicken tikka, better than a bacon sandwich smothered in brown sauce. There they stood, snogging like teenagers in a bus shelter, the heavy metal of his belt buckle digging into her vast belly, mmmgh, slurp, mmmugh, then, 'Mummee, come and wipe my bottee,' and the mood was broken. Anna pushed past the bloke, whose real name was Kevin, and rushed to the bathroom, where Pandora sat with her flowery blue knickers around her thick ankles. Pandora slid off the toilet and bent over so that her mother could wipe her clean: her bottom looked like a great big chilli-filled baked potato. Anna sat there with a load of poohy bog roll in her hand and sniggered, which made the little girl look anxious.

The blokes left at four o'clock. 'See ya,' said Monkey Keanu, and winked.

Anna's husband Chris came back just after six. 'I've picked up some fish and chips,' he said and waited for Anna to be grateful.

The first night the Cunninghams slept in their new house, Anna woke up at three o'clock to see her daughter standing in the doorway of the bedroom.

'For Christ's sake, Pandora, what is it?'

'Done a wee,' the fat child replied, and Anna hauled the cargo of her thirty-two-week pregnancy out of the bed and clenched her teeth.

'Me sleep with Daddy,' said the pudding-featured one, and thudded her way over to where her father lay whistling slightly down his long nose.

'Suit yourself, you little pisser.'

Really, this was all she needed. Vast with unborn baby, a house full of packing cases and a three-year-old who had suddenly decided to deposit steamy, wet patches that stank to high heaven before drying into dark yellow rings on the sheets.

'She's disorientated,' said Chris. 'Children don't like change.'

They don't like seeing strangers snog their mummies on the stairs either. Anna wondered if Pandora had seen her, but she persuaded herself that she hadn't; in fact she almost managed to persuade herself it hadn't happened at all, that she'd just imagined it. But she knew deep down what she'd done; she could still taste his roll-up breath on her lips a week later. Bad Anna.

6

Bleeding Honeymoons

I shouldn't have done it, but I did. That was the first thing I did wrong. I married Chris Cunningham when I was twenty-three.

Why?

Because he was a nice bloke and he had a full-time job like a grown-up. I think he was the first man I'd ever been out with who had an overcoat, a proper one with a silk lining and a chained loop thing to hang it up with. He had money and I didn't; let's face it I wasn't to know my dad was going to cark it a couple of years later and leave me a shed load of cash. If I'd known that . . . Oh listen, if I was a bloody mindreader I wouldn't be where I am now.

I'm not cut out for not having any money. Some people like living on Cup a Soup, wearing lots of jumpers from charity shops to keep out the cold and hand-rolling their own cigarettes. I can't abide all that nonsense. Not that I'm particularly high-maintenance; I'm not one of those women who spends every morning in the hairdresser's then lunches in a restaurant where Lady Di used to go, eating raw fish or stick insects or whatever's in fashion this week.

I'd been out with loads of blokes before Chris and slept with even more; you did in those days. Back in the seventies even nice girls with A-levels were allowed to be slags. He asked me once, 'How many men before me?' I lied, I said, 'Twelve.' He looked a bit shocked, went pink. It's terrible when Chris goes pink, he's one of those strawberry-blond, fair-skinned blokes, losing his hair, and when he goes pink he looks like a giant baby about to burst into tears. His pinkness got on my nerves. When we went on our honeymoon to Antigua he got sunstroke, just lay in our hotel room with his teeth chattering like clockwork mice. I couldn't stand it; in the end I went out, drank a load of cocktails. There was a tequila slammer thing going on, it was fantastic, like being pissed in the middle of a gunfight. I have a horrible feeling I snogged a waiter, which is a bit naughty when you're on your honeymoon, but there you go. I've always been a snogger and unfortunately whenever I snogged Chris, it felt like I was snogging twelve stone of luncheon meat. Christopher's middle name is Robin – I ask you!

I met Chris in a wine bar – that's how people met in the eighties – he was wearing a silly tie and he wasn't my type: he smelt of Wright's Coal Tar Soap and looked like the kind of man who cleaned out his ears with a cotton bud. We slept together that night and he apologised in the morning, said he 'didn't normally do it on first dates.' I remember laughing and saying, 'Really, I expect to do it in the carpark. What am I meant to do, wait till next Friday?'

He laughed then, too, because he thought I was joking and Chris is very polite; he laughs at people's jokes, even when they're not funny, he will laugh to fill silences. I didn't think I'd bother seeing him again, but for some reason I did. He really was very nice; he was straight, solvent and continent – something that should never be underestimated. He was also a gentleman; he lit my cigarettes even though he didn't smoke, and in the early days he always left the room to fart. What more can you ask? I just wish I'd fancied him more.

The trouble with Christopher Robin is that he just isn't very sexy, never has been. He once told me that when he was a teenager nobody fancied him and the only girls he ever got off with were on the verge of alcohol-induced comas; the cider-sodden unlovelies slumped in dark corners at the tail end of parties, with their chewed fingernails and pubic perms. Chris remembers his first French kiss; it was with a girl called Jackie Trennerman, a fifth-form fatty in a cheesecloth shirt and homemade maxi skirt with a frill round the hem. I never met her but I can picture her, slack-jawed on a sofa, bright blue eyeshadow and smudged mascara, Pernod-ed up to the eyeballs, in no state to argue. Poor old pissed Jackie Trennerman. Apparently 10CC were playing *I'm Not In Love* when Chris moved in; her mouth was hanging open anyway so he shoved his tongue right down the back of her throat and inevitably she threw up all over him. Exit Christopher reeking of Pernod and Cheesy Wotsits. He has never been any good at snogging ever since. When Chris kissed me I imagined his tongue in my mouth like an albino slug and it was all I could do to stop myself biting it in half.

My first French kiss was with Janie Conway's cousin on a William Morris print beanbag in their sun lounge. We were only mucking about, fighting over a Blue Ribbon bar, when he started kissing me, and Janie Conway, who was very thin and still wore a vest, started shouting, 'Stop it, Clive, stop it!' The only other thing I remember about the Conways was the big freezer that they kept in the garage. Mrs Conway was very proud of that freezer and would tell anyone who would listen that at any one time there was always a sheep and a pig in it and a hundred and fifty fish-fingers, 'Because you never know.' Oh yes, and she had a funny rake thing for grooming the shagpile carpets. Years later, she got Alzheimer's but apparently she still kept the house very neat; couldn't remember if she'd just cleaned the kitchen, you see, so she did it again. It was sparkling apparently.

My mum was thrilled when Chris and I got together, though I think she was surprised. Up until then I'd been out with all sorts of nutters: mad Irish piss-head poets, Australian junkies, biker boys with steel pins in their legs, inarticulate grunters and shruggers, border-line imbeciles with skinny arses. Men whose life skills hardly went beyond joint-rolling and signing-on. 'But what does his father do?' To be honest I think she'd given up, I was very soiled goods.

I didn't really enjoy my wedding day, I remember feeling rather bored halfway through. It was my fault; I'd kept it deliberately low key because I didn't want my mother interfering. I couldn't be bothered with marquees on the lawn so we did it in a registry office, but at least it was Chelsea Town Hall. It was raining and I remember the wedding party that came in after us looked a lot more fun and had better hats, big ones with feathers. I wore a cream satin two-piece, it was a bit pokey on the hips.

'Do you Anna Louise Redfern take Christopher Robin (snigger) Cunningham?'

'Oh, I suppose so.'

Afterwards, on the steps, some idiot relative of Chris's threw soggy confetti at me and it stained the jacket, which really pissed me off. After the photos (terrible, in some of them I am actually snarling) we all went back to Chris's bachelor flat in Battersea for champagne and something to eat. The cake was this hideous two-tiered affair that Chris's mother had got a girl in the village to make; it was covered all over with those lethal silver balls that break your teeth and the white icing was grubby round the edges.

I don't remember much about speeches, but I do remember that Chris's clan broke out into some ghastly Welsh song which was almost worth it for the look on my mother's face. The next day we flew to the Caribbean, and I started my period ten days early, thirty-five thousand feet above sea level.

Have you ever been to Antigua? It's a dump.

The label on this bottle of wine says that it is a full-bodied red made from Syrah grapes, grown near Narbonne and that it is best served at room temperature. 'This wine is an ideal partner for red meat dishes, especially beef, and it will also stand up to strong hard cheese'. Bollocks to it, I am swigging it out of the bottle whilst eating spaghetti hoops straight from the tin and, personally, I find the tomato-ketchuppy ringworms an ideal accompaniment to the ripe cassis and smooth-rounded tannins of the ripe red wine. It also says on the bottle that 'once opened the wine will remain in good condition for up to two days, if resealed and stored in a cool place'. Well, that's a laugh.

7

Gossip and Gloria

Don't decades fly when you're having fun? It is only recently that every day seems to last two weeks.

I first met Anna about ten years ago when they bought the Pink House. I was rather jealous, I'd always fancied it myself. Not that there's anything wrong with ours, if anything it's bigger, it's just that there's something rather glamorous about having a pink house, very Schiaparelli.

Ours is handsome and solid and it has five floors. I've had the garden landscaped so it's all Japanese, which is fine if you like ponds full of dead koi carp floating belly up and lots of gravel for cats to pooh in, but there you go; the price of style.

The Pink House is halfway up the hill, nearer to the squats at the top than we are. Criminal, isn't it? Perfectly fine Georgian houses at the top of one of the most sought-after roads in South London and they let a load of grubby New-Age travellers take over! All goats in the front garden, white blokes with dreadlocks, blankets over the windows and broken-down cars painted like rainbows – it's always bloody rainbows, isn't it? Anyway, they've cleared them out now and they've been tarted up, so that's sent the house prices rocketing. Sorry, where was I? Ten years ago, you had the grungies up at the top and then a bit further down the coloured houses looking like massive Mr Kipling Fondant Fancies; a pale yellow one, a white one, an ice-blue one and then the pink one. They're well known locally, in fact one of them was used as a location for a film and we all got rather used to seeing that Nigel Havers. Funny little fellow, very thin; looked like he was made out of pipe cleaners.

Back then, I had a little dog, a Westie. It wasn't mine, it was my son Henry's but, of course, muggins ended up walking the silly thing. Mind you, there's nothing like having a dog for getting the low-down on what's happening locally. Dog people are terrible gossips and I do love gossip.

The great thing about dogs is that you can't walk three steps without them stopping for a wee or to smell some other mutt's wee. Gloria was a terrible one for wees; she must have had a bladder the size of a peanut. So she'd stop and I'd stand there, just innocently looking about – admittedly with my glasses on – and it's incredible what you pick up. This is quite a posh road. People don't have net curtains as a rule; we like to show our worldly goods to the passing pleb. What's the point in having a stuffed crocodile running the breadth of your sitting-room wall if people can't look in and say, 'Oh my goodness, they've got a stuffed crocodile'? I find it all quite fascinating, these little glimpses into other people's worlds; a man with his shirt untucked, reaching into the fridge for a bottle of beer after a hard day, a woman with a teething, red-faced baby, standing by the window.

Apparently the Pink House used to be owned by some old biddy, one of those grey-haired genteel types, tea at four in a china cup, old Empire sorts. She lived there with a companion; just two little old ladies, a great deal of carved ebony furniture and a large collection of Buddhas. Rumour has it she went gaga. She started swearing every time she opened her mouth, the silver spoon turned into a sewer, and she began attacking her companion – you can't let them do that sort of thing. Then she got pneumonia and popped her clogs and the house went on the market. I heard all this from the homosexual at number seventy-seven; nice man, died of AIDS about three years ago. It was ghastly, he had this beautiful red setter and a face full of Kaposi's. Last time I saw him he must have weighed seven stone; he blamed it on a Russian sailor. I've no idea what happened to the dog.

It wasn't on the market for long, the Pink House. I watched the removal van arrive and I saw a woman with a fat child of about four and even though she was quite heavily pregnant she moved like a dancer. I was surprised when I saw him, all suited up, and at first it didn't connect that he was the husband. She looked like she should have been married to someone else, like a pop star; someone with a ponytail and Cuban-heeled cowboy boots! But then, lots of couples don't match – me and Nigel for a start. People always expect him to have a younger, prettier wife, but tough, he's stuck with me. Why? Possibly because I turn a blind eye to his unfaithfulness and make the best banoffee pie this side of Milan. Poor Nigel, he thinks I don't know about his extra-maritals. Men can be idiots sometimes. The thing is, it doesn't bother me, I'm not the jealous type. I don't even blame him really; I imagine he has a higher sex drive than I have. I'm rather lazy about sex, it always surprises me when I enjoy it. I don't think I'm as adventurous as Nigel would like; I feel rather foolish in stockings and suspenders, my thighs spill like blancmange over the tops. I don't have fantasies either. To be truthful, I think sex is a beautiful person's game. I'm not saying it should be made illegal if you're not a Calvin Klein model, but there is something rather sordid about middle-aged couples rolling around making loud noises. For example, I can imagine Kate Moss looking rather glorious in the throes of passion, but not Judy Finnegan. Please, don't get me wrong, I have a lot of respect for Judy . . .

Occasionally I can get a bit randy but I always feel slightly embarrassed in the morning and I find having children in the house rather off-putting. Nigel is always trying to make me give him oral sex, which is fine if it's his birthday, but when he tries to reciprocate the favour I am left looking at the ceiling, thinking about food for the weekend and getting the tax done on the car. Anna on the other hand, is a sexual person; she's feline whereas I am rather like an old Labrador. I'd rather have a nice walk followed by a good snooze.

Of course, now that she has let herself go and the sex kitten has turned into a mangy old alley cat, you wouldn't give her a second look. These days she looks like the rest of us; just another middle-aged woman. There are millions of us trudging around, occasionally catching sight of ourselves in shop windows and looking away quickly because it's depressing; we're everywhere, reaching for the size fourteens in Marks and Spencer, buying mince and Migralieve, deciding it's time to have a mammogram – just in case. She's looking worse than me, but then I've always had to make more effort. I've always needed foundation and mascara. Anna used to be able to get away with a smear of Vaseline on her eyelashes, a smudge of lip-gloss and a squirt of perfume; she has taken her looks for granted. She has become the Ugly Duckling in reverse; everything she used to be she isn't any more.

She sleeps so much, it's like having a hibernating tortoise in the house. Mind you, tortoises don't snore. Anna snores like a pneumatic drill and you'd think sometimes that, judging by the vibrations coming from the spare room, there was a load of Paddies in there digging up a road. I used to make an effort not to make any noise when she slept; I would hiss at the children to 'be quiet, turn that bloody television down, take your shoes off.' Not any more, now I bang and crash around and slam doors as needlessly as a teenager.

My jaw aches constantly; my dentist is very concerned he says it's tension – ha, the other day, I took a carton of eggs out into the garden and threw every single one of them against the back wall. Occasionally I bite cushions and rock backwards and forwards like a nutcase. This is what she has done to me.

8

Pat-a-Cakes and Wet Pants

'They're doing ever such a lot to the Pink House; can't be easy for her, looks like she's going to burst any day now.'

Brenda Donahue (number sixty-three) was talking to her son Raymond; he wasn't listening, he was doing something with his Lego, jam all down his t-shirt. 'Mind, it needed some seeing to. Do you remember when we went and had a cup of tea with the old lady and Myrtle?'

'And cake,' said Raymond.

'That's right, dear.'

'Cake with nuts and cherries.'

See he wasn't all sixpence to the shilling; it had been a cake with nuts and cherries.

Brenda had introduced herself to the Cunningham woman just that very morning. 'I'm Brenda Donahue, I live down the road. I've a friend used to live here, not the one that died, no, my friend – Myrtle – was her companion. Years she looked after that old lady. She lives in the Borough now, she says she doesn't miss the stairs – ever such a lot of stairs you've got in that house. I'm the same, spend half my life going up and down stairs like a yoyo; by the time I've got down to the bottom, I realise I've left something at the top. I should be as thin as a pin, can't understand it.' Brenda knew she was prattling.

The woman was good-looking. When Brenda had been pregnant with Raymond she'd worn maternity smocks; everyone did, you didn't go round flaunting your belly. This one was wearing a t-shirt that was so tight you could see her tummy button sticking out through the scarlet fabric.

'Due any day, I see?'

The woman laughed, as if she'd just remembered the big lump in front of her. 'Beginning of June,' she said, and then, 'Sorry, think I can hear the phone,' and she just ran off. Brenda could have sworn she hadn't heard a phone. Oh well, she supposed the young woman had a lot on her plate, she didn't need yattery old biddies wasting her time. Before the door had shut, Brenda had got a glimpse of the hall; all the old wallpaper had been stripped off and the floorboards were exposed. Personally Brenda was a carpet girl.

When Anna had shut the big front door she stood with her back against it, mentally asking God to spare her from the tedious ramblings of little old ladies who were still wearing winter coats in May. The baby was kicking. Chris would say it was because it was a boy and he was going to be a footballer, but it wasn't that kind of kick; it was more rhythmic, like whoever was in there was dancing the cha-cha.

Anna sat on the stairs and thought about baby's names for a while: Orlando, Elvis, Paris, Delilah.

Thinking up baby's names was a great way of tormenting her husband. Chris was wary of extravagance and would tentatively suggest less flamboyant options such as Edward or Victoria. Once he'd admitted to being rather fond of the name Barbara – proof, if proof were needed, that he really didn't have a clue.

For a good twenty minutes she contemplated her navel but even at this late stage, the third trimester of her second pregnancy, with the baby due to make its earthly debut in a matter of weeks, she tried not to think about the actual giving birth bit. Delivering Pandora three years previously had been more of a twenty-hour exorcism than a miracle of nature. Anna had never taken LSD but she presumed that her memories of evacuating Pandora were similar to a bad acid flashback. Imagine a slasher movie set in an abattoir, complete with forceps and men in green gowns with gore up to their elbows. Mamma Cunningham was secretly keeping her fingers crossed for a last-minute Caesarean this time.

In the meantime there was the house to sort out. 'I want it all white,' Anna had told Chris, 'and for a start you can get rid of your mother's bloody dresser.'

Already the Pink House had lost its whiff of old lady embrocation. The sago-coloured Anaglypta had been unceremoniously stripped; she was quite bare now and it suited her.

'My lovely house,' thought Anna.

Most afternoons, Mrs Cunningham lay on a dusty pink velvet *chaise-longue* in the drawing-room and flicked through copies of *Interiors* and *House and Garden,* whilst Pandora sat at the other end of the room watching Pingu videos and eating barbecue-flavoured Monster Munch. The way she ate irritated her mother;

first she would lick the orange crumbs off each savoury snack and then she would individually suck each shape to its pulpy death. When the packet was empty, her doughy face would cloud, genuinely disappointed that the treat was over.

Anna wasn't used to spending so much time in her daughter's company; it was a new experience for both of them and neither was sure of the rules. Dutifully they went through the motions: Anna, bored on a bench watching Pandora in the sandpit, the walk round to Woolworths to buy Fuzzy-Felt, the spat over the pick 'n' mix, the snail-paced trudge home. Yawn. Deep down, Anna was convinced that working was easier than full-time motherhood; she missed the adult world. If the blokes currently installing the new kitchen had been cute, they might have provided a welcome distraction from Spot the Dog jigsaws and cretinous Mr Men stories. But they weren't: one had a hair lip and the other was sixty – dull, dull, dull.

Before Chris had put his big, hairy, yellow-toed foot down, Anna had worked with her friend Maggie, casting adverts from the basement of Maggie's massive Clapham townhouse. Really, it had all been very convenient. What with Maggie having a live-in nanny for her son Joseph, Anna had never really had to deal with Pandora; she'd just handed her over to this well-trained Australian who made sure that both children were fed, watered and exercised. To be honest, Anna was quite shocked when Pandora suddenly didn't need nappies any more; Ozzie Alison had done a good job on the old potty training – it was only now that Pandora had decided to regress. If the problem got any worse, Anna could see herself having to find some specialist shop that sold outsized nappies for the adult incontinent.

Anna felt a pang of temper when she thought about Alison; she knew she should be grateful to the antipodean cart-horse, but the frizzy-haired hired help had recently dropped a domestic bombshell. Alison had told Maggie that with Joseph going to primary school in September, she wasn't prepared to take on Anna's new baby as well as the school run and Pandora. Selfish lump. 'Well, thanks a bunch, lard-arse.'

Maggie had been very apologetic, but, 'You can understand her point of view, Anna.' Bollocks, thought Anna; these girls, just because they are capable of looking after your kids without setting them on fire, think they can rule your life. However, it was a dilemma.

Anna lay watching her daughter. Pandora was busy eating the crunchy bits of snot left over from one of her perpetual colds; she was probably bored. Well, she'd have to stay bored till Chris came home. He was incredibly patient with her, spent hours doing puppet shows or pretending to be a big, barky dog, the latter resulting in Pandora chortling on her back, quivering like a blancmange.

'Woof woof, Pandora, I'm going to lick you to pieces.'

'Tee hee, tee hee.'

Anna wished that sort of thing came naturally to her, but it didn't and pretending made them both uncomfortable. It wasn't as if Pandora was a difficult child; she'd have been quite happy sitting there being thrown pork pies. But she was three now, it was time she went to nursery.

Galvanised into action by the sight of her nostril-excavating daughter, Anna dug out the Yellow Pages and looked up Nursery Schools – Private. There had to be one locally because Anna had noticed a number of pre-schoolers wobbling their way to the top of the hill every morning, all the little Jacks and Jills, Jaspers and Mollys, and then a few hours later wobbling their way down, clutching their sugar paper scribbles and toilet roll sculptures.

Maybe it was the one in Beechwood Road, 'Pat-a-Cakes'? Anna dialled the number.

A Mrs Lomax answered; she was very pleasant, as indeed you would be at the thought of a new 'grand-a-term' recruit.

'Come on up and pay us a visit, bring the little one, see how she likes it. We have lots of lovely fun, as you can hear.' In the background children were singing, 'The wheels on the bus go round and round.' It sounded like a dirge. God, she hated that song.

Anna was actually very lucky: if the Wilson twins hadn't just left due to a family tragedy (Mr Wilson had been made redundant) there wouldn't have been a place for love nor money. Of course, Mrs Lomax didn't impart any of this information to Anna; the whole incident had become rather squalid, what with Mrs Wilson crying on the doorstep, begging for the twins to be considered for scholarships, but before she put the phone down she did remember to ask Anna one vital question.

'Your little girl, she is dry, isn't she?'

'Yes,' lied Anna, 'quite dry.'

At this point, Pandora got up off the cushion she'd been squatting on and the back of her dress was dark with wee.

'Thank you very much, Mrs Lomax, look forward to seeing you tomorrow,' said Anna.

Immediately she'd crashed the receiver into its cradle, she flew at Pandora and like a woman possessed she rugby tackled her to the floor, pulled off the soggy drawers and hit her child in the face, once, twice, three times with the offending knickers.

Anna felt guilty just as soon as she'd finished. 'I'm sorry Pandora, Mummy's very tired. Come on let's get you a milk shake.'

But Pandora didn't want a milk shake, she wanted to lie face down on the sofa with her spotty bum in the air. Anna was so upset that she had to go and sit on the back step and smoke one of her emergency ultra lows. As she inhaled, she apologised to the baby. 'Actually it's your bloody sister's fault.'

Anna decided to leave Pandora with her father when she went to visit the nursery; she was on a mission and she didn't want the leaky Pandora to sabotage her plans.

'I won't be long, I'm just nipping up to that Pat-a-Cakes place. Oh, for pity's sake, put a bib on her, she eats like a pig.' And with that she was off.

Anna had a nice chat with Mrs Lomax, who very kindly offered Pandora a place at Pat-a-Cakes. 'Yeeees,' cheered Anna silently, mentally running round like a footballer with his shirt over his head. Out loud, and as calmly as she could, she asked, 'As from?'

'Well, tomorrow if you like. Of course, I will have to charge the full term's fee, but as you can understand there are administration costs. Oh, and it's fourteen pounds for the pinny.'

She could only offer mornings; Anna had been hoping for full days, perhaps with some after-school activities, say till eightish . . . but it was better than nothing. Fortunately she had the joint account cheque book on her.

'Oh, thank you very much, Mrs Cunningham, I'm sure Pandora will be very happy here. There's a little girl that lives just a bit further down the Grove from you, Georgina Metcalf. I'm sure she'll make Pandora very welcome.'

Georgina Metcalf, daughter of Jo and Nigel Metcalf, sister to Henry, welcomed Pandora by digging her sharp little nails into Pandora's fleshy upper arm and sniggering, 'You can have the peg with the elephant on it.' Georgina was a year older than Pandora, who at three didn't get the significance of the joke; all she realised was that this girl might get nasty, whoops too late!

'Ugh, dirty pig,' squealed Georgina, and she hopped away from the steaming yellow pool that lapped around Pandora's feet. Fortunately Mrs Lomax was prepared to overlook 'our little accident', after all, that poor Mrs Cunningham was enormous with another potential Pat-a-Cakes client and one had to look to the future.

When Anna picked Pandora up at lunchtime, a strange woman with a pudding basin haircut 'yoo hoo-ed' her. Anna smiled vaguely, and dashed off as soon as she could with Pandora's wet pants in a plastic bag. On the way down the hill Anna tried to have a conversation with Pandora about 'lovely nursery' but Pandora wasn't very forthcoming; it was only when Chris got home that she admitted to liking the biscuits at juice-time. He took her up for a bath and put her to bed and Pandora didn't ask for her mother to come and kiss her goodnight. She was whacked out; nursery school can be very tiring.

Further down the road the bob-haired woman aka Jo Metcalf was having an altogether much more difficult time with her daughter. Georgina was monkeying around; she wanted to go to sleep in her Cinderella dress, complete with wimple and veil.

'But the veil might get caught round your neck and you'll choke to death in the night,' explained her mother.

'Don't care,' said Georgina.

'Will she really die?' Henry, Georgina's older brother, was hovering in the doorway, six years old in wire-framed glasses and sharp little knees that had worn holes in his pyjamas. Poor Henry, vole-faced and prone to eczema; he was a terrible worrier. 'If she dies I won't be able to go to school, will I, and we're going to the transport museum, and I really want to go.' He looked on the verge of tears.

Bugger, thought Jo. School bloody trip, packed lunch, damn!

'Listen, miss, you can sleep in the dress but not the hat thing, get it off now. Henry, you go to bed.'

If Jo sounded hysterical it was only because she was. Nigel was late home, she had the attic room to get ready for the new au pair and she knew for a fact she had neither a carton of juice nor a packet of crisps for Henry's packed lunch.

Both Henry and Georgina knew that their mother could only be pushed so far. She was reasonable as mothers go, but she had her limits and now and again (usually every four weeks), she would rear up like a horse that'd gone mad and then crumple down on the floor sobbing into the carpet. Georgina removed the wimple and pretended to be instantly asleep whilst Henry scuttled off to his own room, trailing his bit of blanky.

Jo stomped up to the top floor. The Liverpudlian girl had left burn marks on the dressing-table and there were Tampax applicators and suspicious-looking fag butts in an ashtray under the divan. Jo wished she was the type that could calm down over a nice, fat joint; she'd tried it a few times but it always led to advanced paranoia and having to be led round the block throwing up in strangers' front gardens. She stripped the bed; dirty little slag hadn't changed the sheets once in the two months she'd been with them. Jo swapped the grubby bed linen for a navy blue madras-check duvet cover and matching pillowcase. The new girl was coming over from Ireland, so with any luck she would be one of those poor ones used to sleeping six to a bed and she'd find this little room, with its black and white portable complete with coat hanger down the back, the height of luxury. (Actually when Siobhan arrived two days later, she brought her very own colour telly and a rather swish CD player.)

When all was done and not particularly well dusted, Jo went

downstairs and had a glass of red wine. It was 8.30, Nigel still wasn't home and there was no point waiting for him. She got a Birdseye Lean Cuisine chicken dinner out of the freezer, boiled it in its bag and ate it at the kitchen table; there was a dish of left-over green beans and carrots in the fridge so she dug those out and accidentally ate a Marks and Spencer individual chocolate mousse as she did so. Then she remembered Henry's packed lunch and in a fit of guilt she decided to make fairy cakes; she'd make enough for the whole class and take them up to the school in a Tupperware container. She was a good cook and she tried to be a good mother and wife.

As she weighed out the flour and the sugar, she thought about the Anna woman who had moved into the Pink House; she'd tried to get chatting at the nursery, but the woman was obviously as blind as a bat, just hadn't seen her. Shame, it would be nice to have a girlfriend locally, useful; nice for the kids too. So many people kept moving away, that mad exodus to Norfolk and Suffolk, 'You will visit, it's only just off the A11.' But you didn't because the kids were so travel sick that by the time you'd driven over Tower Bridge they were both honking and spewing bits of carrot down the back of your neck.

Whilst Jo greased a baking tray and heated up the oven, her husband was locked in the ladies' toilet of a tatty old pub off Regent Street. Nigel sat on the toilet seat lid and a girl with a tattoo of a bumble bee on her right buttock bounced up and down on his cock. She had her back to him; all he could see was a lot of hennaed hair and he wished he could remember what she looked like face on. Or maybe it was best this way? He'd undone her bra and it had sort of ridden up around her neck, and her breasts, free from their harness, swayed alarmingly. She was going like the clappers, tits flying all over the shop, and if she wasn't careful, one would lob itself over her shoulder and slap him in the face. He kept trying to catch a nipple but he missed every time. The girl had worked up a bit of a sweat; she was arching her back and making noises like Jo had that time she'd had a pelvic inflammatory infection.

Nigel suddenly realised there was no way this was going to work. He was off his face, pissed and coked up to the eyeballs. Not for the first time did he wish he could fake it like he knew Jo usually did. Suddenly the girl started juddering and yelping and as if his penis was scared of loud noises, it shrank back, like a pensioner hiding in a corner from a robber. She bucked one last time and then, knowing something was wrong, stood bolt upright on her stilettos and said, 'What's happened?' She looked around at Nigel and his little frightened willy and shouted, 'Where's the condom? Eh . . . fucking condom's come off.' It had too.

Suddenly Nigel was very tired. The girl was rummaging in her vagina like she'd dropped a diamond ring down a waste disposal unit; most of her arm seemed to disappear inside of her and her bra was now hooked over one ear. 'Got it,' she gasped triumphantly, and she wiggled the shrivelled prophylactic in his face.

Really, it was time to go home.

Whilst Nigel busied himself with his flies and tie, Jo decorated the fairy cakes.

She went to bed at ten o'clock and at ten past Nigel came through the front door in the deliberate way that pissed people do, being ever so careful to walk straight, speak coherently and not fall up the stairs. 'Bloody mad day,' he intoned, very carefully indeed.

'I'm in bed, I'm exhausted,' yelled Jo, which is, of course, the wife's shorthand for 'so don't start sniffing round my nightie like a cat round a fish shop'.

Wouldn't it be marvellous if, just now and again, couples could communicate without using some sort of code; if Jo could have just yelled, 'I'm really pooped so don't attempt to shag me,' and Nigel could have replied, 'It's okay, I'm not interested, I've had a belly full of lager, a load of class As and some rancid old slag jiggling her fanny up and down my dong for twenty minutes in a public convenience.'

But of course they don't.

So while Jo dozed off and Nigel brushed his teeth until his gums bled, up at the Pink House Chris watched a programme on Rommel and Anna washed the borrowed nursery pants and then ironed them neatly. She wouldn't normally bother, but she wanted to keep things sweet with Madame Lomax.

9

Of Mice and Pigs

Odd the things you start to remember when more important things are too difficult to think about. The past is easier to deal with; I know what happens next. Not like the future. I daren't think about that.

When I was nineteen and before I met Chris, I had an affair with a married man. It's funny, I can hardly remember his face, but I can remember hers, the wife's. White as paper she went, then as dark as beetroot, and the language – I've never heard so many fucks in so few seconds. 'You cunt, you fucking fucker, fuck you, you fuck.' He leapt out of bed like a bolt from a cross-bow and tried to put his trousers on. I always wondered why. It wasn't as if she hadn't seen his willy a thousand times before;

they'd been married fifteen years, they had three children.

Anyway she was a mess. She ate pickled onions all the time, she was addicted to them. He told me she kept one under the pillow to suck through the night like a boiled sweet. Some women don't deserve to keep their husbands.

It never crossed my mind that I'd done anything wrong. After all, why would a man want to make love to a woman whose breath smelt of vinegar? I was the Wrigley's-fresh-breath-Colgate-ring-of-confidence alternative with thin thighs and fabulous tits.

You don't think when you're young and maybe I just never grew up. Chris always said I was spoilt, comes from being an only child; that's why we had to have more than one. To be quite honest I never really wanted any and after Pandora was born . . . well, I was convinced that motherhood wasn't me. Not that I don't love her, I do, deep down and I think, deep down, she loves me. She has to . . . I'm her mother.

I wasn't really ready to have a child. Chris was pathetically broody; I find that peculiar in a man, but there you go. We'd been married a few years, and at first I didn't know what was wrong with me; I was so rough I thought I had leukaemia. We were on holiday, one of those dreary Greek islands with their crappy pebble beaches and loathsome food. Really, how many times can you eat a Greek salad? They're weird aren't they, old Johnny Greek, all those tavernas, all serving exactly the same bleeding thing. If any of them had a brain, they'd open a decent Chinese.

Chris loved the place, kept hiking off to see some ancient pile of crumbling stones whilst I lay face down in the gritty sand, a taste of old pennies in my mouth and the whiff of raw octopus up my nostrils. I should have known I was up the stick, super-sensitive olfactory powers are one of the signs, but I didn't, so I just lay there gagging into my beach towel. I couldn't even drink or smoke; I was allergic to my own duty-free! It was possibly the dullest holiday I have ever had.

It was Chris who first suspected I might be pregnant; something to do with my tits. Not that he put it like that, not Chris, he uses the same language as a 1950s biology teacher. He was watching me putting on my bikini one morning and he said, 'Ah, your cups brimmeth over,'

'Fuck off,' I said, but he was right. I had knockers, not tits, big fat knockers. So we did a test when we got home and guess what? The little dot went bright pink – and so did the other three kits. Bugger.

You'd never think such a small collection of cells could cause so much damage; one summer holiday ruined, thank you very much, things could only get better. But they didn't. I was dragged off to bloody Wales to tell 'Grannie', who suggested names like Gareth and Bronwen.

'Fuck off,' I said under my breath but not quite quietly enough.

'She's very tired,' said Chris.

'She's a bitch,' said his mother, hardly under her breath at all but we pretended we didn't hear anyway.

Some women bloom in pregnancy. I didn't, I felt bloody throughout; my skin went yellow and I had great bags under my eyes, the colour of liver. As for my hair, even Miko the Chinese poof who used to cut it despaired; it just hung in two limp curtains. I also had this boil on my chin that no amount of Clarins would shift. In the end I just gave it a good squeeze every other day and when it looked particularly festering I stuck a plaster over it.

The baby was due in May, 'around the tenth,' they said, 'but first babies are often late Mrs Cunningham.' Fourteen days in this case. I'd started to think it would never happen, that this massive lump in front of me was wind and one day I'd do an almighty fart and the whole thing would deflate. But, of course, it didn't; there was something in there all right and eventually, like the monster from the deep, it came out.

Childbirth is disgusting. I can't stand those types who bleat on about the miracle of bringing a new life into the world. For a start I shat myself; Chris says I didn't but I did. Serve him right for making me eat curry the night before; did the trick though. Lamb rogan josh, that came out first. The midwife was very good, just whisked away the paper sheet and stuck a new one under my bum. Then came baby, head like a bloodied football. As she emerged I heard my perineum rip like old curtains, then the rest of her piled out, like kilos of wet fish, all purple and grey and I threw up over the side of the bed. They said it was the gas and air; bollocks, it was the sight of raw baby. We called her Pandora, though 'bum splitter' would have been more apt.

I had to have seventeen stitches; I'm sure that bit of my arse looks like it's been through a windscreen.

Chris was there, of course, making all the right noises, even when I bit his hand like a ferret and spat fuck words into his sweaty pink face. He adored her on sight and I pretended to, though to be honest I don't think I'd ever seen anything so hideous in all my life. When it was all over and I just wanted to have a bath and go to sleep, they made me feed her; she hadn't been properly washed and there was blood on the matted scraps of her hair. Feeding her was the last thing I wanted to do, but you can't argue with these people, they're very well trained. 'Bonding' they call it, and you have to play along, murmuring words of adoration into the wonky eyes of a new-born stranger. To be honest, given the opportunity I'd have left her on a bus.

I had shoes in my wardrobe that I felt more passionate about.

I never expected to have an ugly daughter; I always expected a small replica of myself, I was shocked when I saw her, like a great big meaty doll, all pink and roly-poly with her ten chipolata fingers and ten chipolata toes. Even the midwife didn't pretend to be impressed, 'She's a whopper,' she said. Pandora weighed twelve pounds, as big as a Christmas turkey. The night after I had her, I dreamt that she was lying naked on a plate, covered in gravy, with carrots, sprouts and stuffing all piled around her like toys in a pram.

I always expected to turn around one day and find the child whose image I carried in my head, the little girl who looked like I used to. But I never did. I was stuck with her, large as life and twice the size. She had my dark hair but Chris's pale skin and her paternal Welsh grandmother's body, short of leg and wide of girth, built to take in washing. Common stock, you see.

Of course, I'd met Chris's family. I knew what they looked like; his bullfrog of a mother, his silent misshapen brother with the ginger fuzz sprouting out of his ears, but I always thought that my superior genes would conquer his, that dark grey eyes would win over watery blue, slim ankles over thick, shapely flanks over massive thighs. My daughter was born half cart-horse and 'plain as a pike staff' as my mother would say.

Chris's father is dead, by the way, nagged into an early grave by his horrible mother. Although officially it says bronchitis on the death certificate, it's still her fault. She didn't let him smoke in the house, and basically he caught his death smoking John Players in the shed, poor bastard.

I was in hospital for five days with Pandora. Course they don't do that these days; they kick you out before the placenta's had time to cool and the baby's still got your pubes stuck behind its ears.

I needed that time in the hospital; for a start, they took her away from me at night, oh merciful release. Chris didn't want them to give her bottled milk, but sod it, they could have given her a family tub of Häagen-Dazs if it had kept her quiet.

Anyway, I couldn't take her straight home, she didn't have anything to wear; none of the new-born size stuff fitted her and Chris had to go out and buy the next size up! Of course, his mother got straight on the train, arrived with a load of home-knitted matinee jackets which brought Pandora out in a rash; all scratchy wool in mustard and maroon. What the hell was she thinking of? 'Is she colour blind?' I asked Chris.

Her other grannie, my mother, sent some exquisite embroidered white rompers from Switzerland, which were equally unsuitable. I gave them to a girl in the same ward; she was only nineteen, had this beautiful baby, tiny with the sweetest face. Adele she called her. Turned out she had a hole in the heart, poor little mite, that's why her little lips were that pretty mauve colour. See, it's not fair, is it? There was me with my mammoth great strong ox of a child and this girl with the damaged doll baby and I still fancied swapping. I've never said a lot of this out loud, it's embarrassing, isn't it? I mean what a terrible thing to say, nobody wants a poorly child really, but then nobody wants a big, blotchy-faced ugly one either.

Babies come in two types: pigs or mice. Mice babies have delicate features, tiny noses and little wisps of hair whilst pig babies have large, red faces and great big thighs and fat noses. I expected a mouse and I got a pig. These things happen and you notice it more and more when it's happened to you. Sometimes when I'm flicking through *Hello!* and there's all those photos of famous telly actresses with their families, now and again I will spot some slab-faced child lurking at the back, looking for all the world like it belongs to the cleaner. Conversely, living in this genetic Pot Noodle that is South London, I have seen the most hideous of toothless crones with delicious moppets for daughters. Mother Nature plays some terrible tricks.

You don't get much wine in a bottle these days, do you? I find myself constantly surprised when another one is suddenly empty. Where did that one go? Hey presto, I'm like a magician.

10

Making Friends and Miscarriages

Part of wanting to be Anna's friend was practical; we both had girls around the same age. Useful, you see? A little pal up the road, jolly handy; we mothers can be quite scheming. In the end it turned out that her Pandora was a year younger than my Georgina but you'd never have guessed, she was enormous. I reckoned she was at least four but actually she was only three. Still, she ended up going to the same nursery as Georgie; it would have been nice if they'd been friends but to be quite honest they couldn't stand the sight of each other even then.

'Hello, Pandora, how are you?'

Silence.

'Look, Georgina's here. Would you like to play?'

'No, go away.'

When Georgina was about five, she said that if Pandora were run over she would laugh. Sometimes I worry about Georgina, she can be very cruel. Every doll she's ever owned has ended up with its limbs amputated, hair hacked off at the roots and scribbled all over with biro. She was the type of child who kicked dogs and pinched babies.

She has the face of an angel and the soul of a prize cow.

I am her mother, I am allowed to say these things. I'm fed up with people talking in half-truths. The truth is I love my family but I know their weaknesses.

So, going back to meeting Anna. As I say, they bought the Pink House and my Georgina and her Pandora were at the same nursery; lovely place, big Victorian villa on Beechwood Road, very Kate Greenaway, all the children wore little red-checked smocks. Private, of course. Sorry if that offends anyone but tough, we're going back to pre-Blair days here and state schools, I used to joke, were so called because they were in a 'right old state'. Pat-a-Cakes, the nursery was called. It's closed down now; tragic really, I mean accidents do happen, but when you're paying a grand a term, you don't expect your child to fall face down into the paddling pool and not get missed till all the others are back indoors having juice and a cheese straw.

I think her name was Katie Robinson; she was only three. Her mother was never the same again, of course, well, you wouldn't be, would you? I mean, Georgina may be going through a vile adolescent stage but I'd never wish her dead, whatever I may say.

The Drowned Tot Tragedy (as the local paper put it) happened after our lot had left, I'm glad to say. It's a private house now, and very nice too. I said to Nigel at the time, 'That's a lovely house. We should go and have a look,' but he just said, 'Whatever for?' He doesn't like upheaval and it's not as if we don't have a perfectly nice house already – and it is nice but it's not as nice as the Pat-a-Cakes place or the Pink House.

Thinking back, I almost stalked Anna. I was always hoping that I'd bump into her and that one day she'd look pleased to see me.

Maybe I was bored, maybe I was lonely. I need friends and my closest girlfriend, Rowena Baxter, had moved to Hastings with a new man. I was a bit shocked to be honest; I know everyone gets divorced these days but it all seems rather unnecessary to me, and such hard work. I mean, I know Roger Baxter was an idiot but it seems a bit dramatic to leave someone who makes over a hundred grand a year for some soppy New-Age hippie type, ten years younger, with a pierced eyebrow. I remember having an argument about it with Rowena, it all got a bit heated. 'I thought if anything I could rely on you,' she shouted. 'Do you realise how unhappy I've been?' I hadn't actually; they had a lovely house and she never had to lift a finger. All she did was bomb about in a convertible Golf. Then she decided to have saxophone lessons – I ask you – and one thing led to another. Henry was extremely upset, he'd been very pally with the eldest Baxter boy.

I took a train down to see her a few months after she moved. It was mad, she was living in this godawful flat and the boys were running wild. She didn't even look the same; she had her hair in a hundred plaits and a ruby stud in her nostril, which to be honest looked plain daft. She sent me a couple of postcards, pictures of seagulls with big scrawly purple ink writing on the back. 'Honestly Jo, I'm so happy'. Maybe.

The other thing that drew me to Anna was that she was pregnant, about as pregnant as I would have been. You realise all this is very private, I don't talk about it. Lots of women lose babies, often it's nature's way. But I think it affects your hormones; don't get me wrong, I wasn't mad with grief, I wasn't thinking about stealing small bundles from supermarkets. It was just that seeing Anna reminded me of how special it is to be pregnant.

It was probably a blessing anyway, that miscarriage. Nigel hadn't wanted a third, they're financially rather draining and we were all nicely sorted, well, past the nappy and colic and sleepless-nights stage.

Actually, that's not quite true. Henry has always been a fiend for night terrors, waking up and screaming louder than any new born; he still doesn't like dolls, trolls or frogs.

I lost the baby at about twelve weeks, it just slid down the toilet and that was that. You can't keep crying over lost foetuses.

I thought she'd be more forthcoming, I was a very friendly face, always smiling always cheerful, 'Yoo hoo, hi there.' But she took a while to take the bait. In some respects I had to woo her. Silly, isn't it? I was a grown-up woman and it was like being back in the playground and thinking, 'That girl looks nice, maybe she'd like to come round to my house for tea and we can prick each others fingers and become blood sisters.'

As a child I got used to hunting for friends; my father was in the army so I moved schools a great deal. I think I went to seven primary schools and three secondaries. That's a lot of 'hello my name is Jo's. My parents didn't allow me to be shy; my mother always said shyness was an excuse for social ineptitude and laziness, and I have to say I agree. I am quite jealous of people who have known their girlfriends since they were in the infants and I have always tried to knock it into Georgina's head that they are to be treasured. But it's no good: Georgina will discard a girlfriend for not wearing the right trainers.

By the time I was a teenager I was quite skilled at the art of being a 'good mate'. I let girls copy my homework, borrow my new top before I'd even worn it, laughed at crap jokes and kept watch for the Silk Cut chicks in the toilets. I was always in the middle, I was never bullied (too tall), never the most popular (too tall) and never the naughtiest (too tall, I would always get caught). I was always part of a group, but I always wanted a best friend, one I didn't have to share. And, even though we were about thirty when we met, I really thought I had a chance with Anna.

Of course, I'd had a few best friend near-misses before she came on the scene. I had some good chums at university in Edinburgh but, of course, once I met Nigel I neglected them; friends are like pot plants, they need nurturing. When I moved down to London (Nigel followed, I knew he would) I lived with three other girls. I'm still in contact with two of them; one lives in Melbourne, the other on a remote Scottish Island. I have never managed to visit either, but I remember their birthdays and of course I send Christmas cards. The other flatmate I lost touch with – accidentally on purpose; her last-known address was scribbled on a scrap of paper, destined never to make it into my Filofax. Helen was hard work; she had an eating disorder and it all became rather depressing. She was so sly; she made out that she was eating massive portions, and she was, but it was just cabbage, mounds of the stuff. 'Oh, I'm so full.' Boiled cabbage, Heinz low-calorie soups, stewed apple and raw carrots dipped in Marmite. Occasionally she would binge and then we would hear the toilet flushing through the night as she brought it all back up. In the end she got so thin that her body grew a layer of down up her arms and down her back, nature's way of keeping her warm I suppose. She looked like a hairy skeleton in ninety-four jumpers, her little chicken-claw hands wrapped around a never-ending supply of Bensons, her fingers so thin that they made the cigarettes look like rolls of wallpaper. Her parents came to pick her up one weekend; she had to be carried like a baby down the stairs by her father. The rest of us waved goodbye from the front step, as if she was going to the seaside, and her mother gave us a look as if it were all our fault. I don't think it was, some people are just naturally self-destructive. Anyway I was very busy; Nigel and I were going to get married and I had a wedding to organise. To be honest, I was rather relieved when the thin girl left; it got me out of having to ask her to be a bridesmaid. She'd have made the photos look very odd.

Anna once showed me her wedding album; she was a beautiful but furious-looking bride, surrounded by fat farmers and squinty-eyed children. 'Chris's side of the family,' she explained.

11

The Arrival of Jedediah

A new kitchen had been fitted in the Pink House. Chris would have liked something traditional, 'The kitchen is the heart of the house,' he'd pontificated. Chris had a habit of talking in clichés; he could be very pompous. Sometimes, when he had something that he regarded as profound to say, you could see him puff up with the importance of it: 'The heart of the house is the kitchen.'

He could have said it until he was blue in the face; Anna disagreed and guess who won? The kitchen was sleek and minimal with stainless steel essentials and a glass dining-table arranged artistically on metal girders. Pandora had already given herself quite a nasty cut on the table but Anna said she would have to learn and that life was full of sharp corners. After all, pain was something that reminded you to be more careful in future; this pregnancy, she reminded herself, was definitely the last.

Anna couldn't understand women who just kept having children, 'you forget the agony as soon as that little bundle is put in your arms,' they whined. Rubbish, Anna could remember every last stitch of Pandora's delivery and here she was about to go through the whole thing all over again. Well, in future she would be more careful; she'd make sure Chris had a vasectomy. She'd do it herself on the kitchen table if there were any argument.

Pandora had sort-of settled into Pat-a-Cakes; the weeing had dribbled to a once a week trickle, so that wasn't so bad. Anyway, Anna had trained her daughter to go quietly and change her own pants if she had an accident. There was always a rolled-up spare pair of knickers about the little girl's person; together they kept the problem under control. Anna also made sure that Pandora didn't have much to drink before she went to nursery; it was better for her to be slightly dehydrated than expelled.

Chris was very excited about the 'new arrival'; if Anna so much as murmured in the night, he'd be out of bed, pulling on his socks and repeating the number of the labour ward like a mantra. He kept the spare set of car keys by the bed 'just in case', and never let the petrol gauge drop below half full even though the hospital was only two minutes round the corner.

A week before the baby was due, Anna caught him making cheese and pickle sandwiches. 'What are you doing?' she asked.

'Emergency rations,' he replied. 'I'm going to put these in the freezer and come the day I shall take them with us to the hospital, just in case it's a long jobbie and I get a bit peckish. Don't want to miss the vital moment because I've nipped to the canteen now, do I?'

'Oh great,' said Anna. ''Just what I need, you stinking out the delivery room with cheese and Branston. Why don't you take a jar of pickled onions with you and have done with it?'

'I need to keep my strength up; won't be much good to you if I'm fainting with hunger.'

Anna was still holding out for a Caesarean. After all, surgeons were much more careful than they used to be, they just slit you neatly under the bikini line; gone were the days when you were left with a whacking great scar across your middle, looking for all the world as if you'd been hacked open with an axe.

Whilst Chris's sandwiches fossilised in the deep freeze, Anna felt like she was waiting for a bomb to go off. Every time she walked Pandora to school, she bumped into the old biddy, that Brenda Donahue woman.

'Hello, dear, still here? Can't be long now, eh.'

It was unbelievable; it was almost the end of May and the wretched woman was still wearing a tweed coat. Every time she saw them she started burrowing in her pockets: 'I usually have a nice toffee. My Raymond, he's a one for toffees.'

Anna hadn't a clue who the woman was talking about. 'She's just cleaned her teeth.'

'Here we are. Well, take it for later, pet.'

The last time they saw Mrs Donahue was two days before the baby arrived. It was June the first and Mrs Donahue wasn't wearing her coat; May was out and she'd cast her 'clout'. Instead she had on a lemon cardigan and she was with . . .

'This is Raymond, my son. Say hello, Raymond.'

Raymond had Down's syndrome, he was about seventeen. Anna had never been more embarrassed in her life; when she finally got home she promised herself that if there was anything wrong with this baby she would drown it.

Later, when she was in the newsagent's, she saw an albino with a hearing aid, so that was two more things to worry about. It was a horrible day and Anna didn't know quite who to blame so she took it out on Pandora and later, when Chris came home, she simply wouldn't speak to him.

On the third of June, Anna went into labour. Chris had the whole thing worked out like a military operation: at 0600 hours they were in the car and on their way to Maggie's in Clapham, where Pandora was to be cared for by the traitor Ozzie nanny. All this had been sorted out months ago. The other option had been to get Nanny Wales, Chris's mother, over from Cardiff Bay. 'You are, I hope, bloody joking,' Anna had blurted. 'I'm not having that Welsh bullfrog in my house, thank you very much.'

'But she'll want to see the baby.'

'Well, she can come up on the coach for the day.'

'She's seventy-four.'

'Like I give a flying fuck.'

So that was that sorted.

By the time they got to Clapham, Maggie was waiting on the front steps; her son Joseph hid behind her, burying the birth-mark that stained his little tea cup of a face in the satin folds of her kimono. Maggie had quite a selection of housecoats, wraps and négligé, today's featured orange chrysanthemums on a shiny black background. It was Maggie's job to be glamorous; second wives cannot afford to let themselves go.

Anna had been having contractions since they'd left Lark Grove; by the time they got to Clapham they were quite regular and as Chris pulled into the gravel drive and turned the ignition off, she was seized by another, 'Ooooohheragh.' There was no time for small talk, not now that Anna was biting hard on the leather strap of her overnight bag and they more or less tipped Pandora out of the car. The child was still in her nightdress; they'd forgotten her bag of clothes, which were by the front door of the Pink House along with Chris's sandwiches. If Pandora was going to get dressed today, she'd have to borrow something of Joseph's. Oh well, he was dainty for five. Maggie took Pandora indoors. 'Isn't this exciting?' she trilled. Pandora had thick, yellow sleep in the corners of her eyes and her hair was all matted at the back. 'Good luck, Anna,' shouted Maggie, wishing it was her that was going to have another baby; she had the money, she had the space, she just didn't seem to have the eggs.

Just two hours later, the phone went. Maggie, Joseph and Pandora were eating croissant in the kitchen, so Allison, the nanny answered. It was Chris; Pandora had a new baby brother, six pounds, four ounces and very blond.

Pandora was dark.

Her father picked her up at teatime; she was wearing a pair of Joseph's shorts and a Club Med t-shirt that Maggie didn't mind if they never got back. All the way to the hospital, Chris talked about the new baby and how 'Pandy' was still Daddy's special girl and that being a big sister was a very important job because babies didn't know anything, not even their colours or numbers. 'This baby must be very stupid,' said Pandora, and for the rest of the journey she counted up to ten and pointed out different coloured cars: red car, blue car, lellow car.

'See,' said Chris, 'that baby's going to need you.'

Pandora had made Mummy a nice card; it had been the nanny's idea. There was glue and glitter all over, it was very special.

At the hospital, Anna was sitting up and the new baby brother was in her arms. It seemed a long time since Pandora had seen her mother. Anna caught sight of her daughter hovering by the door. 'What the hell is she wearing, Chris?' she yawned.

Somehow the special card had got all crumpled in the car and most of the glitter had fallen off; it didn't look very nice any more. Pandora started crying. The baby opened one eye as if to say, 'Do you mind?' Pandora put her face in her father's lap. She wanted to go home and she didn't want that baby to come with them.

While the Cunninghams got used to their recent addition – 'Pandora, watch the baby's head, you idiot!' – further down Lark Grove the Metcalfs had a new arrival too.

Siobhan O'Leary, the latest au pair, had arrived.

At last the Metcalfs had struck gold. Siobhan O'Leary was capable and kind and she remembered to turn saucepan handles the right way round so that the children couldn't pull boiling soup on to their heads. Hoorah for Siobhan O'Leary, she wouldn't take any nonsense from anyone; not even from Georgina, who ran her whole gamut of tricks: holding her breath, getting peanuts stuck in her throat and running round with big sharp scissors on slippy floors. Poor Georgina, she was spinning with exhaustion but she was no match for Siobhan, who could do the Heimlich manoeuvre with one hand and sew on a name tag with the other. Henry was a bit nervous of her at first, but that was Henry. He was a natural born coward, one of life's great snivellers. Ever since he had started primary school he had developed a mind-boggling array of nervous tics, blinks and twitches. His latest fad was washing his hands; twenty times a day they'd be under the tap, first the right, then the left and every night they had to be smothered in Vaseline to stop them cracking and peeling.

Jo was rather relieved that Siobhan wasn't particularly attractive. If one is going to have girls around the house, it's better that they resemble the back of a bus rather than Claudia Schiffer.

Especially with Nigel around; be silly to go offering him temptation on a plate. Jo sometimes wondered if unattractive nannies could charge higher rates, being more in demand than those little frisky little pert-breasted types.

Siobhan could drive, so she ferried Henry to his grey-blazer-with-the-red-piping prep school whilst Jo walked Georgina to Pat-a-Cakes with the dog. It was part of her exercise regime, marred only by the fact that she always seemed to have a Kit Kat or a packet of wine gums in her pocket. (Jo had a theory that calories consumed on the move didn't count.)

It was a while since Jo had seen the Cunningham woman. She must have dropped that baby by now; no doubt she was staggering around like a post-natally depressed cowboy. Poor thing. Jo remembered how she'd been with Henry; it had taken her three months to get out of her dressing-gown. She'd been weepy and confused, convinced she was going mad after she found out it was Thursday when she'd thought it was Tuesday, putting her car keys in the fridge and trying to switch TV channels with her glasses case.

She thought about popping a card under the door offering to take Pandora up to nursery, after all the Pink House was on her way. For a second, Jo imagined Anna all weepy with gratitude, her face blotchy with tears. Just to add to the scenario, Jo gave Anna a big black varicose vein down the back of her leg.

'Hello.'

And there she was, la Cunningham, Mummy Aphrodite in blue jeans.

Jeans! Jo couldn't get into her jeans until Georgina was four. The baby was in a pram, all bundled up in what looked like pale blue cashmere. Surely not; not cashmere for a baby? Was the woman mad?

'Oh look, Georgina, this must be Pandora's baby, er—'

'Brother. This is Jedediah.'

Jo wished she'd had a bath and washed her hair, at least put on some deodorant, the baby was so delicious and so clean.

'Didn't Pandora tell you she had a brother?'

'No,' said Georgina, 'we're not speaking.'

'Ha ha,' the mothers laughed.

'He's ten days old.' Anna was being quite chatty for Anna.

Ten days, blimey, thought Jo. Ten days after having mine, I was still sitting on rubber rings and going to bed with a packet of frozen peas between my legs. 'He's gorgeous.'

To have said otherwise would have been a lie. Mind you, people always say nice things about babies, even when they look like twisted little yellow goblins or chopped liver in a bonnet. But the fact was, and Jo had to admit it, this was the nicest-looking baby she had seen for a very long time. Jed looked like a composite of what babies should be.

For a moment, Jo remembered hers as new-borns. Henry, shy from the start, had even tried to hide from the scan. When eventually it was time for him to put in an appearance, it was as if he'd got stage fright and simply refused to emerge from the wings. In the end the doctors had resorted to attaching a sink-plunger instrument to his skull and had pulled him out with such force that Jo was surprised to see the whole baby emerge and not just a scalp. Mind you, his head had been a very odd shape for weeks, all stretched out like a pillar box. Nigel had always joked that 'at least he'd look good in a top hat'. As for Georgina, well, she was a looker now but at the time she'd been jaundiced and as hairy as a monkey.

'Really gorgeous,' Jo repeated; for someone who was meant to be good with words (a 2.1 in English) she was struggling.

'Yes,' said Anna, 'I think I'll keep him,' and she laughed.

Well, this was nice, having a chat on a sunny day; how fortunate these women were with their children and their big houses. To any passer-by, they would already have looked like friends. Had they been dogs, they would have been sniffing each other's backsides by now; maybe they should have done, in the end it might have saved time. Maybe if Jo had had a really good sniff of Anna she would have detected something untrustworthy about her but, obviously, she didn't.

This was the moment that the ice was broken; from now on Jo thought that it was the thing to do, to run after Anna in the morning to exchange pleasantries, school gossip and cracked nipple tips. Being the more experienced mother, Jo felt in a position to advise. Not that Anna seemed to need much help, that baby was a piece of cake – literally; he was like the nicest bun in a baker's window, all pink-icing cheeks and yellow-cream curls.

They talked vaguely of their husbands. Once Anna said, 'Oh, Chris, he's a saint,' but the way she said it made Jo think that if she looked up the definition of 'saint' in the dictionary, it would say 'congenital idiot'.

Jo took it upon herself to fill Anna in on the who's who of the neighbourhood, after all, the Metcalfs were members of the local residents' association.

'Number seventy-two wears a wig, chemotherapy; the old fellow at number forty-six used to read the ITN news and next door to him there's the Fergussans, she's unbalanced, keeps crashing the car. Don't park anywhere near that Polo, she'll have your bumpers off.'

Jo enjoyed other people's business.

'They're gay at number seventy-seven and the toddler at number nineteen is IVF, not that you'd know, and that woman that used to do the Campari advert lives in the place with the green front door and . . . well, you know me . . . and over the road, you've met Brenda Donahue, the one with the Down's syndrome lad, her husband ran off with a dental hygienist, and next door to her you've got the Chamberlains, they're doctors, which I think is always useful.'

Jo told Anna where the best dry-cleaner was and how there was a woman in the next road who did soft furnishings and was a dab hand at shortening curtains and making loose covers. Jo liked being useful to Anna. 'There's an organic butcher in Trinity Road.'

One day, Anna mentioned that she was looking for someone to help out with the kids, maybe take over the ironing, push the Hoover round now and again. 'Leave it to me,' said Jo, and she was as good as her word; that night she asked Siobhan if she had any friends over in Dublin who fancied a spot of nannying. And, as luck would have it, Siobhan did and that's how Sinaed ended up at the Pink House. Bingo. Good old Jo, three cheers for the busybody, nosy-parker, interfering old bag . . .

Anna was so grateful that she gave Jo a rather poisonous-looking potted plant and asked if she and Nigel would like to come for supper, 'Nothing fancy, I don't really cook. How about next Wednesday?'

'Oh, yes please,' said Jo, and she looked forward to it all week like a fifteen-year-old looks forward to a date with the captain of the school football team.

12

New Babies and Neglected Toenails

I am drinking gin today, mother's ruin. Isn't it a shame that you can't edit your life? That's what I've been thinking; if the last ten years were on tape, I'd just chop out the bad bits and keep in the good moments. That's what they do with films, they leave the shit bits on the cutting-room floor. When I get really upset, I play the nice bits in my head, those 'passing your eleven-plus' highlights. When you think about it, there are very few genuinely one hundred per cent happy times in your life, days you wouldn't swap for the world or even a couple of grand. The clip I play the most in the private screening-room in my head is the day I gave birth to my son – which is strange considering I'd been dreading it for so long.

It was five o'clock in the morning and I knew instinctively it was going to happen, so I just sat at the top of the stairs until my waters broke and the hot liquid trickled down the uncarpeted steps like one of those champagne fountains, and I called Chris. Chris cannot do anything until he is dressed. I swear if someone broke into our house, he would put on his trousers and tie up his shoelaces before tackling the intruder. My overnight bag was in the hall: nightie, toothbrush, sanitary towels, the usual, then we got in the car with Pandora, who was all sleepy and cross, and dropped her off at Maggie's. I reckoned I'd have time to get home, have a bath, a couple of pieces of toast, but by the time we had pulled away from Maggie's, I was having contractions every five minutes and I had to put my feet up on the dashboard and pant. Chris, of course, refused to break the speed limit and we did a steady thirty back to King's College hospital. I remember it was a Wednesday and there was a lot of blossom out. By the time we got there I could hardly walk; Chris bunged me in a wheelchair that had a dodgy wheel and we kept ricocheting off the wall and Chris called it a 'sodding thing', which is quite ripe coming from him.

The baby slithered out an hour later; this little pink eel, like a synchronised swimmer emerging from the deep, he sort of came out with a flourish. 'It's a girl,' said the midwife, and my heart sank to my ankles. Then she said, 'I mean a boy,' and there was my Jed. I swear he had one eyebrow arched as if to say, 'Well how's that for an entrance?' I think he only cried because it was expected of him, but it was a casual cry. I fed him almost immediately; he never slobbered like Pandora, it was as if he was sipping a very good wine. He was graceful right from the word go, he didn't leak or puke, he never had nappy rash or chappy skin, he was honey-coloured with a lick of white-blond hair and the bluest eyes.

My children do not look like brother and sister; they are as different as meat paste and caviar.

To be honest, I hadn't wanted another child but Chris was convinced it was a good idea. I could have cheated, I could have kept on swallowing the little white pills in secret, but that would have meant having sex with Chris for longer. At least if I got pregnant he'd stop snuffling under the duvet like a pig hunting out truffles. I gave in, timed my dates with digital accuracy and pretended to be thrilled when the inevitable happened. At least that was him off my back, or rather my fanny, for a good eighteen months.

Fortunately Chris is one of those men who is squeamish about making love to a pregnant woman; he is of the opinion that his penis might dent the baby's head and therefore ruin its chances of getting a decent degree.

I kept expecting to feel as shitty as I had with the gargoyle but apart from a few weeks when all I could manage was jasmine tea and Ryvitas, I sailed though this pregnancy. Course I used to pretend to be feeling like hell; any excuse to be horrible to my husband, but I reckon I was entitled. He was very good about it, of course, kept wanting to stroke my supposedly aching back. Christ, there is nothing worse, is there, than a bloke wanting to give you a neck massage when he hasn't got a clue what he's doing. Just the thought of Chris's pudgy white hands near my neck made me want to scream. 'Just leave me alone,' I'd spit and he did. You can say one thing for Chris, he's very obedient, and I must admit he was very good with Pandora. That was when they got really close; they still are, they do things together like play chess! They like the same things: marmalade, geography and boring nature programmes. She is more relaxed with her father; she never knows when I am going to leap down her throat. I have done terrible things to Pandora ever since she was really small; when she was a baby, I'd say, 'Come on then, you ugly little shitter, let's change your nappy,' or 'Who's never going to get a boyfriend then? Who's always going to have fat legs, eh?'

When I said these things she'd look up at me with worried brown eyes and you could tell she didn't think it was funny either.

Before she could walk and I had to heave her around in a pram, I would lie her face down as she always had nasty rashes on her cheeks and great plugs of green stuff up each nostril. Sometimes I was rough with her because she was so slow; I'd jam her arms into her coat and shove her feet into her boots and all the time my teeth would be clenched and it was all I could do to stop myself scratching her face.

Once when she was about one and she wouldn't stop crying, I lay her on our bed, put pillows around her and punched them till I was exhausted. Fortunately she had the sense to lie still; if she'd have moved, I'd have got her in the face, smashed out her baby teeth and broken her nose.

See, that's a bit I'd cut out; I'd like to wipe that particular memory right off the tape, that and a million others.

Jed was a good baby; people say boys are more difficult but not my Jed. He was never clumsy like Pandora, even as a toddler he never did stupid things; he never got his head stuck between the banister rails or poked metal objects into plug sockets.

It was Chris who first mentioned that we could do with some help; Jed was a month old and he thought Pandora was in danger of being neglected. I think that it was the day he noticed her toenails that he brought the subject up. He came home from work one evening and when Pandora ran to greet him, her toenails made a scratchy noise on the floorboards. I'd forgotten to cut them and they were exceptionally long.

'This can't go on, Anna.'

We couldn't find the nail scissors, so he sorted her feet out with his teeth and an emery board. I promised to phone an agency, put an advert in one of those magazines, but in the end I just mentioned the problem to that Jo down the road and she said she could fix me up. Some people are like that, aren't they? It's normally the fatter women who are good at responsibility, as if they keep a spare set of organisational brain cells in their buttocks. I only mentioned the nanny situation in passing but she took my number and phoned me back that night; her girl knew another girl and the next thing I knew I was paying for this Sinaed to get the ferry over. Extraordinary really, I mean it was very good of her but I don't much like being made to feel grateful.

The peculiar woman with the Down's syndrome son had given me an evil-looking pot plant just a week after I'd had Jed. 'Congratulations on the safe arrival of your little bundle of joy.' It was the most hideous-looking thing I'd ever seen, so I palmed this ugly aspidistra off on the Jo woman as a way of saying thank you. That should have been the end of it but as I thrust the trif-fid into her arms, I heard myself invite them up for supper! The words fell out of my mouth accidentally; it was only meant in that 'let's do lunch' way, but she looked so pleased I half expected her to roll over and wait for me to scratch her belly. To be honest, I'd liked to have shut the door politely but firmly on this new-found chumminess, but she had her foot over the threshold, 'Super, lovely, supper, when? Wednesday's a good night, would you like me to bring a pudding?' See, I'd only vaguely mentioned the idea of an evening chez the Cunninghams and she was already soaking sponge fingers in Grand Marnier!

13

Fake Tan and Tattoos

I remember not knowing what to wear the first time we went up to the Pink House. It was summer, which doesn't suit me; I go all red and sweaty and freckly like salami, whilst Anna, of course, goes the colour of peanut butter. Winter is better for the fat blonde; we can hide our blubber under layers of velvet and slap on a load of foundation. Blondes look best by candlelight, brunettes can turn their tawny features to the sun. It's not fair, is it?

The night before, I'd had a bash with some fake tan; remember we're going back about ten years and Clarins hadn't got the formula then. I'd made a classic mistake and bought some cheap stuff. I ended up looking like Judith Chalmers emerging from a tandoori clay oven and I'd forgotten to wash my hands, which inevitably turned the dark orange of a tree kangaroo.

Nigel caught me making a coffee roulade and couldn't understand why I was so eager about the whole thing. 'Isn't that a bit over the top? You haven't known this woman five minutes and you're slaving away over a pudding you normally only make for my birthday!'

Then he slugged the Grand Marnier and pretended to be really pissed, staggering round the kitchen swearing and telling filthy jokes. 'What's green and smells of pork? Kermit's fingers.'

'Ha ha, Nigel,' I said. It was an old joke, even then.

At 7.45pm, we left the kids in Siobhan's capable hands. I'd tried to be artistic with a load of flowers culled from the garden but I've never been very good at that sort of thing and what was supposed to look spontaneous and arty ended up looking like a load of broken-headed roses with the mange. Still, Anna had said it was 'casual, just a barbecue in the garden, just the four of us.' As we walked up the hill, Nigel swinging a bottle of well-chilled white wine and me clutching the exhausted flowers and the fancy pudding, I planned interesting conversations in my head, mentally rehearsing those little anecdotes that are useful when things go quiet.

Women do that; we tell funny little stories because we can't remember jokes, I have learnt how to be amusing and make it my job to keep the atmosphere pleasant. I can't be doing with people who sulk in corners.

Anna's husband, Chris, is one of those men who likes cooking, which is a good job because Anna doesn't, she's not interested. The world divides into people who can cook and those who must go to Marks and Spencer. Chris is like me, he's greedy; sometimes I think it would have been nice to have married a man who likes his food. Nigel has a sweet tooth but apart from that he is quite happy with cheese and biscuits, which is a bit galling when you've flogged yourself to death being experimental with beetroot pesto.

So there we were, me with my fake tan and those floaty trousers from Ghost, which are marvellous because they've got an elasticated waist but make your arse look enormous unless, of course, you're extremely thin. In which case you have no need of diaphanous kecks and you can swan around in faded, pink denim cut-off shorts, which is what Anna was wearing. Makes you sick, doesn't it? She'd only had that baby six weeks back.

Of course Nigel perked up as soon as she answered the door. Doesn't take much to cheer up a bloke, does it? The sight of a long-legged lovely in minuscule shorts and a fantastic pair of milk-engorged breasts will do the trick every time. It was obvious she'd just fed the baby, there were damp patches on her pale blue shirt where she'd leaked a little. As soon as she saw Nigel's eyes clock the dark circles, she said, 'Shit, do excuse me, I'll just go and change my top.' When she came down again she was wearing a little yellow strappy vest and below her left shoulder was a navy tattoo of a blue bird; immediately I craved one for myself. I gave her the flowers, the pudding and the wine. 'Blimey, is it my birthday?' she laughed.

The baby was in a basket under a lilac tree in the garden and Chris was hovering over a barbecue; he was wearing gigantic khaki shorts and socks with Jesus sandals and a blue and white striped butcher's apron. Chris is one of those blokes who doesn't care about clothes. However he has outfits for occasions and this was one of his relaxing/mine host/off-duty/out-of-the-office ensembles. He had others for golf, the beach and park walking. On this particular occasion, he wore a baseball cap over his gingery blond hair and smiled a lot. I liked him instantly; he was even sweatier and more freckly than me.

Deck chairs and I don't go and unfortunately I ended up beached in one of those low-slung ones that make you grunt when you attempt to get out of them. Anna sat on a rug with her legs folded impossibly underneath her. 'Origami woman,' Nigel said with approval, and she laughed and ate a pistachio nut. It was then that I noticed that her incisors were rather long and pointed.

They were very generous. For a start there was a glass pitcher of Pimm's and squatting in a large plastic washing-up bowl full of ice at least twelve bottles of beer, plus an open bottle of something Australian on the table. Mind you, to be honest I was more peckish than thirsty and it seemed to take for ever for them to realise that all the pistachios had been eaten and there was nothing left to nibble. Chris must have heard my stomach rumbling because suddenly he yelled, 'Oh Lord, the crudites and dips,' and Anna smirked and said, 'Golly, sorry, Jo, you must be starving.'

It struck me that night how well matched Nigel and Anna were, and for that matter Chris and I; us two raw-boned and clumsy, the other two precise and unsweating. I got taramasalata on my trousers and Chris had ketchup on his chin.

Pandora came out to say goodnight, which she did without kisses or smiles, and when her mother asked her to do the nursery rhyme she'd learnt in school she turned on her fat heel and stormed back into the house. That's when the baby woke up and you couldn't help but notice the difference, him all blond and handsome, the girl all awkward. As she thundered away, I noticed her nightie was caught between the cleft of her buttocks; she was going to have an enormous arse. I felt genuinely sympathetic. I have struggled with mine all my life, my buttocks are like pork panniers; if I sit on a stool, they spill down on either side, therefore I avoid stools. This is what life is like when you are fat; you are forever gauging whether things will take your weight. Big bums even dictate your career choices. For example, I could never have been an air hostess; imagine the chaos, me ricocheting down the aisle knocking people's miniature gins into their laps and collecting mashed potato up the back of my skirt. These days, because I own a second-hand bookshop, I can sit behind a large desk and nobody can tell that I am a size sixteen from the waist down.

We left around 10.30, after all it was a school night. When we got home, I remembered that we hadn't eaten my pudding, it had been left in the kitchen on the sideboard. We'd had strawberries instead: they were rather underipe and she'd forgotten to buy cream. Mine could have done with a little sugar. When we got into bed, I said to Nigel, 'Sweet baby,' but I think he'd forgotten that ours would have been about the same age because he was half asleep and he just muttered something that sounded suspiciously like 'great tits'.

14

Working Lives

Sinaed McKenna had arrived at the Pink House, all twelve stone of her, with seven hair-sprouting moles on her face and all the personality of mashed Weetabix, which, let's face it, was a relief. Au pairs and nannies must be equipped with a sort of sixth sense and an ability to fade into the background when not required. Once their duties are done, they mustn't lie around on the sofa joining in with family life, they must go out, stay in their room, or, ideally, disappear into a puff of smoke.

However liberal you pretend to be, you don't want the hired help being overly sociable, crashing your dinner parties, drinking your port and playing spin the bottle after midnight. Having no personality is better than having too much in these situations.

The nanny can't afford to be too emotional either, that's why you have to be careful with the foreign ones: the sulky Spanish types who mope around with their abundance of body hair and suicidal faces or, even worse, the smiling, nude-sunbathing Scandinavians, the Ulrika look-alikes, with their penchant for eating rollmop herrings topless.

Sinaed McKenna was naturally prudish. She arrived with a stack of big lady's pants and vests, which she wore over an industrial-sized bra, and settled herself into the pale lemon room at the top of the Pink House, with its sloping ceilings that she was forever cracking her head on.

One morning, Anna crept into the room while Sinaed was walking Pandora up to school and literally gagged when she saw what the 'stupid sow' had done to the place: hundreds of photos of flame-haired brothers and sisters, nephews and nieces, had been Blu-tacked to the walls, and the bed was awash with cuddly toys and the vilest crocheted patchwork blanket. Sinaed had turned the place into a Tipperary bedsit, complete with crucifix and rosary beads.

Sinaed liked novelty slippers and wore sweatshirts with cartoon characters on them. She collected china frogs and pigs and Anna had to bite her lip very hard and stick her fingers in her ears when she played her Daniel O'Donnell tapes.

'Ooh, Mrs Cunningham, d'you not know Daniel? The man is sheer genius. And the charity work, ah the fellow is tireless in his efforts for the unfortunate.'

But it was worth it, even if she did dunk her biscuits and bought those odd puzzle books. She didn't bring home strange men or leave amphetamine sulphate lying around. All right, she did drink rather a lot of milk, but it was a small price to pay for someone who cooked, cleaned, washed and ironed with an enthusiasm bordering on compulsion.

Of course Anna had to be quite strict with her about certain matters, the overfeeding of Pandora for a start. 'I'd rather Pandora was given the low-fat spread rather than butter, Sinaed. I don't want her having a heart attack before she's six.' Sinaed was a great believer in dairy products, after all her 'Mammy and Daddy' lived on a farm. Perhaps that was why she was so bovine, Anna conjectured; she'd spent so much time around cows, she'd almost become one. Moo Moo. Sometimes just the sight of Sinaed made Anna want to attack her with the bread knife and occasionally she imagined bringing the big metal toaster down on her head.

Fortunately, before Anna could get violently sick of having Sinaed clomping round the house, both she and Siobhan developed an obsession with West End musicals and spent whatever nights they had off hanging round the stage door of *Les Miserables*. So that was a blessing.

Anna, although she was still feeding Jed whenever she could, gradually weaned herself back to work.

Other people's jobs are a mystery, aren't they? Apart from the simple ones like postman, teacher, dentist, it's difficult to understand what people do for a living; there are so many peculiar things that people actually get paid for doing, like tree surgeons. Once upon a time Anna was going to be an actress but she never had the nerve for it; occasionally she would find herself hot with embarrassment in the middle of the stage, her mouth as dry as sandpaper, and that's wrong, that doesn't happen to Judy Dench.

Anna could never convince herself, never mind an audience, that she was anyone other than Anna Redfern in a wig and a funny pair of shoes.

After her last professional engagement, when she had to dress up as a heap of rubbish for an environmental theatre company, she quit the glamorous world of Theatre In Education and became a waitress instead. Working in the heart of London's glittering West End, though admittedly serving soup and club sandwiches, was preferable to touring round the North of England in a transit van, playing two primary schools a day and having snot balls flicked at you. Occasionally, she went for auditions and once her legs were used in an early eighties satirical sketch show, but it was never going to go any further and Anna knew it, she wasn't a stupid woman. She could have been clever, she could have gone to university and got a second-class degree like Jo had, but she didn't. Instead she landed cat-like on her feet and secured herself a nice cushy job where she could help herself to coffee and smoke if she felt like it.

Anna was lucky to make the move from catering to casting because, let's face it, there is nothing so defeated as a forty-year-old waitress with varicose veins and feet fit for nothing but Dr Scholl's. Anna was good at her job; she'd always had a critical eye. Whenever she looked at people on the street, she knew exactly what they could advertise: some people have yoghurt faces, others are more pant liner.

For a while, she and Maggie had toyed with the idea of their own look-alike agency, but they soon discovered that people who want to look like celebrities have deep psychological problems and it wasn't worth the bother. 'I *am* Cary Grant,' said the bloke with one leg and Anna had replied, 'And I *am* the Queen of Sheba.' They did, however, manage to recruit a Keith Chegwin doppelganger from a bus stop in Battersea, but you can't run a business based on that. So they stuck to finding faces that sold consumer goods, and on the profits of this, they were able to buy the very things they'd helped to promote: beer, tampons, chocolate, cars, tissues etc. All work is a vicious circle.

Chris, of course, worked very hard indeed; he had to, there were a lot of things that needed buying. There was the Pink House, with her expensive tastes and roof-tile habit, Anna, who believed that the money she earned was for shoes and accessories, not petrol or phone bills, and the kids. There were days when Chris was convinced that he was going to have a stroke before elevenses. He worked in the stock market, buying and selling coffee beans mostly. It was very stressful and he often wished he could do what Anna did, just sitting around all day looking at people's faces, deciding if they looked curranty enough to sell biscuits. Chris had to wear a suit to work and sometimes he felt as if his tie was going to strangle him; he could make himself go quite purple in the face just thinking about it. Poor Chris, he was in a young man's game and he felt old for his age; his feet hurt, his sinuses were permanently blocked and he was on a bottle of Gaviscon a day. Secretly he thought about giving it all up and going to live in a cottage in the middle of a field where he could eat roast potatoes all day long.

Lark Grove was full of people trying their hardest, doing their best, keeping the wolf from the door. As we know, Jo Metcalf was the proprietor (courtesy of her husband) of a charmingly run-down second-hand bookshop, 'Chapters', which was mostly patronised by local female art students who would pop in to thieve paperback copies of *The Bell Jar* and anything by Virginia Woolf. Thanks to the bookshop, Jo had read every Jackie Collins book ever published.

Her husband Nigel, an erstwhile Rumpole of the Bailey wannabe, had somehow become an in-house lawyer for the independent television company, Double Ace Productions. You may never have heard of them, but you might have seen some of their programmes: sit coms, satirical quiz shows, topical chat shows, late-night studio audience discussion shows, which inevitably got a bit hairy. Nigel kept an eye on all things libellous, the reins of public taste and decency were in his hands; sometimes he would swap you one 'fuck' for three 'Christ's. Occasionally, he would take a back seat and allow the viewing public to be morally offended; this would result in publicity for the show and with any luck a mention on *Points of View*. Sometimes the job got him down – who was he to stem the tide of filth? Times change, even kids' TV presenters were looking like porn stars, tits hanging out, flashing their knickers, most of them sniffing those giveaway class A sniffs: sniff, giggle, giggle, sniff. There wasn't much that Nigel didn't know about the business, after all, he was a member of a couple of Soho media watering holes, he had seen it all.

Nigel's head was full of slander and litigation; he liked to keep busy. Occasionally when he wasn't, he worried about having contracted a sexually transmitted disease and was forever examining his penis under an angle-poise lamp for 'inflammation and discharge'. So far he had been lucky but guilt is a strangely powerful emotion and now and again his genitals would tingle and he felt as if a million ants were hatching under his foreskin. Nigel, what with his willy-watching and recreational class A drug use, spent an inordinate amount of time in the lavatory.

So, this is how our grown-ups spent their time. Meanwhile, the au pairs picked up towels from the bathroom floor, put the breakfast things in the dishwashers, and did all the jobs that wives used to do, apart from fuck their husbands. Nowhere in either Sinaed's or Siobhan's contracts did it mention husband-fucking.

Of course, the children were busy too; it's not all colouring and Play-Doh being a kid these days. Pandora had letters of the alphabet to trace for homework, tumble-tots on a Tuesday and swimming on a Friday. Georgina had ballet on a Thursday, whilst Henry was learning the French horn. Only Jed, the baby, had nothing to do but gurgle, grow teeth and fill his nappy. Good boy.

15

En Suites, on Breasts and on Ambition

I never used to get tired. I'm not really lazy, I haven't got idle bones. These days I am exhausted as soon as I wake up. In the old days I used to rush around like a blue-arsed fly; that's why I needed help, I couldn't do everything, I needed Sinaed. Isn't it funny? That woman was part of my life for nearly ten years and now I shall never see her again.

I remember what it was like when she first arrived. It's odd having a stranger in your house, you have to remember to put your knickers on when you're running to the bathroom. You can't just sit around biting your toenails and masturbating. Chris was paranoid of course that she'd catch sight of his willy, or worse, that he might accidentally catch her starkers; not the most edifying scenario. She was one of those ginger Irish types, all freckles and white skin, big arse, big tits, but no shape to speak of.

Thanks to Sinaed, I managed to wangle an en suite out of Chris. I tell you, once you've had his-and-hers sinks, you never go back. Cost him a fortune but spared his blushes. I'm not like that, I have always been a bit of a flaunter. Not now, of course, now that I am fat I undress in the dark. But in the old days, I'd strip off anywhere, tits out on the beach, in the back garden, quick flash at the window cleaner. I am one of the few women I know who does not apologise for her breasts. Because women do, they're always going on, 'Oh they're too droopy/small/big.' Well mine were just right; even after breast-feeding two kids I had decent bazookas.

Once I saw the Irish girl's, they were terrible: two big greasy bags of fat with the most disappointing nipples, tiny non-existent pink toggles that looked as if they'd been grafted on from a child's anorak. Don't get me wrong, I'm not a lezzie, though I have been to bed with two women in my life (Lisa and Deboragh as I recall, one thin, one fat, both pissed) neither experience was enough to turn me off blokes. I am a man's woman – truly.

Anyway what was I saying? We had old ginge minge working for us, all rosary beads and chocolate Hobnobs in her bedroom, writing letters home to her childhood sweetheart, not to mention her ma and her five brothers and sisters, who were always having birthdays. That's what I remember about her; when I think of Sinaed, I imagine her at the kitchen table, wrapping up some parcel in brown paper and string, forever licking stamps with her big cow's tongue, slurp, slap, 'Roight then, I'll be orf to catch the post then, Mrs C, don't want our, Seamus/Niamh/Patrick etc. to be disappointed, now do oi?' Mind you, I suppose I was lucky; at least she stayed. Jo's didn't, her Siobhan bogged off within the year, married a bloke in Connemarra and had two sets of twins, one after the other.

Sometimes I wonder what it would be like to have a brother or sister. Would they take my side in all this, would they stick up for me?

I never asked my mother why she didn't have any more children after me; possibly it was because my mother was rather keener on having a life-style than kids. I never bothered to ask if I'd been breast-fed, I knew instinctively that I hadn't.

I think she was relieved that I was attractive; it would never have done to have spawned something that didn't match the furniture. But my mother was still critical in a very low-key way. 'Put your shoulders back, Anna, that's better. Can't have you all hunched up like a baboon,' and then she'd try to smile as if to say, 'You and me, we're in this together.' My mother's smile was never wholehearted; it was designed to look cheerful but not cause wrinkling round the eyes, so it never really went all the way, whereas my father would laugh with his mouth wide open. 'Do you mind, Brian, we don't really want to see your fillings.'

If ever there was the threat of fun, my mother was there to pour cold water on it. By the time I was a teenager my mother was in the grip of what seemed to be a permanent migraine. On the advice of some doctor, she took to doing yoga and meditating and making strange noises; it was as if she was trying to hum the grubby reality of everyday life out of the house. She spent most of her time with her legs wrapped round the back of her neck and her eyes firmly shut. Consequently she hadn't got a clue what I was up to most of the time. She snapped out of it a few years later but there was a time when I'd be coming home at sixteen with my knickers in my pocket; even if I'd worn them on my head and waved used condoms in front of her face, I don't think she'd have noticed.

When I was eighteen I went to drama school. To be honest, I think I only went because I didn't know what else to do and it was a way of getting one up on my mum; she'd dabbled in local amateur operatics and still had the tin of theatrical make-up to prove it: big, greasy, fat crayons of panstick, 'crimson lake' in gold paper and a pat of black eyeliner you had to spit into. I thought drama school was going to be more of a laugh than it was. There were some terrible people there, all taking it really seriously, really believing they were Joan of Arc.

'I am burning. Oh, how the flames lick my heels and turn my knees to charcoal. Alas, I am engulfed.'

Yeah, right.

I loathed improvisation classes; I'd get very embarrassed and feel like I was going to faint. I didn't like fencing either because you had to wear communal masks, full of other people's sweat and dandruff.

I don't think we were a very exciting year; you wouldn't have heard of anyone that was there at the same time as me, though there was a hatchet-faced blonde that ended up in *The Bill* and a bloke from the year below me who was in *Coronation Street,* but I'm fucked if I can remember his name.

Thing was, when I was going to be an actress, theatre was going through that ghastly depressing agitprop phase: lots of ugly girls with hairy armpits and Dr Martens boots. I had a choice; I could get my Equity card by shaving my head, buying a guitar and singing comedy songs about removing men's testicles or I could strip.

I bought a guitar and a spangly bikini and dithered between the two choices. Then out of the blue, I was offered a card in exchange for three months touring primary schools doing Theatre

In Education. It was terrible; it was worse than mastitis, it was worse than putting needles in my eyeballs, it was worse than marrying Chris, and so that's what I did; Anna Redfern became Anna Cunningham.

It was all such a game, being married, playing house, but I never thought I'd still be playing it, year in, year out. I always thought something else would come along. I nearly got parts in a couple of soap operas: I got three recalls for *Albion Market*, I even got an audition to present *The Tube*. I used to be so jealous of Paula Yates; I always reckoned she got the job because she'd sucked off Bob Geldof which, even if he is a bit of a whiffy old tramp, was groovier than being married to a prematurely balding fat bloke and living in South London.

I had an agent, you know; Gareth Fergusson. Never heard of him? Complete alcoholic, embarrassing really – all big talk and fuck-all action. Scottish bloke, swore he was best mates with Billy Connolly, greasy little liar. Anyway, a couple of years later he went and croaked it, coke-induced heart attack. I went to the funeral, more out of nosiness than sentiment, and guess who wasn't there? That's right, his best mate Billy Connolly. I think that's when I really fell out of love with the business, not that I'd ever been particularly passionate in the first place. That was my problem, I think; there was nothing at the time that I wanted badly enough.

There aren't very many options for an out-of-work actress who can't type; inevitably I fell into the second oldest profession in the world: waitressing. Chris wasn't keen, oh fan that fire.

Actually, I could understand his point. For a bloke in the City it's one thing introducing your wife as an actress, but saying, 'Meet my wife, she picks up other people's dirty plates,' is something else entirely. If you are introduced as an actress, people immediately jump to the conclusion that they must have seen you on the telly and they start making wild guesses: 'Weren't you that girl in *Boon*?' etc., but if you're a waitress, the conversation grinds to a halt and they start looking over your shoulder hoping to see someone who writes books or does something interesting.

Not that waitressing isn't fascinating, it's hilarious. The amount of spitting that goes on in people's food! In the past I have been known to grab small handfuls of pubic hair and deposit them under puff pastry lids, and never once did I wash my hands after I'd been to the toilet, not even after I'd done a poo. It made me laugh. Everyone was at it: bogies, fag ash, great oysters of phlegm, and this was a posh place too.

I only did lunches; tips were better at night when everyone's more pissed but Chris liked me home in the evening. I used to nick provisions from the restaurant for our tea, mostly stuff like smoked salmon and fancy cheese; he went mad when he found out. For a moment I thought he was going to march me back and make me own up! Just the sight of him all swollen up with self-righteousness and indignation made me laugh till I wet my pants. Christ knows why he didn't give up on me. The restaurant was called The Blue Mandolin; course it went bust but that was the eighties for you. It's a tapas bar now, serving little oily bowls of hideous fishy things with glassy eyes that make your breath smell.

I've always nicked stuff – only little things. I've even stolen from friends. I remember Jo moaning on about losing a marcasite brooch, course she blamed the cleaner. Think I've still got it somewhere. Never worn it, that's not the point. It wasn't like I needed it, Chris was forever buying me little treats; soon as he knew I was pregnant he bought me a pair of diamond earrings. Serve him right if I have a miscarriage I thought. But I didn't, even though once, when I was really panicking about everything,

I drank a load of gin and had a bath that was lobster-killingly hot. But it refused to let go and slide out, that baby had taken root like a great big barnacle in my womb. Nothing I could do was going to shift it.

Back then we lived in a Victorian semi in Herne Hill. It was all right, it was just identical to all the others and the day I came home from hospital with Pandora, I decided I just didn't want to live there any more.

Poor Chris, he'd gone to so much effort; there were yellow roses to greet me and he'd gone to Marks and Spencer and bought all sorts of delicious things you could just put in the microwave. His mother had been up and had filled the freezer with vile lamb concoctions, all grease and bone, which I chucked in the bin. 'She was only trying to help,' said Chris. 'Fuck off,' I said, but he didn't mind because I was 'obviously suffering from post-natal mood swings'. Well actually I wasn't, I was suffering from a badly stitched fanny, having him for a husband, living in a boring little semi and the disappointment of that hippopotamus of a baby.

When the fuss died down and people stopped popping by with presents and cards and flowers and Chris was at work doing whatever he did and I was just stuck there with blob features, I thought I might go mad. It was such hard work. I never even had the time to sit down and enjoy a good shit; all I did was run around with my shirt open. She wanted feeding constantly and she was so greedy she'd guzzle away and then puke it all up again. I remember thinking, well here's an eating disorder in the making. Anyway, it didn't seem to matter how much she regurgitated, she got bigger every day. You could practically hear her putting on weight and it drove me mad.

I made up my mind to get a job, a proper one. It made sense, but I was clueless about what it might be. I was virtually unemployable and I knew Chris wouldn't let me waitress again. I was on the verge of giving up when I got a phone call from a girl I'd been at drama school with – Maggie Nichols. I remembered her because she'd been the most spectacularly awful Alison in our feeble second-year production of *Look Back in Anger*. Poor Maggie, with the West End having resolutely turned its back on her and the words 'We'll call you' echoing in her ears, she'd ended up in casting. For a couple of seconds, I let my imagination place me as the lead in a new female detective series, a sort of Miss Marple in suspenders; the reality was less exciting. She needed an attractive-ish woman for a BUPA catalogue, you know the sort of thing: woman in lipgloss lying back on clean, white sheets having just had an operation which, judging by her face, was slightly more enjoyable than a West End musical followed by dinner in a posh restaurant. In the end, despite spending thirty-five quid on a new nightie – I was determined to be professional about this – I didn't get the job; apparently I didn't look happy enough! Well, *quelle surprise*. But I did get chummy with Maggie again and it's odd how things work out, isn't it?

Since I'd last seen her, Maggie had married this photographer, bit older than her, rich you could say, massive house on Clapham Common. He'd been married before, to one of those sixties junkies who used to float up and down the Kings Road in floppy-brimmed hats and no shoes. They had one daughter – almost grown up – then he met Maggie and dumped the missus, basically because when he married her she looked like Brigitte Bardot and twenty years on she's still a ringer for her which, if you've seen any pictures of Brigitte in the last ten years, is not altogether a good thing. When blondes go, they really go. So, doggie Bardot fucks off to live in Ireland on some commune for knackered wives or something, the daughter lives in Paris and is doing her own thing, our David Bailey of Clapham moves Maggie into the mansion on the Common and they have little Joseph.

By the time I met Maggie's son he was three years old. He's sort of cute but has a birthmark on his cheek, one of those port wine stain thingies; they don't show up on scans you know.

This photographer, by the way, used to be quite shit-hot: loads of album covers in the seventies, big awards, couple of coffee-table books, that sort of thing, which is why the stupidly massive house, complete with studio and office space downstairs. But Mr Trendy Snapperoonie couldn't hold on to his Kodak crown, and Maggie, who has never been stupid (which is probably why she never made it as an actress), started a model-cum-casting agency in the basement. Joe Public, she called it, after the little one. Not that she could give him any work, not with that port wine stain. I suppose he could have got away with his profile but his port wine stain was on the good side.

You don't need all this, do you? All this information; it's giving me a headache trying to remember everything. All you need to know is that I started helping her out. It was perfect, I really liked that job. Maggie says I can go back any time; she's got someone else filling in but only because she had to. Joseph is fifteen now. Last time I saw him he had a bolt through his nose and three metal spikes sticking out of his chin; I suppose it's to detract from the Vimto stain that's still there on his cheek.

Funny really; there we were, two young mothers, kid each, and we'd be doing loads of castings for baby stuff: catalogues, nappy ads, Calpol, but we could never cast our own children, they were like little monsters in the attic.

Later, when I had Jed, and it was obvious that he was perfect model material, Maggie wouldn't let me, said it wasn't fair on the others. Jealous cow.

16

Mother's Help and Mango Chutney

I never intended to sit down for a living, but that's what I do. I work in my second-hand bookshop and for ninety-five per cent of the time, I sit on my derrière. Years ago, before I had all the confidence knocked out of me, I used to pretend to be a writer with one hand in the biscuit tin, the other hovering over a keyboard.

Nigel bought the bookshop. It's a converted stable and Americans, if they ever find it, love it. It's very 'quaint', which is a euphemism for 'damp and smelly'. I have to force the shop to make money because if I fail, Nigel will have won. I tick over . . . I should have done better. I was really rather clever at school; there was only one girl in my class who got higher grades and in the end she went mad, took off all her clothes on an intercity train and tried to jump. She was halfway through her second year at Oxford. The only reason she didn't manage to kill herself was because a load of squaddies sat on her; she was naked and wriggling all the way to Waterloo.

I am cleverer than Anna; she has a diploma in drama, I have a 2.1 in English. I should have written a novel by now. A long time ago, I had a few articles published in various women's magazines, pithy social comments about 'shopping trolleys with wonky wheels' and the 'hilarious consequences of being married with kids'; you will have read this type of garbage countless times. Some people are better at it than others and become minor celebrities on telly panel games; I didn't because, let's face it, I wasn't that funny. I never got beyond the 'Doesn't it drive you mad when they squeeze the toothpaste from the middle of the tube?' level of wit and I will admit now that on at least three occasions I banged on about 'the missing sock syndrome'. I wasn't very original, shall we say. I also had a go at writing children's books but they were rejected. Ditto a radio comedy drama and several plays.

Because I have always pretended to be a 'working mum', I have always had help; lots of those soppy au pairs that you get really cheaply because they all have some personality disorder. Really, the girls I've been through. I've had the lot: idle slags, lying cheats, chat-line addicts, petty shoplifters, sulkers, whingers and worse. I had one that used to tie Georgina by her plaits to the banister rail and another who was forever forgetting to do the kids' laundry. Once she sent Henry to school wearing a pair of her knickers; you can't do that to an eight-year-old boy – not when he's got swimming anyway! I mean, it's funny now but at the time they drove me mad. Some people are really lucky with their staff, I'm not. I counted them up the other day, the au pairs, the cleaning women; I got to seventeen and I know I missed out a couple. And for what? So that I could have a 'career' that in the end came to sod all. The way I see it is that we're the only generation of women to be caught out, the only ones who will ever buy the 'having it all' myth because it's nonsense really. The next generation won't bother; they'll revert back to being wives and mothers and lying on the sofa every afternoon watching Bette Davis films and eating chocolate gingers. Well, they will if they've got any sense.

Siobhan was the best au pair I'd ever had, which is why, of course, she stayed for just twelve months. Unbelievable. Anna, of course, was far jammier with her Sinaed; the girl stayed year in, year out, putting up with dreary Pandora – for Jed's sake, I suppose. Anna was never particularly nice to her; there was always an atmosphere when the two of them were together. I don't think Anna liked anyone who sucked away some of her son's affection. She could be quite snappy with Sinaed; once, when she was pouring cream over a bowl of fruit salad for Pandora, Anna knocked the jug clean out of her hand. It smashed on the floor, there was cream everywhere and all I remember was this terrible silence whilst Sinaed cleaned it up. It was Jed who made things better whenever Anna was in a mood; he would gurgle and clap and sing for her, he was a consummate performer; by the time he was two he was quite the vaudevillian.

I wasn't surprised when Anna told me how she'd nearly been an actress, and to me, doing what she ended up doing – working in casting – sounded rather glamorous. But, to be honest, most things are glamorous compared to sitting by an electric fire, flogging Agatha Christies.

I always thought she'd get Georgina in for something; at one point they were handling the Ladybird children's clothing company account; Georgina would have been ideal, it was obvious. But she never did.

We met the woman she worked for once; it wasn't a very successful evening. We have found over the years that it's better with just the four of us, strangers upset the balance. This particular night – I think it was Anna's birthday – there were the six of us having an Indian takeaway up at the Pink House. I told you Anna can't cook, so I'd made her a cake; one of those strawberry and shortbread jobbies, fiends to get right, and I'd been working all day, but it was her birthday and I think sometimes it's nice to make the effort. So we took it up the hill and there were these ghastly people, this hairy over-the-hill photographer and his incredibly silly wife: Mike and Maggie. I've got a thing against people with beards anyway so I loathed him on sight, bombastic, patronising old git; and she was unbelievably precious, called everyone darling and chunnered on about colonic irrigation, which is out of order when you're eating an Indian takeaway. I've never been able to face a murgi masala ever since. She was too thin, a little red-haired sparrow of a thing, top to toe in Versace, her scrawny shoulders tanned into leathery submission. I didn't know who was meant to be impressing whom, it was all labels and name-dropping and sharing boats with Richard Branson. Well, you can't compete with that sort of thing. The whole atmosphere was out of kilter, so I started knocking back the booze and ended up having some stupid row with beardy bloke about Northern Ireland. I accused him of being an IRA sympathiser and it all got rather ugly. I can't remember getting home that night but I know somehow I'd managed to get mango chutney in my bra.

We didn't talk about it afterwards; occasionally Maggie and Captain Birdseye, as I called him, went over for supper and occasionally Anna and Chris went to Clapham but we never did the sixsome thing again. She's called a few times on the phone recently and I let her talk to Anna; I leave the room out of politeness but sometimes I am tempted to snatch the receiver out of Anna's hands and beg Maggie to have the wretched woman at her house. Only I can't, she's just had a lump removed from her breast and I think she's under enough pressure. I have noticed, however, that Anna never asks her how she is. Do you see what I mean?

I don't have an au pair anymore; haven't for several years, not since Georgie started secondary school. I have done with young women in my house. Siobhan was the last decent one and she left nine years ago. These days I have Sue, who is older than me (just), with grandchildren, who live in Bromley. Sue has diabetes and a council flat on the North Peckham estate, but is none the less completely trustworthy. She comes in every day at around three and does housework and ironing and keeps an eye on the kids, who get dropped off via an elaborate school run at four-ish. Sue stays until either Nigel or I get home and if it's after eight o'clock and it's dark we get her a cab – good help is hard to find. Sometimes I give her blouses from my wardrobe. She is efficient and businesslike and does not want to get too involved; she has her own family, her own friends, her own troubles, but she doesn't bang on about them, not like some I know. Sue's granddaughter, Jade, had a meningitis scare a few months back, but she came to work anyway. The woman is the salt of the earth; at Christmas, not only do I give her good quality bubble bath, I give her a cheque for one hundred pounds.

Sue doesn't clean the spare room, it's not part of her job; what could she do with that room anyway? I have lost track of how long Anna has been staying but I know the place is beyond mere Mr Muscle; it needs fumigating, it needs the rat-catcher in. Anna has become domestic vermin.

17

Playtime For Grown-Ups

Jo was depressed. Her chocolate consumption had escalated to dizzy heights: some days it felt as if the blood in her veins was ninety-eight per cent Cadbury's. The eighties, that decade of greed and ambition, shoulder pads and champagne, were nearly over – and what had she achieved? Matrimony, kids and a fat arse. Still, you couldn't blame Thatcher for everything.

Jo's literary dreams were collapsing around her ears; she kept getting rejection slips, and the features editor of *She* magazine had described her most recent article as 'trite and immature'. Jo wondered whether it was the colour of the walls in the study that was putting her off; the paint chart had described it as 'Georgian Red' but it had turned out more 'Abattoir Brown'. It was so dark that even when the sun was beating down outside she had to have the electric light on. Her desk was awash with scripts and ideas for novels but it was just too hard; maybe a children's book would be easier, an alternative alphabet book? Jo started making notes: A is for Aardvark, B is for Botulism, C is for Crap, maybe it wasn't such a good idea. Nigel had been right, as usual; it was a good job she had the bookshop to fall back on. Sometimes Jo didn't want to do anything. It would be nice occasionally to just get back under the duvet and sleep the afternoon away, but Siobhan was forever hoovering the stairs and you couldn't pretend to have a migraine every day.

It wasn't that Jo saw Anna as a sort of hobby, but cultivating the new friendship was a welcome distraction.

People never bothered so much with friends in the olden days, they were too busy bringing coal in from the shed, boiling pigs' heads and darning socks; life was too short for friends. Nowadays it is important to have a wide and varied social circle; ideally this circle should include ethnic minorities, a couple of professionals, at least one or two with letters after their names, and a smattering of interesting types who make hats or sell handmade jewellery in Camden.

'This is my friend Ingrid. She's Polish, does a lesbian highwire act.'

'Oh, well done! Meet Mimbib, Ethiopian Jenga champion of the world.'

Poets count for several points, as do those loaded chums who own a place in Tuscany where you are always welcome in the summer. Conversely, you should take away points for being matey with traffic wardens and tax inspectors.

For some being popular is more important than for others. Some people view friendships as a matter of convenience; their 'friend' has a car and can therefore be relied upon for lifts. Traditionally women are more friend-friendly. They are also quicker to make enemies. Men aren't fussed; they will happily talk to strangers or to no one at all. Men will work side by side with old Perkins for twenty years and still not know if he has a middle name. Most women aren't like that, they will meet another woman at the bus stop and within twenty minutes they will know how many abortions they have had and where they bought their shoes.

Jo needed Anna more than Anna needed Jo. Back then anyway.

Anna Cunningham wasn't big on girlfriends, never had been. Women being the betraying sex, she was suspicious of her own gender; had been ever since she was little and realised that other girls can be very spiteful, especially if you have something they're jealous of: long hair, pink ribbons, a fun-fur coat or a silver charm bracelet.

Consequently by the time she was in her twenties Anna didn't have very many friends at all. You know what it's like, you move they move, you don't return the fifth phone call – whatever: divorce, disease, car crashes (RIP Jessica and Steve, cut down in their prime by a pile-up on the M1), all these things can limit your social circle.

Anna's husband Chris, however, was more congenial than his lovely wife, and occasionally Anna would have to accompany him to dinner parties where she would look rather bored and smoke, if not between mouthfuls, then at least between each course. It was the common consensus amongst Chris's colleagues that Old Cunningham's missus, despite being a foxy lady, was 'a bit like hard work' and, of course, their wives despised her. 'She's a cold fish, that one.' And she was.

People had to persevere with Anna; she took stamina and, as

luck would have it, Jo had always been the determined type. She had made up her mind that the Cunninghams would come for supper.

Jo fetched a couple of cookery books from the kitchen and curled up on the study floor. It had been a couple of weeks since the barbecue up at the Pink House; Jo blushed when she remembered how she hadn't taken her glasses and at the end of the night, when it had gone rather dark, she'd picked up a spare piece of meat only to find that she was chewing an old oven glove.

Prawns in cocoanut and chilli? You had to be careful with prawns, people were allergic to sea food and that was the last thing she needed, Anna rolling round the floor in the throes of an encephalitic fit. Not that Nigel would mind, especially if she was wearing a short skirt. Jo was a bit worried about Nigel; he kept having nosebleeds and he couldn't quite meet her eye over the breakfast table. Oh well, she thought, he won't leave me; if he leaves me I shall have the house and he'll never see the children again. It was as simple as that.

The next thing she knew she was lying on the carpet with her thumb in her mouth and it was gone seven o'clock. Bugger.

Jo hadn't seen Anna for a while, though she kept bumping into Sinaed with Pandora in the park; it was very frustrating. 'Say hello to Anna for me,' she would instruct the girl. Eventually she scribbled an invite on the back of a postcard and shoved it under the front door of the Pink House; she would have liked to have rung the bell but she didn't have the bottle. Jo was surprised at herself, she wasn't normally this dithery. 'Come round to ours,' she'd written, 'we owe you. How about Thursday?' And she printed her telephone number in big figures at the bottom. Anna didn't call back until the day before, which was hideously rude, but she was very charming and said, 'It would be really nice.'

Anna forgot to tell Chris about supper with the Metcalfs until he came home twenty minutes before they were expected. 'So you better hurry up and have a shower, you stink like a polecat. Go on, hurry up.' Ten minutes later he came down wearing a Hawaiian shirt. 'Take it off,' Anna said, 'you look like a fat Timmy Mallett.'

The Cunninghams left 'the girl child' with Sinaed.

'Daddy, don't go. Daddy, don't leave me.'

'Shh, sweetheart, we won't be far away.'

'Come on, damn you, we're going to be late.'

It was one of those late summer, early September evenings, with the sky dark yellow and heavy overhead, all swollen with uncracked thunder. Between them they carried Jed in the Moses basket, his dark lashes crashed out on his peachy cheeks. Chris had the beginnings of a migraine, a combination of the weather, work and eating only chocolate bars for lunch. Anna was in a strange mood, as if there was an electrical current running though her and some of the wires were dangerously loose.

'This is it. Bloody hell, pampas grass – how very suburban.'

Chris didn't understand what was wrong with pampas grass but he kept his trap shut. Anna could be very critical; if she didn't like something her lip would curl back. There was a lot of lip curling that night.

'You can't have Designers Guild curtains just anywhere,' Anna explained later. Actually, Anna was right, the curtains were a mistake; ditto the three-piece suite and the hall carpet.

'Come on down to the kitchen,' said Jo. She was wearing a white apron like a proper chef, complete with blood stains; she was obviously nervous because her voice kept going very high, shrill as a budgie's. 'I was hoping we'd be able to eat in the garden but, never mind, we can have the French windows open so we'll be semi-al fresco thingummybob. Drink, drink, what would you like?'

Nigel was standing by the sink with a gin and tonic; he raised his eyebrows instead of saying hello and Chris bumbled over to shake his hand, which seemed to take Nigel rather by surprise.

They put the baby under the table and Jo told them a story about some other friends who had once done exactly the same and had driven off at midnight forgetting the child, who was found the next morning eating left-over breadsticks.

It didn't ring quite true. 'You are a liar, Jo,' said Nigel. 'They didn't actually leave the kid, they just nearly did.'

Jo was trying too hard, her hair was plastered to her forehead and there were wet patches under her arms. 'Yes, well . . . hummus anyone?' She had made it herself so it was thick and lumpy. Chris said it was delicious and Jo went pink. 'Nigel was meant to bring home some special olives from Soho but he forgot.' At this Nigel pretended to be retarded, which was quite funny.

The Metcalfs' kitchen was what Chris thought a kitchen should be: kids' drawings all over the place, the fruit bowl was full of broken biros and bruised bananas, and there were novelty fridge magnets and heavily stained cookery books, all sticky with wine and gravy. Serious-looking pans hung from metal hooks above a big red Aga; there was even a rocking-chair with a patchwork cushion on it. Anna thought it was all rather grubby: the tea towels were all scorched and the glasses were smeary. When Jo opened the fridge to get out some butter, a bluebottle swarmed out and they all had to pretend not to notice.

The conversation took a while to get started; like an old Hillman Imp it kept having to be kick-started, only to end up going down a cul-de-sac.

'So, Chris, tell me, do you like Woody Allen?'

'Um, yes, Nigel, I do. Wonderful stuff. And you?'

'Er, no.'

Jo had made a vast tortilla, which was a shame because Anna wasn't fond of eggy things. 'I'll just have some bread and salad, thanks.'

When Jo got upset about Anna not eating enough, Nigel said, 'Give her a break, Jo, not everyone has the appetite of a navvy.' Which was a bit below the belt because Jo's eyes smarted and she turned the same colour as the Beaujolais.

Excess alcohol eventually came to the rescue, of course, and in the end they were setting fire to Ameretto papers and listening to The Clash. Jo used up some of her best anecdotes, but it was worth it when Anna nearly fell off her chair laughing.

A disaster had been averted, a-six-out-of-ten-could-have-been-better kind of an evening suddenly turned into an eight-out-of-ten-let's-do-this-again night.

The friendship was coming together, the first few stitches had been made; it could still have fallen apart at this point, unravelled, frayed or snapped, or both parties could simply have lost interest, but for some reason it didn't.

The relationship between the Metcalfs and the Cunninghams was like a jigsaw puzzle of a messy abstract painting; you had no idea why those pieces should fit together but they did.

18

Tics and Tequila

I feel terrible today; every organ feels like it's bursting with black pus. I keep waking up smelling alcohol oozing from my pores, my tongue as thick as a bedsit carpet after a student party. My nails are broken and I can almost hear the little thread veins around my nose exploding. Hey ho, the present is too uncomfortable; let us get back to the glorious past.

After we'd had the barbecue in our back garden, the Metcalfs invited us down to their place. Chris was enthusiastic; he liked Jo. 'Jolly decent type, good fun.' I wasn't that bothered to be honest, though I found Nigel mildly diverting; there was something rather dirty about him that appealed to me.

We left Pandora with Sinaed but we carried my Jed in the

Moses basket down the hill; I was still feeding him at night. In fact, I fed him until Chris said that it was getting bizarre and that if I didn't stop soon, I'd end up feeding him through the school railings at playtime. So?

They obviously had money, but they'd gone a bit wrong with the décor; they'd overdosed on peacock green, and the furniture was a mishmash of every style imaginable: seventies beanbags jostled with Victoriana, and she'd gone mad with the curtains – you can't put Designers Guild just anywhere. I kept my trap shut, obviously, but a cheese plant – really! Cheese plants are only ever acceptable in a dentist's waiting-room.

They were fiends for photos, every spare surface had a silver frame on it. That's when I noticed how pretty Jo must have been when Nigel first met her. She was laughing in a plum-coloured Laura Ashley satin ball-gown, with her yellow hair in a shaggy perm; still plump but at least two stone lighter than she was now. He, of course, had improved with age, shaved off that silly half-hearted tash and grown out of his red leather tie phase.

We went down into the kitchen; she had one of those pointless, massive great Agas which are fine for keeping premature sheep warm but useless for anything else. Poor Jo, she was sweating like a pig in labour and there were dark rings under the armpits of her denim shirt. Jo has a tendency to perspire; she's not as whiffy as she used to be but back then she smelt a bit. Sometimes, when she laughed, waves of BO would waft from her armpits and I'd have to sit a little further away. Of course, she's changed a lot; the other day she went mental when a side plate I'd been using as an ashtray wobbled off the arm of the sofa and left a trail of mayonnaise and ash down its pristine, burnt orange velvet sides. 'Bloody hell, Anna, watch what you're doing! You're worse than Henry!' She is not as chaotic as she was, neither is she as forgiving. She is impatient of me; she has stopped bringing me milky drinks when I cry out in the night.

We ate at a scrubbed pine table. The plates were yellow with blue rims; there are still a couple of them left, but they are chipped now and the glaze is crackled all over.

Nigel opened the French windows on to an elaborate patio; Jo said they'd just had it landscaped, it was 'Japanese'. It was a fucking mess actually.

I can't remember what we ate. Back then I didn't have much of an appetite, not like Jo; she was so greedy, she always had cake crumbs stuck to her lipstick.

The kids made an appearance, of course, looking like a paedophile's wet dream meets Enid Blyton; all pudding-bowl hair cuts and freckles on their dinky little noses. Georgina was wearing a tutu over her pyjamas and insisted on dancing. I could have hit her for being so much prettier than my own boot-faced heifer, but you can't do that sort of thing. Instead I comforted myself that Henry's chin was rather absent and he had one of those funny blinky tics that nervous children have.

Jo drank a lot, which isn't her style: beer then wine, white then red. It was as if she was trying very hard to relax and couldn't quite manage it. When we should have gone but we couldn't because great plops of rain had started to fall, she got out a bottle of the stuff that has a dead worm in the bottom and started to tell the same story she'd told us earlier. This was Nigel's cue to make a big pot of black coffee. So we sat there till the rain stopped, drinking the coffee, and for a moment I thought that Nigel was playing footsie with me under the table; we were all pretty smashed. When we left, Jo was eating the kids' supply of chocolate buttons; she was hiccuping and pretty unsteady on her feet. Nigel saw us out and when I turned to wave to Jo in the basement kitchen, I saw her with the bottle of tequila to her lips; she didn't see me. I only ever saw her that pissed a couple of times. It would be nice to get smashed with Jo again but she has taken to drinking Aqua Libra of an evening and her personality has become all buttoned-up – dull, dull, dull. Jesus, I have three mouth ulcers and they are fucking agony.

When I was a teenager, I drank cider and vermouth, and sometimes I would fill a medicine bottle with a mixture of whatever I could lay my hands on, pilfered from the myriad of bottles that my parents kept on the sideboard. Pernod and advocaat is a lethal combination, let me tell you.

There was a lot more ceremony to drinking in the old days, more paraphernalia: ice buckets, cocktail shakers, a hundred different glasses for highballs and sherry, lager and gin. My parents kept little jars of maraschino cherries and cut lemon slices, bottles of ginger ale and bitter lemon. As a child I loved the smell that hung over the house the morning after they'd had a drinks party, that fug of cigars and stale perfume, Dior and ash. Of course, I'm going back to the days when bags of crisps came with little blue twists of salt and grown-ups drank standing up, the ladies complimenting each other on their hair and the men discussing motorcars and the male 'perm'. There was none of this casual screw-topped wine slugged out of chipped beakers and drinking beer straight from the can.

On the very rare occasions that I endured a visit to Chris's mother in Wales, I found the lack of alcohol somewhat difficult to deal with; she kept a couple of bottles of Guinness in the fridge for Chris, but disapproved of women drinking. On more than one occasion, I almost said, 'If I didn't get pissed, I wouldn't be able to fuck your son,' but I never did; I just took my own supply and made Chris have sex with me under her roof. He didn't like it and I had to grit my teeth, but it was worth it, just to know that she could hear us banging away, with the headboard knocking chunks of plaster out of her crappy walls.

19

Pilfering and Pudding

I wonder when dinner parties were invented? Everyone has them now; they are part of the social dance of the middle classes, the on-going tit-for-tat ritual. The gradual forming of friendships over too many glasses of red wine drunk too late into the night. The probing and collecting of information that makes people believe they know each other really well, only nobody does; most people are strangers – even to themselves.

It doesn't matter how many weekends spent in drafty Yorkshire cottages and New Year's Eves you spend together, the fact that you buy birthday and Christmas gifts for each other, the favours you do in the name of loyalty. Everyone has a hidden core, a little nugget of their personality that is best kept secret.

Like me and my chocolate habit; no one really knows how many Twixes I can shove down my throat, I frighten myself sometimes. Once I ate Henry's Christmas selection box all in one go; on Boxing Day he opened it up only to find that it had been ransacked.

We gradually got to know each other's stories. Anna was an only child. They are a particular breed, not used to sharing; you have to excuse the only child as they are used to being spoilt. Chris has a brother who lives and works in Wales and is apparently, according to Anna, 'rather odd'. I have a brother too: he lives abroad in Hanover with his big-breasted German wife and their two little boys. I would like to see him more, but we are all so busy. They send photos, which is nice. Nigel is an only child but only by accident; his sister, the beautiful Elizabeth, was killed falling from a horse when she was eighteen and just about to go to university to study languages. I have seen photos of her, she had everything to live for. Life is very cruel. Nigel was there when they turned off the life-support system; they donated her eyes and her organs. Sometimes I wonder whether Elizabeth's death is the reason why Nigel messes around with young girls. Once, when he was very pissed, he told me he used to dream about making love to a girl who looked up at him with his sister's yellow-green eyes. There's nothing you can really say when your husband tells you something like that, so I kept my trap shut and pretended not to hear

Georgina has Elizabeth's eyes, not literally, obviously; when her paternal grandmother saw her for the first time, she kept saying, 'Elizabeth, Elizabeth,' but that's where the similarities end. Apparently Elizabeth was a bit of a goody-goody: Girl Guide, Duke of Edinburgh Award blanket knitter, you know the type. My Georgina is a self-centred, two-faced little vixen – I'm not being horrid, I'm trying to be honest.

Nigel's parents live in Edinburgh now, in one of those rather grand, grey-stone Victorian jobbies, and his mother takes comfort in Catholicism, whilst his father takes comfort in Southern Comfort and reads books on battleships. We do not visit often. His mother is the saddest person I have ever had the misfortune to spend Christmas with; she keeps a plait of Elizabeth's dark brown hair in a glass case on the stairs and eats mostly dry oatcakes.

My parents live in Wiltshire. My father is the nicest man in the world; he is a retired brigadier and grows his own vegetables, which my mother insists on distilling into alcohol – her courgette wine is particularly vile and has to be drunk with several sugar cubes in each glass. She doesn't drink as much now, not since half her stomach has been removed, but she still smokes thirty Benson and Hedges a day and her white hair has a dark yellow nicotine streak at the front. My parents are involved in several good causes and both play a mean hand of bridge. They still love each other; I have seen them holding hands walking round the garden. They look like a slightly geriatric version of the Start Rite logo.

Anna's mother is by all accounts a beauty, but she is absent, as mother and grandmother. Occasionally, the most gorgeous table linen arrives from Switzerland, but she never visits; apparently her second husband has had open-heart surgery and isn't able to fly. I mean, it's all very well having hundreds of lovely napkins but it's no substitute for a mother's love, is it? Her father is dead, typical eh? Blokes always peg out first, they can't stand responsibility, can they? It's like now, even though Nigel is fed up to the back teeth with Anna, he can't bring himself to say anything; he doesn't want a scene. 'Not yet,' he says, 'give her a little while longer.' I think he thinks, 'There but for the grace of

God go I'. Not that he is a religious man, it's just that he knows he has been lucky, he has got away with his mistakes. It has been a while now since Nigel has come home smelling of guilt and other women's knickers.

So it went on, the Cunninghams and the Metcalfs. It was all so convenient; we fitted into each other's lives like cold hands into warm pockets. In the winter, we went out for long walks followed by big pub lunches, comfortable enough to steal the pickled onions off each other's plates: 'Get your thieving paws off my silverskins.' In the summer, we'd go to Battersea Park: 'Last one there's a cissy.' Anna could play tennis; of course she could, anyone with legs like that is bound to find an excuse to wear a tiny pleated white skirt. Nigel can play too, and they would thrash each other round the court, whilst me and Chris sat fatly watching, discussing new fashionable restaurants, keeping an eye on the kids.

I think we were nicer as a foursome than individually; that often happens when you are with other people, you behave yourself better. Not that we didn't row, we fell out over all sorts of things and privately we probably all harboured mean thoughts about each other. You do though, don't you? However much you like someone, occasionally you will find yourself thinking, 'Oh you sly bitch.' Once I lost a marcasite brooch, nothing special, just a memento of my grandmother. Anyway, I was convinced it was the cleaner, sacked this perfectly good Venezuelan girl – hysterical she was – but, 'No,' I said, 'how can I trust you if you pilfer my things?' I told the agency and everything. Course, a few months later I was in Anna's bedroom trying to find a safety pin and there it was, in a little cut-glass bowl on her dressing table: my little marcasite butterfly. I never said anything. In some respects I thought it was my fault; if I hadn't had so much pudding, the button wouldn't have popped off my skirt and I wouldn't have been sniffing around for a safety pin.

Looking back, it's as if she really didn't have a clue as to what was right and what was wrong. She was born without guilt glands, she is physically and emotionally incapable of feeling remorse, she cannot blush and she will not take responsibility for the bad things she has done; nothing is ever her fault. Anna has no moral backbone. It's all so obvious in hindsight.

Attractive people tend to get let off the hook, don't they? Good looks are a sort of alibi, it's the thick and the ugly that get caught. Anna was so pretty that you forgave her for being nasty sometimes. For example, it always worried me how much fonder Anna was of Jed. I felt sorry for Pandora, though to be honest she was a difficult child. I'd try to cosy up to her but she blanked you out, made you feel daft for trying. I think she only really liked her dad. Once, I remember, we all traipsed off to the seaside; it was October but freakishly hot, so we went to Broadstairs and ate fresh crab and chips. It was about a year after we'd met; Jed was toddling. So there we were on tartan rugs, all buckets and spades, looking like something out of 1963. Anna had built this fairy sandcastle. She was so good at that sort of thing; it had turrets and was decorated all over with shells and ring pulls and fronds of seaweed, it really was very pretty. There was a photographer on the beach and he asked whether we minded him taking some shots of the kids, and as he didn't look like a pervert, we said, 'Fine, go ahead.' One of the pictures ended up on the front page of the *Daily Express*, something about it being 'The Hottest October Day in Thirty Years', and there was Anna's sandcastle and the kids: Jed looking like an angel, Henry looking earnest digging a hole and Georgina mid-arabesque holding a spade like a wand. Only Pandora was missing, but if you looked very closely you could see the shadow of her fat leg.

Her mother was always trying to cut down her sweetie rations; it was always,'How about some nice raisins, Pandora, or an apple?' But of course the kid never wanted nice raisins or an apple, not when all the others had Toblerones and ice-creams. It is easy to see the faults in other people's children, much harder to face up to the problems of your own, like Henry twitching and stuttering. Anna imitated him once; it was cruel but we all pretended it was funny – even Henry, who laughed and laughed but blinked and twitched twice as much as normal whilst he did so.

20

Sausages and Paper Hats

Life went on, down Lark Grove, as life has a habit of doing. Nothing stays the same for ever, certainly not the Pink House. Anna had it all done before you could say Sir Terence Conran; it was very tasteful. In fact, *House and Garden* gave it a four-page feature and the clever photographer, with his fish-eye lens, managed to make the proportions look even more grandiose in print. There was a lovely picture of Jed on Anna's knee and a very flatteringly blurred one of Pandora jumping up and down on her bed.

Chris wasn't around for the shoot, he was at work, and by the time he came home, the photographer and Anna had polished off a bottle of champagne and Anna was wobbling around trying to make popcorn in the microwave whilst the photographer, whose name was Denzil, smoked dope on the sofa. Chris was rather brusque with Denzil, not surprisingly; you can't trust a man in leather jeans, especially not one with such a large bulge around the crotch area. Denzil left pretty sharpish, after all, his girlfriend was nine months pregnant. What was he thinking of?

Sometimes Chris thought his wife was a witch; she didn't use her powers very often but when she did the spell was all-powerful.

That night, Anna dreamt of the photographer and laughed out loud in her sleep. You don't have to be fully conscious to be unfaithful.

Chris hardly noticed other women; occasionally in the summer he would observe that young girls seemed to be unfettered around the bosom area, but he found it quite easy not to stare, unlike Nigel who was tortured by the sight of anything eminently fuckable and had the erections to prove it.

Late summer gave way to autumn. Anna placed a bowl of shiny, brown conkers on the kitchen table; you could barely walk down the Grove without them falling on your head. Jed was pink-cheeked in Baby Gap, Pandora even fatter of leg in the woollen tights that the weather demanded.

Anna, despairing, took her daughter to the doctor to discuss her weight. 'Honestly, Doctor, if I didn't know it wasn't possible, I would swear I can hear her skin stretching.'

It was a lady doctor; she was quite pleasant about it. She asked Anna a lot of questions, weighed Pandora and said, 'My, you are a strapping lass, aren't you?' Like it was no bad thing and with any luck she'd be playing rugby for her country in the not-too-distant future.

There wasn't much Anna could do; Pandora was a 'big, heavy-boned child', but maybe she should switch to 'skimmed milk, swap biscuits for fruit and make her run around as much as possible'. Then the nice lady doctor gave Pandora a lollypop for being 'such a good girl'. Anna waited till they were out of the surgery before snatching 'the bloody thing' out of Pandora's sticky hand and chucking it in the bin.

As if it were any consolation, Pandora was doing very well at her nursery school; Mrs Lomax said she was a clever girl and that her number and alphabet skills were easily those of a four-year-old. 'Like her bum,' muttered Anna, under her breath.

Anna was enjoying being back at work. They had a huge Malaysian Airlines advert to cast and for days hordes of little Orientals would pitter-pat down the stairs into Maggie's basement office; some of the women were so beautiful, Anna would have quite happily taken them home and hung them on the wall.

The Cunninghams were invited down to the Metcalfs for Bonfire Night; it was just a small do. Unfortunately Jo had invited the Donahue woman and her Down's syndrome son. 'Raymond loves the fireworks,' twittered Brenda. Anna avoided them as much as possible; Raymond couldn't even spell his own name with a sparkler and the sight of his big pink tongue hanging out of his mouth reminded her of seeing a dog's penis when she was very young. Nigel's friend Roger Baxter turned up, the one whose wife had run off with the hippie. He had his sons with him for the weekend and his new girlfriend cried when her beige suede boots got muddy in the garden. 'I just can't cope,' she kept saying, and when Jo offered her a spare pair of wellies she wailed, 'But these are a size nine – I'm only a three and a half.'

Jo made mounds of sausages, which meant that Chris and Pandora were happy. Anna stayed indoors with Jed; he didn't really like loud bangs, his little arms would fly up in alarm every time a rocket went off and his denim-blue eyes would pop wide open. Jo fed him in the sitting-room, and at one point was surprised to see Nigel and Roger enter the downstairs lavatory together. Ah-ha, now that was interesting. Anna had never been averse to the occasional toot, so it was obvious that they were doing coke. Anna made a mental note to quiz Nigel on the situation as soon as she finally gave up breast-feeding Jed. Chris was very averse to drugs; when they knew she was pregnant, he'd stood over her and forced her to throw her private stash down the pan. It was one of the reasons that he hadn't liked her waitressing; kitchen porters are fiends for the old white stuff. Somehow Anna knew Jo didn't have a clue about Nigel's little habit. Well, she could keep a secret if he could.

Later, when all the kids were in the playroom watching a video, the homosexuals from number seventy-seven turned up, bearing bottles of vodka, and started dancing to the Gypsy Kings in the kitchen: 'More like Gypsy Queens,' they screeched. Raymond, of course, got overexcited, so Brenda took him home – which was a relief.

As soon as the whiff of gunpowder and sausage had evaporated, it was Christmas; the Metcalfs' house now smelt of cinnamon and rum. Jo made her own cake; it was traditional. She also baked her own mince pies, though Nigel once made her cry when he told her that they weren't a patch on Sainsbury's. Jo took the festivities rather seriously and sprayed twigs and ivy from the garden with silver spray and placed them in a large vase on the mantelpiece; she arranged holly around the mirror above but it kept sliding down. Nothing ever looked quite how she imagined it would look; she didn't have the knack.

Georgina played Mary in the nursery school nativity; Pandora was the donkey. Jo and Anna sat next to each other. All the parents had to sit on nursery chairs; Jo's creaked every time she moved to take another photo of bloody Georgina who, if truth be told, was rather rough with baby Jesus, picking him out of the crib by his hair and dropping him on the floor when they took their curtain call. Many of the mothers were moist-eyed throughout the proceedings; Anna wasn't, so she lent her tissues to Jo who blubbed until her nose swelled to three times its normal size.

Joe Public closed down for Christmas. Maggie was off to the Caribbean, she needed the break; she'd been on IVF for months and nothing seemed to be happening.

Anna went to town on the house. Christmas was a good excuse to spoil her rotten; she was as ornate as an Indian bride, garlanded and sparkling with fairy lights on every floor. Anna remembered to buy a tree – it was over six feet tall – but she forgot to order a turkey and on Christmas Eve, when she popped up to Sainsbury's, there were none left. She bought the largest chicken she could find, a bag of Brussels sprouts and a box of Paxo. She'd rather have had a smoked salmon bagel any day. Jo joined the queue behind her. 'Mad, isn't it? I've been here four times already this week. I forgot the chestnuts.'

'I forgot the turkey,' Anna sniggered.

So it came to pass that the Cunninghams spent Christmas Day down at the Metcalfs. It was a huge success with only a few smacks: one on the hand for Georgina, who had pierced Pandora's leg with a cocktail stick, and a whack on the bum for Pandora for whining.

Jo didn't quite manage to take her apron off all day. She was so busy, what with wrapping bacon round little chipolatas and making proper brandy butter, that she didn't get round to putting on any lipstick and her face was as red as a hundred-metre hurdler's. Nigel had bought her a butcher's block; Anna said, 'If

Chris bought me one of those, I'd put his head on it.' Some women are destined to receive breadbins and ironing-board covers, others, like Anna, get little leather boxes lined with blue velvet containing diamonds and pearls. 'Gorgeous earrings,' Jo said, and when she bent over to inspect them closely, her head as large as a big pony's, Anna noticed that all the pores around her nose were wide open. It wasn't Jo's fault, it's what happens when you have to keep sticking your head into boiling hot ovens. Jo smelt of gravy and turkey gizzards, Anna smelt of advocaat with top notes of cranberry (Jo had made a big jug of sea breeze).

It was a good day. Anna was glad that she'd remembered to wrap up a tablecloth her mother had once sent her, for Jo, and that Chris had been persuaded to donate his Trumpers aftershave to Nigel. 'You can't just turn up empty-handed.' Henry had been thrilled with his five-pound note and . . . well, Georgina would just have to lump the spare copy of *Cinderella* that Anna had found under Pandora's bed. 'Don't like books,' the little cow had sulked. 'Only because you can't read,' her older brother chipped in. Anna gave Henry one of her rare smiles at this point; usually she just ignored him. Shame his eczema had flared up.

There was a bit of a to-do when Jo brought in the flaming Christmas pudding; when she put it down on the table her paper hat fell into the flames and was engulfed. 'Wear mine,' said Nigel. Anna didn't wear a paper hat, so for the rest of Christmas dinner only she and Nigel looked like they didn't have learning difficulties.

When dinner was finished, Anna cornered Nigel on the landing and, after a whispered conversation into his ear, he passed her a miniature envelope and she disappeared into the bathroom, carefully locking the door behind her. They had such fun that night. Nigel got 'Twister' out and he and Anna contorted themselves over the coloured spots until they were all weak with laughter.

The Cunninghams only left because Georgina 'accidentally' shut Pandora's face in the dividing doors. It was gone eleven.

These things seal a friendship: port and Grand Marnier, jokes from crackers, walnuts and chocolate liquers.

Chris felt a bit guilty for having such a good time because his mother had put the phone down on him for neither inviting her to the Pink House nor visiting Wales. 'Tough shit,' said Anna full of festive spirit, literally – Nigel had been rather generous on the drinks front. That night she let Chris fuck her; well it was Christmas. It was a shame she sobered up halfway through and remembered he wasn't Val Kilmer.

21

Nits and Nonsense

I wonder how many meals we have eaten at the Metcalfs' kitchen table. Certainly more than I ever prepared at the Pink House. I told Chris when he asked me to marry him that I wouldn't be cooking. I said, 'I will perform fellatio, I will have sex in public places and at home with the lights on, but I don't do cooking.'

There's something very smug about women who can cook, isn't there? As if without them the rest of us culinarily backward types would starve to death. Bollocks, have you been to Marks and Spencer recently? You can eat your way around the globe: a prawn masala here, a lamb teriyaki there. Anyway, I like sandwiches.

My mother made chutney once; she wore her chutney-making outfit as she did so, a green and tan ensemble with a jaunty red head scarf tied gypsy style, as if to match the tomatoes. After several hours hovering over the bubbling goo with a thermometer, there were jars of it everywhere, fermenting under little grease-proof circles. It all went mouldy: my father and I much preferred Branston.

When I was a waitress, all the chefs I ever knew were mad. They were like the drummers in rock bands: on drugs and in the throes of divorce. I have never met a 'normal' chef.

I only ever had one pinny. We had to make one in domestic science at my soppy girls' school; mine took three and a half terms to complete and even then I got in trouble for appliquéing it with sequinned butterflies. They liked you to conform at St Augusta's.

We did do cookery, I remember now; if pushed, I could prepare a light supper on a tray for an invalid and I can do jelly. Our first cookery lesson involved washing up in the correct order and taking care of bone-handled cutlery. After that we moved on to 'a hot milky drink' – I ask you! Pandora, of course, loves to cook. She didn't realise until she went to nursery that you could actually bake cakes at home. Mind you, a big packet of ready-to-roll pastry and a handful of currants kept her quiet. She used to make mournful-looking pastry people with unhappy smiles.

Jed liked icing biscuits; he was always very artistic. Even when he was very small he liked a variety of colour on his plate: a slice of cucumber, a wedge of tomato – by the time he was three he was quite fussy about garnish. My son had sophisticated tastes for a toddler: smoked salmon, black olives, Parma ham and he loved lobster. When he was six, he suddenly realised the connection between skippy white lambs and the gristly mince that his paternal grandmother boiled up and refused to eat it. Of course, she reckoned I'd put him up to it. I didn't . . . well, I might have just mentioned how sad it was that those dear little baa lambs ended up being wrenched as babies from their mothers, dragged into filthy abattoirs and electrocuted to death.

I make beautiful salads; presentation has always been very important to me, I have an eye for detail whereas Jo hasn't got a clue. When we were all friendly and jolly we used to joke about Jo's food presentation, we used to give her marks out of ten. She never got higher than four. We used to think she found it funny too, only I don't think she did; once, when Nigel gave her two out of ten for a very sloppily served goulash, she went mad, took our plates off us and chucked the whole lot in the sink – which was daft, it was far too chunky to go down the plughole. Then she started shouting, 'You cunts, I've slaved my tits off making this and all you lot do is sit there and criticise. Well sod you.' And off she stomped. Nigel said it was probably 'that time of the month' and we all had beans on toast. I made it, I got nine out of ten for presentation: I put a sprig of parsley and an olive on each serving for a laugh.

She was a great one for making cakes; she made all my kids' birthday cakes, right from when they were very small. It was ridiculous, all they wanted was a cartoon thing from Sainsbury's, you know the sort, yellow sponge, jam in the middle, a billion E numbers. But oh no, Jo had to martyr herself on that stupid Aga and kill herself making something that wasn't a patch on the commercial ones. When you're six, you couldn't give a shit about lightness and texture; all you want is a cake that looks like something you recognise off the telly. None of us were ever grateful enough. She was in a no-win situation, she hadn't got her priorities right: all the time she was cooking Nigel complicated things involving ducks and guinea foul, he'd much rather she'd taken the time to give him a blowjob. Men like Nigel don't want their wives with suet on their noses, they want them lightly scented and preferably with their legs round the back of their head.

Going out for a meal with Jo was purgatory, she just couldn't relax and enjoy it. She couldn't get over the fact that restaurants could charge seventeen quid for something she could rustle up for three. That's why she always tried to get her money's worth, eating all the bread in the basket, making sure if I left anything on my plate it was put in a doggy bag. Embarrassing really. She couldn't eat oysters either, that's how frigid she is; Nigel and I used to order them just to make her gag. No wonder Nigel bought her kitchen equipment for her birthday and Christmas presents; if he'd bought her anything else it would have ended up covered in gravy. However much perfume Jo put on you could always smell garlic underneath.

I laughed when she told me she'd been a head girl; it made sense. She was the most reliable person I had ever met; 'sensible' to Jo was a compliment. She kept ant powder and she had a proper first aid kit in the kitchen, she knew how to use bandages and, deep down, she would have liked one of the kids to have fallen into a pond so she could demonstrate her mouth-to-mouth resuscitation technique. She loved a good crisis: picking glass out of a cut knee, removing splinters. When Pandora got nits, Jo sorted it out, she had all the gear. She was really very happy raking dead eggs out of my daughter's hair with a nit comb. She liked doing all the things I hated, she was alkali to my acid. She was the best mother I had ever met, I suppose.

I think she would have liked a third child; she told me once that she'd 'suffered' a miscarriage. The verb 'suffered' is always used when it comes to losing babies, isn't it? Though I'm sure there are as many relieved 'mothers-not-to-be' as disappointed ones. She is forty now, but she still keeps the old cot in the attic and once I found her crying because all of Henry's and Georgina's baby clothes had been eaten by moths. I have always been more ruthless with my past than Jo; she has always been the type to keep shoe boxes of mementoes: Mother's Day cards, hospital wristbands, Georgina's first pair of tap shoes, all the sort of rubbish that I would put in the bin. When her children were small she had their feet cast in bronze – not literally, ha ha.

22

Responsibility and Rennies

It wasn't like it was easy, you know, me being the one in charge all the time. I was, I organised everything, muggins here, without me there wouldn't have been all those so-called good times. It was me buying the turkeys, peeling the potatoes, boiling the giblets, setting the table. I bought bigger pans, I made sure there was a beaker round here for Jed, a plastic one with a spout. I accommodated them, I kept in Rennies for Chris! I really worked at our friendship, I really thought it would go on for ever; that one day, when the kids were all grown up and at university . . . Oh yes, I had that planned in my head. Henry at Edinburgh studying archaeology, Georgina at Bristol doing some media course, I thought maybe we would still be together, the four of us, getting old, going on exotic holidays, cruising down the Nile, the boys in panama hats, us girls in floral frocks with hankies tucked into our sleeves.

I've been a fucking fool. Okay, we did get something back, like the table linen that Anna fobbed off on me from time to time: I made all the right noises, 'Oh look, it's so lovely,' but I knew she thought it was naff. We have wasted so much time on that family, and reels and reels of perfectly good film capturing their daft antics.

I was the head girl at school. I've always been thoughtful, well-meaning, I've always tried hard. Don't get me wrong, I have a temper, my children will vouch for that. I've chased Georgina around the house enough times, threatening her with a wooden spoon, and there have been a number of incidents when I have broken Henry's Airfix models out of sheer spite. Ask my husband. I know I'm not the easiest person to live with; I suffer from ghastly PMT and when everything gets too much for me and I sob and bite my knuckles. But it's only a couple of days every month and for the rest of the time at least I try to make up for being occasionally hateful. My family have homemade cakes and hand-blended soup; when Henry's eczema gets bad, who is it that puts on his ointment? Me, of course.

Men are rubbish, aren't they? What do men do? Do they take the children to the dentist, optician? Do they check their heads for lice and test them on their French vocabulary? Do they know when it's swimming, rugby or Beaver scouts? Do they fuck. Men only take responsibility for that which directly affects them, like making sure they know what time the Grand Prix starts and if there is cold lager in the fridge. We're supposed to be grateful, of course, that they're not beating us or forcing us to have anal sex before breakfast. Well, it just won't do.

I know a woman who is my age and is not married and has no children. I always used to feel sorry for her, now I am not so sure. She leads a supremely selfish life, never off that Eurostar. Her shoes are by Emma Hope, her dressing-gown by Georgina Etzendorf; she lives in a doll's house in Chelsea, just a ten-minute stroll from Harrods, where she buys sushi from the food hall. Her house, although minute, is worth more than ours; she has silky wooden floorboards and a beige suede sofa, everything is caramel, cream or taupe. In the winter she wears cashmere and in the summer she wears linen. There is nothing in her life to confuse her; she listens to Radio 4 or opera and spends her evenings, should she choose to stay at home, curled up on that suede sofa, reading, wrapped in a pashmina, nibbling sushi, sipping whiskey and ginger. She collects amber necklaces and spends Christmas in the Bahamas, she has no pets and has on many occasions refused to be a godmother. I do not blame her. I am sick to the back teeth of everything and everybody, not even chocolate can cheer me up. I opened a packet of Jaffa Cakes this morning and only managed two.

I couldn't begin to tell you how many diets I have been on. I have eaten only grapefruit and boiled eggs, dissolved Slimfast shakes into skimmed milk, counted calories, trimmed the fat off my ham, weighed my potatoes and, most recently, attempted the cabbage soup regime – a terrible American invention resulting in a meagre three-pound weight loss and borderline incontinence. It is only recently that I have realised that the greatest appetite suppressant is abject misery; without really trying my waistbands have become loose and I no longer have to lie on the floor to zip up my good Agnès b black trousers. Not that I would recommend this particular method of shedding flesh to anyone. Life is so much harder when cheesecake isn't the solution.

I have started going swimming three times a week, in the evenings. I like to get out of the house. I like it best when the pool is almost deserted and you can watch the night turn the skylights dark blue. It is an old-fashioned pool and I am grateful for the lack of wave-machines and inflatables; occasionally an Elastoplast will float by my face, but on the whole it is quite clean. I see the same people: the man with one leg and the very old lady with the saddle-bag breasts and the long brown nipples that point to the floor. After I swim thirty lengths, ten crawl, ten breast stroke and ten lying on my back, I spend a long time in the shower. I condition the chlorine out of my hair, apply lotions and potions, fruity-smelling concoctions of mandarin and cocoanut that remind me of cocktails drunk a long time ago. Sometimes even when I am dressed, I sit in one of the cubicles with the door bolted. I like to think no one can find me. Once I fell asleep and when I woke up, the cleaners were mopping the floors and talking of hysterectomies. The other night Georgina said she might come with me. I said I'd rather she didn't and her eyeballs bugged out of her head. Poor Georgina, I haven't as much time for her as I used to; in the old days, I would help her with her homework, colouring in her geography maps, blue for the sea, green for the land. Once I made her a wattle-and-daub house for a history project. Yesterday, when a button fell off her flares, I made her sew it back on herself – she took twenty-five minutes to thread the needle. As for Henry, he has turned into a pupa never emerging from the chrysalis of his bedroom. Our home has turned into a rooming-house full of disgruntled tenants and I am the bad-tempered landlady.

23

Skating and Scalping

When Georgina Metcalf was seven years and eleven-and-a-half months old, she decided she would rather Pandora Cunningham did not attend her eighth birthday party. 'It's my party, Mummy, and I don't want old stinky-pig Pandora.' It was a very embarrassing situation. Jo solved it by physically forcing her daughter to write out an invitation and Georgina wept furious molten tears as her mother's big, chapped hand propelled her own smaller fist over the paper. 'Dear Pandora, please come to my party at Streatham ice rink and afterwards at McDonald's, on March 16th at 1.30pm, love Georgina'. When Pandora received the invitation, it was all smudged and crumpled. 'I don't want to go,' she told her mother. 'Well, you're bloody well going and that's that,' Anna replied.

Come the big day, Anna forced her daughter into some sensible skating trousers and a polo neck jumper that Nanna Wales had recently seen fit to send. The sweater was a peculiar shade of vomit with thick purple stripes around the neck and it brought Pandora up in blotches. She'd have been more comfortable wrapped up in hessian.

At precisely 1.25pm on March 16th, Anna frogmarched Pandora out of the house. Jo had tied pink balloons to the front door to add a note of gaiety to the already desperate proceedings.

Georgina thought the balloons on the door were 'pathetic'. She had got a new bike for her birthday, which was a surprise; what she had wanted was a CD player and a telly for her bedroom. 'It's got loads of gears,' Jo kept saying, 'you'll be able to whiz up really steep hills on it.' Georgina rolled her eyeballs. Fortunately Nigel saved the day by presenting his daughter with a large box containing an ice-skating tutu. It was ridiculous, Georgina had been ice skating precisely three times. Jo was so angry, she burnt all the 'happy birthday' croissants and Nigel had to go to the garage to get some more.

Henry had bought Georgina some bubble bath from the Body Shop because that is what brothers are forced to do.

Children's birthday parties are notoriously fraught. By ten o'clock, Jo had swallowed enough Migralieve to kill a rhinoceros, but she kept smiling – that frightening, teeth-baring grimace that mothers pull when they are millimetres away from committing infanticide.

Four little girls were dropped off by their mothers/au pairs at 1.30, which meant that, including Georgina and Pandora, there were too many to safely squeeze into one car. It was a good job that Anna had offered to help out with transport. (Actually she hadn't, Chris had offered her services and now there was no wriggling out of it.)

Bummer, thought Anna as she rolled up at Jo's.

Pandora went to the same school as Georgina but because she was in the year below, she didn't know any of these girls. Anna couldn't tell them apart, they all looked like miniature Kylie Minogues, if such a thing is possible.

Jo had her head girl hat on; it made her shout more than was strictly necessary and adopt a curiously strained, old-fashioned jollity. 'What fun,' she kept bellowing, as if by saying it with enough decibels over and over again she would manage to convince herself. 'Who wants to come with me and who wants to go in Pandora's mummy's car?' Jo yelled, as if offering the invitation to the tramps in the park half a mile away.

'I want to go with Georgina,' unisoned the titchy Kylie clones. They all had their hair in high bunches and Anna could have sworn one of them was wearing lipstick. Georgie, Lottie, Becky, Jessie and Ruby looked like they were in some pre-pubescent girl-band dreamt up by a paedophile. Pandora could have been the roadie.

'Well, I haven't got enough seatbelts for you all and if any of you go through the windscreen, then what would your mummies say,' retorted Jo at full volume.

In the end, Anna took Georgina and Pandora. It was an uncomfortable compromise and all the way round the South Circular the girls exchanged not a word. Anna put the radio on. 'It's my party and I'll cry if I want to . . . '

The ice rink wasn't a particular success. Georgina was overexcited in her white spangly outfit and spilt coke down it, which made her sob for a good twenty minutes. All her little cronies gathered round in a sympathetic circle, though a couple of them looked rather pleased. Pandora had to wait ages for her size-four hire boots; all the other little girls took a one or a two. It was three o'clock by the time they got on the ice; twenty minutes later they all wanted to come off but Jo wouldn't let them. In fact she decided that she and Anna would have a go. There was no arguing with Jo when she was in this mood, so Anna dutifully borrowed a pair of skates and, thanks to a misspent youth, was soon doing graceful laps around the rink whilst Jo clutched the sides, her legs buckling, her ankles like Bambi with elephantiasis. At least this gave the little witches something to laugh at, and they all gathered round Jo hooting with gleeful spite.

Anna, in a fit of maternal bonding, tried to help Pandora; she held her daughter's hand and managed to get her moving. Pandora was so grateful that she tried really hard. Her boots were killing her but it didn't matter; she had her mother to herself and she was easily the prettiest and best mum in the whole wide world. 'Good girl,' Anna said, and Pandora glowed; maybe when she was eight she would have a white sparkly skating outfit. At that point she forgot to concentrate, and turning her blades to avoid an empty crisp packet on the ice, she brought both of them crashing down. 'Fucking hell, Pandora, you great lump. I could have broken my leg.' And the mood was broken.

The day went on for ever and Jo was exhausted. It was mad; in her day birthday parties involved a quick round of musical chairs, a hilarious game of pin the tail on the donkey, pass the parcel and then home with a piece of birthday cake wrapped in a red paper napkin. This lot wouldn't be seen dead playing pass the parcel, unless of course the prize was a Gameboy or an all-expenses-paid trip to Orlando by Concorde.

At McDonald's, Anna and Jo sat away from the girls. There

was a bit of nonsense about spitting through straws at Pandora but Jo soon put a stop to it; all straws and drinks were swiftly confiscated. Her headache had returned with a vengeance; with any luck it would turn out to be a massive cerebral haemorrhage creeping towards her brain and within minutes she'd be dead and out of this hell.

The journey home was like a rewind of the journey there. Back at Lark Grove all the other little girls were stopping-over for the night. Anna popped into Jo's for a quick cup of tea. She had somehow managed to catch Jo's headache as if by osmosis. 'Got any Nurofen, Jo?' she begged, desperate to go home. Half a cup of Earl Grey later, when she went to find Pandora, she discovered her sitting on the landing outside Georgina's bedroom, the door firmly closed. Suddenly livid, Anna stormed into Georgina's room; the micro-bitches were painting their nails and Georgina's Barbies were all over the floor. Anna went up to Georgina and, with her lips close to the child's ear, said very quietly, 'Happy birthday, you bitch.' To give Georgina her credit, she didn't even flinch.

Anna marched up the hill towards the Pink House, with Pandora having to trot to keep up; she didn't slow down until they were safely through the front door and in the hall. At that moment, Jed came running down the stairs and flung himself at Anna's feet. 'Look what Daddy did,' he said, convulsing, and lifted his head. Chris had taken him to the barbers; all his blond curls were gone. Her lamb was shaven and shorn and all forlorn.

Pandora stood back and held her breath as her mother flew up the stairs two at a time, swearing her head off. Halfway up she changed direction, came careering back down, down to the basement where the kitchen scissors lay innocently in the drawer under the cooker. Anna grabbed them by the handle. 'Chris,

Chris,' she was yelling. He should have known by the tone of her voice to have taken cover, to have hidden in the wardrobe, rolled up in the spare duvet, in the attic with the ladder pulled up safely after him, in a tree at the bottom of the garden, behind a chimneypot on the roof. Like a fool he came bumbling out of the study, only for his wife to take a flying leap at him. Before he could defend himself, she was scalping him and locks of gingery hair were falling to the floor.

24

Fat Daughters and Fake Daughters

I dreamt about my children last night: Pandora had sat on Jed and squashed him to death, it was awful.

Pandora's fatness and her clumsiness never seemed to bother Chris, but she drove me to distraction. Mealtimes were purgatory, even when she was very small, the mess she'd make; sometimes to punish her, I'd wipe her face hard with a stinking, sour dish-cloth, pushing it hard against her fat mouth. She always had bits of potato in her hair, chocolate down her front, jam on the pale balloons of her cheeks. Jed was exactly the opposite; I never had to bother with a bib or put newspaper under his high-chair like I'd had to do with Pandora. He was the sort of kid who could eat an ice-cream in the back of a car and you'd never have to use a single wet wipe; Pandora on the other hand would need hosing down. Of course, being left-handed didn't help and I think I probably made her nervous; that's why she'd drop things. Life has always been difficult for Pandora. Of course, now I wish I'd been nicer to her, now that I have started to spill things down my front we might have more in common. She might even feel more relaxed, seeing me like I am now, with a bandage round my ankle from when I fell down the stairs the other day, the dollop of mustard on my t-shirt, and the dandruff on my shoulders. I've never had dandruff before. I also have a liver spot on my hand and last week, when I was absent-mindedly chewing a Werther's Original, I heard a splintering sound in my jaw and when I spat out the sweet I saw that half a molar had broken off. I have always been proud of my teeth, losing them is a shock. I should go to the dentist, but a little swig of whisky is very good for toothache. I remember my father telling me that.

To be honest, I can't go and see my dentist; he is a very good-looking man and I wouldn't want him to see me like this. Anyway, it's quite comforting putting my tongue into the hole where the tooth used to be and swilling whisky around its jagged remains.

Pandora had three fillings by the time she was eight; Jed has none.

Chris worries about Jed because he thinks he is gay. I have spent a long time thinking about this, whilst I swig whisky and curl my tongue around my broken tooth. Chris thinks Jed is gay because once he found him wearing one of Pandora's bras with the cups full of toilet paper, pretending to be Melinda Messenger. He also he wears perfume behind his ears and a thin silver chain round his ankle.

Once, when he was very little and I was very bored, I dressed him in one of Pandora's old frocks; my mother had sent it over from Switzerland for Pandora but she was too beefy to squeeze into it. It was white with smocking and pink daisies embroidered into it. Jed's hair was quite long so I put a yellow ribbon in it. I just wanted to see what it would have been like to have had a pretty daughter. I shouldn't have done it but I couldn't resist. When he was dressed, I put him in the car and we drove to a supermarket out in Surrey Quays and I did my Sainsbury's shop there instead of at my usual. I put him in the trolley and called him Perdita. Everyone smiled at him, old ladies stroked his cheeks and said he was a 'proper little princess'; course, I went and fucked it up a bit, slung the usual boy pampers in the trolley. At the check-out the girl said, 'Don't you want girl nappies?' I had to pretend to be all vague and ditzy and lied too much about Perdita being up all night teething and me losing my marbles. A nice, peroxide blonde went and swapped the nappies for me, which meant I had to go home, switch Perdita for Jed and nip down to the chemist for the right kind. I didn't know what to do with the girl nappies so I put them at the back of the airing cupboard and tried to forget about them. Funny, I'd forgotten all about that. See, that's the good thing about doing nothing; it gives you time to remember things that never made it on to photos, the stuff that can get forgotten because there is no evidence to remind you.

Last year we had to go and 'have a chat' with his headmaster. It was laughable really; apparently Jed had been caught skipping down the corridors and had on a number of occasions licked other boys' necks – 'uninvited', added the headmaster, in a voice which suggested that Jed had been going round fisting other boys without their permission. Chris and I had a row about it in the car afterwards; he went on about Jed not liking 'normal boy' things like trains and cars and fossils and football, which was silly; Jed is interested in football – he had an enormous poster of David Beckam above his bed. He's just sensitive and a bit flamboyant and he started to lisp when he was about six, but all kids have funny habits. Jo's Henry used to do that awful blinking and Pandora went through a phase of clearing her throat all the time which made me want to punch her. Anyway, I don't care if he is gay; they can be very amusing and they're always clean. Chris said I encouraged him, just because once I painted his toenails and bought him a Baby Spice pillow case. I nearly told him about the time I took him out dressed as a girl but I realised he wouldn't see the funny side. He's so straight is Chris, it's the Welshness in him, that Methodist streak. No wonder I had to find excitement elsewhere.

After the 'little chat' with the headmaster, Chris tried to do a load of father–son bonding; dragging Jed off to football matches, buying him a cricket bat. He didn't want a cricket bat, he wanted a Barbie Dream World camper van with matching accessories. I got him one a couple of Christmases ago, he had a great time with it. Once, when I was tidying it away, I saw that he'd dressed up Action Man in one of Barbie's disco outfits, and instead of a grenade, he'd got his hand curled around a pink evening bag. I thought it was hilarious. Chris went all red and cross, but the way I see it, if there were more boys around like Jed, there'd never be another war. Life would be one long round of cocktails and women would wear hats again. I miss Jed. We used to share a bath and he'd soap my feet and then I'd do his ten perfect toes, all painted silver. Fuck it, my tooth is really hurting and the whisky is all gone. I have noticed that Jo has stopped restocking the booze cabinet. They used to buy wine through the *Sunday Times* wine club; whole cases would arrive and there was a metal rack full of Italian reds and Australian whites. Now she buys five bottles a week from Sainsbury's, mean cow. Another funny thing I have noticed is that she has started screwing the lids back on to the spirits very tightly; no wonder my teeth are cracking up.

25

Cry Babies and Little Cows

She fell down the stairs on Tuesday. Her ankle puffed up, so I made a cold compress of frozen peas and found an elastic bandage; she is becoming a liability. I'm sure it's better now but she refuses to take the bandage off and makes a big show of limping around. Maybe it's really broken but I'm beyond caring. I have spent so many years being concerned about other people's well-being.

When your children are small you worry about whether they are developing normally: Henry was slow with his teeth and for months I imagined him raw-chinned and dribbling well into his teens. Georgina missed out the crawling stage and I was convinced she had something wrong with her legs. You fret so much about the physical side of things, the running out into the road, the falling off climbing frames, picking up AIDS-riddled needles in the park, that you forget about their personalities, though the signs are there right from the beginning.

For example, Henry was a crybaby, a thumb-sucker, frightened of the dark, of big barking dogs, of things that went bang in the night. He had a 'noo noo'; lots of children do, but I have a horrible feeling that he still has it, an ancient piece of silk that lined his cot blanket. When he went to school, I wouldn't let him take the whole stinking rag, so I cut a piece off, got the nanny to hem it and he was allowed to keep it in his pocket. When he was about nine, I told him that if the other kids found out about 'noo noo' he'd have seven bells kicked out of him.

Henry is sixteen now and occasionally, when I look in on him sleeping, I have to remove his thumb from his mouth. He is still frightened of dogs, he was even nervous of Gloria, the silly little mutt that I bought him to get over his fear. But I reckon what frightens him most now is girls. Who can blame him with a sister like Georgina, who would be funny if she wasn't so frightful?

The trouble with Georgie is that because she has always been beautiful, she has never had to make an effort and she has taken her looks for granted. Even when she was little and people told her how lovely she was, she would give them a withering look from her buggy as if to say, 'I know. Whilst you with your moles and whiskers and skin tags are quite hideous.' Everything is 'gross' to Georgina; I, of course, am mega-gross, whilst poor Henry, with his pustulating skin and the carbuncles on his neck and his diminutive chin, is not just 'gross' but a 'gimp' and a 'retard' and a 'mong'. Georgina spends hours in front of her mirror, but she has no reason to panic, she is passing through puberty without a blemish. I don't worry about her taking drugs, she is too vain, after all, sniffing glue gives you sores around your mouth (I have read the pamphlets). But I do worry about how nasty she can be. If life were really fair, if karma actually worked, then whenever Georgina was beastly, a boil would erupt on her lovely face and her ears would fill with blackheads. But then nothing's fair, is it?

Georgina doesn't care about anyone but herself: she would never pause and consider vegetarianism like so many other girls her age, she couldn't give a shit about animals, she is turning into the type of woman who will wear real fur. She runs with a pack of similar teen witches, all mobile phones and sniggers, minds full of pop music and fashionable labels. I could shake her at times, shake her till her belly ring falls out. She had that done behind my back; I didn't notice for ages, not with everything else going on.

It would be simpler if I was just jealous of her; the way there is that gap between the tops of her tweezered legs (Georgina is not daft enough to take the razor to her pins), the way her stomach sprouts from the top of her jeans as slender as a spring onion, the thinness of her arms.

Fat arms have always been my downfall – along with the other bits. I have always had what I call primary-schoolteacher arms, the ones that wobble like tripe in a breeze. Georgina, despite doing nothing but sitting on her behind talking to her cronies, is honed to the bone, her ankles, knees and elbows are sharp. Mine are round and blunt and I have footballers' knees. She says she wants to be a model; I wouldn't be surprised if this happens, just a little disappointed because she plays thicker than she really is, filling the margins of her exercise books with hearts and cartoons of girls in flared trousers. She knows every lyric to every pop song, but refuses to remember her prime numbers.

When I was her age, I had a paper round and a Saturday job; Georgina has an allowance and will not so much as vacuum her room to earn it. She spends our, sorry 'her' money on glitter nail varnish, hair mascara and henna tattoos. When I was fourteen, I had my school uniform, two pairs of slacks complete with stirrups and a black velvet pinafore dress for best. Georgina owns half of Top Shop. Her father indulges her, of course; they sneak off together and come home with wedge heels and diamante hair clips.

Soon she will be going out with boys; there will be grubby paw marks on her little white bras and I will die a thousand deaths. When I find myself thinking like this I am shocked. I have become a born-again prude: bad language makes me wince, people spitting on the street make me gag and recently, when I was on a tube and the couple opposite me started kissing, I had to change seats. I have been thinking about taking up tapestry.

I nearly had a cigarette on Tuesday; I haven't smoked for four years. I took one of Anna's Silk Cut out of a packet she'd left in the kitchen and I went into the garden, but by the time I'd come back in and found some matches, the craving was gone – thankfully, it is a disgusting habit. Instead I ate a peach and congratulated myself on the clarity of my taste buds and the fact that I was eating fruit. Then I walked round to Brenda Donahue's house and had a cup of tea with her. Raymond was having one of his bad days and sat on the sofa picking his nose. It is a terrible thing to admit but sometimes I need to be reminded that other people are worse off than I am. Brenda admitted that after her husband left her she had contemplated putting a pillow over Raymond's face and jumping out of the window.

26

Skinny-Dipping and Sangria

The first time the Cunninghams and the Metcalfs went on holiday together, Jed was just a toddler and Anna was very frightened that he might drown. Jo had hired a villa in the north of Majorca with a pool, which was marvellous but meant, of course, that there had to be an adult lifeguard on duty at all times.

Nigel was also rather worried about going to Majorca; he'd been to Magaluf as a teenager and the pal he'd gone with had returned home with genital warts. Genital warts were one of Nigel's phobias, they have to be burnt off and can re-occur for life. To Nigel, the mere mention of Majorca conjured up sexually transmitted disease. His suspicions were confirmed when they boarded the plane at Gatwick, only to find it was full of *Sun*-reading common types demanding lager on a 10am flight – and that was just the women. Nigel thought they all looked as if they were riddled with genital warts.

He needn't have worried. Majorca is an island of two halves: the peasants stay down in the south, where they eat egg and chips and turn geranium-pink in the sun, whilst the middle classes stream up to the north, with their factor thirty and their Booker-nominated novels. It is just the way things are. Possibly there is some village in the middle where people dither between *The Birdy Song* and Martin Amis.

It takes less than three hours to get to Majorca but when the plane touched down some people started clapping! Nigel almost fainted with embarrassment. Chris, however, forgot that clapping was very *infra dig* and joined in, which meant that Anna had to punch him rather hard in the stomach.

Jo was horribly nervous about the whole thing; choosing a holiday is an awesome responsibility and the flight unsettled her. Jo didn't like flying. Anna loved it and when the plane hit turbulence halfway into the journey she yelped with laughter, whilst Jo tightened her sphincter until you could have sharpened pencils with it, and clutched her copy of *Hotel du Lac* to her chest rather as if it were a bible. Jo took charge of all the passports, all eight of them – even Jed had his own. Anna's passport photo managed to look as if David Bailey had been operating the photo booth, whilst Jo's made her look like her father in drag.

They travelled in convoy from the airport in two hire cars, and only had to go round the one-way system twice before they found the motorway. The villa was just outside of Puerto Pollensa on the north-west coast and half a mile down a dirt track, off the main road. Jo was so tense that she gnawed her bottom lip and it took two days for the indentations from her top teeth to wear off.

It was a relief when the villa finally came into sight; a two-storey traditional stone finca-style suntrap, complete with a cartwheel bolted to the side wall.

Hoorah, hoorah, let the holiday begin.

Of course, it's not as simple as all that. The welcome box of groceries consisted of white bread, six eggs and a tub of margarine. So Jo offered to pop to the supermarket. 'No, really, it's got to be done.' When she got back everyone was in the pool eating egg sandwiches, but she pretended not to mind and prepared a tray of gin and tonics, making sure she got the extra strong one.

It was the first time they had seen each other wearing so few clothes. Jo found it all rather traumatic. She made sure she never lay on the sun lounger next to Anna: the contrast would have been too stark, Anna visibly turning copper in a scarlet bikini, Jo with her dingy flesh the colour of old bra straps, barely contained within an old Marks and Spencer swimming costume with built-in cups. Ah well, at least Chris was in no better shape, with his spindly legs, his big fat belly and the large gelatinous moles on his back. 'Ugh,' said Georgina when she saw them. She was six, Pandora five, Henry eight and Jed just two. Nigel, of course, with his university rowing-team body, looked just fine in his Speedos. The only bulgy bits on him were his genitals, something Anna couldn't fail to notice. 'Your Nigel's got a fair-sized knob,' she remarked casually, over a dish of roasted almonds.

The villa had three bedrooms; the plan was that Anna and Chris should have the big one with the en suite because they needed the extra space for Jed's travel cot. 'It doesn't seem fair,' Chris said. 'After all, Jo, you organised all this, you should have the big room.' But Anna had already taken their bags up and arranged her toiletries in the little fake marble bathroom. There was another bedroom with two sets of bunk beds, which was ideal for the bigger children, so that left the smallest room with the twin beds and cat-flap-sized window for Jo and Nigel. It wasn't ideal: Nigel was slightly claustrophobic and down the corridor Pandora, disturbed by Henry's nocturnal jabbering and occasional screams, decided to wander in to Chris and Anna's bed every night and wedge herself between them like an electric fire. The sheets were nylon and Anna thought she might suffocate.

'Next time you book a holiday, Jo, make sure the bloody place has got air-conditioning.'

She wasn't being ungrateful, Jo persuaded herself, she was just tired. None of them got much sleep. They attempted a couple of daytrips but it was easier to stay by the pool and pick lemons from the trees in the garden. Sometimes Jo thought it would be nice to go out for dinner; it was quite hard work feeding people three times a day and none of the kids liked the same thing. When she wasn't cooking or shopping or washing up, she was on lifeguard duty – after all, she was the strongest swimmer. Jo found herself constantly running around in her flip-flops; one day she stubbed her big toe so badly she took the nail clean off. Nigel kept telling her to 'chill' and occasionally she had to hide herself away in the laundry-room and have a little cry whilst she sorted out the washing. 'Just chuck your stuff in with ours, I might as well do it all together.'

Jo and Anna went to the Wednesday-morning market in the town together. It was meant to be a special 'girl treat' but Jo found herself buying figs, tomatoes, cheese and artichokes, whilst Anna bought a leather belt, some shoes and a turquoise bra and knickers set. Still, you can't eat lingerie and everyone agreed that the artichokes were delicious.

Two weeks flew by. On the last night they drank every drop of alcohol they had left and ate their farewell barbecue by the pool. Once the kids were asleep they kept drinking, not even bothering to tidy away the supper plates. They were laughing a lot and at midnight Anna stripped down to her new turquoise bra and knickers and dived into the pool. The next minute, they were all in; the boys were stark naked and when Anna threw her soggy underwear on to a deckchair Jo found herself doing the same. Unfortunately the cold water sobered her up and she suddenly felt vulnerable and embarrassed.

Jo got up at 5.30 the next morning; their flight was at 10.00 and there were still the dinner plates, the barbecue grill-pan and a broken glass to clean up before they left at 7.00. It wasn't fair to leave everything to the maid. In the end, she needn't have been in such a panic, the flight was delayed by three hours. 'I knew it,' said Nigel. 'See, Jo, you had time to creosote the fence.' He was trying to pretend he didn't have a hangover, but they all felt terrible and Chris had to go and be sick whilst Anna bought some cigarettes in the duty-free.

But it was a fabulous holiday, and they all decided to do it again. Over the years, the Cunninghams and the Metcalfs rented villas in Majorca, a gite in France, a farmhouse in Corsica and a converted windmill in Tuscany. Jo organised everything. Once she put her foot down and said it was up to the boys to arrange the accommodation. It was a disaster; they ended up in a godforsaken bungalow in Brittany, where it rained every day and they decided to get the ferry home before someone got stabbed to death with the bottle opener.

Sometimes Jo dreaded these holidays; they were so much effort. She had to make sure Henry had enough asthma inhalers and then there were travel sickness pills to remember and Elastoplast, insect repellent, antihistamine cream, sun-block and after-sun,

Calpol and then, of course, the dinghy. That bloody dinghy. It was her fault, of course, buying one built to last, sturdy as a U-boat. Every year she wished it would get punctured beyond repair, but no, every year it had to be found, packed, inflated and then at the end of the holiday deflated – which took four hours – and even then it was always wet so she had to remember to have enough bin liners to wrap it up in. Still, it wouldn't be the same without the dinghy. What else would Anna have to lie in as she bobbed about the pool drinking cheap Spanish champagne?

Often Jo's irritable bowel would flare up and she would have to sit on the lavatory for hours on end, listening to everyone else having fun outside. But at least while her colon dithered about trying to make up its mind whether to auto-strangulate or just fall out completely, she had time to plan what she should cook for supper. Her only concession to being on holiday was buying shop-bought mayonnaise.

Over the years, evidence of these trips accumulated in both households: a pair of pink flowery flip-flops, a couple of straw hats, little ceramic bowls that looked like lettuce leaves, pebbles and shells. In the old days there always seemed to be sand at the bottom of their suitcases, but Jo's toenail never really grew back.

27

Sex in Solihull

It's hot today and I have nothing to do except sit in the Metcalfs' garden with a wine box, thinking of other summers. This is the worst one I have ever had. I'm not even brown and I am always brown in the summer.

The first time I remember going abroad was when I was twelve, and I had a yellow, crocheted bikini just like my mum's. We went to Majorca. I've been back there since with Jo and Nigel, Chris and the kids; for two weeks we rented a villa with a pool, in the north of the island. I'm going back about eight years, Pandora must have been five and Jed two. We had a good time, apart from the day I slapped Georgina and Jo caught me. It's not on, I suppose, leaving a bright red slap stain on your best friend's daughter's cheek, but she deserved it. She was being vile to my Jed, taunting him with a bottle of Ribena; holding it high above his golden head, so his little fists were outstretched and his face coloured raspberry with fury. She'd sat on my Ray-Bans and sniggered when they cracked. I was livid with her, but the juice incident was the last straw. I was watching them out of the window and I remember charging out of the kitchen like a bull on heat and before I knew it I'd given her a real crack across the chops. At that moment, Jo came out of the little laundry-room.

'Anna, you've hit my child,' she said. There was almost enough disbelief in her voice for me to say, 'No, I never.' Georgina was bawling her head off.

'I'm sorry, Jo,' I said, 'but she was being such a cow to Jed.' At this point, Pandora waddled by; she had a big bruise on her arm. 'Bloody hell, Pandora, what have you done now?' I shrieked. She was always in the wars: lumps on her head, scabs on her fat knees.

'Georgina bit me,' she replied.

Well, fair's fair, really, a slap for a bite.

Jo decided we were all tired and hot and bothered and we should all make friends. Huh, fat chance. Georgina has never liked me, little minx, but at least we knew where we stood.

We have laughed about this incident since but I have noticed over the years that whenever it is my birthday Georgina never joins in singing, 'Happy birthday, dear Anna,' she just mouths the words. Spiteful little bitch. We're all going on a summer holiday – only I'm not.

I lost my virginity in the summer holidays of 1973; I was fifteen, he was twenty-two. I wore denim shorts with embroidered flowers on the bum, great big cork wedges and halter-necked tops tied up with string, which was always coming undone; it was part of my charm, I was a delicious parcel all ready to be unwrapped. As I recall, I'd progressed from snogging to petting quite rapidly. Nice boys were always shocked when I allowed them easy access to my pant area; they were used to being swatted off like flies. Not by me; I would breathe in, allowing them extra fumbling space, making it easy for them to undo the top button of my Farah jeans. To be honest, I scared most of them off.

I suppose I got bored of nice young men who couldn't look me in the face once they'd put their fingers in my knickers. By the time I was fifteen, I'd grown out of the local youth club and the parties that were supervised by nervous parents who would frisk the boys for alcohol and made sure the lights were kept on so that things didn't get out of hand when the 'teenagers' played spin the bottle.

I started going into town after school and hanging out in a cafe called the Purple Fountain. It was full of what my mother would call 'low life', which was the point of it really. It wasn't just me, a bunch of us went, rolling over our school skirts at the waistband to make them shorter, playing the schoolgirl thing to the hilt: hair in high bunches, sucking on lollies, jailbait with a school motto emblazoned on the breast of our blazors, *Semper Paratis, Semper Volens* – always ready, always willing – you're not kidding!

Vic was a part-time Hell's Angel, part-time newsagent; his dad had a paper shop and if Vic got up early enough to take in the morning delivery then from four o'clock onwards he was free to wear a ripped leather jacket with a skull and crossbones badly painted on the back. He didn't actually have a motorbike but he had a helmet and a metal pin in his leg from the time he came off his mate's Harley. Vic spent a lot of time in the Purple

Fountain; he spent most of his money playing Alex Harvey Band numbers on the juke box, drinking coffee and eating cheese toasties. He had a cannabis leaf tattooed on one forearm and the name of his girlfriend, Linda, on the other. Both were homemade and the L and the i of Linda were a bit close together so it looked like Under, and that's why everyone called Linda, Under. Most people had nicknames: there was Spider (a thin bloke), The Bleeder (a haemophiliac), Gobber (because he did) and Spunk (no explanation necessary).

Mostly I went to the Purple Fountain with a girl called Karen, whose parents had recently got divorced thereby giving her *carte blanche* to do whatever she liked, and Melanie, who nobody noticed wore a brace because she had the most enormous pair of tits. We were all fifteen, pockets full of Polos and ten No. 6. I lied to my mother that I was in the netball team and we had practices after school. On other occasions I said I had projects to do and had to go to the library. Mum suspected nothing, she had other worries: my dad was playing around and she had a touch of arthritis in her right hand that was making the jewellery business a bit tricky. She took up yoga, and got so good at meditating that as she sat with her legs in the lotus position she never really knew what time of day it was, never mind what her teenage daughter was up to.

Vic called me the Schoolie and teased me, spraying strawberry milkshake at me through a straw. 'Stop it, Vic, you big bully,' but my eyes would be bright and I'd start flicking my hair the way girls do when they're excited. When 'Under' came in, Vic would switch his attention swiftly over to her. She worked in a supermarket and would come straight to the Purple Fountain after her shift; sometimes she still had on her salmon-coloured nylon overall under her fringed leather jacket. Under was nineteen but she still got spots. They were particularly bad just before her period and there was a recurring one just above her lip; a vast yellow head surrounded, as if in obeisance, by a crop of lesser yellow heads. Apart from her dodgy complexion, not helped by the thick layer of orange panstick she used as a concealer, she was a very pretty girl, 'in an obvious sort of way' as my mum would have put it, Meaning she was blond and had big blue eyes and puffy pink lips. But she was getting wide around the bum from sitting down all day and the pockets of her Levi's had begun to bulge. Vic and Under lived together, that was how serious it was. Under ignored us schoolies, she had her own mates: Big Tina, Gail and Mad Liz. Mad Liz was the most frightening, because she was.

It was hot, the summer I lost my virginity, and because it was the school holidays I divided my time between the open-air pool and the Purple Fountain.

I had plenty of money: when my allowance ran out, I'd filch fivers from my father's pockets. Dad didn't have a wallet, he believed in fistfuls of cash and left little heaps of screwed-up notes and coins all over the place.

I had a pair of pink heart-shaped sunglasses, a purple shiny bikini and a tan that had been kick-started by ten days in Ibiza with my parents. Me, Karen and Mel would meet up at the pool around midday, the sun glinting off Mel's brace, and we'd arrange ourselves in the same corner every day. It was a camp made up of brightly coloured towels, suntan lotions, cans of Coke, teen magazines and a portable radio. All around the pool were similar camps: the teenagers occupied the northern territory at the deep end of the pool by the slide and diving boards, whilst families with little kids congregated by the shallow end near the cafe. It was an unwritten rule, but none the less obeyed; occasionally a stray dad-type would take a stroll through the teen section, only to return back to family base with an aching heart and a semi hard-on.

The cafe served burgers and chips and sandwiches on white bread, cheese and cucumber, egg mayonnaise or ham and tomato, but we never ate much, maybe a strawberry mivvie – melted ice-cream running down your cleavage. It wasn't the done thing for girls to be seen eating in public. It was one thing to nick the odd chip off a bloke, but to eat a whole carton – gross. So the holidays slid by and oblivious to melanomas we rolled around like spit-roasted baby pigs basted in Ambre Solaire. Poor Karen was a bit gingery and her naturally sago-coloured skin burnt badly and she peeled like an old fence. I, meanwhile, turned the colour of tinned sausages.

At around four we'd get changed, stuffing soggy towels and bikinis into plastic bags, and cycle off to the Purple Fountain. We'd leave our bikes a few blocks away; it was seriously uncool to arrive on anything that had two wheels and no carburettor. The Fountain was on a back road parallel to the high street and the pavement was wide enough for everyone to splay out on the concrete. Occasionally there would be complaints and the cops would come down and chivvy everyone inside, where the air was thick with blue smoke and the sticky tables thick with flies.

The girls' toilets were awful in the summer. I would concentrate on the graffiti and inhale my wrists as I read, 'Alice Cooper Rools', 'Mel for Spider', 'Vic and Under true luv 4 ever'. Ha, thought little old me, one foot against the door as it had no lock and trying not to pee on the seat, 'true luv 4 ever'? I would see about that. I had seen the way Vic looked at me. Push-over.

We had to wait until Under went on a training course for two days in Preston. She decided to stop over with her sister – first mistake. Her second mistake being not giving Vic a blowjob before she left. By four o'clock that thundery Wednesday afternoon, his balls were aching, and all I had to do was walk into the Fountain for him to get a gravity-defying erection.

We couldn't go back to his place, 'it wouldn't be right,' he said, but Sam the bloke behind the counter, dispenser of milkshakes, toasties, smutt and innuendo, and purveyor of the finest foreign pornography, had a couple of rooms above the Fountain; nothing fancy, but the weasel owed Vic a favour, it would do. By five o'clock, he had smuggled me through the kitchen and up the back stairs. He'd borrowed a johnny from Spider, I wasn't nervous. When he took off my clothes, I stood back and let him look at me, brown and white like a trifle with two cherries on the top. You'd never have known I hadn't done it before.

Who knows what would have happened if Under had not found herself throwing up on the second day of her course. 'Food poisoning,' she told her sister. 'Food poisoning my foot,' said Elaine, who had three kids. 'You're up the stick, love.'

Vic told me all this in whispers; he came to meet me after school. He said he 'couldn't finish with her, the pregnancy was confirmed, and for all he was a bastard, he was not a cunt.' He married Under in the September and had the reception at the Fountain. I wasn't there; Mad Liz had seen me creeping down the stairs with my newly broken hymen and Vic behind me doing up his flies. Mad Liz might have been mental on account of the metal plate in her head but she wasn't thick. She collared me the next day and told me if she ever saw me in the Fountain again, she'd put a Stanley knife in my face. Eight months later Under and Vic had a baby girl; they called her Suzi after Suzi Quatro, but unfortunately she grew up to have a lazy eye and fat legs.

Funny all these details that keep flooding back. I can remember the moles on Under's arms, the scar in Mad Liz's hairline; I can remember these things but sometimes I struggle to get a proper picture of my own children in my head and I have to go through the Metcalfs' red leather photo albums to remind me of myself.

28

Sani Lavs and Dead Rats

When I was a child, my mother and father had a caravan; it was the smallest caravan in the world. I believe it was called a Sprite 400, which was very apt considering it was only big enough for elves. I loved that caravan. At night time the dining-table swivelled down into a miniature double bed for my parents, whilst my brother and I wriggled around on shelves disguised as bunks, farting and giggling into our sleeping bags. There is something very comforting about sleeping in a caravan, especially when it is raining and you feel you have your whole world safe and sound around you. Everything is simple – maybe that is what I should do, buy myself a caravan and park it in the middle of nowhere.

When I remember those holidays I can conjure up their tastes and smells: my mother's fruitcake, the pale caramel plastic plates and the funny toilet full of blue liquid and turds, which my father would have to empty every other day. A Sani Lav, I think it was called. Once we went to the Italian lakes. My brother and I had a lilo and a kitchen porter from one of the posh hotels on the lido used to push us far out into the water; I remember him because he had several fingers missing on his right hand.

My parents didn't approve of hotels; hotels were for cissies. They didn't do luxury and we only got ice-creams if we were really good. I must have been sixteen before I swore in front of my parents and even then I was sent to my room. I'm not sure my children could cope with the sort of lifestyle I had; if you so much as mention a game of scrabble to Georgina she goes running off to call Childline with accusations of abuse.

I once tried to get them to play a game of pontoon with matches like we used to, but Henry pretended to fall into a coma. Maybe I'm just remembering the nice moments. All families are a bit quaint, aren't they? We've all got secrets. When I was a kid my mum went through a phase of drinking very heavily. This was thirty years ago when addiction wasn't as fashionable as it is now; these days dependency is *de rigueur* and I am getting slightly bored of it.

My mother's drinking was very confusing; we kept it quiet. Wives of brigadiers are not supposed to crawl under the eiderdown every afternoon, listening to *Woman's Hour* with a bottle of vodka. My dad, despite being totally at home ordering hundreds of men to march in unison, hadn't got a clue what to do with her. 'Now now, darling, let's not get silly.' Being the practical type, he took pre-emptive strike action, starting with installing a fire extinguisher in the bedroom, so that if she did nod off with a

Bensons in her hand then at least she could put the bed clothes out before the curtains went up and she set fire to the whole house.

My brother and I were put on 'watering down duty'; it was our job to pour down the sink half the contents of every bottle of spirits that we found and then proceed to top them up with water. He even screwed down the lids so tightly that she would have to wrestle the bottles open with her teeth; consequently there were bite marks on the lids of the vodka and the gin. Between us, we managed to keep the problem in check, it was only at the occasional 'do' in the officers' mess that she had to be watched. Once, at a Christmas party, she got a bit out of hand, waded into the string quartet that were providing polite background music for the evening, seized the cello and proceeded to ride it round the room as if it were a wild pony, neighing and whinnying with abandon. Eventually she came a cropper on a vol-au-vent and skidded across the parquet floor into the French windows. She was quite badly cut and even now, living quietly in rural Wiltshire, she still has a thick purple scar on her chin.

We all have secrets: the funny uncle with the wobbly knee that you weren't supposed to sit on. Any family, if you go back far enough, has someone that barked at the moon. On my husband's side there's a great-great-grandfather who gambled away the family silver, put a shotgun in his mouth, pulled the trigger and somehow missed his brain. He lived for several months with a massive hole in the top of his head, his meninges blowing in the breeze. Or so the story goes. We all have a little bit of bad blood, skeletons in our cupboards. It's just that Anna's came tumbling out all at once, and now that it's happened, it seems like she needs gluing back together. Like a gorgeous piece of china, she'll never be perfect again.

We shan't be going on holiday this year. What with one thing and another, part of me is a little bit relieved. It's not easy keeping everyone happy; Henry and Georgina have reached that difficult age, even the old yellow dinghy has had its day.

I can't remember how many holidays we had with the Cunninghams; they became rather a habit and not necessarily a very good one. Maybe I should have nipped it in the bud a long time ago. Even the first time we went away together, when everyone was on their best behaviour, there were ugly moments. Like the time I walked out of the laundry-room and saw Anna strike Georgina crack across the face. There I was with a bundle of their bloody towels that I'd put in the machine with ours, and she was hitting my child. I was livid and shocked but I let the incident go; there'd been some fuss earlier about Georgina breaking Anna's sunglasses and if I had to be honest I'd have to admit that Georgina had been a prize bitch to Pandora ever since we'd got there. She had to be watched, did Georgina; she enjoyed tormenting the Cunningham kids and sometimes on that holiday she'd embarrassed me. She was a six-year-old bully with the face of an angel in a polka dot bikini.

The other thing I remembered was that it was always me who had to go to the supermarket, sometimes twice a day. I shopped, Chris was in charge of the barbecues, Nigel took care of the booze and Anna . . . well, Anna sunbathed really, and occasionally chopped up a tomato or put olives in a dish. Christ, some of this has been my fault. I have let her get away with her nonsense for years and bloody years.

There was another incident that I'd forgotten up until recently. It suddenly resurfaced and it made me feel quite queasy just thinking about it. Halfway through that first holiday, we'd driven out to a beach and it was right at the bottom of about three billion hairpin bends. 'Mum, I'm going to be sick!' (Henry) – I can still hear the panic in his voice. When we got there, it was perfect: secluded, deserted, golden sand, real postcard stuff. We unpacked the boots of the cars, put out our towels, made our camp and the kids were mucking about with a Frisbee when Georgina started screaming; she'd skidded in the sand and buried beneath its soft grains was the rotting corpse of the most enormous rat.

Something horrible always has to happen, doesn't it? On the way back, Henry did throw up; he said ever since he'd seen the rat he kept imagining it in his mouth. It wasn't a very successful day and to make it worse I started to peel like an old snake. Guess who had to clean the sick out of the car? That's right, me. Do you know, I have been thinking of having 'sucker' tattooed on my forehead.

29

Naughty Nigel

Nigel George Metcalf married Josephine Alexandra Travis way back in the autumn of 1982. The bride wore a vast cream satin meringue of a dress, which increased her volume and dwarfed her dainty new spouse.

He was a phenomenally unfaithful husband; from the moment their engagement had been announced in the *Scotsman* and *The Times* he was at it, fornicating at any opportunity, like a rat up a drain. Now, in 1995, he was halfway through his second decade of adultery. Older, but no wiser, Nigel, daddy to Georgina and Henry, had been playing away from home again: two blowjobs and a shag in the shower. The latter had been rather unsuccessful, Nigel had slipped on a bar of soap and it had all become rather undignified. Naturally he felt bad about it, he always did; sometimes it was debatable whether the snatched moments of illicit snatch and the gonad-exploding ejaculations were worth the days of torment afterwards. This time it wasn't just the guilt, he also had a very tender bruise on the back of his head.

Nigel Metcalf was a terrible one for casual sex (and by that we don't mean nonchalantly having it off in an old cardigan with leather elbows, while smoking a pipe and holding a cup of tea in one hand and the *Evening Standard* in the other). He just couldn't help himself; he was as greedy with strange women as Jo was with chocolate, gobbling them up regardless of whether they were past their sell-by date, belonged to someone else or showed signs of having already been half chewed and spat out by a previous consumer. Just as Jo battled with her weight, Nigel fought with his libido.

Nigel viewed his penis rather like a Ghurkha does his sword; whenever it was unleashed, it was duty-bound to plunge itself into the sticky reaches of some tart's juicy love box. In the same way that Jo could never resist that extra biscuit, Nigel could never resist another portion of female flesh. If sex on the side contained as many calories as chips, Nigel Metcalf would have weighed forty stone.

These extra-maritals normally happened when Nigel went away on business; he wouldn't have dreamt of being unfaithful within his own postcode, you don't shit on your own doorstep. Anyway, it wasn't as if he ever had affairs, not proper ones. There was no real intimacy involved, it was just a matter of sex, a more sloppy grunty form of shaking hands.

Blondes, brunettes, redheads, thin, fat, tall, short, smelly, bandy . . . On occasion, Nigel's quality control slipped rather badly and he would wake up wondering if he had accidentally booked himself into Battersea Dogs' Home.

The trouble with Nigel's job was that there was ample opportunity for this kind of behaviour. It wasn't as if it cost him anything, it was all on expenses: hotel rooms, bar tabs, continental breakfasts. The only thing Nigel had to fork out for was condoms and these days most of the women he picked up seemed to carry their own.

There was a woman in Newcastle who had popped a prophylactic into her mouth and within five seconds of unbuttoning his flies had expertly managed to deposit it on Nigel's penis. It had been a shock, especially as the condom had been a liquorice-flavoured one and had turned his appendage the dark grey of a rotting corpse. 'Forty quid, darling,' she'd rasped after.

Nigel had slept with all sorts since he had married Jo: skinny, sickly seventeen-year-olds in empty padded bras, improbably large-breasted thirty-year-olds that left fake tan stains on the bed sheets, swarthy brunettes with scratchy stubble on their legs.

Once in a hotel in Wales, he had managed to persuade a pair of nubile twins to join him in his room for drinks from the mini bar. It was only in the cold light of day that he realised there was no way these women were twins; it was obvious – one being a good twenty years older than the other. 'No,' the younger one giggled, 'course we're not twins. She's my mum.' And the two of them rolled around, laughing down their matching piggy noses whilst Nigel choked on his Alka-Seltzer.

Part of the problem was that Nigel liked his cocaine rather too much. There was always a small wrap of paper tucked into one his Savile Row suit pockets, a little origami envelope of his old friend 'Charlie'. Daft, of course, for a lawyer to dabble in illegal class A narcotics. Nigel had a lot to lose and every time he blew his nose and his handkerchief filled with blood and stuff that looked suspiciously like cartilage, he was reminded of this fact.

He had panic attacks in the night and often woke up sweating, convinced he could smell the sex on him; some of the women Nigel fucked weren't particularly clean. With his nostrils drenched in their smoked-salmon scent, he would often creep off for a 3am shower, loofah-ing himself long and hard. Sometimes he wished his penis could be involved in some kind of industrial accident; he'd be much better off without it, and it wasn't as if Jo would miss it.

Nigel loved Jo, Nigel needed Jo; he knew that without Jo the dark side of Nigel Metcalf would come slithering out and within months he'd be freebasing and fucking fourteen-year-olds. Sometimes Nigel frightened himself . . . time for a quick toot. Snnnnnnnnnnnghhh. Ah, now that was better.

When Nigel felt normal he blamed his wife; it was her fault really. Jo was bloody lucky to have him, he was a good-looking man with a large earning capacity, a good pension and a whopping great life insurance policy. She was a jammy cow and just once in a while it would be nice if she showed some gratitude, if she would take her nose out of whatever soppy women's book she was reading at the time and suck him dry. The least a man should expect from a wife is weekly oral sex, given willingly with a smile and a swallow. Whenever he did force Jo's head down beneath the duvet, she would re-emerge, her job done and immediately run to spit out his sperm in the sink. Where's the gratitude in that?

Nigel would put money on Anna being a swallower, Christ knew what she was doing with Chris. He was a nice bloke and all that, but just like Jo he'd married out of his sexual league.

Sometimes Nigel had uncomfortable dreams about Anna; subconsciously he had fucked her on many different occasions. The first time was over his own kitchen table whilst the others ate pineapple upside-down pudding and held up marks out of ten for stamina and agility.

For a good few weeks after this dream, Nigel had found it difficult being in the same room as Anna, but he kept his dirty imaginings to himself. You don't go round touching up the missus's best mate, however much her tits looked like they were begging to be bitten hard.

Now and again he would allow himself a wank over her, there was something about her arse that made him want to spank her. Because he rationed his Anna wanks, Nigel liked to give himself free rein over what he would like to do with her, and it always shocked him by how violent these fantasies were. He saw himself pulling her around by the hair, ripping the buttons off her shirt, but the picture that always made him come was of Anna, her face all bruised and bleeding, taking him in her mouth. By the time he had this scene in his head, he was pulling at his penis in a frenzy muttering, 'Fucking bitch,' with every stroke. Was he mad?

It always mildly surprised Nigel that when he next saw Anna after an 'Anna wank' she wasn't covered in bite marks with his fingerprints around her neck.

Sometimes he thought she was egging him on. When they first met the Cunninghams she was positively flirty, but it had worn off and nowadays she treated him like a brother. Hey ho, incest was always an interesting option. In the meantime, there was the guilt of last week's conference totty to get over and the promise of that new researcher to come. He would also have to be more careful; that Carol had left scratch marks on his back and a small love bite on the inside of his thigh. Nigel decided to give his ravaged back an alibi by scratching it more and insisting to Jo that she'd switched washing powders and that he must be allergic to whatever it was she'd bought.

'Don't be daft, it's the same stuff I've been using for years.'

Had Jo been the suspicious type and inspected Nigel's scratches under a magnifying glass, she would have seen for herself the tell-tale slivers of plum-coloured nail varnish embedded in the welts. As it was, she gave him a spoonful of Piriton and told him not to be 'so wet'.

Nigel didn't discuss his extra-curricular activities with Chris Cunningham – they didn't talk about that kind of thing. They didn't talk about much; it's difficult to get chatty when you've very little in common. Anyway, it's not the done thing for a man to say to his wife's best friend's hubby, 'Fucked your missus last night, up against the pantry door, she was begging for it. Only a dream mate, no hard feelings.' It just wouldn't do.

So, they talked about other things – thank the Lord for the weather. 'Brrr, chilly out, no wonder your wife's nipples are sticking out like' – whoops, stop it.

30

Soho Surprises

I knew that Nigel was unfaithful to Jo because she told me. I wasn't surprised, but I pretended to be outraged on her behalf. She'd been drinking when she blurted it out. We were staying in a converted watermill somewhere that I don't remember the name of; Jo had organised it, seen a picture in *Elle* magazine and got on the case. She's a great organiser is Jo, or she was; these days she has lost the will. The party days are over but back then we were always having fun.

There are photos of us mostly laughing: Pandora, beginning to lose her baby teeth, a big, ugly yellow adult tooth sticking crookedly from her gum. Jed at three, with his bleached sweet-corn grin; they look so young. It's probably only seven years ago but it feels like seventy. I remember the mill had a games room up at the top and there were thousands of dead flies on the windowsill. I don't know why but these things just stay in your head, like stains on your best dress.

The kids were in bed and the boys were playing pool in the games room and Jo and I were clearing up the dinner things. She was tipping all the leftover wine from everyone else's glasses into hers and I was rolling a very small joint, because sometimes I do. It was just after Christmas and we'd brought all our leftovers with us; there was a big whiffy Stilton on the table and a tin of Quality Street, mostly full of empty wrappers. Suddenly she just came out with it, 'He isn't faithful to me, you know, Nigel fucks around,' and she sang the last bit in a really bad Marianne Faithful kind of voice, and I knew that once she'd finished the red wine she'd start on the port. I wasn't quite sure what to do or say apart from, 'Jo, I'm sorry, he's an idiot,' which, of course, he wasn't, he was a good-looking bloke in his thirties with a fat wife. 'I don't mind,' she said, but she stabbed at the Stilton and a big chunk of it avalanched off and then she sat there eating cheese and chocolates and told me what she knew. It wasn't much, just the usual: hotel bills, odd phone calls, occasional scratches on his back, it was familiar stuff. Whenever my father embarked on a new liaison, you could tell by the amount of talcum powder he put in his socks; I remember the cloudy footprints he'd leave as he walked from the bathroom back to the bedroom, the gargling with Listerine, the mints in his pocket, the giveaway singing of odd songs. When he was fucking a woman called Jennifer, he'd bellow *Jennifer Juniper*, the Donovan song, and my mother's eyes would roll.

She told me about how Nigel had dreamt of fucking his sister, which even though I was a bit stoned I recall thinking was a bit kinky. Once she'd started telling me about it, she couldn't stop; her tongue went flip flap in her mouth and all these words came tumbling out. Apparently they were never really serious, just silly little slags. It had started before they got married. She'd had a cousin to stay in the little flat she'd shared with some other girls in Gypsy Hill; it was someone's twenty-first birthday and she'd caught him with the cousin on his knee. He said he'd just been messing around and it was just a laugh so she forgot it and married him. She didn't ask the cousin to be a bridesmaid and her auntie had been really pissed off and sent them a really horrible set of glasses as a punishment. They had pictures of people playing golf on them.

I got a bit confused at this point so I just made a lot of comforting noises and she blew her nose on a tea towel and said that it didn't bother her that much and, anyway, didn't it happen all the time? I could have said, 'No, Chris wouldn't dream of it,' but I didn't see why I should make her feel worse. She was heading for one hell of a migraine anyway, what with the crying and the red wine and the chocolate and the cheese, so I rolled another joint and she filled her lungs to the brim even though she's never been any good with dope.

The next day, we all set off for the beach; we were in convoy, us behind the Metcalfs and suddenly Nigel pulled the Volvo on to the grass verge and Jo got out and threw up all over a bush. We pulled up behind and waited till she'd finished honking – the bush looked like yellow and purple snow had fallen on it in the night – then we drove off.

I saw Nigel with one of his girls once. I was walking down Old Compton Street and I needed a wee, so I nipped into a pub; it was just before Christmas and the place was chocker with office-parties types. Nigel was sitting in a corner with a skinny redhead squashed up next to him, and even though they were trying to be discreet her coat had slipped to one side and I could see that he'd pulled up her skirt and wrenched down her tights and knickers, which were all bunched up around her thighs, and that he was finger-fucking her. I didn't know what to do, so I went to the ladies' and just sat there on the loo thinking. I almost didn't realise that I'd started my period; I'm really vague about these things, I have an extremely erratic cycle and I wasn't prepared. Bloody Christmas, bloody Nigel, bloody bleeding. I folded a load of bog roll up to be getting on with, left the cubicle and started wading through my bag for some change for the tampon machine.

That's when the red-haired piece came staggering in, pissed out of her head and all her buttons done up wrong. She got out the old repair kit, a battered little black nylon make-up bag, and started weaving in front of the mirror trying to get her plum-coloured lipstick back on straight. I asked her if she had any change for the tampon machine and she fished for her purse but all her money had fallen out of it and into the lining of her bag. She started to empty the bag on to the floor, all bits of tissue and pens, fag packets, lighters, chewing-gum and tatty old cheque books. She had the hiccups, so I kept saying, 'Don't worry, forget it.' But she kept insisting, 'Hold on, jussst hold on,' and there's this shit all over the floor and she's wobbling about until finally she goes, 'Ha,' and waves a tampon at me. The wrapper was a bit torn and it looked pretty grubby but I took it anyway. I went back into the cubicle, sorted myself out and when I came out she was in a heap over her bag. She'd nodded off; she had half a Christmas cracker in one hand and her purse in the other. I took the purse, all fat with credit cards and the change she'd tried to stuff back in it, and dropped it into the bin where the sanitary towels go. Then I lifted the plum-coloured lipstick and fucked off out of there.

I never said anything to Jo and I didn't mention it to Nigel and I certainly didn't tell Chris. For a start, what was I doing wandering round Soho three days before Christmas? Well actually, husband dear, I was buying black crotchless panties, and lager-flavoured booby drops and glow-in-the-dark condoms. For I too had begun to be naughty.

31

Drugs and Duty

When I think about it, I told her all my secrets. She has seen me off my face, crying my eyes out, spilling my emotional guts, but that's me, I'm a blubber and a blabber. She isn't, she's as closed as a mussel, as dark as a horse.

Nigel once accused me of being a little bit in love with her, which was stupid, and anyway he only said it to detract from the real argument, which was something to do with him lying to me again.

I always knew, you know, about his girlies. It was just that I never wanted to give him the satisfaction of realising that he could keep on being unfaithful and I'd keep on letting him get away with it. I always hoped he'd get it out of his system and now he has. What the silly sod never realised was that after the children were born, he lost his place in the pecking order; they came first, simple as that. I always wanted a family, and I would jump through hoops of fire to keep mine together. I have never had the slightest desire to tear things apart. Why should I? It's not as if I went into this marriage with my eyes shut. By the time I met Nigel, he'd already fucked three of my friends, one of whom attempted a paracetamol overdose thanks to his Casanova tendencies.

I think if you marry a man who is better looking than you are, you have to put up with the consequences. All that mattered was that he didn't take the piss. I knew Nigel was sexually sneaky but as long as he didn't do it in our bed, as long as he didn't get emotionally involved, I could stick it. In some respects, I would rather Nigel have a quick knee-trembler in a lift with a gorgeous blonde than he started taking the same woman out for lunch three times a week, just to talk. I have always been able to comfort myself that Nigel's floozies were never an intellectual match for me and that after a few hours with some brain-dead bimbo, he'd be glad he had me to come home to. I might not have big tits but I've got a very impressive vocabulary. Without me, Nigel would fall to pieces. I give his life the safety perimeters that he needs. Nigel has to be reminded when to eat, when to go to bed. Without me he wouldn't eat vegetables, he'd have rickets and scurvy, and then who would love him? After his sister died and his mother's heart dried up like autumn leaves and she had no emotion left to give him, he needed another mum. I have been a very good mother to my husband and these days I am very pleased to say that he is being a very good boy, he is concentrating better and has stopped being so silly. Nigel has grown up.

Some people take longer to grow up than others; men especially tend to be socially arrested at about the age of four. Becoming an adult is all about self-realisation and that can be a terrible thing. It's always a blow to find out that you aren't anything like you dreamt you'd be. When I was young, I thought that when I got to about thirty everything would slot into place, that miraculously I would be able to put my hair in a French pleat, speak Italian and wear cashmere sweaters in shades of caramel. The reality, of course, is very different: my hair remains both lank and flyaway, the only Italian I have learnt comes from the back of a pizza menu and I am more likely to be found wearing an acrylic mix than cashmere. One just has to get on with it, tripping over furniture, spilling beetroot and mispronouncing pasta dishes.

I think we all have roles to play; once we get over the disappointment of realising that we are never going to be supermodels, famous lady novelists, astronauts or whatever, then it is time to abide by the rules of compromise. Most of us are nobodies. Apart from a few soap stars and a handful of pop singers, we all have to come out of the playground of make-believe eventually and take our responsibilities on the chin. You can't have excitement all the time; too much fun and too many sweeties only lead to tears before bedtime. Children showing off are bad enough, but adults who do it need to be smacked.

I didn't have a clue about Nigel's penchant for drugs, not for years. Obviously I noticed that he sniffed a lot and that sometimes he couldn't stop talking, but even when I kept finding bank notes all curled up at the corners I didn't really put two and two together. You wouldn't, would you? What does your husband do? Coke mostly. I'm sure he was terrified of me finding out. Which I did, of course, thanks to Anna

It was some time last year. I noticed them conspiring in a corner and then she left the room. I gave her a few minutes and then I followed her up the stairs. When I found her, she was in our bedroom, bending over the dressing-table. 'Anna,' I said, and she turned round, a five-pound note still hanging from her nostril. 'Oh Jo,' she said grinning, and the note dropped to the floor. As she bent down to pick it up, I saw the white powder in a little square of lined paper behind her, next to my collection of perfume bottles. One of Nigel's suits was lying on the bed; she re-folded the piece of paper and put it firmly back inside the jacket. It was Nigel's best suit, the one from Kenzo and she arranged it neatly on to the hanger then hung it back in his wardrobe. 'It's only a bit of fun,' she said. 'Don't have a go at him, everybody does it.' I sat on the bed and she sprayed herself with my L'Eau D'Issey. 'Really, Jo, I think it's best we keep quiet about this, don't blow it out of proportion. We're having such a nice time.'

We went back downstairs. The mother of a friend of Georgina's had stayed for supper after taking the girls to see a film; it wasn't a good time to make a fuss. When everyone went home, I went back up to our bedroom, got the cocaine out of Nigel's jacket pocket and waited for him to come up and explain himself. He was very apologetic; he even managed to squeeze out a few tears. It wasn't a regular thing and he could easily stop. I think he was relieved that I knew because while I hadn't, he had no reason not to do it. I was very patient. I reminded him that he wasn't a rock star, that he was a man in his forties with two children and a very good job. I told him that he couldn't afford to be such a pathetic idiot and he agreed. As far as I know, he hasn't touched it since; but then for far too long I have given everyone the benefit of the doubt.

I have been thinking a lot about duty recently; nobody believes in it anymore. When I was a child I never enjoyed seeing my father's mother because she was old and smelly and gave you thruppenny bits in a soiled handkerchief all stiff with snot, but it was our duty to see her and so we did. Children today know nothing about duty and I think it might be too late to teach them the fundamentals. They know nothing of people who are not as privileged as they are, they have no idea what it is to wait for anything, to save up, to be grateful. At the end of the road, behind us and round the corner, are hundreds of council flats, full of kids whose toys come from car-boot sales. However, there is a form of apartheid going on and we have never allowed them to mix in case their watches got stolen.

I have a horrible feeling we might have spoilt them. None of them are quite right; you could not, with your hand on your heart, say that any of our children is a well-adjusted, healthy, happy, normal individual: Henry is weak, Georgina is a bitch, Pandora is a miserable lump and Jed, well Jed is queer. Nature or nurture, it doesn't really matter, whether what happens to our children is genetically predisposed or taught to them in the home, it is still the parents' fault.

We have failed them. Even when we were making them happy we were damaging them. Sometimes I think about how we could have done it differently, how we could have stopped them watching so much telly, forced them to have hobbies, made them go to Sunday School, set the table, empty the bitty bucket, play the piano. But we didn't. I have always been too tired to be strict. I have let my children get away with letting their swimming things turn mouldy and losing their fountain pens and Gameboys, I have let them drop towels on the floor and take food up to their bedrooms. They have become like animals in a zoo; God knows how they will cope when they are set free into the wild. They can only make Nutella sandwiches and heat pizzas.

I have come to the conclusion that as mothers and wives we have to set an example. It is our duty to behave ourselves, to follow the path of least embarrassment and I'm not just talking about wearing stupid hats or singing on the street. Anna has not been dutiful.

32

Blood, Blood and Blood

They were all getting older. Age creeps up on you; one day you bend down to tie up your shoe and you find yourself thinking, now is there anything else I can do whilst I'm down here? Women usually fare worse than men in the ageing process, just take a look at the newscasters on the telly. Middle-aged men, despite their spaniel jowls and pink-tie tendencies, manage to achieve some headmasterly gravitas, whilst women of the same age get a faraway, desperate look in their eyes as if they might be about to bolt off to some Caribbean island and marry a twenty-year-old native with a spear and a hundred conch shells round his neck. It's that 'last chance' time.

Jo thought it might be a good idea to learn conversational

Italian, Chris bought himself some golf clubs, Anna began to moisturise her neck and Nigel started taking ginseng and a fungus which he kept in a jam jar in the fridge.

The men were beginning to notice how much unnecessary hair kept sprouting from their nostrils and ear holes. What a silly notion. You want hair on your head – anywhere else is an unwanted bonus. Hair is very tricky, always too much or not enough. Anna tweezered her newly sprouted grey pubes until she got bored and shaved the whole lot off. Chris found this disturbing; she had the body of a mature woman and the fanny of a lap-dancer. Meanwhile Jo's thighs continued to quilt like an old-fashioned eiderdown.

The children were growing up too, physically anyway. At eleven, Pandora accidentally went to school in a pair of her father's black leather lace-ups and didn't notice until breaktime when Amanda Govern said, 'Jesus Christ, look at the state of Cunningham's feet.' You must try to avoid wearing men's shoes when you go to an all-girls day school for the over-privileged, if orthodontically challenged, bitches of South London.

Cross-dressing was never so accidental with Jed, who was causing much consternation for wearing clip-on earrings. The teachers' staff room divided into those who thought he should be free to express himself – 'He's only eight, we mustn't stunt his creativity' – and those who thought, 'He needs all this willy woofter stuff slapping out of him before he grows up to be a fully confirmed fudge-packing pillow-biter.' There was never any doubt that Jed might be going through a phase; it was as plain as the navy mascara on the tips of his lashes that here was a boy destined to be 'light across the carpet'.

Georgina, unbeknownst to her parents, had enjoyed her first snog. Henry was still waiting, though he practised hard enough, giving his pillow a 'right seeing to' most nights.

They were all having lunch together at the Metcalfs'; it was Easter and therefore traditional. Jo had bought a big piece of lamb from the organic butchers but she'd misjudged the timing slightly and it wasn't cooked all the way through. When Nigel pierced its side with the carving knife, a lot of oily pink blood oozed out.

'Ugh, gross,' squealed Georgina.

'Practically still bleating,' Nigel muttered.

'Lovely rare spring lamb,' said Chris, who being Welsh liked to assume he knew about these things, 'with lovely new potatoes, petits pois and mint from the garden. Yummy scrummy.'

'Oh please, Chris, we can see what's on the table, none of us have suddenly gone blind overnight,' Anna snapped.

'I'm blind,' shouted Henry in a stupid voice. 'I'm blind.'

Then Jo, in a sudden fit of temper, got hold of one of the serving spoons and hit her son smartly on the nose with it. Henry was always prone to nosebleeds, so then there was him and the lamb leaking crimson corpuscles all over the shop.

'Well, get some ice then,' shouted Nigel, and Jo went lolloping off to the freezer whilst Chris attempted to drop his car keys down the back of Henry's neck and Anna shouted at him for being a 'twat'.

'Put your head forward, Henry, then pinch it hard at the bridge,' she instructed. Henry tipped his head directly over the dish of peas and the sudden whiplash movement resulted in a fresh outpouring of blood, like the explosion of a bottle of tomato ketchup which has been vigorously shaken without previously checking that the lid is screwed on properly.

'Ugh, Henry, you bloody pig, look at the bloody peas,' screamed Georgina rather aptly. Jed at this point was inhaling the insides of his wrists for all he was worth. Sunday lunch was turning into something rather biblical, what with freshly slain bleeding sheep and ashen-faced bleeding teenage boys; had Anna any pubes left, she wouldn't have been at all surprised if they had spontaneously combusted in some sort of burning-of-the-bush homage. This was the New Testament as written by Stephen King.

Jo came limping in with a tea towel full of ice; she'd banged her leg on the pedal of Georgina's bike as she ran through the utility-room to the freezer. Her big white calf was already coming up in one of those unsightly bruises that only the very pale must suffer. Jo had skin like the inside of a pear.

'Put your head back – back Henry! Will you put your head back, you're bleeding all over the tablecloth.' It was one of the Swiss ones that Anna had once given her. You can't scrub blood out of delicately embroidered Edelweiss and it was a terrible mess.

Then Chris had one of his brainwaves. 'I know what gets bloodstains out,' he exclaimed, as pleased with himself as Einstein must have been when he stumbled across the theory of relativity. 'Ash, ash gets bloodstains out!' With that he grabbed the brimming ashtray that contained Anna's countless Silk Cut stubs, all Paloma Picasso lipstick-stained at the end, and upended it over Henry's O-rhesus negative splodges.

At that point, Anna reared up like a circus pony. 'You cretinous freak,' she exploded, 'ash is for silver, it's salt for blood,' and Nigel, who may as well have joined in, ran to get the Saxa, which he proceeded to throw with liberal abandon over the ashy blood. Whatever happened they might as well have just buried the tablecloth in the garden; it looked like evidence at a murder enquiry.

Henry's nose just would not stop bleeding, he began to look quite green about the gills. 'If he pegs out, Mum, can I have his bedroom?' quipped Georgina, who received a quick backhander from her mother.

Then Henry began to cry, which was embarrassing because he was almost fifteen. 'Right, hospital,' Jo decided. 'Sorry everyone, and I'd made such a lovely pudding. Nigel get the car.' But Nigel had had too much to drink, so Chris offered, but then he couldn't find his car keys, which were eventually discovered down the back of Henry's underpants. So off they went, Nigel, Chris, Jo and Henry. Anna offered to stay and hold the fort, which was ever so good of her.

Only Anna's idea of holding the fort and Jo's were two rather different things. When they got back from casualty at six, having seen some of the more depressing sights of South London, i.e. a man with a broken bottle sticking out of his head, and a small child in a methadone coma, Jo couldn't believe what Anna hadn't done.

The Jackson Pollock table-cloth was still *in situ,* the salt, ash and blood had soaked into dirty pink mounds, the lamb, as if forensic had insisted it should stay where it was, was sitting there like a Cluedo corpse with the knife still in its back. All that was missing was a few chalk outlines and you'd have had a marvellous opening sequence for an episode of *Inspector Morse*.

The Cunninghams had gone home. Jo was pissed off, she didn't like Georgina being left 'home alone'; it wasn't that she wasn't old enough, it was the fact that Jo didn't trust her. Not as far as she could throw her.

Chris left almost immediately. The rhubarb crumble that Jo yanked out of the Aga could have been anything – incinerated cat judging by the state of it.

When Jo quizzed Georgina later about why no one had thought to save the crumble, Georgina smirked and replied airily, 'Oh we had another little drama straight after you left.'

Apparently Pandora had stood up to carry some plates to the

dishwasher and when she turned around Anna had noticed the red stain on the back of her yellow jogging bottoms. Pandora had started her periods. Anna had gone quite loopy about the whole thing and dragged her home for a bath.

Well, really, thought Jo, it had been like an abattoir at their house today.

Pandora was mortified. She hadn't felt well all day, what with the lamb and Henry's nose haemorrhaging long stringy blood clots and then for her worst nightmare to come true. She wasn't the first in her class to start but judging by her mother's reaction, she was a medical phenomenon and belonged in the *Guinness Book of Records*.

'Periods . . . but you're not even twelve!' Anna had stuttered, as if it should be illegal, never mind physically impossible. 'The very idea. In my day you didn't come on till you were nearly fifteen. I haven't got anything you know.'

Georgina had some mini Lillets, more for practice than anything else.

'I don't think Pandora can cope with tampons yet,' Anna snapped.

'Suit yourself,' replied Georgina, 'I was only trying to help. I suppose you'd rather she had one of those lovely big sanitary towels that everyone can see you've got on because it's bigger than a nappy and makes you feel like you've got a week's washing stuffed down your knickers? Or maybe you'd like her to fashion her own protection out of rags that she can rinse out every night like they used to in the olden days, and then she'll stink and loads of flies will buzz around her knickers?'

'That's enough, Georgina,' said Anna firmly. Pandora was wide-eyed in horror. It was worse than that scene in *Carrie* where Sissy

Spacek gets bombarded with jam rags, thought Anna. 'Jam rags' – now she was resorting to the playground language of her teens. Anna found some stick-on towels at the back of Jo's linen cupboard and threw one into the bathroom, where her daughter sat dripping miserably on the loo.

Pandora wished this could have happened at school where the nurse, despite having a hairy chin, was a lot more sympathetic than her mother. 'Have you got any Nurofen?' she ventured.

'Yes, thank Christ,' Anna replied and promptly threw the last two down her neck.

Jed was loving it, the absolute toe-curling horror of it all: Pandora's humiliation, his mother's embarrassment, it was enough to give a boy an 'overexcitement tummy-ache'. He sat in Jo's bedroom, pretending to smoke one of her eyebrow pencils, whilst he watched his reflection retelling the story in her dressing-table mirror.

'And then she stood up. Well, the back of her was drenched in girl gore, the red tears of the fairer sex's monthly weeping.' Yes, that was rather good. Jed's prose was a very purple purple.

By the time Chris got home to the Pink House, at around 6.30 Pandora had gone to bed. 'It's very tiring being a woman,' his wife reminded him, whilst Jed sniggered and repeated his mother's words in the Lady Windermere voice he'd been practising for weeks. 'It's very tiring being a woman, positively exhausting, what with the old menstruation. Takes it out of a girl, don't ya know? All that ooozing one does on one's monthly.'

Anna threw the *Sunday Times* supplement at him, whilst Chris looked as dazed as the bloke in casualty, the one with the bottle of Beck's jammed into his skull.

'Oh, poor period pants Pandora,' sang Jed.

33

Trouble With Miss Toilet Duck

That Sue woman, the one they employ to keep an eye on things, is getting increasingly on my nerves. We do not speak. I flick V-signs behind her back and she clatters around when I am trying to nap. I know her type, she is of the 'you make your bed and you lie in it' persuasion, and so I do, lie in my bed that is. Often I take food up to this little room and I crouch under the duvet feeding myself treats. She doesn't approve of this, doesn't Miss Glade, Miss Toilet Duck, Miss Hoover Bag and Wax Polish. She can fuck off, the frizzy-haired gargoyle. I know her routine well enough now to sneak downstairs when the coast is clear, when she is busy chipping the dried shit off the inside of the lavatory bowl in the upstairs bathroom. Then watch me fly down the stairs into the kitchen where I arrange a tray of tortilla crisps and Battenburg cake, bagels filled with cream cheese and pastrami, dill pickles and Jaffa cakes. I like the combination of sugar and salt and I don't bother with things that require cutlery.

I keep emergency rations under my bed: a bag of Doritos and a jar of salsa, one of those kiddie-size packets of Frosties – just in case – plus a corkscrew, a can-opener, a bottle of wine and a tin of Carnation milk. Survival rations.

I do not like this Sue woman. To make her life more difficult I flick ash wherever I go; it's her job to keep the place spic and span so I am careless with toothpaste, clumsy with the coffee jar, thoughtless with pans of boiling soup. I leave apple cores in hard to reach places and spread crumbs far and wide. When she comes to the house, she puts on an apron over her tracksuit – it makes her look like a nurse, silly cow. Jo told me recently that her granddaughter was very ill. Good, I thought; if my life is going to be screwed up then it's better if other people suffer too. Jo has taken her side in our little game of domestic war. Yesterday she left me a note, which said: 'Dear Anna, please try to remove your clothes from the washing-machine when they have finished their cycle. There are four other people in this house and all of them have shirts, socks, pants and tights that need washing!!! Love Jo.'

She added the exclamation marks to make it sound more lighthearted but there was nothing funny about that note. I was so cross I went round the house removing batteries from everything that is battery-operated: radios, torches, Walkmans, Nintendos, alarm clocks, and after that I was quite hungry. Because Sue hadn't arrived, I was able to have a nice leisurely breakfast. I decided to eat in the dining-room and used the china service they keep in a big glass-fronted mahogany cabinet. I had freshly squeezed orange juice, Alpen, scrambled eggs, bacon, toast with butter and then two croissants with some blackcurrant preserve from Harvey Nichols and a banana. It was quite exhausting carrying all that lot from the kitchen in the basement up to the dining-room on the ground floor. I also had a glass of port, which was just sitting on a silver tray on the sideboard with a label round its neck that might just as well have said 'drink me'. Afterwards, I was too tired to take everything back downstairs, so I just left it, closed the dining-room door and went and had a bath in Jo and Nigel's en suite. I will not use the children's bathroom; the grouting is mouldy and the floor and towels are always wet. Anyway, the sight of Georgina's tiny discarded knickers depresses me.

It's strange living in someone else's house. I have found out so much more about these people; I know them so much better than I did when we were just friends.

In Nigel's study I have found evidence of the affairs that Jo told me about. There are a couple of alarming Polaroids. You cannot see the girl's face because in one she has her naked back to the camera – she is kneeling and her hands and feet are bound with silk scarves – and in the other all you can see are a pair of obviously very young breasts, across which the word 'slut' is written in red lipstick.

As for Jo, apart from hundreds of photos taken when she was young and had a perm as silly as her smug grin, and a little silver box containing the children's baby teeth, there is a box file brimming with birth certificates, school reports, all the pieces of work she had published before she realised that she wasn't Julie Burchill, a blue leather dog collar (Gloria died, she was run over by a motorbike, terrible mess, right outside our house), her wedding garter (I presume), two pregnancy-testing kits, the positive dots long faded, but nothing incriminating, no skeletons, nothing that could get her into as much trouble as I have been. Her yellowing school reports say that 'Josephine is a polite and helpful member of the form with a mature outlook that belies her years'. Miss Goody Two Shoes.

It is an interesting hobby, sneaking round another family's home. Medicine cupboards for a start are fascinating; the Metcalfs have at some point suffered from worms, styes, nits, thrush, cystitis, warts, chesty coughs, dry coughs, tickly coughs, there are greasy jars of Vicks and Vaseline, tubes of Golden Eye ointment, throat lozenges, anti-chloraseptic sprays, sun-lotions, protector factor twenty-five for her, eight for him, after-sun, fake tan (ha), hair removing cream and eyelash dye. Jo is a hoarder. I found three Christmas puddings at the back of her kitchen cupboard last week; one was a luxury number from Marks and Spencer. They last for ever, Christmas puddings. I popped it in the microwave, it was delicious. And being the only one eating it, I got to keep the genuine silver sixpence for good luck. Ha!

34

Poltergeists and Other Problems

If I didn't know better, if I didn't know it was Anna, I'd think we had a poltergeist. Stuff keeps disappearing: batteries and light bulbs, mayonnaise and bottle openers. She takes things and puts them somewhere else. The other day I found our passports in the airing cupboard; that is not their place, I keep important documents in a file in the study. When I went to put them back there, I found a couple of dirty Polaroids propped up against the Apple Mac! I returned them to where Nigel had hidden them all those years ago, in the back of his *Comprehensive Guide to Infectious Diseases*. It wasn't as if I hadn't seen them before, I even knew who the girl was. I bet her breasts aren't as good as they were then. I believe her name was Sonia. It doesn't matter any more anyway, Nigel has stopped tomcatting around, at least for the time being. It's as if he has seen what happens when the boat gets rocked and he no longer wants to get wet. He has aged almost overnight; he wears glasses now and his hair is thinner. As if to make up for it he is thicker round the waist; he takes solace in litre tubs of ice-cream instead of little lines of cocaine.

Just for once, I would like to be alone in my own house. The kitchen is full of everyone else's debris, cartons are put back in the fridge with half a centimetre of juice in them, empty Marmite jars are returned to the cupboard, the laundry-basket is crammed with other people's dirty knickers, there are shoes all over the stairs and no one ever puts a CD back in its case.

Sue, despite being a treasure, cannot control our mess. The other day she found a mouldy apple wrapped in a tissue on top of the pelmet in the sitting-room – whoever put it up there must have used a ladder. It never used to be this bad. Every now and then I try to blitz the place and I stampede from floor to floor, demanding that bin liners are filled and taken to charity shops. Only I never have time to take the damn stuff to Oxfam, so the bin liners split whilst they wait in the hall and gradually their contents get redistributed around the house all over again. We have too much stuff: there is a bike in the basement that Georgina has ridden twice, and a rowing machine in the utility-room that Nigel barely managed to get the packaging off. In the pantry, hanging from a nail, there is a plastic bag full of other plastic bags that I always forget to take to the supermarket, there are Wellington boots by the back door that the children have not been able to squeeze into for ten years. I have kept the high-chair – what the fuck for? In the big chest of drawers in the kitchen, there are Play-Doh machines and kiddie pastry cutters and a thousand dried-up felt-tip pens; in one of the drawers glitter has been spilt, in another there are hundreds of envelopes of photographs that are too hideous to stick into albums, Chinese takeaway menus from places that shut down five years ago and a game of Monopoly with its silver boot and top hat long lost.

Mess never used to bother me; I prided myself on my Bohemian outlook. My onions on strings, copious bottles of red wine, half drunk, the corkboard inches deep with invites and post-cards, kids' drawings, school memos and scraps of paper with telephone numbers on. See how busy and popular we are? Sterility and order made me suspicious; tidy people were anal and dull. Life was all about big, chipped, steaming casserole dishes, brim-ming with meat and bubbling sauces, candles dripping wax on to the table-cloth, music playing and me a bit pissed, swaying as I brought through big bowls of buttery mashed potato and peas that I'd bothered to pod myself. I can't be bothered any more. I hardly cook these days; last week I found some mince at the bottom of the freezer and for a second I thought I would make a big shepherd's pie like I used to, all brown and crispy on the top, and we would all sit down together and eat it, me and Nigel and Anna and Chris and the kids. Then I remembered that those days are over; I chucked the mince in the bin and we had cheese and crackers and a cup of tea in front of the telly.

Nigel's not bothered about proper food, Georgina's on a diet, Henry only eats baked beans and Anna prefers to eat in her room. It's a wonder we haven't got mice – we probably have. My house seems to be deteriorating around my ears: the lino in the kids' bathroom has curled up like stale cheese sandwiches, the boiler groans as if an old man with lumbago is stuck inside and the cold tap in the kitchen has begun to run brown water.

I keep having these dreams where I live in a beach hut all by myself, with just a hammock and a rush-mat floor. These days I go to bed very early; if I haven't been for a swim, come 9.30 I'm in the bath. It would be nice to relax but I know Anna's been in there: dark pubes in the soap, a can of lager teetering on the cistern, cotton-wool balls on the floor and, balanced along the side of the bath, a row of toenail crescents that I know she has bitten off with her teeth. It's like getting into a tub after a filthy dog.

She used to be so groomed, with her elegantly arched eyebrows and her smooth brown hands, her oval fingernails with their cuticles neatly pushed into place. Anna was the only person I ever knew who bothered to remove the hard yellow skin from the soles of her feet, and when she painted her toenails she used a rubber toe divider so that the varnish didn't smudge. Even her underwear was lovely, all silk and multi-coloured, lacy bras, expensive; the sort of thing you have to go to special shops in Knightsbridge for. Nowadays, well, the state of her pants – they're worse than mine. I'd be too embarrassed to use them for dusters.

35

Olive Pips in the Pipes

There was a funny noise in the Pink House: a rattling and scraping of metal and stones, followed by a dull whining – and it wasn't Pandora. Anna tracked it down to the dishwasher, 'buggering sod.' The thing had been playing up for weeks, not doing its job properly, pebble-dashing everything with a fine spray of cement-like muesli that had to be scraped off by fingernail. Anna wrestled the stupid appliance open, it was even worse than usual; not only was there the now familiar high-fibre, gritty veneer over everything, but the baked-bean pan still contained some anaemic-looking washed-out beans. In fact, by inspecting each individual item in the wretched machine, you could tell exactly what the Cunninghams had been eating over the last twenty-four hours. Here, a dollop of brown sauce, there, the dried mucus of a Marks and Spencer fish in white-wine sauce; she'd need an industrial floor-sander to clean this lot. Anna was so cross, she snapped the stems off two rather smart wineglasses as she manhandled them out of their wire restraints. 'Shitty Mcshit.' Anna was a good swearer, she enjoyed blasphemy. 'Fucky dingnuts and bastardy cunt-holes.'

It was time she had a brand new kitchen anyway. Chris was so tight. The place was looking positively eighties; white goods were so naff. Anna decided she'd have new silver Smeg everything, so that was ten grand spent before ten o'clock in the morning, mentally anyway.

Deep down, Anna knew she was on a loser; she'd just conned Chris into buying her a new Polo. Like, huh, big deal, it wasn't a convertible Mercedes, just a bog-standard, bottom of the range hatchback, it didn't even have a poxy sunroof. The trouble with Chris was that he actually enjoyed being mean; she'd seen him in the supermarket, hungrily eyeing the shelf of knock-down-price dented tins, the sell-by-today-or-get-chucked-away goods. Whenever Chris got the gleam of parsimony in his eye, it was Anna's job to poke it out; she'd buy caviar, even though she didn't like it, ready-to-bake potatoes from Marks, a pair of ancient Chinese baby shoes from an antique market, an empty gilt canary cage.

'My mother,' he always said, when she chucked away a roast chicken having cut off only the breasts, 'would have fed the four of us on that for a week. Boiling bones, Anna, that's the trick.'

'Fuck off, Chris. If you wanted to marry your mother then you should have looked for some fifteen-stone amphibian with facial warts and pants that smell of old cabbage,' Anna retorted. She only said it because it was true.

Well, this wouldn't buy the baby a new bonnet. It was all very well sitting there thinking about what a cheapskate her husband was; before she went out on the lesser silver-fronted Smeg hunt, she had this old heap of shit to get fixed. Anna kicked the dishwasher shut. Right . . . Yellow Pages. She dug the directory out from under a load of *Smash Hits* magazines (Jed's) and flicked through; there was quite a choice. Had Anna a guardian angel, then maybe she'd have been steered towards any other number in the Electrical Appliances Repaired section, but she hadn't and she wasn't: all she was armed with was a badly bitten ballpoint pen. Peckham Premiere Services, No Hidden Extras. She drew a ring around it and dialled. Oh oh, chongo.

Three rings . . . four . . . five, she was about to put the phone down and try Old Kent Road Electrics when someone answered.

'Allo.'

'Oh, hello.'

'Yeah?'

'Hello, yes, I've a dishwasher – Hotpoint – on the blink, making noises, generally playing up and giving me gyp.'

'Well, we can't be doing with gyppy dishwashers.'

'No, we certainly can't.'

'Is it plugged in?'

'I'm not a complete fucking idiot.'

'Orl right, luv, calm down. Address?'

'The Pink House, Lark Grove.'

'Yeah, let's try an' narrow it down a bit, luv. What number?'

'It hasn't got a number, it's the pink house, you can't miss it.'

'I'll send someone round, be about an hour. Give me your phone number, luv, in case he can't find you.'

'If he can't find me, then he's certainly not capable of mending a dishwasher. In fact, I wouldn't trust him to be able to wipe his own arse.'

Anna put the phone down but not before the man on the other end of the line breathed, 'Snotty bitch.'

Over at Peckham Premiere Services, Ray told his son-in-law Danny to get his nose out of this morning's page three and his arse into gear. 'Some stuck-up-sounding posh bird got gyp with her dishwasher. Hey nonny, lick my clit,' he affected in a very posh voice.

Danny could have done without any call-outs this morning at all; he had a stinking hangover, one of those ones when if you move your head too quickly sick comes up your throat and you have to swallow it back. It was his missus, Carlene, driving him to drink; that was the only problem with working for her dad, he couldn't exactly come in of a morning and start slagging off the silly mare. He just didn't get what was with Carlene at the moment; she was a lovely-looking girl but she wasn't looking after herself. Ever since baby Ted, she'd just stopped making any effort. It was all she could do these days to put deodorant under her armpits. She'd not been shaving either – now that made Danny heave; if he'd wanted a wife with hairy pits, he'd have married one of them lezzie tennis players. It just wasn't like her.

After the first kiddie three years back, she been straight down Weight Watchers, getting rid of that baby gut. This time she'd just not bothered; it was very worrying. Her roots were about ten feet long an' all, it was embarrassing. Course, her old mum dying hadn't helped, she'd been ever such a good nanna before the cancer got her. One minute it was just her arm all swollen up, next she was a goner. Still, there was no reason for Carlene to let herself go, her mum wouldn't like it, very proud of Carlene she'd been. Course with Nanna pushing up daisies there was no one to look after the kids while Carlene went to the hairdresser's, it was a vicious circle, but there was no way Danny could see it was his fault. Maybe he should buy her some perfume, a pair of naughty knickers, cheer the silly moo up. Danny couldn't abide moody birds; the way he looked at life you could have a laugh or you could go round being a miserable cunt. He lifted his eyes from 'Leanne, 19, from Stockport'.

'All right, Raymondo, where to?'

'The Pink House. I'm a name not a number.' Ray went into his *Prisoner* routine, only Danny wasn't old enough to get it.

'The one down Lark Grove?' he guessed.

'In one.' Now Ray was being that bloke who does the darts scores.

See, reasoned Danny, Ray hadn't let himself fall to pieces; he'd only been a widower a couple of months, it was his missus who had kicked the bucket, but he wasn't sitting around moping. He was getting on with it, having a laugh, like now; he had loads of voices did Ray, his Loyd Grossman was spot on, he should have been on the telly.

'What do you reckon?' Danny asked. 'Bit HRT?' This was their code for women who were past it and bonkers to boot.

'Borderline,' his father-in-law replied.

Danny barked and pretended to be a mad dog with rabies, cos that was what old birds were like, present company's dead wife excluded. Danny wouldn't mention his Carlene problem to Ray. Wouldn't do to go upsetting the old man, he had enough on his plate. Nah, he'd sort his missus out tonight, he'd do the whole thing: bottle of wine, Chinese takeaway, then he'd give her a good shagging, none of this 'I'm so tired' nonsense. Maybe he'd make it two bottles of wine to be on the safe side.

Danny got into the van. It wasn't far to Lark Grove; he'd had a few jobs up there before; they all had dishwashers, them posh types . . . and nice coffee and fancy biscuits. He'd fixed a washing-machine down there not six months back. The daughter had been off school, wandering round in her Rug Rats t-shirt, glimpse of pink knickers, little slag; he'd seen her, the way she'd come over all daft just cos there was a bloke in overalls down in the kitchen. Her mother hadn't liked it. 'Georgina, if you're so poorly I think you should get yourself back into bed.' 'Schoolitus,' she'd whispered to Danny, and the girl had gone deep pink before fleeing upstairs. He'd seen flashes of her bare legs through the banisters. He'd have fucked it, if it hadn't been about fourteen. Mind you, how old had he and Carlene been? Fourteen, fifteen? Danny shifted in the driver's seat. He was going to have to get laid tonight, it had been almost a week. His nuts felt like spacehoppers.

Back at Peckham Premiere Services, Carlene's dad contemplated attaching a piece of hose (there was plenty of it about, rubber tubing being integral to the business) to the exhaust of his Rover Vitesse. But, as he reminded himself in his Harry Enfield 'only me' voice, 'You don't want to do that.'

It was 9.57am when Danny knocked on the door of the Pink House.

36

Or is it Mrs Cuntingham?

I can remember what I was wearing when I first saw him: old Levis and a long sleeved t-shirt with butterflies all over. When I answered the door it felt like I must have put the t-shirt on inside-out and the butterflies had come alive and entered my ribcage. I remember looking at my feet and thinking, Oh good, I've painted my toenails. They were bright red. It was 10.00 in the morning, by 10.30 we were kissing in the kitchen and by 10.35 he had come in my hand. But at least he'd fixed the dishwasher. There were seven olive pips lined up in a row on top of it. 'But it needs a new motor,' he said, 'I'll order you one. Should be ready this time next week. Would that be convenient?' As he said that, he leant forward and twisted my nipple hard; I wasn't wearing a bra. I gave him a cheque from our joint account and he said, 'Thank you very much, Mrs Cunningham,' and for a moment I thought he said 'Mrs Cunt-ingham' but he couldn't have really. When he'd gone, I sat on the Victorian rocking horse in the kitchen and finished myself off – heigh-ho Silver! I didn't suffer any guilt, I never have – such an exhausting emotion. To be honest, I think adultery made me a nicer person. I remember making chocolate Rice Krispies cakes with Pandora later that evening and I managed not to shout at her for dropping a load of Rice Krispies on the floor.

I have always liked secrets; they are delicious things to roll around the back of your mind. When you are having normal conversations with people, it's nice to have pictures they can't see playing on the private screen of your brain.

His name was Danny, he was never a Daniel. Daniels are solicitors; they have clean fingernails and silk pocket handkerchiefs. Dannies, however, have rough hands with calluses that ladder your tights.

When he left that first morning I realised, just before I set off to Maggie's, that there was a dirty oil mark on my t-shirt where he'd pinched my breast. Obviously I got changed.

I have been thinking about why it all happened and it's not just my fault. I have been trying to sort out the reasons in my head and I have come to the conclusion that apart from the olive pips, society is to blame. Let's put it this way . . . I have made notes, in fact I have written an essay on the subject; it's a shame I wrote it after a bottle of red wine and my handwriting had gone to pot, but this is the gist of it:

Most people are capable of running two personalities, especially women. In the olden days, they didn't have time, they were too busy handwashing clothes and losing fingers in the mangle.

These days, thanks to electrical equipment, vacuum cleaners, dishwashers, freezers etc, we have the time to be duplicitous. We have mobile phones on which to make whispered assignations, we have cars and can meet men in far-flung parks, we have our own passports, we have the freedom to completely fuck ourselves up – if that is what we choose to do.

Women didn't really meet men in the olden days, not men they didn't know; they didn't have as many things in the home to break down. It was just the postman and the milkman that came to call – and look at the reputations those guys had! It is difficult for women not to meet men these days. We have jobs where motorcycle couriers come in like gladiators, with their helmets under their arms, still vibrating from riding large motorbikes; there are pizza delivery boys and tennis coaches and gym instructors, chiropractors and shrinks. We have become a sex-obsessed society. It gets to the point where whenever a strange man comes to your door you can't help but imagine what he would look like coming into your face!

There, you see, I have given this some considerable attention. Maybe I shouldn't have written it out in the back of Georgina's English exercise book because when I tried to rip it out, all the other pages came loose and I found myself having to throw the whole lot in the bin.

I am not trying to make excuses for my behaviour, but I do believe that some of us are more prone to slaggery than others. They will probably find a gene one day, they've found one for everything else: shyness, homosexuality, alcoholism – there is, no doubt, a gene that makes you predestined to be a crap dancer.

My problem is that, apart from Chris, I always fancied baddies. However I am not stupid, my self-preservation button was always slightly bigger than my self-destruct button – up until now, that is – and I knew that you flirted, snogged and occasionally shagged the baddies but you should marry the goodie. Chris is good through and through. I always suspected that I was morally dysfunctional but I thought if I stuck with Chris his goodness would wear off on me, that I would catch niceness as easily as the flu. It nearly worked.

You would never have guessed from looking at me that I had the slag gene; I have always been rather classy. I do not have bleached hair and I have never felt the need to totter around on stilettos with my knickers showing and my tits out on display, but I probably give off a smell. It's always been there: I remember even when I was a very little girl and my mother took me to see Father Christmas in a big department store, when I sat on his lap he got an erection. I was only seven, it wasn't my fault.

Pandora has not inherited my latent nymphomania. No doubt one day she will marry a Welsh farmer with a big red face and they will wear their Wellington boots inside the house and have lots of children as broad as they are tall. Jed, on the other hand . . . well, it doesn't bother me what Jed is like, though as soon as he started showing the signs Chris got all uptight. Silly sod. One day when Jed is rich and famous, he will escort me round town on his arm, and I will drink champagne at first nights and eat those little filo pastry parcels that you can fit in your mouth in one go. Of course, by this time I will be slim and elegant again and all this will be forgotten.

That stupid cleaning woman of theirs left a can of air freshener, some furniture polish and a duster outside my room the other day. Ugly old hag.

37

Sex and the Ex

I have been trying to think, really racking my brains, but to be honest, I have only ever had it off with three people in my entire life. Maybe it's my turn next. Maybe I shall go loony and jump the milkman, offer myself round the neighbourhood. There is a nut house locally, maybe I should shag a couple of inmates, get my average up. I know people are at it all the time, slobbering over each other, tugging at buttons and hooks and eyes; I have watched Channel 5, you know. Maybe I'm the freak, the foolish, faithful, long-suffering wife. But quite honestly, I just don't fancy anyone. All right, there's something about Robbie Williams that makes me want to feed him hot buttered toast while I'm in my nightie, but that's as far as it goes.

I wouldn't know how to go about having an affair. I haven't the pants for one. I buy nice, fresh white cotton knickers from Marks and Spencer that come up over my tummy and cover my pubes. I feel chilly in a small brief and cannot cope with thongs. I have always been taught to keep my kidneys warm; we have a history of trouble in that department on my side of the family.

I was eighteen years old when I lost my virginity. I was the head girl of a girls' grammar in Hampshire and he was the head boy of the neighbouring boys' grammar. Sweet really: we discussed it fully and he came with me to the local clinic for advice on contraception. See, I've always been responsible. His name was Michael Granger, his middle name was Jonathan and he was a Capricorn.

We did it at his parents' house – they both worked – it was half past four on a Friday afternoon. Afterwards he read me some Keats and then we both sat down at the dining-room table and revised for our mock A-level exams. I tested him on his Spanish vocabulary and he tested me on the Treaty of Versailles. We may have had a cup of coffee. When his mother came home from work, she asked if I wanted to stay for tea. I didn't really because she was a chiropodist and I always worried about whether she'd washed her hands properly. But I said, 'Yes, that would be lovely,' and we had fish pie. I suppose we were rather unexciting, but then again I think there is something to be said for unexciting.

I never had an orgasm with Michael Granger, but then I wasn't really expecting one. I remember it being quite pleasant but rather messy; there was rather a lot of mopping up with tissues to be done afterwards.

Michael and I planned to go to the same university but he flunked his A-levels and ended up at Manchester Polytechnic. I visited him a couple of times; he was living in this hall of residence and had decided to go all punky. He met me off the coach once wearing a red-and-black striped mohair jumper, which was rather a shock: I never managed to visualise him in anything but his navy blue school blazer. I went to Edinburgh and in my first year I didn't look at anyone else: I was being faithful to Michael. Daft really, as the third time I visited him in Manchester he'd got involved with an older woman, well, a second-year student who was doing drama. Her name was Yvonne Sticky, she had a peroxide bouffant and a red PVC jacket. She was a part-time punk poet and rumour had it she drank absinthe. Whatever, I met her once; she was very sweet but her teeth were badly stained and I wondered what Michael's mother would think of her shoes – they were green snakeskin stilettos. She wrote me a punk poem of apology. It went:

I never meant to nick your Mick,
I wouldn't have done it,
but he's got a big dick.

He hadn't actually.

So I went back to Edinburgh and for the next year I had a rather bizarre relationship with one of my tutors. He'd have been struck off now, but back then in the late seventies it was one of the perks of the job. He was a very lazy man and he was rather impotent. I think it was Glenn who put me off oral sex; he'd have me down there for hours trying to coax his reluctant willy into a semi-hard-on. It never worked: in the end he'd just fold it in and I'd make the sort of noises one would make had one suddenly been penetrated by something the size of a small walrus. Men never know when you are faking, their egos won't consider it. Glenn had a coterie of us adoring girlies; he also had a very clever wife who worked in the same apartment. Alicia, her name was. They had a daughter called Lettuce. Obviously I realise now that the man was a complete wanker.

I met Nigel in my second year. He'd been to Aberystwyth but had transferred after his sister's death as he wanted to be closer to his parents. He had this terrible air of tragedy about him. I'd never met anyone with a dead sister before. Men, if you need to pull, invent a deceased sibling or cancer-stricken parents or a touch of leukaemia. Us girls are suckers for a sob story: that's why junkies get laid.

We were friends before we were lovers. I'd found him trying to walk up Dundas Street; it's very steep and he was very drunk. It was his dead sister's birthday and he was raving outside an Italian restaurant I'd been to with some friends. I knew where he lived so I took him home. It was a long walk, with him taking three steps backwards to two forwards; they call it the Dublin shuffle, don't they?

He had a first-floor flat off the Cowgate and he needed help up the stairs. I put him to bed. He was crying so I sat with him all night, then slipped off at about six in the morning. I had an essay to hand in; old head girl habits die hard.

The next time I saw him he was snogging a friend of mine in a club.

I waited a long time for Nigel; I mopped up his sick three times before I even got a kiss, but I got him in the end.

He won't ever leave me, I know that. I gave his parents their grandchildren, and despite the fact that my horrible spoilt brats never ring or write to say thank you for those Scottish five-pound notes that come through the post every month, there is a mutual gratitude thing going on. I give them a reason to get up and go to the post box; it's not much but it's better than nothing. If

Elizabeth had lived, she would no doubt have had several beautiful and talented children of her own, but she didn't.

I am Nigel's parents' only link with the future. Mind you, Elizabeth carried a donor card and there are, no doubt, grateful recipients out there using her second-hand vital functioning organs, her corneas and valves: Elizabeth continues to play her trump cards from the grave. Maybe one day some child who received Elizabeth's heart will turn up and claim my children's inheritance. These things strike you in the middle of the night.

38

Shag, Shag, Shag

It was a very naughty thing to do. Once was bad enough but they kept on doing it, Danny and Anna, Anna and Danny. Feverish, ferocious fucks in the middle of the day and not a word to anyone. Had Danny passed Anna on the street, he wouldn't have guessed she'd be such a rude lady. But she was; she was a dirty one, that Mrs Cunningham.

He'd asked her once how old she was. 'Nearly forty,' she'd smirked. It didn't bother him; on the contrary, older birds tended to be more grateful, they tried harder.

Danny knew these things. When he was fourteen, his sister's pen-pal came to stay, all the way from Stockport. 'Stockport!' sneered Danny, 'don't you mean Stockholm? What's the point in having a pen-pal from Stockport?'

'Shut up, you spaz,' his sister had replied. 'Be mental writing to a foreigner, you wouldn't know what she were on about.'

So Brenda had come down from Greater Manchester on the coach, and before she'd been at theirs three nights she'd popped his cherry – ever so quietly mind, as Danny's kid brother had been asleep on the bottom bunk below. It hadn't taken long: by the time it was over his sister, who was busy in the bathroom getting ready to go out, still had her electric curlers in. He would always be grateful to Brenda with her big spotty face and her battered-sausage breath.

For ages the piece of chewing gum she'd taken out of her mouth as she taught him ''ow to French kiss proper' stayed stuck behind his bedpost. Now and again, when she'd gone home, he'd reach out and feel it, just to remind himself that it had really happened. Yes, older women were just fine in Danny's book, though obviously you had to draw the line somewhere; you didn't want them without teeth and knickers full of biscuit crumbs, there had to be a limit.

Not only was Anna older, she was posh – an added bonus. Posh birds in Danny's experience were mad for it: they played better games, bought you expensive gifts, talked dirty (sometimes in French) and occasionally took it up the arse.

Carlene wasn't taking it any which way and Danny was reduced to having a J Arthur in the marital bed whilst his once well-and-truly-up-for-it missus faked being asleep. Danny refused to skulk off to the bathroom; it was his house, he could wank wherever and whenever he pleased. Danny had a theory that if you kept sperm too long in your testicles it could go bad.

It wasn't Carlene's fault: she was missing her mum and she hadn't felt right since baby Ted had been born eighteen months ago, so she ate biscuits and drank big litre bottles of Coke and stopped wearing the kind of clothes that had made Danny proud to say she was his wife. Danny didn't like it. He liked it when all his mates wanted to shag her, which a couple of them had, but only with his permission and only once he'd set the video camera. Poor Danny: his once lovely busty better half was drooping in front of his eyes. He was going to buy her a boob job for Christmas. That would make her feel better.

In the meantime, there was always Anna. Anna who waited in the Pink House.

Anna was getting ready for a little bit of afternoon Danny delight; whilst her lover sat in traffic eating a McDonald's down the Walworth Rd, she depilated and deodorised, and dithered between the black bra with the red lace or the red bra with the black lace. She opted for the latter – the matching knickers were clean. She pulled on a pair of tight navy Levis and a white shirt – it wouldn't do to look like she was trying too hard – then she practised pulling sexy poses in the mirror, making sure he'd get an eyeful of the red bra. The jeans were rather tight. Damn Chris and his enchilada fixation: they'd had a Mexican last night and she could feel the refried beans fermenting in her bowels. Concentrating hard, Anna let rip with an almighty deafening fart, above which she could barely hear the doorbell ring. 'Oh God, oh God.' She quickly sprayed the room with Thierry Mugler's 'Angel' and galloped down the stairs. Calm down, Anna, don't run.

'What is it this time, Mrs Cunningham?' asked Danny.

'It's the washer in the en suite, the taps very stiff.'

'Maybe I should have a look at it.'

Anna followed him up the stairs; it was all she could do to keep her hands off his arse.

They walked though the bedroom into the en suite. It still smelt a little of 'Angel' though no undertone of fart, Anna was relieved to note. He carried his toolkit with him and it was only when he slung it down on the tiled floor and shut the door that she allowed herself to breathe. Danny had a smile like a baby wolf; a number of women had commented on this before. He gave her the baby wolf smile from under his long, dark fringe and hooked his finger through one of the belt loops on the waist-band of her Levis, pulling her towards him. 'Who's a naughty lady?' Me, me, me, Anna wanted to scream and laugh at the same time, but she controlled herself. There is a fine line between farce and fantasy. Within seconds, Anna's white shirt was on the floor and Danny's flies were unzipped; had this been a cartoon his cock would have sprung from his Calvins with a loud 'Thwaaang'.

He didn't even have to push her head down, she was on the floor before you could say 'fellatio'. Calm down, Anna. She was too keen, taking the whole of Danny's knob in one go, too much too quickly. 'Don't gobble, Anna,' (her mother's voice in her head). Anna felt herself gag, an enchilada taste rose in her throat – oh no, what if she threw up, spewed on his cock? Relax, she wouldn't. She knew what she was doing, she was a forty-year-old woman, after all.

She opened her eyes briefly and caught sight of herself in the mirror, slurping away like a child on an ice lolly, whilst a man whose surname she did not know held her tightly by the hair.

So while Anna had her face tenderly slapped by a plumber who did not pronounce his aitches, her husband Chris dealt his coffee-bean deals and sweated heavily. This was no job for a fat man in his forties: one day, he thought, he might self-combust with stress. It was not unusual for men in this line of business to go mad. 'Remember Simpkins? Messy business. Workmate, colleague, lovely wife, two little girls, place in the country, good bloke, forty-eight paracetamol, died three days later – kidney failure, conscious to the end.' Hell . . . Chris could smell the panic coming off him in waves. All he wanted to do was go home.

Fortunately he didn't. Danny left at three o'clock but before he walked out of the front door, Anna gave him a cheque for sixty pounds. Well, if it made her feel better. Danny pocketed it; he had the Carlene 36DD-cup fund to think of.

Anna went back upstairs, removed the lipstick from round her ears and generally tidied up. Now that Danny was gone, she could fart away, so she sang and she farted and she farted and sang. They were due down at the Metcalfs' later; they had this year's summer holiday to discuss. When the kids got back from school, Pandora asked why she was home. 'Been to the dentist,' her mother said gaily. Really, she'd have to start thinking of some more original excuses.

By the time Chris came home, she was in the bath; she made sure she had turned the lock, she wanted some 'quiet time' to re-live the afternoon. Chris kept banging on the door, 'ANNA, IS MY GREY JUMPER DRY? ANNA, ARE YOU GOING TO BE IN THERE ALL NIGHT, ONLY I'D QUITE LIKE A SHOWER. BUGGER OF A DAY, Middle East crashing all over the wretched shop, fucking appalling headache, probably some giant blood clot creeping towards my brain, nothing lethal just enough to render me blind and incontinent, not dead, no such luck. Oh sweet Jesus, cords have shrunk. ANNA THESE CORDS HAVE SHRUNK, WHAT THE HELL HAVE YOU DONE WITH THEM? Can't be me, can't have piled on that much timber, not in ten days. Been eating less than the hamster;

skimmed milk, wholemeal bread, well sod it, tonight I'm off the diet, tonight I shall gorge. I shall have seconds, thirds and fourths, then I shall come home and have cheese and crackers and cornflakes, if I feel like it. ANNA, ARE YOU LISTENING? I THINK I'VE GOT A BRAIN TUMOUR. My right arm's been tingling all afternoon and I can't do my trousers up, HELP ME ANNA!'

Anna, behind the safety of the locked door, pulled stupid faces at her husband. Oh, fuck off, Chris, you great ape, just fuck off and have a nice quiet coronary in the corner, there's a good boy. 'I'M WASHING MY HAIR,' spunk in it, Danny cum, full of protein, ha – won't need conditioner then. He should bottle it, I'd help him fill the containers, 'BE OUT IN A MINUTE,' hmmm, tanned hard-body Danny, cock like an eel, freckles on his back, snogarama, sore lips, do call again, Danny, do come and screw me another day, come soon, Danny, ha, come in my mouth and my hair, 'I HAVEN'T FUCKING TOUCHED THEM,' been too busy being a bad girl to do housy things, too busy being a dirty bitch. Say it again, slap my face and call me a dirty bitch, write my name on a toilet wall, 'HOLD ON, I'M COMING.' I wish.

And Anna got out of the bath, all clean and shiny.

While the Cunninghams and the Metcalfs ate Jo's famous scallops in ginger with noodles, Danny was back in Nunhead. He was bored. Carlene was pretending to have nodded off in the marital bed; she had three-year-old Roxanne tucked under one wing and baby Ted under the other. Poor Carlene, she was boiling hot and her left arm had fallen asleep under Roxanne's heavy, sweaty head but the rest of her just wouldn't. Danny sat downstairs, drank a can of lager and watched the Fantasy Channel. There was a foursome going on but it wasn't his cup of tea, the presence of the blokes was off-putting. Danny couldn't be arsed watching other men having a better time than he was. Eventually he turned off the telly, crept upstairs and folded himself into Roxanne's little pine bed. Under the Tellytubby duvet, it smelt of soap and wee and wherever he lay his head there was a Barbie.

39

Not in Front of the Hamster

It is a long time since I have had sex, or even a snog for that matter. It's not like I'm not used to it: sometimes me and Chris would go for weeks without doing the deed – but that was only because I didn't fancy him. 'I've got a headache, I'm still on my period, go away Spam man.' Poor Chris, his cock must have thought it was in permanent hibernation.

There is nothing quite like being in lust, is there? The anticipation of being touched by someone who has you trembling and dripping at their mere thought, who can make you come without touching you.

Sometimes I have orgasms in my sleep – nature's way of compensating, I suppose – and on occasions these orgasms are so intense that I wake up biting the inside of my wrist and moaning. Sex was never very wonderful with Chris: just the sight of his gormless face on the brink of orgasm put me off. That's why I would always position myself face down, doggie style, so that I could roll my eyes and pull bored faces into the pillow whilst he jabbed away tentatively from behind. Once he slipped and his cock entered my arsehole – he was mortified. I was very briefly thrilled. He was always too gentle for me: if only he had slapped me and pulled my hair and sworn into my face, I could have stood it. Plus he always had too much spit in his mouth. The world divides into those who can snog and those who can't: kissing Chris was like kissing a Labrador and sometimes I'd get so furious I would bite him and dig my nails into his pudgy flesh. He thought I was getting carried away by the expertise of his lovemaking and laugh this embarrassed half laugh as if to say, 'There you go, missus, how's this for a good time.' It wasn't.

Jo and Nigel still have it off: I heard them the other night. I sat on the stairs listening to the grunting – it was so funny – 'Ungh, ungh, ungh,' like a couple of sumo wrestlers fighting in the dark.

Their son wanks a lot: I have seen him. He does it into a school sock and when he thinks no one is watching he attempts to burn them and bury their remains in the garden. The other day his mother asked where the hell all his school socks had disappeared to, and I had to bite the insides of my cheeks so that I didn't laugh out loud. He went the colour of cranberries, spotty Herbert. Mind you, I bet it's great for the rosebushes.

The girl is probably still a virgin; she is only fourteen after all. She thinks too much of herself, that one. I hear her talking to her friends on the phone: they are all spoilt and rich, and imagine that life is going to be like that film *Clueless,* and on their seventeenth birthdays they will get walk-in wardrobes and a convertible. I have read Georgina's diary several times; it is the usual teenage mush. She gives her friends marks out of ten for looks, clothes and how wealthy their parents are. From her diary, I have managed to glean the fact that she intends to lose her virginity to a pop star, someone called Ritchie from a band called Five. She has a poster of them on her wall and I drew pimples and moustaches on the Ritchie geezer – she went mental and blamed Henry. He could have done it, of course, he snoops around her room often enough. I know because at the back of his wardrobe I found a pair of her knickers – oh, and the instruction leaflet from a box of mini Lillets. What a Mata Hari I have become.

It was very simple conducting the affair. All I had to do was make sure that Sinaed was kept busy every Monday morning, so I started sending her to the supermarket. Normally she went on a Friday and it meant that by the weekend we were down to dried pasta and bottled sauces, but what the fuck. I'd give her long-winded errands: the car needed washing, clothes had to be taken to the drycleaner. She also had an aerobics class on a Wednesday afternoon, so that was another window in my diary. Work was easy to bunk off: I started to have a lot of fictional root canal treatment, smear tests and such like. Sometimes he'd pop over for a ten-minute quickie first thing in the morning when Sinaed was doing the school run and Chris had left for work. They start early in the City; he was out of the house by 7.30.

I knew he was married, he told me. Her name was Carlene and they had two children: three-year-old Roxanne and a baby, Ted. He said his wife had been a looker but had let herself go after the second baby and didn't like going out. From which I gathered she had a dose of postnatal depression. Perhaps I should have been more sympathetic.

We did it all over the place. With Chris I have only ever done it in bed; he would never dream of taking me by surprise over the sink in daylight. Danny and I did it upstairs, downstairs, on the stairs, in the cellar where the cobwebs are. We did it in the bath, in the marital bed and several times on the floor in Pandora's bedroom, with the hamster awake and watching us with his beady brown eyes. We used condoms: I was phobic about them not being flushed away properly. Sometimes, when they didn't go down after more than two flushes, I'd fish them out of the bowl, wrap them in toilet paper and put them down the waste disposal unit.

He wasn't thick, he was funny and he made me laugh. Sometimes I bought him things, a silver chain, but he told me not to because Carlene was the jealous type and he didn't need the agro. It was Carlene's dad who ran the firm, he had to be careful. Well, so did I, I had a bigger house and nicer things. I had more to lose than he did. He told me where he lived and I drove past a few times; it was just a little Victorian terrace, with a peeling front door and a broken toilet in the front garden. Once I saw Carlene; she looked like a Third Division footballer's wife. She had a big chin and her black roots badly needed touching up. She was wearing a pair of faded jeans that were pulling round her midriff and when she lifted the baby out of the buggy her top rode up and her stomach was all loose.

40

Cause and Effect

My whole life is on hold. I would like to have people over for dinner but she'd be there, freeloading the booze, hiccuping and being tragic, embarrassing everyone.

I'd quite like to go away for a weekend but we can't leave her. It's only temporary but temporary has turned out to be too long. I'm not equipped to deal with this, I do not have the patience. I'm neither a nurse nor a therapist, in fact I'm not sure I can even play the best friend for much longer. It feels like a horrible rehearsal for other future nightmares: having my mother come to live with us – or Nigel's! Thank Christ we are rich, and come the day we can stick them in a home. Anna is only forty-one and she isn't mad, despite evidence to the contrary; she has just had a hard time but we are all suffering.

Last weekend, Nigel and I went out for the night. We have to have some life and it's important to know what's going on in the real world. We went to see that play *Art* in the West End. Some American friends had invited us. Their son is at school with Henry and they live in one of those mock-Georgian houses behind electric gates in Dulwich, but are never the less very nice people. Americans tend to be, don't they? After the theatre (marvellous, seventy-five minutes without an interval), we went out for dinner to one of those new fashionable restaurants; it was full of thin thirty-four-year-old women looking a bit like Gwyneth Paltrow. We ate complicated food on big white plates, drank expensive wine and, to cap it all, our lovely, loaded American chums insisted on flashing their platinum Amex card and paid for the lot. For the first time in months I felt like we were having fun. We had normal conversations about school fees and mortgages and the use of magic realism in literature.

By the time we got home, it was past one o'clock and Anna was splayed out on the sofa with an empty bottle of Malibu, and a dish of half-eaten Frosties on the floor. She was wearing my best satin wrap, a pair of ancient high-heeled Jimmy Choos and a hat Georgina had bought for a fancy dress party, a little pill box thing with a veil. Apart from a shoulder-length pair of earrings that I didn't recognise, she was otherwise naked; the dressing-gown had fallen open and you could see her pubes running riot like ivy over the tops of her fat legs. Nigel said, 'Ugh,' and we threw a tartan rug over her and left her to sleep it off.

When we went to bed, we had sex. We were both quite pissed and the kids were staying with friends; we were consenting adults fornicating in our own house. I think it got quite noisy.

I don't mean I was yelping and howling, that's not really my style, it's just that I'm quite heavy and the bed creaks. Afterwards, I went to get a glass of water from the kitchen and Anna was on the stairs. She gave me this filthy wink and I noticed her left breast was hanging out of my kimono and I knew she'd been listening and masturbating in my Jimmy Choos. I was livid. 'What the hell, Anna?' I hissed, and she just giggled and started to crawl up the stairs with her bottom up in the air. As she turned the corner on to the next landing, she farted and collapsed in fits of laughter. I was so cross that instead of having the glass of water, I went downstairs and finished off a bottle of white wine that had been knocking around in the fridge for a few days. The next day I felt like shit. Anna didn't get up at all.

Once, when I was a teenager and studying French for O-level, my father thought it would be a good idea to do one of those foreign exchange jobbies and a miserable girl called Veronique duly arrived from Toulouse.

'Would you like to go ice-skating, Veronique?'

'Non.'

'Would you like to go to the cinema?'

'Non.'

Would you like to take a running jump, you dreary frog? Obviously. I never made the return trip. She stayed with us for two weeks and it felt like a year; Anna has been here for less than a month and it feels like a lifetime. I try to put it all in perspective: whenever there is an earthquake and thousands of people lose their homes I know I am relatively well off, but one's sympathy wears thin. It's like the Serbian refugees who clean windscreens down at Vauxhall; I no longer feel guilty when I set my windscreen wipers off at them.

Henry and Georgina have begun to loathe her. Georgina never had much time for her anyway but now when the two of them are in the same room, you can cut the atmosphere with a chainsaw.

'Anna, have you been in my room?'

'No, what would I want to go in your room for?'

'You've been spying on me. You're sick.'

'Jo, can you ask your daughter not to address me in this fashion, like I'm some scullery maid?'

'Leave Mum out of this, I'm talking to you.'

'Oh, la-di-da, Miss Hoity Toity. You want to watch this one, Jo, paranoid if you ask me.'

'Mum, she's been going in my room.'

'I never. She's a liar, Jo, vicious little alley cat.'

'Mum, tell her she can't talk to me like that. She's bonkers, Mum, and I'm sick of her. She nicks my sweets, Mum, and she touches my things.'

At this point, Anna started to imitate Georgina talking in a really het-up, high-pitched way.

'Just stop it, the pair of you,' I bellowed, and Georgina went flouncing off.

'It's not fair. I hate you, Anna, and I hate you, Mum.'

When I went up to talk to Georgina later, she'd cut her fringe really short and was crying on the bed begging me to make it grow back. There are some things mothers can't do, but she sat on my knee, even though her feet dangled on the floor, and she let me give her some love. Actually, the new fringe suited her and I noticed that a few days later all her friends had cut their fringes really short too. Georgina will always bounce back. Henry, on the other hand, is bottling everything up; consequently his skin is worse than it's ever been. Anna, of course, takes great glee in noticing every new pimple.

'Blimey, Henry,' she says, 'I thought it affected your eyesight not your complexion.'

I have no idea what she's talking about but I wish she wouldn't tease him, he's very sensitive, is Henry. He's started doing the blinking again and he hasn't done that for a couple of years.

41

Pandora's Tale

Pandora was lying on her belly on the bedroom floor. She took up a lot of space, her big white legs stretched out behind her. Pandora's socks lay in wrinkles round her ankles; she would rather they stayed up. Neat girls wore their socks pulled firmly to the knee; Pandora's socks were frayed from constant hitching. She was writing an essay about 'My Family'. All children are made to do this at some point, it helps the school to know what they're dealing with. Teachers these days are trained to pick up any sign of domestic impropriety. Pandora's pen was sweaty in her hand.

'My name is Pandora, I am twelve years old and I am fat. I am fat because I like to eat things that are bad for me and I eat things that are bad for me because it upsets my mother. Every time I open my mouth and put in something that leaves me with sugar on my lips, I can feel her cringe.

'There are photos of me when I was a baby and my mother is holding me on her lap. She looks uncomfortable, like she'd rather I'd go and sit somewhere else. To be fair, I don't look that comfortable either, but as I cannot crawl, never mind walk, I am stuck. I used to think that maybe she brought the wrong baby home from the hospital, only she didn't because I look a bit like my dad and a bit like Nanna Wales. I've got two nannas. Nanna Wales, who lives in Wales and Nanna Geneva, who lives in Geneva, makes sense I suppose. I've only seen Nanna Geneva about three times, she has very thin legs and wears high-heeled shoes. Nanna Wales wears slippers'.

Pandora screwed up her first attempt, lobbed it into her Spice Girls waste basket and began another.

'My name is Pandora Cunningham, I am twelve years old and I live in a pink house with my mother and father and my younger brother. (So far, so good, no cats out of the bag there then.) My mother is called Anna and my father is called Chris. My brother is called Jed, which is short for Jedediah, he is nine and my mother loves him more than me because he looks like an angel in a nativity play'.

Whoops.

She started again.

'My name is The Blob, that is what they call me at school'.

Pandora gave up on writing about 'My Family'. She took her hamster out of his cage. He was quite new; hamsters usually live till they are three, which meant that Nibbles could safely expect to live for another two and a bit years (if only). Pandora loved Nibbles and she loved her father; she loved her mother but she wished that Anna wouldn't shout into her face with her teeth all clenched and bits of spit coming out. She loved her brother too, but quite often she wished he'd never been born.

Sometimes Pandora liked to imagine that she had a life-threatening illness and that her mother stood by her hospital bed and wept, 'Oh, Pandora, my darling child.'

Pandora tried to count her blessings: school was horrible but sometimes they had chocolate sponge with custard at dinnertime; her mother was mean but occasionally suffered from bouts of guilt and bought her anything she wanted, her dad was the best dad in the world and Siobhan was okay.

'Pandora, Jed, supper,' her mother was shouting from the basement. There was no real urgency, Anna didn't cook, not properly, not with butter and flour anyway; the Cunninghams were on a health kick and Pandora had been put on a diet behind her back. It was a Tuesday night; tuna salad with baked potatoes.

'I wouldn't have any butter if I were you, Pandora, try a little yoghurt instead.'

Pandora would have killed for a pizza. As she got up from the floor, her big knee knocked over a tin of Coke –

'Pandora, the diet ones are for you.'

– and huffing a little, she bent down to mop it up with the leg of her pyjamas before it made her collection of *Mizz* magazines go all soggy. Pandora liked *Mizz* magazine but whenever she filled in the personality tests she always came out as a Dreary Dora or a Sulky Suzie; just once it would be nice to score a Fun-time Fi Fi. As she reached for the empty can, Pandora found a little cardboard packet with coloured balloons on the front. Durex flavoured condoms. Pandora shuffled backwards; somehow she managed to kneel on her protractor and it cracked sharply. She knew what condoms were for, she saw the film last term. She knew about AIDS and how not to get pregnant, and sperm and ovaries; what she didn't know was what these condoms were doing in her bedroom. Because she didn't know what else to do with them, she put them back under her bed and went downstairs for dinner.

Jed was already sitting at the table. 'Hello, Mrs Stinky,' he said cheerfully. Jed was wearing his school uniform, but under his grey trousers peeped a pair of his mother's Agent Provocateur fluffy mules, pale pink satin with marabou trim.

'They were in the sale,' Anna had said when Chris found them in a box in her wardrobe. 'I couldn't resist them – must be going mad in my old age.'

Jed didn't want tuna salad, so Anna had made him some tinned spaghetti with grated cheese heaped all over it. The children's father was out on business, 'clogging his arteries, no doubt, with red meat and creamy sauces.'

Pandora chewed her potato. One side of it had gone all hard, her mother had cooked them in the microwave again. She said they didn't taste any different but they did.

Anna was looking very pretty today, prettier than any woman of forty has a right to do; she could easily pass for thirty-four.

Anna's looks were a combination of luck, genetics and that little extra which if packaged could be labelled 'triumph'. It was only when Anna caught sight of her daughter chewing that her mouth became pinched, and for a moment she looked a bit hard. Anna was thinking that when she was Pandora's age she was in Ibiza wearing a yellow, crocheted bikini and how overnight her schoolgirl buttocks tied up in canary-coloured string had become like magnets to any red-bloodied male on the beach.

After supper, Pandora retreated back into her bedroom. She said she had a history project to finish, but all she did was squeeze four large blackheads out of the side of her nose, and count the condoms in the packet: there were four of them.

She was just going to go to bed when she heard her parents arguing she couldn't help it, her mother was really yelling. Pandora crept across the landing and listened at the door, trying not to make snuffling noises when she breathed. Pandora suffered terribly with her sinuses.

'I've never heard so much bollocks in all my life.'

'Please, Anna, just calm down. There's obviously some cause for concern.'

'"Some cause for concern". Have you heard yourself? You sound like an idiot.'

'Please, Anna.'

The door was slightly open, Pandora could see her parents' reflection in the big mirror over the mantelpiece: her father looked crumpled and worn out, her mother was red in the face and she had both her hands on her hips.

Pandora knew what they were arguing about; it was Jed. Pandora's brother had been in trouble at school for 'behaving in an inappropriate fashion', in other words, he had been mincing around like Noel Coward *in utero*. Pandora wondered what it would be like to have a normal brother, she had read about them in books. Little brothers should be cutting up worms, eating ants and kicking footballs through greenhouse windows, not swanning around the house reeking of lady's perfume, wearing a velvet Alice band, 'My Alice band,' fumed Pandora, as she tried to tiptoe away as silently as her size eight, big black regulation lace-ups would allow.

'And I wish you'd stop lurking around poking your big fat nose into everyone's business.'

Her mother came flying out of the bedroom.

'I was just—'

'Just nothing.'

Pandora withdrew. What she really needed was some Nurofen.

Pandora had period pains again and she hated them. Jed wouldn't want to be a girl if he knew what it was really like. Pandora lay on her bed, face down with her knees pulled up under her chest and undid the button of her school skirt. 'Not fair.'

A few minutes later, she heard her father coming out of the bedroom. He knocked on her door and she wished he didn't have to, he never used to, not when she was a little girl and could still fit on his knee. Pandora thought that growing up was rubbish.

'Can I come in, Pandy?'

Pandora kicked the packet of Kotex Maxi Pads under her bed. 'Yeah.'

So he did, her lovely dad, with his shiny pink face and the nose that didn't suit either of them. He sat on her bed, on top of a pile of clean laundry including a bra, which was a bit embarrassing, but they both pretended not to notice and he said, 'Sorry about, you know.'

'Iss okay.'

'How's school?'

'Iss okay.'

It wasn't really but she couldn't go telling her dad that no one wanted to sit next to her at lunchtime, and that she always had to play goalie in hockey because she was the biggest in the class and that when the left-hand lens fell out of her glasses and cracked in two on the floor everyone laughed.

'It'll all get sorted out,' said Chris, and Pandora knew that he meant Jed. 'Just a phase, he's going through.'

'No it isn't,' Pandora wanted to say. 'You know it and I know it; Jed's a fairy fudge-packer.' But she didn't.

'Come down and watch some telly?'

'In a bit.'

Pandora could feel the sticky wetness of her towel and much

as she'd like to have had a nice chat with her dad, she really needed to get to the bathroom.

Chris glanced over at the homework that lay open on her desk. 'Anything interesting?'

Pandora reached out and shut her history book before her father noticed her teacher's red pen scrawl at the bottom of the page. It wasn't her fault it was so messy, Daniella Trent had kept nudging her all through the lesson and now she had to write it out again.

'Fire of London,' she said.

'Ah, Pudding Lane. I can take you to see where it started. Would you like that, just you and me?'

'Yeah, yeah, whatever.' God, if he didn't go soon, the red stuff would leak through on to her pants.

'Rightio,' and he shuffled off, pulling the door shut as he went.

Pandora bent down to retrieve the Maxi Pads; the condoms were still there. Pandora counted them again: one, two, three, four. Before she could ask herself what she was doing, she had picked up a safety-pin that was lying on her bedside table (the zip had gone in her jeans), and pushed the sharp end into one of the condoms; it was the lime-flavoured one. Then she put the packet back and, grabbing the packet of Kotex, she galumphed to the bathroom. Just in time. Christ, it took three flushes to get rid of the used pad.

42

Bondage and Lies

Chris never suspected a thing, even when Danny, for a laugh, made me phone him while we were having sex. I was very clever and very careful most of the time but I had to watch myself; once I was doodling and realised that I'd covered the front page of the *Telegraph* with his name and hearts: Danny, Danny, Danny, in big loopy letters. I burnt the paper and went out and bought another copy.

There were several near-misses: Jo came round once and I sat chatting to her whilst Danny shivered with a hard-on under my bed for twenty minutes. Twice he was leaving as Sinaed was coming home, and once Chris was off work with diarrhoea and he called by; I told him he'd got the wrong house and he winked and left.

I was his 'Posh Fuck', his 'Lady Muck', his 'Mrs Nympho-Bitch'. These do not sound like terms of endearment but they are when they are slurred into your hair when you are blindfolded and tied to the bed with dressing-gown cords. Sometimes there was a lot of tidying up to do after Danny had paid a visit: scarves to be put back in drawers, bicycle pumps returned to their rightful places, underwear, handcuffs and vibrators hidden in plastic bags inside other plastic bags and tucked to the back of the wardrobe. Oh, naughty, naughty me, what a bad girl I have been. Looking back, I was living two lives. It wasn't like I was shagging my lover every minute of every day – I still went to work, I put petrol in the car, got money out of the bank and bought microwave meals for my family – it was just that once or, if I was lucky, twice a week, a man who was married to someone else, a bloke who held his knife like a pen, a true blue-collar geezer, would come round to my house and fuck me senseless. I knew it wouldn't go on for ever, it wasn't like we were going to run away together; I don't see why it all had to get so dramatic and silly. In France these situations are normal, everyone is unfaithful and there is something odd about you if you aren't.

I have taken to reading those magazines, the ones full of stories from real-life readers writing in with their true-life tales of human misery: My Husband Turned Me Into A Human Fire Torch, I've Got Three Vaginas, My Mother Is A Man, all that sort of stuff. I have arranged to have these delivered, along with Georgina's *Smash Hits* and Henry's step-by-step guide to 'understanding the human body'. They make me laugh and, God knows, we all need a laugh.

I had an affair with a stand-up comic once, well, it wasn't once, it was about twenty times. Boom, boom. I'm not lying. It was Nigel's fault, he asked us to a recording of some late-night comedy show down at the telly studios on the South Bank. I have never been so bored in all my life. This is a warning: never be part of a studio audience. They treat you like shit – retarded shit at that – you are made to work harder than the performers, whooping and whistling and clapping like lobotomised sea lions. There was a woman with a big arse in maroon leather trousers waving a big piece of cardboard with 'applause' on it, and under that board she had another one that said 'louder' – stupid old tart. She was old enough to know better. You couldn't even go out for a pee; it was like being held hostage, but worse because you knew there weren't crowds of people storming the British Embassy, demanding that you should be released. Afterwards, there was a party in what they call the 'Green Room'; plastic cups of white wine, little bowls of Bombay Mix, oh, the glamour. In the TV studio, his suit had looked quite expensive; close up it was cheap and you could tell that in a few years' time, when the little-boy Irish charm had worn off, he'd be seedy, his hair would no longer flop across those green eyes and his thinness would become mean-looking.

I am good at judging how people will look in the future; it's part of my job. Blonde women are the worst, they go off like fruit; one moment they are ripe and their skin is plump and full, the next they are rotting and the skin has become withered, baggy and bruised. They don't just go off, they ferment.

Paddy Burns was his name. I took his number for professional reasons: Mags and I were casting a big soft drink commercial and we were looking for quirky types. He didn't get the advert but he came round to the house and we had sex whilst Jed took his afternoon nap and Sinaed was at jungle gym with Pandora (I thought it would help shift some of the beefiness off her legs – fat chance). It was never going to be anything serious. His cock was long and thin like his nose, and he wore horrible underpants.

The sex wasn't very good: perhaps he was the sort of bloke who would have been better with an audience. Still, it passed the time, they haven't got much to do during the day, stand-up comics; they watch daytime television and try to write jokes about *Countdown* on the backs of envelopes.

It fizzled out quite quickly. A few months later I saw him on a late-night television programme, wearing the same cheap suit and doing a routine about having sex with an older woman. It was all about how difficult it is to maintain an erection in the face of cellulite. I knew it wasn't me he was talking about because at the time I didn't have cellulite, but I still felt pissed off.

Some years later when Sinaed showed me a photograph of her cousin's wedding in Dublin, I was sure I could spot him in amongst her brothers; he had on the cheap suit and because his hair was receding, he looked like a big forehead on legs. I am glad he never made it.

43

The Definition of Nymphomania

We never knew she was being silly. When the Danny thing eventually came out, she told me about the others; she didn't really count the ones she hadn't had full sex with. Anna has Clintonesque morals: snogs and hand jobs and the occasional bit of oral don't count in her book, so really, apart from Danny, there'd only been one other, a stand-up comic; and even he didn't really count considering she'd never achieved orgasm with him.

Apparently I'd come round once, interrupted one of their *Confessions of a Plumber* scenarios. I'd borrowed her hand-held mixer to make meringues and I'd popped by to return it. I don't know why, she never used it; all Anna ever needed in the kitchen was a can-opener. Anyway . . . she answered the door and all the time we were having coffee in her kitchen, he was hiding naked under her bed. She said that when I left she realised that her shirt was buttoned up all wrong and her lipstick was smudged. I hadn't noticed it makes me feel stupid; they must have laughed together when I'd gone. Silly old Jo, she hasn't a clue.

She has told me everything now; she has told me things I don't really need to hear. She has filled me in on every fuck, down to the very last detail. She has said that the sound of his voice made her want to insert objects into her vagina; that once he phoned her and when she put the phone down she realised she'd been 'pushing a courgette up and down her cunt'; that he literally made her drip. 'Women ejaculate too, Jo. I'd be so wet I thought I must have pissed myself.' She is drunk when she tells me these things, how he would push her against the wall and pull at her clothes, how once she wore Pandora's gym skirt and he came all over it and Pandora thought she must have spilt some yoghurt. When she told me this she laughed until a bit of sick came out of the side of her mouth and I had to put her to bed again.

She has described his cock to me – length, girth, balls – his smell, the way their teeth would smash together, the rawness of her lips. I have told her to stop on numerous occasions, but she insists. She has told me how they had anal sex and that 'Really, Jo, you should try it.' I told her I didn't think it was me. I wished she would shut up; it was a Sunday evening, we were watching *The Vicar of Dibley*, there was no need to tell us. Nigel hid behind the *Observer*, thank Christ the kids were in their bedrooms. When she talks about having sex with Danny, she touches herself. 'My nipples, Jo,' she says, 'were like truck nuts as soon as I saw him. He hardly had to touch me and I'd come.'

So now do you see why we don't have friends round? You can't subject normal people to the pornographic rantings of some mad old tart. You can imagine it, can't you? Anna in mid-flow, 'And then he'd shoot his spunk in my face, hot jism in my eyes, and call me a dirty bitch. Pass the beans, vicar.' See, it's not on.

And all the time this was happening, all the time she was having to wash spunk out of her hair in the middle of the day, none of us had a clue. We still had our kitchen suppers and talked about the kids and new cars and where we wanted to go for our summer holidays. To tell you the truth, what sticks in my craw is that even now, after everything that has happened, she has never really said sorry. She has cried and ranted and raged but she has never really apologised and I'm getting bloody fed up with it. I don't want to hear about how he'd take her on the kitchen tiles, how she would kneel on all fours whilst he fucked her from behind and spanked her arse with a spatula, how she would anoint her nipples with peanut butter and let him chase her round the house. I can buy tabloid newspapers if I want salacious tittle-tattle in my own home.

I am turning into Mary Whitehouse; I have started to despair of soap stars fucking page three girls and cocaine-fuelled sex frenzies involving footballers and single-parent strippers. I have started reading a lot of Jane Austen. I have come to the conclusion that there's a world of difference between being a twenty-something flibbertigibbet and a forty-year-old stupid slag. Anna is too old to be behaving in this ridiculous fashion.

Nothing like this ever happened when my parents were in their forties; London might have been swinging but everywhere else it was business as usual. Only, maybe I'm wrong? Something keeps bubbling up at the back of my brain. It was a long time ago: I must have been about ten, my brother eight. We were living in Berlin and it was Christmas and suddenly on Christmas Day two other children arrived on the doorstep and we had to give them some of our presents. Two little girls, I can't remember their names, one was about five and the other was even younger. I gave the older one a set of pencils with Japanese ladies' wooden heads on the end. She said something about her mummy running away with 'Uncle Bernard', but it didn't make much sense to me at the time. They stayed with us that Christmas night, the two of them shared my bed; two little blond heads, one at either end. I slept on a camp bed in my father's dark green army sleeping bag, which was too hot, and anyway, it was hard to sleep because the phone kept ringing. In those days, that was unusual; people didn't use the telephone like we do now. Back then, if you wanted to call someone, you had to go and sit in the hall at a special table and 'speak nicely and clearly'.

Their father picked them up the next day. My mother was a bit embarrassed because she was making us egg-fried bread in her dressing-gown and slippers.

'Is she back?' my mother asked.

'She's back,' the man said, 'but for how long is anyone's guess.' He had scratch marks on his face.

Some months later, my father had to give evidence for one of his lance corporals who was being court-martialled for trying to kill another soldier. During a discussion of this case at the supper table, my mother muttered the word 'nymphomaniac'. When I asked her what it meant, she replied that it was a word used to describe a woman who consorted with men regardless of their class or social status. Everything fits together in the end. Those little girls will be in their mid-thirties now and their nymphomaniac mum will be a pensioner.

44

Plumbing the Depths

They had nothing in common, Danny Leigh and Anna Cunningham: he liked salad cream, she liked mayonnaise, he liked Dairylea, she liked Brie. Once she made him a cup of Earl Grey tea; he said he'd tasted better puddles. Another time she mentioned Shula Archer and he hadn't got a clue who she was talking about; Danny had Sky Digital and had never read a John Updike book in his life. Instinctively they knew their boundaries: Anna didn't mention metaphysical poetry and he didn't talk about football. If she did use a long word he would say, 'Swallowed a dictionary?'

Sometimes he was moody and Anna felt nervous; on these occasions she would try very hard indeed, literally bending over backwards to please him. Anna had always been very supple at school, but when you're forty, holding yourself in the crab position in some desperate bid to enact the Kama Sutra, takes its toll. There were some days when, after a particularly hectic Danny session, her legs would buckle as she walked down the stairs.

She was terrified that he might get bored of her, so she bought a French maid's outfit and let him drag her round the house on the end of a lead. She was utterly at his disposal, and sometimes he was terribly ungrateful; once, when she was giving him a blowjob, he reached inside his jacket pocket and proceeded to eat a Ginsters cheese pasty whilst her tongue performed acrobatics over his genitals.

'Close your eyes,' she said, 'and count to three hundred and fifty then try to find me.'

She hid behind Pandora's curtains, quivering, whilst he made a couple of calls on his mobile and swigged milk from the carton in the fridge. Eventually he found her and, pulling her across his knee, he gave her a good spanking with Pandora's hairbrush. 'Not too hard,' she squealed. After all, how does one explain bristle marks on the bum to one's husband? 'Oh sorry, darling, I must have sat on a hedgehog.'

Just when they were getting down to business proper, he started talking about her daughter.

'How old is she?'

'Pandora? She's twelve.'

'Might have to come and sort her out in a few years' time,' he'd sniggered. 'Is she like her mother? Is she horny?'

'No.'

'Come on, I bet she's a right little goer.'

She was standing in the middle of Pandora's bedroom, bent double, holding on to her heels with her bum in the air and staring at the carpet, whilst Danny penetrated her from behind. Suddenly she felt all cross and rather foolish; she was wearing some of Pandora's school uniform, the shirt knotted under a new purple satin underwired bra, black fishnets and most definitely non-regulation scarlet patent stilettos. Pandora's blazer smelt ever so slightly of school dinners. In the background, a Wallace and Gromit alarm clock ticked both gormlessly and efficiently.

'Oh yeah,' he monotoned, 'like mother, like daughter, maybe I'll have you both.'

It was rather difficult balancing like this; at any moment Anna could have toppled headfirst on to the hamster cage. She had to concentrate but it was tricky and what with Danny mumbling on about fucking Pandora, it was all rather off-putting. Suddenly she heard her voice go all posh and strict. 'I don't think you will.' Blimey, she sounded like her old headmistress, and with that, Anna stood upright, yanking up her purple pants, and showed Danny a particularly hideous school photo of Pandora that had been laying face down on the bedside table. 'There,' she snapped, 'that's Pandora.'

'Oh,' he said. There was a lime-green condom hanging off his knob. 'Is she adopted?' he inquired.

Anna pretended to laugh it off but she was close to tears; for a moment she felt like one of those desperate women who go to fancy-dress parties as St Trinian's schoolgirls under the misapprehension that they look sexy and cute, when in reality they looked like frightening old whores. What was she doing?

That was the last time they used Pandora's room, which was probably a relief for Nibbles: hamsters are nocturnal, they don't like being woken up at eleven o'clock on a Thursday morning by men wielding hairbrushes and women dressed up as schoolgirls going, 'Aaaagh, oooh, aaagh.'

When Danny had gone, Anna hung the school clothes back in Pandora's wardrobe and scoured the room for tell-tale signs of fornicating plumbers. Danny was a sod for leaving his Rizla papers lying about, he was getting careless. Just a couple of days ago as she and Chris had settled down for the night, she'd stretched her legs out in the bed and her foot had come in contact with one of Danny's socks. Carefully she had curled her toes around it and surreptitiously dragged it up the bed until she could reach it with her hand and quickly squash it under the mattress. They had to be more careful. Just as she was about to leave the room, she noticed Nibbles hanging upside down in his cage, à la Olga Korbut with testicles. As hamsters go, he had a lot of personality. Anna remembered when she'd bought him: £3.99 from Peckham market. He'd been a present for Jed, but Jed had gone off him; he hadn't liked cleaning out the wet wee-wee sawdust so consequently the cage had begun to stink.

'Oh, just let me do it,' Pandora had huffed, and Nibbles had become both her responsibility and little furry friend.

He was sweet. Anna knelt down; her joints cricked alarmingly, oh great, just what she needed, old slag's knee! 'Hello little fellow,' she said, and as she opened the cage she noticed the packet of condoms lying under the bed. 'Fucking hell, Danny, you thick twat.' She scooped them up; she would chuck them out of the car window as she drove over to Maggie's. Just then out of the corner of her eye she saw a beige blur streak out of the bedroom door. 'NIBBLES!'

Anna spent the next forty minutes running round the house, still in her fishnets and high-heeled red shoes, trying to corner the hamster. It wasn't all fun and high jinks having an affair.

Whilst Anna captured domestic rodents, Danny sulked in his

van. Anna had stopped paying him a call-out fee. You can't make a living out of shagging frustrated housewives.

Two roads away in the converted stable block, Jo sat in her second-hand bookshop and thought about Georgina. More precisely she thought about what she had seen Georgina doing at the bus stop yesterday afternoon. She had been kissing a black boy. Jo hadn't told Nigel; he would have had her locked up in a convent. It was all very well for him to have the morals of a tom cat, but if he thought his precious daughter was out necking on the streets of South London he'd bust a gasket. After all, he didn't pay two grand a term for her to fraternise with local comprehensive scum.

Bloody Georgina. If she hadn't lost her brand new DKNY trainers, then Jo wouldn't have thought to pick her up from school so they could go and buy some new ones.

'But you're not having another expensive pair, Georgina.'

'Oh, that's right, let's go to Woolworths and get some revolting cheap ones.'

'We're not made of money.'

'Just don't go on, you're so boring.'

She shouldn't have bothered; she should have left Georgina to play games in her lace-ups, but no, she'd closed up the shop early, gone to meet her at school; only there had been road-works at the top of the hill and she'd been late. Georgina was already waiting for the bus, her tongue rummaging round the tonsils of a strange boy. He was much taller than her, she'd been on tiptoes. As Jo drove past she was so embarrassed, she sort of ducked.

Maybe it would be better if she just kept her trap shut, let the girl get it out of her system. To be honest, Jo felt vaguely sorry for anyone who got involved with Georgina; she was vile.

Just then, old Mrs Donahue came in; Raymond was at his adult education centre. 'Your friend is having ever such a lot of problems with her plumbing. I've seen that white van outside hers three times in the past fortnight.'

Brenda bought a job-lot of Catherine Cooksons; she liked a nice romance. Don't we all, thought Jo.

She was going to ask Anna what was wrong with her plumbing next time she saw her, but what with one thing and another, she forgot.

45

Ending in Tears

I wasn't well on the last day I saw Danny. It was a flu thing; I lay in bed sweating, with my head throbbing and my limbs feeling like rusty tractor parts. Chris was very good, of course; he's marvellous when people are ill, he likes to fuss around. He ran me a bath, changed the sheets on the bed and brought me up a tray of weak Earl Grey tea and some Alpen in a dish with blue flowers all over. He did it properly; Chris is the only person left alive who still bothers to roll up napkins and put them into rings. I lay back on clean white sheets, all talcum powdery, and knocked back a couple of paracetamol with a gulp of orange juice, shuddering as I tasted the bitterness beneath the chalky coating. The Alpen tasted nasty too, as if the milk was off, and I spat it back in the bowl. I cleaned my teeth and felt like I could be sick if I moved my head too quickly. Chris phoned Maggie to say I wouldn't be in. I knew she'd be pissed off because we had hordes of accordion players coming in for an Austrian beer commercial.

Chris delivered a wet kiss on my cheek and my stomach churned, then he disappeared off to work and Sinaed took the kids to school. As soon as I was alone in the house, I started to feel better. I had a nap and when I woke up it was 10.30. Sinaed had started beginners' feng shui at a local college; she'd made some cronies and I knew they all went to the wine bar for lunch. It was all so simple. I called him on the mobile; he was short with me. I should have told him not to bother but I didn't, I asked him to come over at lunchtime, 'I've some pipes that need tinkering with.' When I put the phone down, I could smell the sweat on me again so I took a shower; the light in the en suite is very cruel; my face was the colour of old parsnips and my moustache looked more pronounced than normal. I decided to bleach it, do my eyebrows; I had plenty of time.

It's not as simple as you'd think, being a brunette: we are descended from the same ape as Sean Connery, hairiness is an occupational hazard. I attacked my eyebrows with some ferocity, tears welling up with every pluck, then I slathered my top lip with Jolene creme bleach. My hair needed something doing with it, I'd hennaed it for ages but it had become coarse and gingery. I made a mental note to have it dyed black: I wanted it sleek, like a bird's wing. I was just going to wash it when the doorbell went. It was twelve o'clock; I should have remembered Danny is working class, they take their lunches earlier than us, and it's not lunch, it's dinner. They're another race altogether, common people, they have different habits; they eat more fried food, drink milk out of the carton and shovel their peas. Danny ate meat pies and Ginsters sausage rolls from garages.

Hearing the doorbell was a shock. I literally flapped like a starling trapped in a chimney. I wiped the bleach off my lip with a corner of the bedspread and threw myself into a green towelling robe. With hindsight it would have been more sensible to have pretended not to be in, to have preserved the myth, but I pelted down the stairs and as I opened the door, the spring sunshine hit me between the eyes. Immediately the lyrics of that old Rod Stewart song flooded my brain: 'The morning sun when it's in your face really shows your age,' and I could see it in Danny's eyes; I was no longer Francesca Annis to his Ralph Fiennes, Benjamin's Mrs Robinson had morphed into Maggie May, dog-rough, been round the block once too often, flea-bitten and mangy. I swear he jumped, then he said, 'Jesus, Anna, are you all right?' I tried to hang back into the shadow of the hallway I caught sight of myself in the mirror: the Jolene creme bleach had reached mid-cycle and the result was a tangerine caterpillar under my nose. The battle was lost: I was forty with a bilious stomach and badly dyed hair. It was time to retreat.

'It's all right, I've fixed it,' I yelped. At that moment his mobile trilled, and as he turned to answer it, I shut the front door and sat behind it weeping. Through the letterbox I saw him walk quickly down the garden path – he didn't look back – the phone still pressed to his ear. It was 'so over', as they would say on *Friends*. When I'd stopped crying, I went down to the kitchen and sat on the wooden rocking horse. I had a glass of Alka-Seltzer in one hand and a pickled gherkin in the other. I couldn't even be bothered to have a wank.

Men don't dump me as a rule; I think it was the shock that made me cry. I have chucked loads of blokes in the past. I was well on my way to getting rid of Chris when suddenly he asked me to marry him! I don't know why but instead of saying, 'Don't be pathetic, we could never make each other happy,' I said, 'Yes.' He didn't kiss me; he seemed a bit stunned. He just stood there rubbing his hands together and saying, 'Splendid.'

It should have been me that called it a day with Danny. His departure was too casual; I would have liked a better goodbye scene to remember. I fantasised about how it should have been: me breaking the news as gently as I could, the look of anguish on his face, his refusal to let go, the tears, a lingering farewell kiss, an anguished howl, perhaps a sickening crunch as he drove the works van straight into a wall. But no, he had walked away with what looked like a jaunty spring in his step. No doubt he was whistling as he rounded the corner.

I wasn't the first, he'd admitted that to me. There had been a French widow in Clapham, a newly wed in Lewisham and any number of eager divorcees from Nunhead to the Isle of Dogs.

I had nothing left of him. A few days later I hunted round the house, searching for evidence to prove he'd actually existed, but apart from the nylon sock under the mattress, I couldn't find anything: not a hair from his head, not a roll-up butt that he'd sucked, not a crumb from one of his cheese pasties. Danny Leigh had left the building and my heart was in pieces. Boo hoo, boo hoo.

46

Anna the Abhorrent, Georgina the Grim

Apparently it just fizzled out. Isn't that always the way? Love affairs are like fireworks: the more spectacular they are, the quicker they burn out. It's the dull ones, those short squat no-threat-to-anyone types that go on for ever. Course, I never knew when it was over because back then I didn't even know it had begun. She just didn't tell me anything about it and I'm the sort of person that people tell things to. I can't walk down the street without complete strangers filling me in on how their dialysis is going or what colour paint they've decided to do their kitchen. Once I was nipping to the shops and a woman told me how her next-door neighbour threw snails over the party wall and what should she do about it? Sometimes I think I must look like a walking Citizens' Advice Bureau.

Years ago when I was a student living in halls of residence, people were always knocking on my door, crying and carrying on. I was always very good at dealing with the emotionally bruised. I used to keep a jar of instant coffee in the little locker by my bed, along with a tin of powdered milk and a box of tissues. I was always sympathetic, my shoulders damp with the tears of forlorn first years: 'He's finished with me, Jo, and I can't bear it.' I was a right little agony aunt. I used to think that when I had children I would be so understanding of them; they would be able to tell me anything. Huh. My children are secretive: Henry has always been too embarrassed to tell me the truth and Georgina too duplicitous.

Maybe I would have noticed if I hadn't got quite enough on my plate: I was worried sick about Georgina and the black boy – wherever I went there seemed to be teenage girls with massively distended stomachs. I got quite paranoid about it.

Looking back, Anna did seem very tired and a little depressed. She stopped taking quite so much care of herself. Once I almost passed her on the street, she looked positively bedraggled: all the detail had gone out of her, her hair didn't look clean and her fingernails were grubby. One thing I do remember is that she suddenly started eating puddings. That's not like Anna, she was always more savoury of tooth – she had good meat-eating canines – but once I had them round and she polished off the tarte tatin! I didn't say anything but she just kept pouring cream over her plate until the pie was almost floating and the cream swum off the side. Afterwards, she had to undo the top button of her jeans. Nigel said something around that time, something about her going off, looking her age all of a sudden. But that often happens to women when they hit forty; it's as if the struggle becomes too much and they can't be bothered to hold in their stomachs any more, gravity takes its toll, you develop jowls and that extra flap of skin oozes out from under your bra strap and all of a sudden you feel self-conscious in a sleeveless frock. Nature is very cruel, and if there is a god I don't think he likes women very much.

To be honest, I didn't have very much time to worry about Anna: I had enough problems of my own. The bookshop had flooded; I had a whole load of Graham Greene first editions gone to papier mâché. Henry was being bullied at school and Georgina was basically being even more Georgina-ish than usual. She was hanging out with the black lad and I knew that she was smoking. I was exhausted.

See, that's what I can't understand: how she ever had the time or the energy for an affair in the first place. I certainly couldn't have managed it. Anyway, the last thing I want to do when I have some time to myself is have sex. I'd rather sort the laundry cupboard out.

She asked me a few weeks ago if I ever masturbated; I told her to stop showing off. It's not as if I haven't, we've all had a fiddle, but she kept going on, about dildos and vibrators – she said you could buy all sorts of things from these sex catalogues. I said the last thing I got from a catalogue was a navy button-through linen dress from Next. Really, other people's sex lives are as dull as their holiday snaps.

He was much younger than her of course, fatal mistake. If I were to embark on an affair, I'd make sure it was with a seventy-year-old with cataracts and a heart complaint; at least you'd stand some chance of being left something in the will. Another thing, I don't think I could get particularly intimate with someone who hadn't gone on to higher education; call me a snob, but I like a man with letters after his name. By all accounts this Danny was almost illiterate.

'What did you talk about?' I knew as soon as I said it that it was a silly thing to ask.

She sneered and replied, 'We talked about how he was going to fuck me into the middle of next week.'

'Charming,' I replied. I have never gone for bits of rough, though I will admit that there are two young men who wash cars in Sainsbury's carpark and when the weather is good they take their shirts off and . . . well, now I'm just being silly. To be honest, I don't think I've got that air of promiscuity about me; I have always been the kind of woman who can ask for a pound of sausages without the butcher smirking.

If Nigel died, I can't actually see myself in bed with anyone else; I couldn't be bothered to go through that stage one of a relationship again; all that gargling with breath freshener before bed and trying not to fart. I think I'd rather live on my own and learn the Latin names for plants. I'd like to be able to look at the sky and say with confidence, 'Oh my goodness, a chaffinch.' Hopefully I shall have grandchildren, and when they come to stay I shan't have a television and they will be happy to paint water-colours and make gingerbread men. It would be nice to have another go with a fresh set of children. If I had another chance, I'd be really strict: they would go to bed early, eat at the table with cutlery and I'd force them to go to art galleries. I used to like going until the children spoilt it, rolling round on the floor being bored. What every art gallery needs is a large supply of full-length body callipers on castors that you could hire to strap your child into. Then you could wheel them around and force them to look at the paintings for as long as you deemed neces-sary: five minutes for a Monet, three for a Frank Auerbach.

Obviously each calliper would have to come with some leather head-harness that ensured their eyes would be kept open and their mouths firmly shut.

In the end, I had a word with Georgina about the black boy; she tried to deny it at first. 'I never, it must have been someone else.'

'Georgina,' I said, 'give me some credit. You are my daughter, I'm your mother, recognising you goes with the job.' In the end she owned up; I wish she hadn't, she told me he was sixteen and he lived on an estate at the Elephant and Castle. We made a pact; as long as she didn't let him touch her, as long as it was just holding hands and kissing, then I wouldn't tell her father. There have been times when I have longed to read her diary but I know I mustn't. Anyway, I am too frightened about what I might read. I have done with interfering in other people's lives, I don't care what anyone does any more. I just don't want to know.

Some Jehovah's Witnesses came to call; I told them I was Jewish but to come back when my friend Anna would be around as she was very interested. I am becoming spiteful: it is her fault.

Now that I have begun to dislike Anna, I feel as if she has played a big trick on me, that all the fun we had was a con. Once you have fallen out of love with your husband you can divorce him; you should be able to divorce your friends. I would rather like an official piece of paper that stated that Anna Cunningham and I, Joanna Metcalf, are no longer best gal pals; she no longer has the right to my sympathy, time, loofah or Marmite. I want to stand up in court and renounce our friendship; I am bored of her and I don't want to play any more. Loyalty is overrated, friendships are like gardens: sometimes you need to prune them, cut out the dead wood, get rid of those strange weeds that take root and upset your foundations.

I have been a fool. If I have my time again I will make selfishness an art form, I have learnt a lot from Anna. Compassion has become an albatross around my neck, pecking at my heartstrings till they have been quite eaten away by bad temper and resentment.

Do you hear me Anna? I used to be a nice person. Hell, I think my period is due.

47

Carlene Finds Out

It would have been all right if Carlene hadn't found out. It was over and done with weeks ago. Danny hadn't even thought about her, the woman in the Pink House, he'd gone off her. It's like Indian takeaways: you have the same thing for months on end and suddenly you just can't face another chicken korma.

Carlene was feeling a bit better. She had begun doing aqua aerobics and since baby Ted had finally cut his back teeth, he'd started sleeping through the night. She was singing as she sorted through the laundry. Danny's denim jacket could do with a wash, it could go in with her jeans and Roxanne's little denim pinafore with the red flowers all embroidered round the hem. Danny had got her a really good second-hand washing-machine with built-in tumble-drier, so she didn't have to go pegging stuff out any more. It was a lifesaver, 'specially when Ted had been poorly – sick and shit all over everything – she could just bung it all in the machine and it came out looking like new. Carlene spent a lot of money on her kids' clothes, she liked them to look nice.

She was listening to the Golden Hour on Radio 1: 1988, that was the year she'd started seeing Danny. She knew all the words to the songs so she sang along as she emptied his jacket pockets. 'I should be so lucky, lucky lucky lucky.' She wasn't a plumber's wife for nothing: Carlene knew better than to clog up her precious washing-machine with lighters and bits of old change. There was a screwed-up fiver in one pocket and an empty packet of Smints; in the other there was a ounce of Old Holborn, a used tissue and a cheque for a million pounds!

What?

Sorry?

I beg your pardon?

'Pay Danny Leigh one million pounds for services rendered'. The bottom line had been filled in with red biro kisses and exclamation marks and it was signed simply 'Anna'. Carlene sat down in the green plastic laundry-basket and blew her nose on one of baby Ted's sour-smelling t-shirts. The cheque trembled in her hand.

The handwriting was all slanty, and in the space under the box where this 'Anna' had scribbled all the zeros, two names were printed in black capitals: Mrs A Cunningham and Mr C R Cunningham. It was a joint account. She and Danny had one, there was fuck all in it, 'specially as they'd just put a deposit down for a week's holiday in Corfu – ever such a nice hotel, all white with a special pool for kiddies, with slides and a little thatched hut where you could buy piña coladas with umbrellas and paper parrots sticking out. She was really looking forward to that holiday; she'd already bought Roxanne her very own Barbie beach towel.

Carlene went into the kitchen. She hadn't even had her breakfast; there were two pieces of toast gone to asbestos in the toaster. She threw them in the bin and turned off the radio. Roxanne was at play centre and baby Ted was asleep in his buggy in the hall, his pudgy little hand curled around a Jammy Dodger. Carlene stood in her own kitchen as if she were in a play and couldn't remember what she was meant to do.

There was a big lump of cheese and the pulpy bit of a tomato on the draining-board from when she'd made his sandwiches, the bastard.

But she wasn't surprised, not really; state of her at the moment, she looked more like his mum than his missus. Before she did anything else, she ran upstairs and opened the wardrobe so she could look at herself in the full-length mirror. She took off all her clothes and stared; it wasn't very nice. There were red marks around her belly from where the elastic of her knickers dug in and livid stretch marks around her breasts. When was the last time she'd been down the tanning centre? She was so angry with herself that she bit her forearm and only when she stopped did she realise she was screaming. 'Hush, hush now love.' God, she wanted her mother. Her mother would have known what to do. She'd have sorted it out, taken Carlene to the Blue Water shopping centre, had a spot of lunch and a nice shop, bought something from Marks for tea, come home and watched the soaps. Carlene hoped they had *EastEnders* in heaven; her mum would be that bored if they didn't.

She got dressed. 'Stupid, stupid, stupid.' For a moment she forgot where she'd put the cheque. It was in the kitchen, by the cheese. Carlene picked up the cheddar and squashed it with her hands, fingernails full of whiffy wax. Then, wiping her hands on the back of her leggings, she went to find the phone directory, mentally chanting the alphabet in her head. C was the third letter in, near the front then: Cunliffe, Cunnane, Cunnew, Cunningham, there were nine C Cunninghams, but only one C R Cunningham. It was very easy; this Cunningham couple lived at the Pink House, Lark Grove, SE5. Easy peasy, lemon squeezy. There was an *A-Z* somewhere; Danny was forever leaving them at home and having to buy new ones. There it was on the stairs; everything ended up on the stairs: piles of clothes, toilet rolls and toothpaste to be taken up to the bathroom, kids' toys, the place was a fucking tip. A, B, C, D, E, F, G, H, I, J, K, L. Carlene went through the letters, out loud this time, in the same sing-song rhythm she'd learnt at school. Danny had been at her primary, a year above. Danny Leigh, Danny Leigh. They all used to do handstands in the playground and the boys threw stones at their knickers. Once he'd won a prize for a painting competition; it was of a footballer skidding towards the net. Years later he admitted he'd traced it; he was a liar and a cheat. She remembered him going up for his prize in assembly, that cocky swagger, his mates jeering; he got a book token, you should have seen his face drop. He must have been ten. It was no good, you couldn't stop loving someone just like that.

It wasn't that far, Lark Grove, she could get a bus to the bottom and walk up; she'd be back by the time Roxanne finished play-group. She stuffed the *A-Z* into the string bag that dangled off the buggy and left the house. The mangled cheese lay on the kitchen floor and the Zanussi Turbo Dry was left with its soap-powder drawer pulled out and its door agape like a surprised mouth. Carlene walked down to the bus stop. It was scribbled all over; years ago someone had written 'Sex? Fuck my mum', and it was still there. Mad round here, thought Carlene; she was sick of it, been here all her life. She wanted to move out Purley way, get a nice modern semi, start again: only this time she wouldn't be a miserable cow, she'd do him nice dinners, chicken with gravy, and she'd be all smiley and come the night time she'd have a see-through lacy negligee and she wouldn't be too knackered and she'd let him snog her, even if he'd just had a fried egg. Be all right in Purley. Just then Ted woke up, waaaaagh, waaaagh, bloody men thought Carlene, and the number twelve came round the corner.

It isn't easy getting on a bus with a buggy and a screaming red-faced toddler, but there was a little old woman who gave her a hand and then squashed herself down next to Carlene on the bottom deck, even though there were plenty of empty seats. 'He's a bonny lad, I never had any of my own,' she chirped. Oh, here we go, thought Carlene, just my luck, another of them nutters from the loony bin. That was another thing about living round here, the psychos, all running round shouting their nonsense. When they moved to Purley, she'd get Danny to buy her a little runaround, one of them little Puntos, and she'd never have to get on a bus again.

Baby Ted's nappy felt heavy under her arm. 'Think he might have crapped up, love,' said the old woman. 'See, that's something I've not minded missing out on. Mind you, the old man's skiddies were bad enough,' and with that she pulled out her handkerchief with its smell of lily of the valley, and spent the rest of the journey with it pressed up to her nose. 'Pooh, what have you been feeding him, love? Don't half pong? Still, least you know it's him. When you get to my age and you get a whiff of shit, you think, oh here we go, that's the last of me faculties gone for a burton,' and the old lady cackled. 'Eh, you've got to laugh, 'cos life's one long turd, dear, then you die.' This last thought set her off again. 'Hyukhyukhyuk, I'm seventy-two and I've still got all me own teeth. I've not gone gaga yet, and I've not got rubber sheets on me bed like some of them. Mind you, half of them are just lazy; rather lie there in their own piss than get up and visit the kazi, idle buggers.'

'Do you happen to know what the nearest stop for Lark Grove is?' Carlene asked.

'Do I,' the little woman snorted. 'I used to live there, big posh house, with my friend Lady Edwina – though she weren't no friend, she were a right bitch.'

There, thought Carlene, I was right, raving bonkers this one; unfortunately the petite pensioner seemed to be able to read her mind.

'I'm not fibbing, love, a pink house it was, I'm popping up there as it happens, see my friend Brenda; she's a nice woman, got a mentally retarded son, Raymond. I'll walk you up, love, mind I'm only going to number sixty-three. I don't like going up by the Pink House, gives me the willies. Here we go, darling, this is us.'

The old lady helped Carlene with Ted again. For an old woman she was quite strong: like a miniature lady wrestler, she began to kung fu the buggy till it popped open. 'There you go, pet.' Carlene put Ted into the buggy; he was too heavy to carry, his nappy would have weighed at least a stone by itself. 'My name's Myrtle,' the old woman informed Carlene. 'Can I push?' Carlene relinquished the buggy handles to the wiry Mrs Pepperpot character.

'I'm Carlene and this is baby Ted. Mind the dog shit!' Dog shit apart, this was a very nice road. It wasn't like most places in the neighbourhood, it was like being on holiday in another town.

All the front doors had steps going up to them; some of them had rinsed milk bottles standing guard on the top step. Carlene didn't realise that people still got milk delivered; the last milkman round their way had got stabbed over his yoghurt money and that put a stop to that.

In one of the front gardens, a grey-haired woman was kneeling on the grass, picking up snails and throwing them into a shallow wooden basket. Her front window was open and from somewhere indoors, Carlene could hear that tune they used to advertise pant liners – or was it Cadbury's Flake?

'Nice here,' she said to Myrtle. She wished she'd put on some better shoes, the ones she was wearing were all cracked and you could see the bulges of her toes through them. 'So you lived in a big Pink House?' The way she said it sounded like she was talking to Roxanne. Mind you, Myrtle was probably only a couple of feet bigger than Roxy.

'I did too, so there,' snapped Myrtle. 'When the old lady snuffed it, some bloke and his missus bought the place. My friend Brenda says they've done it up very modern inside. They've a little lad too and a girl.'

'That's like me,' said Carlene, and she went on to tell Myrtle about Roxanne and before she knew it she'd told Myrtle all about her mum dying.

'Oh dear,' said Myrtle. 'Would you like a Pontefract cake?' She offered Carlene a paper bag; all the liquorice had stuck together.

'No thanks,' said Carlene, 'I'm on a diet.'

Suddenly Myrtle stopped walking. 'Well, this is where my friend lives. Nice meeting you dear. Ta-ta little chap,' and she popped a Pontefract cake into Ted's mouth, which made him cry his eyes out. 'See, I'd have been rubbish with kiddies.'

Carlene took the dribbly black sweet out of Ted's mouth but

he kept on spitting as if the taste was still there and all the spit was dark grey so that was his nice pale blue t-shirt all messy. By the time she had sorted out the traumatised toddler, Myrtle had disappeared inside a bright yellow door. Batty, that one, Carlene reckoned, and she pushed Ted further up the hill. There was something very familiar about the coloured houses, Carlene was sure she'd seen them before. She stood on the opposite side of the road and wondered what she should do next. There was a silver Polo parked in the drive; she could slash the tyres, but she hadn't brought any slashing equipment. Damn.

One moment she was standing against some railings on one side of the road, the next she was knocking on the front door of the Pink House and there was a roaring in her ears like she was standing under a waterfall. A big ginger-haired woman answered the door. 'Yes?' she said in a funny accent. What was it, was it Scottish? No . . . Irish, this woman was Irish. Danny didn't like ginger nuts, apart from Nicole Kidman, and there was no way this woman could be mistaken for Nicole Kidman, even on a foggy night and from a distance. Who the hell was she? Carlene opened her mouth, she had no idea what was going to fall out of it, 'Is Marsha in?' Marsha – where had that come from? Carlene didn't know any Marshas; neither did this woman judging by the confusion on her face.

'Marsha, no.'

Carlene had another go. 'Marsha Cunningham?' she garbled.

'No.' The ginger piece shook her head. 'It's Anna and Chris Cunningham that live here.'

Suddenly there was a voice coming from upstairs, 'Who is it, Sinaed?' and a pair of feet appeared on the top stair; they were wearing little snakeskin kitten-heel boots under blue jeans. They came down a step.

'Wrong address, Mrs C,' this Sinaed shouted over her meaty shot-putter's shoulder.

'Did you put the car keys back?' asked snakeskin boots.

'Yeah, in the bowl on the mantelpiece.'

As Sinaed turned sideways, Carlene got a glimpse of the hallway; it was big enough for a piano, an old one painted white, with pink candles in holders on either side. The floor was uncarpeted, plain scrubbed boards, like on a boat, and there was a dark wooden table pushed up against one wall under a big gold mirror with its frame all peeling and the glass all mottled. Probably an antique, Carlene thought.

'Sorry,' the redhead said in that voice that made Carlene think of pints of Guiness, 'I t'ink you've got the wrong house,' and she shut the door.

Carlene looked at her watch. It had been a present from Danny; he'd lifted it from the bedside table of a loft conversion in Clapham. Nearly time to collect Roxy, she'd make it if she was lucky, if she ran. Carlene trotted down the hill and crossed the road to the bus stop. Come on, bloody number twelve, come on, come on, as if miraculously a large, red double-decker bus would streak round the corner like a race horse on its last lap of the Grand National. It didn't; she waited twenty minutes, weeping hot tears of frustration and fury. That bitch in the snakeskin boots didn't have to wait for poxy buses, not Lady Muck, oh no, she'd just park her size ten bum in the driver's seat of her Polo and vroooom off, bitch, bitch, bitch.

She was twenty minutes late picking up Roxanne; they tried to fine her a quid. 'Fuck off,' said Carlene, and they decided to let it go this once. By the time the three of them got home, the shit in Ted's nappy was squashed as flat as a pancake; it looked like pastry pooh that had been flattened with a rolling pin and it reached from halfway down his legs to the small of his back.

Carlene didn't know where to hide the cheque. In the end she slid it behind a framed photo of her mum; Danny would know better than to go mucking about with that. In the photo, Carlene's mum was smiling and pointing at the camera; she had Roxanne and baby Ted on her knee and her arm looked quite normal. It had been less than a year since it had been taken. Had he been fucking that Anna cow back then?

48

Appetite Vs Libido

Things were very dull after Danny stopped coming round to play. It meant I could concentrate on work a bit more, but wouldn't you just know it, as soon as Danny was out of the picture, Maggie went and found a lump in her breast and got completely hysterical about it. I told her it would be something and nothing, but whenever she thought I wasn't looking she would slide her hand down the inside of her top, surreptitiously checking to feel if it was still there.

'Normally I get a bit lumpy just before my period, but they die down. This one's just stayed; it's hard.'

'Does it hurt?' I asked.

'No,' she replied.

'Well then, what are you moaning about?'

Only I was wrong. Lumps aren't like hearts; it's the ones that don't hurt that you have to worry about.

So she went to the doctor and the doctor wasn't happy, so she went to a clinic and the clinic wasn't happy, so she went into hospital and she had the lump removed and you'd think that would be the end of it but no, she had to have a course of radiation or something and she said it made her feel sick and the business started to suffer. We just weren't delivering; she kept turning things down because she didn't feel as if she could cope. I thought she was being a bit selfish really, and I was a bit pissed off because she didn't trust me to handle everything. In the end I confronted her about it, and she went mumbling on about me not having been 'one hundred per cent committed recently' and blah blah blah.

Then she went to have a lie down. She was really low; her hair was coming out. I didn't think that was such a bad thing; she had a nice little face and I'd been telling her to have her silly hair cropped for ages.

But I still went in; I still sat there, whilst she lay upstairs not talking to anyone. I sat in that bloody office and waited for calls that hardly ever came. I mean, they'd caught it early enough, she was going to be fine; it wasn't as if they'd had to take the whole tit off or anything really dramatic. Sometimes I'd get so bored, I'd creep up to Maggie's kitchen and have a little pick at whatever was in the fridge. She'd lost her appetite so Mike kept going to posh delicatessens and buying her little treats: roasted artichokes in olive oil, fat Greek olives and lashings of smoked salmon, mmm yum. I developed a real taste for mini stuffed vine leaves and chicken tikka pieces. I think that's when I started to put on a little weight. It didn't seem to matter: I wasn't seeing

Danny any more, I wasn't competing with a young man's body, I wasn't making love in broad daylight. So what if I ate chips? I have never had a weight problem until recently.

The truth of it was that I was bored. There're only so many shoes you can buy on a reduced income, and now that Maggie and I weren't getting any big contracts, I was down to pennies. Obviously I still had a joint account with Chris, but he was so mean, scrutinising every bill like a hawk. 'LK Bennett, how much?' I've always used my own money for treats, it saved explanations. Household bills were Chris's concern; every penny I ever earned I always frittered on myself. I had the most marvellous shoe collection: some weren't practical enough to be called shoes, you couldn't walk in them. I had kitten heels, stiletto spikes, chunky wedges and a pair of suede JP Tod's in every colour available. I had delicately embroidered dancing pumps and big, black leather motorcycle boots; even my slippers were little, gold-beaded extravagances.

But shoes are pricey and donuts are cheap. You can buy donuts everywhere: little mini jam-filled ones from Marks, great big custardy ones from the local garage. When you haven't been in the habit of eating confectionary, it's quite a surprise to find out what a variety there is. Before Danny left me, I could take or leave chocolate. There were new bars on the block that I'd never even tasted: fabulous concoctions of shortbread and toffee crisp, nougat and hazelnut. I began to collect empty wrappers in the bottom of my handbag. It was always a shock to find them there; it was like having another woman's handbag. It was as if my taste buds, having lain dormant for so long, had been brought back to life and after years of denial and neglect required constant stimulation. As my appetite increased, my libido shrivelled; sometimes I thought my clitoris might have simply dropped off, dead as an old tooth. When I pictured it, I conjured up one of those disgusting pellets that owls regurgitate.

For a while after Danny dumped me, I made sure that I continued to look fabulous, just in case he popped by. A little Touche Eclat under my eyes; my father's famous purple bags were beginning to stake their inheritance, whilst the pinched little furrows that I was used to seeing on my mother's face invaded mine. A couple of times I caught sight of myself and had to look again to check it was me, and when I had to admit ownership of my reflection I would pull in my stomach and put my shoulders back before I dared look again. Jed started to peel skin care samples out of my glossy magazines and suggest I 'at least give it a go'. There is not much to do for a woman in her forties when her career has curled up its toes, her children are at school and she has a big strong Irish girl running around doing all the domestic paraphernalia.

I started going to the cinema, secretly in the afternoon, a big tub of popcorn on my lap, a bucket of Coke by my side. Sometimes, in the dark, I would unbutton my jeans; the zip had started to leave a livid indentation on my belly. For the first time in my life I bought myself a pair of trousers with a drawstring waist; I kidded myself they were fashionable. Ha, let me give you one piece of advice girls: once you can fit into a pair of size ten Levi's, make sure you wear them every day. It's a bit like touching your toes; if you don't do it on a daily basis, there comes a time when it's physically impossible. I tried on my jeans the other day: I just about got them over my knees. I don't cry as a rule, not over silly little things, but I broke down and sobbed over my 501s.

49

Ifs and Buts

I sometimes wonder what our lives would have been like if we had never met the Cunninghams. It's as if ever since we became friends, all this became inevitable. It would be nice to cheat fate now and again. If we hadn't moved down from Scotland after we graduated, if we hadn't been able to afford Lark Grove, if Georgina had gone to the state nursery. So many ifs and just as many buts.

Time goes so fast, like the blinking of an eye. One moment you have twenty-twenty vision, the next you can hardly see the E on the optician's screen. Like with the kids: one minute they are so tiny, the next they are stashing pornography under the bed (Henry) and whiffing of Silk Cut (Georgina).

You can't freeze time; this is something I have had to learn. If I could, when would I have stopped it? Before Nigel was unfaithful? No, because then we wouldn't have had Georgina; oh yes, he managed to slip in a quick affair whilst I was still breast-feeding Henry. I never for a moment thought it wasn't my fault. I think I've always taken the blame. Sometimes I think that if I had been a better friend to Anna, if she had trusted me more, she might have told me what was going on and I could have controlled it. I could have sat her down and weighed up the pros and cons of the affair.

Pro: you are having wonderful sex.

Con: it's with someone else's husband.

Pro: it's doing wonders for your skin and hair.

Con: you will get found out and it will end in tears.

People get up to the maddest things. Read the problem pages in the tabloids and decide whether to laugh or weep. Tabloid people are forever having it off with their boyfriend's dad or their sister's husband; they never know who the father of the baby might be or what colour it's going to turn out.

Compared to most, my life has been quite dull: three lovers, one husband, two children, one miscarriage, parents still alive, one appendix scar, myopia, cellulite, thin hair, fat thighs, brittle nails. That's me. Many people ricochet through their lives lurching from one disaster to another; I'm just not the type to go looking for trouble. There are so many good books one can read instead.

I shoplifted when I was a teenager – there, at last something to blot my copybook. I wasn't very good at it though, I was too short-sighted. I remember once I was trying to nick a chewing gum from the wire rack next to the till: I leant close and managed to swipe a Juicy Fruit but as I turned to leg it, the wire rack containing the gum got caught on the button of my jacket and I had to run down the street with this bloody contraption bouncing off my chest, leaving a trail of Wrigley's all the way to my backdoor. I never did it again. My father would have had me put against a wall and shot.

Nigel's past has been very different from mine: one dead sister, two living-dead parents, numerous one-night stands – ah, but only one wife, and, as far as I know, just the same two kids. He also has an ex-cocaine-problem, two crowned teeth, a widow's peak and a recent astigmatism in his left eye.

Anna's past is a hundred lovers, one red-haired husband, two children – one fat, one thin – a thirty-fag-a-day-habit, an escalating drink problem and the ability to be a thorough pain in the backside. She also used to be beautiful, funny and on occasions incredibly warm. She used to dole her kindness out to me in small portions at irregular intervals: just when I was becoming starved of any affection from her, she would laugh at one of my jokes or stick up for me or say that I looked nice. The rationing of her compassion made me want it more; I'd bask in it when it was delivered. She did the same with Pandora, occasionally giving the child her full-on love and attention. She could make you glow.

Maybe that's why I wanted her to be my friend. I have never been short of love; I was very secure as a child. My mother, despite being a bit mad, loved my brother and me to pieces, and my father was devoted. I was always popular at school. Nowadays shopkeepers and neighbours like me; where I live loads of people say hello, 'Hello, Jo, hi there.' Anna was like a difficult dog: the fact that I knew I was one of the chosen few, that she wouldn't bite me, made me feel special.

I remember Brenda Donahue talking to me about Anna years ago. 'She's a good-looking girl . . . ' and the sentence hovered in mid-air. 'But,' I added for her, 'she's lacking in the compassion department, went back for seconds in looks and couldn't be bothered to queue for kindness.' I'd have liked to have tried to explain Anna to Brenda; the fact that she only liked attractive things and how ugliness bothered her. But it would have sounded rude; she'd have realised that I was talking about Raymond. Raymond will be thirty next year; his heart is in a bad way. He has never bothered me: his skate-on-a-plate eyes, his untrained erections and dribbly mouth, he is just Raymond, but I knew he upset Anna. Anna once asked me, if I was to get pregnant again and I found out there was something wrong with it, would I keep it? It depends, I replied, I could cope with missing limbs and deafness, possibly mild brain damage – a sweet little blind one. What about you, I ventured? 'Well . . . If I knew it was going to have red hair, I'd have an abortion.' She must have noticed my face because she added, 'Just joking.' Back then, when I gave her the benefit of the doubt, I believed her: now I am not so sure.

Everything Anna has done to amuse herself has backfired. Thank Christ the kids are away for the summer. I miss them horribly, even Georgina's tantrums. They have gone to stay in Devon with some people who, to be honest, we don't know very well. Sometimes I feel sick when I think about it. When I waved them off, I thought if anything happens to them, if they are killed on the motorway, then that will be it: I shall simply slit my wrists. I wouldn't have to think twice about it; I would hack at my veins with a rusty baked-bean tin lid, if I had to.

The strangers to whom I have entrusted my children are called the Morrises. Their son Matthew joined Henry's class last term, a nice lad by all accounts; they have a daughter too, an eleven-year-old who will be going to Georgina's school in September. I met the mother, Angela Morris, at Henry's sports day. She sat next to me and roared encouragement at her son for two hours; neither of our husbands was present. We had tea together afterwards in the funny Turkish cafe near the boys' school. I liked her because even though she'd just had a cream tea, she ordered one of those peculiar Turkish cakes that look like shredded wheat drenched in honey. She got a good deal of the cake stuck in her big horsy teeth. The boys sat at a table as far away from us as possible, sniggering and eating sugar lumps. The girl, who just the previous day had had four molars removed in preparation for a brace, was stoically reading a book about ponies with a hanky clutched to her mouth; she was still bleeding slightly from the gum but she didn't complain. Lucy, she was called. I liked her, she reminded me of myself as a child: slightly overeager, the opposite of Georgina, who has been practising ennui since she could walk. By the time we'd had four cups of bitter black coffee and the caffeine rush was affecting my pulse, she'd offered to have Henry for a few weeks in the summer holidays, 'We have a farmhouse in Devon.' I never thought I'd take her up on it; I didn't think that I'd end up begging her to take Georgina too. But I did; it was the only solution to our domestic madness. I had to do something. I realised it was the only sensible option when Anna quite calmly announced over the breakfast table that, 'Whenever you make love to a man, you should wait until they are on the brink of orgasm and then shove your finger right up their bumhole, as it makes for a more intense sexual experience.' It's not the sort of thing teenagers need to hear, not when they've got their GCSEs to worry about. Thank God Henry sat his exams before all this blew up in our faces: The Geneva Convention, Dickens' use of simile and the declension of Latin verbs are confusing enough without the distraction of some pre-menopausal harpy rampaging round the house.

Sometimes you have to trust your instincts; Angela Morris seemed a capable woman, there was a no-nonsense way about her. 'You mustn't worry about them,' she said. 'I've managed to drag my two up without losing any limbs.'

'Ha ha,' we laughed, but I had tears in my eyes.

50

Carlene's Revenge

Carlene was not having a good time, in fact she couldn't remember the last time that she had. A little blister that had come up on Roxanne's belly had evolved into full-blown chickenpox. Big weeping sores covered the child's entire body; she looked like something special effects would dream up for *Casualty*. They were up her nostrils, in her hairline, on the roof of her mouth, up her bum and under the soles of her feet. Danny said that if she scratched them and ended up scarred it would be Carlene's fault. All she could do was soak 'the spotty one' in calamine lotion and cut her nails very short so that she couldn't tear her skin. On the third day of spilt Calpol and no sleep, baby Ted woke up with one of the blisters on his eyelid; within an hour seven more had appeared. You could see them surface; by lunchtime he was infested. Poor Ted, he cried and cried and cried until they all had headaches and Carlene felt that she'd gone blind in one eye. Sometimes she got migraines.

Danny was useless, of course; he was terrified that he might catch it.

'You must know if you've had chickenpox,' Carlene yelled.

'No, I don't,' Danny yelled back, and he went stomping off to the pub. When he got back, he was in a much better mood; according to his mum they'd all had it. 'All three of us and it was Christmas *and* the sitting-room ceiling fell down, so I don't know what you've got to moan about.' But he decided to sleep on the sofa anyway. 'Them sheets could do with a wash, Carlene.'

Roxanne was back in her own bed. Some of the scabs were starting to fall off, leaving little crusty lids all over the house. Ted was sleeping in with Carlene: he was hot and fretful and he couldn't suck his dummy because it hurt his mouth. Carlene's head was getting worse. At midnight she threw up. She needed some Migralieve; if she didn't get some, she'd be like this for days. She woke Danny. 'Please, Dan, can you get me some pills for my head? It's killing me.' But Danny couldn't take the van to the all-night junkie chemist down the green, cos he'd had too much to drink – couldn't risk losing his licence, be mental. So Carlene took the van keys, and even though she could see out of only one eye, and it was the short-sighted one, she didn't bother fetching her glasses. Carlene was wearing a stinky pair of leggings and an Arsenal shirt; just before she went out, she put a beige bat-winged leather jacket on top – good, now she looked really horrible. As she left the house, she banged the door on purpose hoping to wake baby Ted. She paused under the front door; the bedroom window was directly above. SLAM. One, two, before she'd counted to three, he was off – waaagh – sounding like the beginning of a seventies glam rock song by The Sweet. Carlene scuttled down the path and locked herself into Danny's works van. There was shit all over it: empty Coke cans, burger wrappers, polystyrene coffee cups; he was a pig. Her dad's van wasn't like this; his was all tidy, just a bag of wine gums in the glove compartment.

Carlene was not a great driver: she was too cautious, she didn't like overtaking and she didn't really like turning right into oncoming traffic. Sometimes she arranged her journeys so that she only had to turn left. Still, at midnight it was quiet, she could be back in twenty minutes.

The junkie chemist was no more than half a mile away; it stayed open twenty-four hours, doling out methadone prescriptions for thin people with twitchy faces and blue marks down their arms. Smack heads were the pits. Danny's little brother was on it; they'd not seen him since Roxanne was a new-born and he'd come round and nicked the baby listener.

She drove the back route, avoiding the big hill that sometimes meant having to put the handbrake on and then having to decide when to release it. Carlene hated hill starts; she was unconfident about what her father had referred to as 'biting point'. She always had to hold her breath on an incline.

'Packet of Migralieve, mixed, a large bottle of baby Calpol with sugar and I'll have them bibs.' They were on offer: five bibs for £3.50, just little cheap, thin towelling ones. She hadn't a clue why she was buying them; she used a plastic one for Ted, a blue one that curled up at the end so all the bits dropped into it. Sod it, she could pay by cheque. She picked up a Rimmel eyeliner and a pearly pink nail varnish.

'That it?'

'Yeah.' There was no one else in the shop. The girl behind the counter was Asian, tiny thing, looked about fifteen, but there was a big Alsatian dog curled up on the floor by her feet. Not very hygienic. Carlene didn't like dogs, she always told Roxanne not to pet them; she didn't need her face chewing off even if it was going to be covered in big chickenpox scars. Carlene got back in the van and took three pink Migralieve out of the packet. There was a big plastic bottle of water in the passenger footwell; she wrestled off the lid and was just about to swig some down when she realised it was turps. She needed a drink but she wasn't that desperate. She threw the pills down her throat dry and managed to swallow them without choking. Then she drove round the roundabout twice, for the hell of it, and headed home.

She would have turned right, she would have gone back the way she'd come, but suddenly there was a big lorry and she didn't think she'd get across the road in time so she turned left. She could still get back on to the main road if she went up the hill, past Sainsbury's and over the top way. Carlene gripped the wheel as tightly as if she were on a fairground ride as she drove up the hill. She didn't know how she'd done it, but she'd got into a filter lane; she wanted to go straight on but she couldn't, and when the arrow pointing right turned green, she followed its direction. Where the hell was she? She took the first turning on the left and stopped the van. Before she even looked for an *A-Z*, she knew where she was: she was at the top of Lark Grove and she could see the Pink House.

Carlene sat for a good thirty minutes just thinking and painting her nails with the new nail varnish. It was quite nice; she didn't often get time to herself. She saw something slope across the road; the pills were beginning to work, she could see better out of her left eye now. It was a fox, an old one, its red fur tinged with grey, with something in its mouth. She hoped it wasn't a rabbit; when she was a little girl her pet bunny Rosemary had been killed by a fox. Her dad hadn't let her see. He'd gone out with a mop and a bucket and some newspaper. Later she'd lifted the lid off the dustbin and there was all blood and fur poking out of the paper.

It had been a long time since Carlene had been out this late; these days she was forever nodding off halfway through *The Bill*. She was so tired and she was so miserable: no wonder her husband had . . . It was nearly one o'clock and she wondered if Danny was worried. She doubted it; he'd had a skinful judging by the state of him.

A couple were walking up the hill; they were staggering slightly and they kept stopping to kiss each other, every five steps a snog. As they drew up almost level with the van, they started groping under a street lamp. She could see the white of the girl's skin as her t-shirt rode up. There was a smothered giggle and they were gone. She and Danny used to be like that.

Suddenly Carlene got out of the van. It wasn't her idea, it was as if she were being operated by someone else. It was like when she was little and her dad had got her a load of string puppets, marionettes they were called, they had wooden heads: one was a girl who looked like Heidi with yellow plaits, the other was a boy with a green felt hat. She'd played with them for ages till the strings got all tied up and they were more trouble than they were worth. Funny, she'd forgotten all about them.

By the time Carlene stopped thinking about puppets, she was halfway up the steps of the Pink House. What on earth was she doing? Actually, she was opening the packet of bibs – which was a bit silly because the nail varnish was still tacky – then she realised she was soaking the bibs with the turps. What a strange thing to be doing. It was like she was following some half-forgotten recipe, she had all the ingredients, she'd even brought the bottle of turps from the car – what on earth for? Oh yes, to soak the bibs: one, two, three, four, five – now what was meant to happen? She had five soaking bibs. Tie them together, that was a good idea. They had different coloured strings: red, blue, yellow, green, orange. There that was that bit done, what next? Nothing, nothing would have happened next, but the lighter was in the pocket of her leather jacket, so she pushed the bibs through the letterbox and set fire to the one on the end; it was the one with the orange trim and a picture of building bricks badly printed on the front. They weren't very good bibs, see the way they caught fire. You wouldn't want one of those around a baby's neck. The bib blazed for a second then it died down; there wasn't much of a flame, just a blue flicker, be out in a minute. No harm done, and Carlene sniggered at the thought of old snakeskin boots coming down in the morning to find a load of soggy bibs all tied together like bunting for a babies' carnival.

Back in the van, she giggled all the way home. At one point she went through a red light, which made her laugh even more. This was great, she didn't even have a headache any more.

When Carlene got home, Danny was flat out on the sofa, fast asleep with his hand in his underpants. Carlene took another couple of Migralieve and got into bed. She slept very well for the first time in weeks. In the morning Roxanne climbed in under the covers and said, 'Pooh, Mummy, you smell funny.' It was the turps. Carlene sniffed her hands. Oh well, forget it; it was over now.

Only it wasn't. It would have been, but what with one thing and another, events last night had shunted into each other like cars on a fog-bound motorway. If the bibs hadn't been on offer, if they hadn't been so absorbent, if the bottle of turps had been water, if a lazy teenager hadn't just hours before shoved a whole bundle of Indian takeaway leaflets through the letterbox of the Pink House, if the varnish on the hall table had been fire resistant: if, if, if, if. But they were, it hadn't, he had and it wasn't. Oh dear.

51

Down the Ladders

It had been a normal Friday evening, nothing untoward. The usual Indian takeaway in front of *Frasier*, bed by eleven; life isn't very exciting when you are no longer fornicating with the odd job man. I had the chicken jalfrezi, Chris had his biriyani, the kids shared a korma and we all had pilau rice, poppadums, cucumber raitha and sag bhajee. With Sinaed away in Ireland I didn't even bother to tidy away the foil containers; I thought, I can do that in the morning. I was planning to do rather a lot of things in the morning: I wanted to go to Gap to sort out the kids' summer clothes as it was nearly the holidays. We drank lager and then I had some red wine: I wasn't very pissed, I just had to be a bit careful going upstairs. Chris stayed downstairs for a while: maybe he watched a documentary about lesbian porn stars on Channel 5, but he probably didn't. I heard him lock up; by the time he got into bed I was already rolled up like an armadillo on my side of the mattress. I hadn't cleaned my teeth and the Indian was causing havoc with my lower intestine: I was pumping out long quiet farts, it must have been like getting into a train carriage full of sarin. He read for ten minutes; one of his boring hardback books about World War Two fighter planes that he gets Jo to buy for him from book fairs. His gold-rimmed glasses had slid down his nose, and the way he was propped up gave him a quadruple chin. Eventually, he turned off the light and rolled on to his side, taking all the duvet with him. Snnnprr Snrrr prrhhh, pffff, pafff. He snored and I farted.

The next thing I remember was the smell of burning and a crackling like crisp packets. 'Chris.' I poked him hard. I have a better sense of smell than he has. 'Chris.'

'Ungh wha . . . ungh.'

'Chris, wake up. I think the house might be on fire.' Well, that did the trick; he was out of bed like a nuclear rocket, a semi hard-on poking out from under his belly like an exclamation mark!

I couldn't remember what I was meant to do; I couldn't remember if it was a good idea to open the windows – then I realised that I couldn't because they were locked anyway.

'I'll get the children,' he said, but he put on some trousers first. The lights weren't working. 'Wet some towels,' he shouted, and I tripped to the en suite thinking, see, this extra bathroom was a good idea after all. I picked up a bundle of towels, dropped them in the bath and turned the cold tap on full. He grabbed one and wrapped it round his face, and then he opened the bedroom door.

I could see the smoke. I could see an orange glow; it looked like a sunset in Fiji but it smelt like the end of the world. I could tell it was just the ground floor but I didn't know how fast it would travel. I was actually very frightened. I have never wanted to die by fire or by water; when I do die, I want it to be very quick.

The children were terrified; Pandora seemed to have lost the use of her legs and Chris carried her into our bedroom. Jed followed clutching his jewellery box. Fortunately, Chris knew where his mobile was; it had been charging, so he grabbed it off the floor and called the fire brigade. I am sure they could hear Pandora screaming in the background; maybe they even heard me tell her to shut up. They certainly took it seriously. Chris had a quick look down the stairs; you could feel the heat rising and it was very difficult to keep calm. He came back into the bedroom and said it wasn't going to be possible to get out.

I think that's when I had to run to the toilet; I had rather bad diarrhoea. I only just made it and, wouldn't you know, there was no loo roll. Oh great, I thought, the indignity of it: dying with a shitty arse. I grabbed the shirt I'd been wearing earlier and used that – shame really, it was a nice one from Liberty's. Chris wedged the rest of the wet towels into the crack under the bedroom door and then we sat and waited.

Jed started singing *Ten Green Bottles* but he stopped at nine. I don't know which was worse: listening to Jed singing in a rather high-pitched overwrought way or the silence that followed, during which we could hear the house blister. Pandora started praying: 'Our father who art in heaven, Hallowed be thy name, Thy kingdom come, Thy will be done, For ever and ever, Amen,' which added a weirdly surreal touch to the proceedings. Chris kept saying, 'It's all right, chicken, we'll get out of this,' and then he had us strip the bed and start tying the duvet cover to the bottom sheet, which I think was therapeutic rather than useful.

We heard the siren before the fire engine came up the street; it was very reassuring. We all gathered at the window and watched it pull up outside the house. The lights in the windows opposite came on, and within seconds people were streaming out of their houses. The firemen were shouting and Chris took the angle-poise, from his bedside table, and put it through the glass so that it was dangling out of the smashed window, still attached to the plug in the wall. 'We're up here. There are four of us. Please hurry!' and Pandora added a few self-conscious 'helps'. The ladders clattered up the side of the house. Our bedroom has two big windows; Chris had broken the one on the left, the ladders went up under the one on the right and a man's voice shouted at us to move away whilst they knocked it out. There was glass all over and Chris threw the duvet and my lovely satin bedspread on top of the big jagged shards so that we didn't cut our feet. In a crisis he was proving to be very sensible. It was odd seeing the fireman talking to us at the windowsill; it was rather as if he'd popped up for a chat. I felt bad that I hadn't got a cup of tea for him. 'Shall we have you out then?' He had a Northern accent – they're always rather comforting, aren't they? 'We'll have you down in a jiffy, let's take the little lad first,' and Chris picked up Jed and passed him out of the window as if he were a roll of lino. The fireman seemed to carry him down under one arm. I could hear people clapping when they got to the ground. 'Right, who's next?' He sounded like a grocer serving people in a shop, 'Pound of tomatoes, love?' Pandora suddenly froze on the windowsill; I might have given her a little push. 'Go on, Pandora. Do you want your father and I to burn to death?' She cut her leg climbing out; the fireman actually had her over his shoulder, her big fat bum in the air. Another fireman came up for me; I think the first one had probably slipped a disc carrying my daughter to safety.

Suddenly it all became more urgent: there was a massive crack from somewhere below and flames shot out, lighting up the garden and the faces of the crowd on the street. They had the hoses going; it was very loud but I heard Jo shouting, 'Anna, Anna.' I'd pulled on a denim skirt earlier and I had to hitch it up around my middle as I climbed out on to the ladder. The man held me tightly round the waist; I could feel the spray of the hose as we slithered down, and suddenly I was in my front garden. The front door was lying flaming in the hallway and the stairs were being eaten alive. I must have fainted because the next thing I knew I was lying in an ambulance and as Chris came staggering up the steps Pandora threw herself at him. 'Hush, chicken, hush. Didn't I tell you it was going to be okay?' Then they closed the doors and the ambulance pulled away; after all, there was 'no point hanging about,' as the paramedic in the green overalls said, 'it wasn't a pretty sight.'

By the time we got to the hospital, I was cursing myself for not having my handbag; I really could have done with some lipstick and a comb.

52

Luck and Ladybirds

Living where we do, one gets used to hearing sirens, seeing flashing blue lights whizzing up and down the road. I have seen policemen leaping out of their panda cars, grabbing at legs fast disappearing over garden walls. There's a lot of it about: burglary, drugs, knifings – they say most of them have guns nowadays. You have to be careful; if in doubt, keep your trap shut.

I have stopped shouting at strangers for dropping litter. I never used to be nervous. Last week, I was walking up the street and a lad on a pushbike cycled past on the pavement, shoving me into the wall. 'You're a big lad,' I shouted, 'ride your bike on the road not the pavement.' I expected him to flick me a V sign and keep going, but he didn't; he wheeled the bike round and rode back at me. Once we were level, he gobbed in my face. I could taste his spit on my lips and all sorts of things like hepatitis B went through my mind. Three times he spat, calling me a cunt and a bitch. I remember saying, 'Come on, let's not be silly.' I sounded like Penelope Keith, all posh and ridiculous, but I was very frightened, and he was younger than Henry. In the end he rode the bike hard at my legs and told me how next time he would stick a knife in my face. I was too scared to go home in case he was watching to see where I lived; I just kept walking till he'd gone.

We have been burgled twice but compared to other people we have got off lightly: no pooh on the walls, no tortoise in the microwave, no budgie's head upon the pillow.

I knew a woman who went away to Morocco; when she got back someone had been in and nicked the marble fireplaces, the chandeliers, the dining-room table with six matching chairs, a massive statue of a lion from the back garden and a couple of bay trees. Now you can't imagine that lot being easily fobbed off in the pub.

My car has been broken into three times; they always leave my tapes, though personally, I can't see what's wrong with Kirsty McColl and the *Eurythmics Greatest Hits*. We do what we can: window locks and mortices, handbags under coats, jewellery hidden, lights on timers and alarms all over.

Nah nee nah nee nah nee – whenever I hear a fire engine, I always remember the rhyme, 'Ladybird, ladybird, fly away home, your house is on fire, your children are gone.' When I was little, I thought ladybirds must be the saddest creatures ever. It's everyone's worst nightmare fire, isn't it? Especially in these big, tall houses that we live in, with their narrow stairs and locked windows overlooking concrete paving and spiky railings. A long time ago

I bought a smoke alarm, but I took the batteries out because it kept going off whenever I fried bacon. Now I have one on every landing, but I still get up in the middle of the night to check the ashtrays, make sure the iron isn't on and that the cooker is off. With Anna the way she is, you can't be too careful.

You'd have thought she'd learned her lesson, waking up like she did at two o'clock in the morning, the walls on fire, smoke billowing up the stairs, her children asleep on the floor above.

She must have panicked. They say that when aeroplanes crash, they go down much slower than you'd think; people have time to crap themselves and scribble notes to their loved ones. Anna told me that Chris put on his trousers before screaming to the children, then he went to get them by crawling up the stairs with a wet towel around his face, even though it wasn't strictly necessary.

Once I set the chip pan alight, and for some reason I threw a tea towel over the flames and that just lit up too, like one of my Christmas puddings smothered in too much brandy. In the end I threw the whole lot into the fishpond; it went up like a bomb, so that meant there were three more dead carp in the morning.

When Georgina and Jed were in their parents' bedroom and the lights weren't working, Chris managed to call nine, nine, nine on his mobile. Anna said that he was very polite. 'I'm sorry to trouble you but my house is burning down and I'm stuck on the second floor with my wife and our two children, so if you wouldn't mind sending the lads round,' or words to that effect. Nah nee nah nee; three of them came swooping up the hill, emergency lights flashing like a junior disco. Nigel woke up first; he said he realised it was our street because people were coming out of their front doors and running up the road. Some of them were in such a hurry, they left their doors open. Oh silly billies. If someone had access to video playback of the street's activities that night, apart from the fire dancing round the Pink House, they would have seen a couple of lads dart into the Gregsons' and dart out again. They got away with a leather coat that was hanging over the newel post and Mrs Gregson's handbag, containing two hundred quid sterling, six hundred in traveller's cheques and two flight tickets to Gozo. Having your handbag nicked is inconvenient at any time, but the fact was that the cash and the tickets were a wedding present for their eldest daughter who was getting married the very next day! I heard all this second-hand a few days later. You have to laugh, it wasn't even the thirteenth: it was 2.00am on Friday the ninth of July.

We arrived, Nigel, Georgina, Henry and I, just as the ladders were going up the front of the house. I had a thick layer of moisturising night cream on my face and no shoes, but at least I'd remembered to put on knickers under my nightie. There was quite a crowd. The police had blocked off the road at the top and the bottom and were shouting at everyone to stand back. 'Get back. Please stay well back.' It was horribly exciting. You could see their four little white faces at the window, banging on the panes of glass. Window locks, you see; and you never keep a spare set of keys to hand, they're always downstairs in the fruit bowl, aren't they? They got Jed out first, women and children and all that. The nanny was away; I'm not sure where hired help comes in the pecking order. It was just like something out of *London's Burning*, and all the women were in a lather. It's a cliché about the sexiness of the fireman, but it's only a cliché because it's true. When they got him down, people started clapping; knowing Jed he'd have liked to have gone back up for an encore, but they carried him off to an ambulance and by the time they'd done that, Pandora was down too. The fireman had smashed the bedroom window and a jag of glass had caught her fat leg so it was bleeding quite badly, but apart from that it seemed to be going very smoothly.

When another fireman brought Anna down, she stood for a second in the front garden, looked back at the house and fainted on the spot. For a second I thought she was putting it on, but it was quickly obvious that she wasn't and really, you couldn't blame her; they'd kicked down the front door and great clouds of black smoke were pumping out of the hallway. As the water hit the flames there was a hissing noise, like adders in a frying pan. It wasn't just the heat, it was the noise and the smell. I suppose people got quite used to this sort of thing during the blitz.

Chris climbed down the ladder himself, with the fireman shielding him like a dad in case he fell; he had his weekend chinos on and a shirt but no tie, and you could see that he was shaking. They put a blanket round his shoulders and helped him into the ambulance. As it drove away, there was a terrible splintering sound and from where I was standing I could see that the staircase had collapsed on to itself and a new lot of flames sprang up out of nowhere, reminding me of those kids' birthday-cake candles that go out then relight themselves – which is supposed to be funny but is actually incredibly irresponsible of the manufacturer.

Afterwards, when the fire was truly out and all that was left was a black soggy mess and a stink of something like burnt hair and damp school blazers, we went down the hill to Brenda Donohue's and drank coffee and brandy. I think we all needed it. Raymond was very overexcited; Brenda was having a terrible job trying to get him to go to bed and at one point he got a bit violent and punched her in the face, poor Brenda.

When you think about it, there is bad luck lurking behind every closed door.

53

The Morning After

Myrtle phoned Brenda Donahue; she got Raymond, who held the phone upside down and kept shouting into the earpiece, 'Big fire, very hot, big strong firemen, all better now.' Brenda eventually wrestled the receiver off her son. 'Yes? Oh, Myrtle, oh, I'm so sorry. It was such a lovely house, and the wisteria, well, I know, such a shame, such a crying shame. We all saw it, you know, the whole street was out; it was like the Queen's Silver Jubilee. The Metcalfs came back for coffee and we had a stiff drink. Jo was beside herself, they're very good friends . . . Yes, the Cunningham woman, that's right, no, no one hurt, not badly, but they were taken to hospital, just a precaution. Yes dear, you must, I've some prawn won tons in the freezer, Raymond doesn't like them. So how did you hear? I was going to call, but we had such a late night.'

Myrtle had been watching the television. After the main news it was time for a regional update. 'And now the news and weather, wherever you're waking up this morning.' She recognised the Pink House immediately, like a mother who recognises her charred child in the burns unit – what the devil? Myrtle sat on her little divan bed, with her tights in one hand and a digestive biscuit in the other, staring at the television.

Carlene had seen the news as well; she was just about to switch over to the cartoons when the man said, 'And a mystery inferno in South London.' Danny had gone to work; it was eight o'clock. She switched over anyway; she'd rather watch vintage *Tellytubbies*. Later when she popped out to the shops with Roxanne, she picked up a copy of the local paper: 'Electrical wiring was most likely to have caused the inferno. The family survived the blaze and are recovering in King's College Hospital suffering from shock and minor smoke inhalation. Once again the Chief Fire Officer stresses the importance of smoke detectors in the home and it was thanks only to the prompt action of the local fire brigade that a major tragedy was averted.' Next to the article was a recipe for roast pigeon breasts in Pernod with fennel.

Carlene didn't know how she felt, so she decided not to think about it. She walked the kids round the market and splashed out on a very smart suitcase with wheels and a pull-out handle for their holiday. When Danny came home, she was in the kitchen cooking fish-fingers for the kids; the grill pan needed a good clean and at one point a curled tongue of flame leapt out from under the hood as if a fire-breathing lizard had been hibernating inside.

'For fuck's sake, Carlene, what are you trying to do? Burn the place down?'

Did she blush when he said that?

Carlene's hands shook as she cut up baby Ted's fish-fingers, the blackened surfaces splintering under the knife. In the end, she mashed them up in ketchup with a fork. Danny kept sneaking off to watch the telly but by the end of the day the Cunninghams' fire was no longer deemed newsworthy: after all what's one dead hamster? Nibbles had been trumped by the mugging of an old lady by a couple of teenage girls in Lewisham.

Over at King's College Hospital, Chris was rather enjoying his sponge and custard; he never got custard at home. Anna wasn't eating so he ate hers as well. Chris felt fantastic: he was alive, his family were alive, he hadn't let them perish. He was a man, a man who would rebuild his home and be a better person as a result. 'As long as we're all right,' he repeated. 'They're only things; we can buy more things, we're insured, darling. Everything will be all right; they just need to get to the bottom of it and then we can start again.' This is what happens to some people after a nasty shock, they feel immortal. Chris was enjoying every second of not being dead. As for hospital food, well, all that rubbish about it being inedible; it was manna, that's what it was, pure ambrosia. Well, he was right about that.

Jo phoned the hospital.

'Are you a relative?'

'Yes, I'm Anna's cousin,' she lied.

'Actually, it doesn't really matter: visiting hours are between six and eight.' The nurse was rather casual about the situation, as if this sort of thing happened every day in a busy London hospital – which, of course, it did. Jo felt that she was being short changed on the drama front; in some respects it would have been more exciting if the Cunninghams were perilously high up on the danger list, hovering on the brink of death and being artificially respirated in intensive care, rather than strolling round the ward, borrowing change for the payphone and complaining about the antiquity of the dog-eared magazines in the waiting room. 'Really,' Anna whinged to nobody in particular, 'what is the point of a 1993 copy of *Vogue*? It's so misleading.'

The fact that she was lucky to be alive and reading, that her eyeballs hadn't turned to liquid in the heat of the blaze, was beginning to escape her. Anna was getting used to being 'lucky to be alive', in fact she was getting thoroughly bored of it. It was time this farce was over and they could get back to being normal.

Still, Jed was enjoying himself; he'd got friendly with a young porter called Errol. Errol had two earrings and a bleached Tin Tin quiff; after lunch he took Jed into the little room where they kept the vases (jam jars and other assorted receptacles) and gave him a good tickling – after all, patient morale is very important. They were all bearing up very well, apart from Pandora who had sunk into catatonic gloom and hadn't spoken ever since Jed told her that Nibbles had been prematurely cremated. 'Poor old Nibbles, I think I heard him screaming.'

The fire officer turned up to have a little chat with Anna and Chris: had alcohol perhaps been partaken of? Might a rogue cigarette have rolled between the floorboards? Could one of the children have been playing with matches? Yes but not much, no and no. Before the officer left, Chris, trying to look dignified in a pair of frayed pyjamas with yellow stains around the crotch area, gave a small thanks-to-the-boys-in-blue speech, during which

Anna managed to yawn three times. Enough was enough; Chris was in danger of getting emotional. She interrupted him. 'We will be able to go home, won't we? We can live in it? I mean, it might be a bit smelly but we have still got a roof over our heads, haven't we?'

The fire officer's left eyebrow shot to the top of his forehead. 'Oh no, Mrs Cunningham, I don't think you've grasped the gravity of the situation. Yours, I believe, is a Georgian property: horse hair in the wall cavities, dry plaster, grease and fluff beneath the floorboards – like living in a tinderbox. I think it will be a good few months before your house will be structurally sound enough to inhabit.'

That was the first time that Anna cried, and once she started, she couldn't stop. In fact she got a little bit hysterical and the nice nurse had to give her a special little yellow pill.

'Think it's just hit her, sir,' hazarded the fire officer, backing out of the door, whilst Anna did her mad woman in the attic routine. Eventually the little yellow pill performed its magic and for the rest of the afternoon Anna slept, Pandora stared at the wall, Chris composed letters to his insurance company and Jed chased Errol in and out of the service lifts.

Jo turned up at visiting time. Nigel would have come but he had to deliver Georgina to a party in Fulham. Typical, thought a still semi-sedated Anna, that child would disco dance at a funeral. Jo had decided to deal with the Cunninghams' trauma in a practical fashion. Like refugees, there was no point in buying them flowers, they needed food and clothing and cash; so she'd nipped to British Home Stores and bought them each a set of underwear and a tracksuit. When they put them on, they looked like some weird religious cult with an unhealthy obsession for table tennis.

Chris loved his. 'Jo, you're so kind,' he stuttered, genuinely touched; he even had tears in his eyes. 'We'll pay you back. Unfortunately I seem to have left the house without my wallet, ha ha.'

'Oh, Chris,' said Jo, in a deeply sympathetic way.

Oh, Christ, thought Anna; if he was going to continue this brave little soldier act she would have to kill him. Momentarily she allowed herself to imagine what would have happened if Chris hadn't made it out of the bedroom window: she'd be a widow now, hmm. There was something rather appealing about widowhood; those Scottish ones on the telly adverts seemed to have a fantastic time smirking round hedgerows in hooded capes, looking for all the world like they were off to fuck the gardener in the orangery.

Jo handed Chris an envelope containing two hundred pounds in twenties and a little leather purse full of coins, 'for the phone and the chocolate machine.' There was something rather smug about her tone: she'd remembered everything, what a good friend she was. Chris's gratitude was in keeping with someone on dialysis who has just been offered a new kidney; if he said thank you one more time Anna would have to avail herself of one of those cardboard hats that the hospital supplied for patients to be sick into. After Jo had exhausted her supply of charitable goodwill she went home, but not without promising at least twenty times to do everything she could to help in the difficult time ahead. 'Oh, I'm sure we'll muddle through,' Chris vowed bravely, and he reached for Anna's hand to demonstrate their mutual determination to battle on, only to find that it was balled tightly into a fist.

The doctor came to check them out just before supper (coley bake with broccoli followed by tinned mandarins in jelly; Errol managed to sneak Jed an extra jelly). Mr Samarawickreme said that, all things considered, they had been very lucky, and it was all that Anna could do not to scream into his face, 'Lucky? Lucky is winning the National Lottery on rollover week, not having all your earthly possessions incinerated, you cunt.'

'So,' continued the doctor, having satisfied himself of their physical well-being, 'you can go home tomorrow. Whoops, sorry, you can't, can you? Well, I'm sure you'll sort something out . . . family . . . friends.' At this point he would normally mention the social services but there was something about the Cunningham woman that made the words 'DSS accommodation' stick in his throat. 'Well,' he continued, 'good luck,' and with a swish of his white coat he was off.

Chris had a plan up his sleeve. Really, he pondered, there was nothing quite like a near-death experience to make a chap fire on all cylinders; most invigorating. The plan involved going away for a week; he'd seen the hotel in a magazine in the television lounge, and as long as it hadn't gone dramatically downhill in the four years since the glowing reference had been issued, it would be just the ticket. 'All creature comforts in this idyllic setting close to the Dorsetshire coast, discreet yet efficient service, choice of inglenooks and open fireplaces, original flagstones and aged beams, duck pond, resident peacock and lovingly attended lawns (croquet on demand). The Pocock Arms: old-fashioned charm with a modern twist'. Yes, see, it would all be fine. Truly they were blessed. They had each other, they had the Metcalfs, they had lovely new tracksuits and a leather purse full of loose change; people have conquered the world with less, mused Chris.

It was only in the middle of the night when he realised he had no smart tie to wear in the exclusive à la carte restaurant that his confidence wavered. As he tossed and turned under patched and faintly blood-stained sheets, stamped 'Property of K. COLL. HOSPITAL', he couldn't remember if peacocks were good or bad luck.

54

Amateur Dramatics in Dorset

Chris got on to the emergency American Express service and dramatically gulped the story into their sympathetic ear. I must say, they were very impressive: a brand new platinum card was dispatched by motorcycle courier the very next day. It's amazing what a small piece of plastic can achieve – and I'm not just talking about vibrators. Chris hired a rather swish blue people carrier and decided we should all go on holiday.

We went to stay at the Pocock Arms, a very swish country-house hotel near that chalk giant with the big willy, Cerne Abbas or something. Dorset anyway, and given the circumstances we were having quite a nice time. When they knew what had happened, the owners, Bill and Heidi, upgraded us into a suite:

two bedrooms, a living-room and a fabulous bathroom complete with a Jacuzzi. Of course, in return for this generosity we were meant to look a bit stricken and miserable, which is hard when the sun is shining and you have a heated outdoor pool and tennis courts at your disposal. Luckily, Pandora managed to look traumatised enough for all of us; she was in mourning for Nibbles, even her appetite was suffering. I tried to explain that he was probably about to die anyway. They only live about three years do hamsters, and old Nibs was getting on; but it didn't seem to do much good. She moped around like a character in a Greek tragedy, wringing her hands and only eating one piece of toast at breakfast.

Because the weather was so lovely, I went into the nearest town to buy swimming costumes for us all. There was a half decent Marks and I bought myself a size twelve one-piece; I've always found their size tens a bit tight round the bust but I got a shock when I tried to get it on. Since Danny had stopped coming round, I'd been eating more than usual, and all that comfort eating had taken its toll. The backs of my legs looked like Shirley Temple's face: all dimples.

I was too embarrassed to go swimming, so I thrashed Chris round the tennis court instead. I was starving afterwards. We had tea on the lawn; scones with jam and clotted cream, yum. I was really enjoying myself till Chris, taking advantage of my good mood, tried to put his arms around me and started saying things like, 'It'll be okay, we'll come through this, you'll see.'

'I know,' I snapped, and wriggled away from him. I felt like a claustrophobic ten-year-old trying to get away from a cloying grandmother.

I must say, the service at the Pocock was wonderful and the food, well, they don't give those Michelin stars out for nothing and the Pocock had three. We'd just had dinner (monkfish and langoustine risotto – delicious), when the call came. It was the police. They had found out who had tried to burn us in our beds and would we 'mind very much if a detective came down to talk to us tomorrow'? Chris took the call and he said that it wouldn't be a problem and why not come for lunch as they did very good bar snacks at the Pocock?

'Did they say who it was?' I asked, and Chris said the officer hadn't felt 'at liberty to divulge that information', and even though the Armagnac and prune parfait was very nice, I couldn't finish it. I felt a bit odd. I felt like I had the night before I married Chris: sort of sick and full of trepidation. When the kids had gone to bed and I was still trying to get to sleep in our four-poster (I'd eaten the little chocolate they put on the pillow – nice touch), Chris started banging on about who the arsonist might be. He presumed it was one of the nutters from the loony bin round the corner: a bloke, probably schizophrenic, probably high on drugs, and he went into one of his pompous speeches about how although everyone slags off the police, we still have the best law enforcement record in Europe. Fortunately, I nodded off before he started backing this theory up with statistics.

The next day was cloudy. Chris tried to get the kids to do some schoolwork; he set them maths and gave Pandora an essay to write, then he got into a state about how thick they were and it all got a bit tense. It's funny how quickly you get over the shock of nearly losing them; we'd managed to be nice to each other for nearly five days and the strain was starting to show. Jed sloped off and it wasn't until the policeman arrived that he re-appeared; he'd made up his face with felt-tips. He'd made rather a good job of it too, but his father was livid. I swear he'd have taken Jed's red lips and green eyelids off with a blowtorch if there'd been one lying handy. The policeman's name was Detective Inspector Randolph – 'Call me Alan' – and he had one of those moustaches that only really straight policeman think might be a good idea. He was shorter and fatter than I expect a policeman to be and his nails were badly bitten.

We talked in the conservatory. The kids were sent up to their room and we could hear them bickering all the way up the stairs: 'Move it, fart arse,' 'Shut it, poof.'

Once we'd ordered some coffee he got straight down to business. 'Well, Mr and Mrs Cunningham, you'll be relieved to hear that a woman has been arrested on suspicion of AWI, by which we mean Arson With Intent. She was taken into custody yesterday and will officially be charged in court this week. Considering the seriousness of the matter, bail will not be applicable and I should imagine she will stay in Holloway until time of trial. Shouldn't be longer than a couple of months.' At this point one of the little waitresses came in with a pot of coffee on a tray, all set out nicely with macaroons.

'A woman you say, Alan,' mused Chris. 'How bizarre.'

I ate a macaroon and kept quiet; I knew the policeman was going to say something that neither of us particularly wanted to hear. I looked out of the window. A little Japanese couple had just arrived in matching Burberry macs. She didn't look the type to fuck plumbers; you've no idea how much I wanted to swap places.

DI Randolph sipped his coffee neatly, so he didn't get it clogged up in his moustache, and arranged his face into an expression of seriousness. 'That's right, Mr Cunningham, and there's no easy way of saying this, but from all accounts this was a personal vendetta, your wife being the target.'

It was bloody ridiculous. It was like an amateur production of an Agatha Christie play: there was a silence, I reached for a biscuit.

Chris picked his jaw up off the carpet and said something like, 'Bloody hell, Anna, what's been going on?'

'Is her name Carlene?' I ventured. Honestly, it was mad; I could feel this bubble of laughter coming up my throat. I coughed to get rid of it and a spray of macaroon came out of my mouth.

'Maybe you and your wife should have a little chat. I'll be in the bar. The Cumberland pie looks jolly nice,' said the inspector, and then he waddled out.

I don't need to go into details here; suffice to say that by the time Alan Randolph had demolished his Cumberland pie and a large slice of Bakewell tart, my husband knew that he was married to an adulterous slag and, thanks to my shenanigans, our beautiful home had more or less gone up in smoke.

I wasn't prepared for his reaction; his face went the colour of blackcurrants and a vein stood out on his forehead. I watched it pulse. I had seen my husband upset before, of course I had, like the time someone scraped a key down the side of his car and when the tax people confused him with another Chris Cunningham and sent him a bill for forty-eight thousand pounds – but I had never seen him like this. Fury seemed to percolate through him. 'You have spoilt everything,' he spat. I didn't know what to do with my hands; I really could have done with a cigarette. I had to sit there and watch my husband erupt like a volcano.

The worst thing was that he didn't want to see me, he said he couldn't bear to be in the same room. 'Go away, Anna, get lost.' He actually told me to fuck off! It was really uncomfortable; we were in the public lounge and there were other guests present. Heidi and Bill came running through to see what all the fuss was about; you expect a bit of effing and blinding in a Salvation Army hostel but not a nice country hotel. Bill took Chris into his office for a brandy.

In the end it was decided that I should get a lift back to London with DI Randolph and that Chris would stay in Devon with the kids. I think Bill and Heidi had decided this might be the best solution. I was summoned to the office.

'What are you going to tell Jed and Pandora?' I asked.

Chris had his back to me. 'The truth,' he replied, and he banged his head against a filing cabinet on purpose.

'Please, Chris, wait till I've gone.' It was strange to hear myself begging him to do me a favour and it was even stranger to hear him say, 'Don't you dare tell me what to do, you bitch.'

I called Jo from the payphone in the bar; Alan Randolph was paying for his lunch. When he saw me, he pretended to be very interested in the contents of his wallet. As I waited for Jo to answer, he brushed past me. 'Just going for a quick Jimmy Riddle, see you by the car in five.' I nearly asked which car, but there was only one panda in the drive.

I eventually tracked down Jo at the bookshop. She said, 'Anna, it's in the papers, it was a woman. You can't credit it, can you?' I asked if I could come and stay; that I needed to be in London, things had to be sorted. 'Darling, of course, stay as long as you like.' I bet she regrets saying that now.

While I was speaking to Jo, Chris must have gone upstairs to tell the children what I'd done because as I walked out through the hallway, Jed came flying down the stairs and slapped me in the face. Pandora stood behind him; she looked at me but she didn't speak, then she turned around and disappeared back up the stairs. 'You bastard, Chris,' I shouted. The little Japanese couple who were now checking in at the reception desk appeared rather shocked; their mouths formed two perfect letter 'O's. I shrugged and tried to affect nonchalance as I was escorted from the premises by a plain clothes officer.

Suffice to say, no one waved me off. In the car, Alan Randolph put on Radio 5; he made it quite clear that he didn't want to talk and he only took his hands off the steering wheel to pick his nose. It was a very dull journey and because I had to sit in the back like a naughty child I felt rather queasy.

55

Gin and Sympathy

It didn't make the nationals because no one was killed (apart from the hamster, poor Nibbles), but there was a photo in the *South London Sparrow*, and a big headline saying 'Mystery Blaze'. Anna was described as a housewife in her forties, which she wouldn't have liked.

I went to see them in hospital. Anna managed to look glamorous even in one of those hospital-issue nightdresses. We went to the dayroom so that she could have a cigarette; she was very quiet and put the stub out very carefully. Jed was having a fantastic time doing handbrake turns in a wheelchair; he was full of it. Pandora was asleep and when she woke up Jed broke the news about the hamster and she turned her face to the wall and fat tears oozed out of her eyeballs. I offered her a Kit Kat but she didn't want it.

On the Sunday before they set off for a week's recuperation in a posh hotel in Dorset, they came over to ours for lunch; I did a lovely poached salmon with parsley mash and mange tout, followed by one of my famous summer puddings.

Everyone down the road had rallied together and bags of clothes had been deposited round at ours over the weekend. Some of them were quite nice; I bagsied a Jean Muir cardi and a pair of leopard-skin flares for Georgina – I knew Pandora would never be able to squeeze into them. Anna turned up her nose at most of it, but I saw Jed swipe a purple Lurex V neck.

They left at four; it was a bit of a relief as they were just starting to realise what they'd lost. Throughout lunch, Anna had kept dropping her knife and fork and saying things like, 'Oh no, my Kenzo jacket,' and Chris had lost a first edition copy of *The Wind in the Willows*, which he got a bit upset about.

Apparently the fire officers had been to see them at King's. The ground floor had been completely gutted and further up the house there was smoke damage and structural problems; the kids' bedrooms were relatively unscathed and if the hamster hadn't been left on the first-floor landing, it would have been all right. Poor Pandora, even Georgina felt sorry for her and gave her a big pile of old *Smash Hits* to read in the car.

By the Wednesday they knew who'd done it. That did make the papers, well it would! It's not every day a twenty-four-year-old attractive mother of two is taken into custody on an 'arson with intent to endanger life' charge. She is in Holloway now, this Carlene Leigh. I bet you there's some hairdressing scheme going on in there and by the time she goes to court they'll have touched up her roots. Juries don't trust women with long black roots; it's that Myra Hindley thing.

She called me from the hotel. I couldn't really understand what she was saying but I got the gist of it. I was glad Anna was coming to stay, it would be nice. Doh.

She arrived in a police car, with just an old copy of *Country Life*; not a spare pair of knickers or a wash bag, nothing. It was just gone six, so we laid into the gin and she told me what had been going on.

'See the thing is, Jo, I've been a bit daft with this bloke Danny. I had an affair and that's why the house got burnt. It was his wife; she came round that night and tried to kill us all.'

Well, what do you say?

I remember Nigel was late home, so me and Anna and the kids had supper; just pasta with pesto, green salad and some French bread. To be honest, I was a bit pissed by the time we sat down to eat and Anna was reeling. I made her go up and have a bath. I laid out my rather sweet, white broderie anglaise nightie on the spare bed and she popped down for a Cointreau; but I tell you, she was in that bed and fast asleep by 9.30.

I had filled the kids in on some of the sketchier details before supper. I think it made them nervous because every time they looked at each other, they started laughing. Then Henry farted and Georgina got a bit hysterical. At one point I thought Anna was going to punch her; they've never really got on, those two. When Nigel got in just after ten, I sat him down in the drawing-room and told him everything that she'd told me. 'Mad tart,' he said, and I didn't know whether he was talking about Anna or Carlene.

I was hung over to the teeth the next day; I couldn't even drive the kids to school, they had to get the bus. Before I went to work,

I called Sue to warn her not to be surprised if she found Anna wandering round the house. Later she told me that when she'd arrived, she'd found 'Mrs Cunningham' asleep in a deckchair in the garden, with an empty bottle of Cava. To be honest, it's been going downhill ever since: she is pissed most of the time, she is ungrateful, she doesn't lift a finger to help and I have started to hate her. It's a terrible thing when you want to smash your best friend's teeth out. There have been moments when I have wished that the whole lot of them had been burnt to death. It would have been easier; we could have grieved and remembered the good times.

I still can't believe it's happened, it's all so ridiculous. If it were on the television, no doubt starring Kevin Whately and, oh, someone like Dervla Kirwin, I would find it hugely amusing. Unfortunately this is no telly drama, we are not actors and at the end of the day we can't go back to our normal lives. It just goes on and on.

56

Retribution

Chris was very, very angry indeed. It wasn't an emotion that he was accustomed to feeling; he'd always been such a reasonable chap. 'Good old Chris' – well, not any more. Fury had him by the horns, he was like a wounded bull: wild-eyed, hurt and bellowing.

People who are used to being angry are also used to getting over it. They are familiar with the stages of rage: the flaring up and the smashing of plates, the swearing and spitting, followed by the sulking and silence. Anger is like a force ten gale: eventually she exhausts herself and as the storm clouds blow over, the huge ranting waves of rage become little ripples of resentment and gradually the tide of emotion ebbs into the final stage of forgiving and forgetting . . . till the next time.

But Chris couldn't get over it: his whole body seethed, his blood bubbled in his veins. Obviously he maintained a civil veneer to the staff at the Pocock and he apologised to Heidi and Bill, the understanding but embarrassed proprietors, about his Tourettish outburst in the lounge. But at night, when the children were asleep and he was drinking whisky by himself, he could taste his own bitterness.

Chris had fallen out of love with his wife; he had never really liked her, not really, but he had always loved her. And now he didn't; it was as simple as that. The bubble had burst and now that he didn't love her he hated her and he wished her dead. He pictured her in a car crash, her blood-soaked body mangled over the central reservation, and doubted that he would bother attending her funeral. In his mind, he killed her in every conceivable way: sometimes she fell down lift shafts, her dying screams echoing in the metal void, other times he saw her stumbling off a crowded tube platform, headfirst into the path of an oncoming train – but no, decapitation was too good for her, too quick, too easy, so Chris put her into a hospital bed and had her dying grotesquely, slowly and painfully of some terrible bone cancer. Because he wanted her to suffer, he decided to finish her off with the flesh-eating disease, necrotising fasciitis, so that she could watch and smell herself decomposing while she was still alive. He imagined her toes putrefying one by one, the gangrene galloping up her legs and her vagina rotting like an old cabbage. He became quite medieval in his torturous fantasies: she should be pulled apart by wild horses, burnt at the stake, stoned to death, but before she was killed he would like to tie her naked to a cart and drive her through the streets of London with a sign around her neck proclaiming her guilt.

But even if she didn't die, even if he didn't put his hands

around her neck and gouge her eyes out with his thumbs, then he wanted her to be lonely, he wanted her to lose her looks and to be unhappy, he wanted her to know that she was unloved. After all, who really loved Anna? Not her mother, not really; there was only him the children and, well . . . Jo, he supposed.

He had told the children. He had surprised himself. The Chris he used to be would have minced his words, sugared the pill, but he hadn't: he told them that their mother had betrayed them. He hadn't even waited until she'd gone like she had wanted him to; he blurted it out while she waited for the policeman to powder his nose and pay for his bar lunch. He was glad when Jed had run down and slapped Anna and he was glad that Pandora didn't even want to say goodbye. Anna didn't deserve Pandora's affection; she'd never given Pandora any. Everything was a lot clearer now that he didn't have to make excuses for her, now that the devotion had evaporated. The truth was that she'd treated her daughter like shit.

As for Jed, well, maybe he would forgive his mother but that was his business and, as if hit by lightning, Chris suddenly realised that he and his son wouldn't have much in common in the years to come; Jed could do what he liked.

It was quite frightening this new-found clarity, this sudden ability to see things as they really were and not how they had all pretended them to be. Chris felt like an actor who had suddenly departed from a long-running soap; he didn't have to play that part any more and it would be interesting to see who he would stay in touch with. Pandora definitely, but as for the others, the bit-players and walk-ons, he wasn't that bothered if he never saw them again. Maybe Jo, he genuinely liked Jo. But as for Nigel, when had he and Nigel ever been really close? They'd affected an almost theatrical mateyness but they'd never really enjoyed their scenes together, it had always been rather 'eggy'. Chris suddenly saw his relationship with Nigel as if through the eyes of a hypercritical theatre critic: 'Unfortunately the characters playing Chris and Nigel were never particularly convincing, leaving the women to take centre stage'.

His mother had been right all along: he should never have married her. She was a nasty piece of work; she was bad like something out of a children's fairy tale, wicked to the core. 'I told you so,' his mother said when he rang her, whisky-sozzled at midnight. 'Why don't you come home?'

Why don't I? thought Chris. Yes, he decided he would go home; he would take his children to Wales, even though his mother's house was cramped and smelly and had horrible furniture. Chris's mother lived in a bungalow full of crocheted mats and knitted dolls. It was the absolute opposite of the Pink House and therefore just what he needed.

Chris decided (halfway through a bottle of Johnnie Walker) that he wasn't going to try any more; he had tried and tried for twenty years and where had it got him? An unfaithful bitch/cow/slag of a wife and a load of stuff he'd never wanted in the first place that had ended up being burnt! So what was the point? He made up his mind that he wasn't going back to work, sod it, why should he? Fuck the job. He didn't know what he would do, but his brother had a farm. He could work on a farm, he didn't need much money: what had he ever spent on himself? He'd done everything for her, the strumpet/harpy/whore. Enough was enough. Pandora would be happy in Wales, it would be easier for her; after all, there were a lot of fat plain girls in Wales.

As for Jed, well, it might just be the answer; some good clean country air might blow away his Nancy-boy cobwebs. For a second he imagined Jed with a collie dog and a stick but this illusion was shattered when he looked over at his son who was busy colouring in designer outfits for a paper dolly that he'd made. Jed was talking to himself, 'Ideal for a premiere or even a smart luncheon.'

Pandora was writing a letter to her mother. She had locked herself in the bathroom and sat on the toilet with a biro and some of the Pocock Arms' complimentary notepaper balanced on her knee. 'To my mother', she scrawled. 'I hope you rot, you are a fucking bitch and my dad is worth a hundred of you. I never want to see your stupid face again, I never want to hear your voice, I wish I had any other mother but you. Yours with disgust, the girl who used to be your daughter'. That was all she needed to say. When she had finished not signing any kisses, she ripped the letter into little pieces and flushed it down the toilet, wishing that it was her mother's head.

Jed, meanwhile, continued to colour in; he'd designed a pink ball gown with a nipped-in waist, trimmed with diamante. As he added a black lace bodice, he wondered if the plumber had been cute; was he a blond or was he a brunette? According to Jed's imagination, he was a blond and when he went to work he took off his top and his shoulders were broad and strong with little gold hairs glinting sweatily.

Jed was wrong. As we know, Danny had very dark, almost black, hair, which at the moment he was in the process of tearing out. What had his silly mare of a missus done?

The consequences of Carlene's actions were devastating for Danny. Now that she was in prison he had two kids to look after – on top of all the house crap. For all that Danny knew how to mend a washing-machine, he had no idea how to load one. Carlene's dad was being useless: course Danny could have time off, but he'd be buggered if he was going to pay him. After all, it was his fault that Carlene was languishing in Holloway. Carlene's dad had stopped joking. All his funny voices died in his throat.

When the police had turned up at the door – bang, bang, bang (Danny hadn't got round to fixing the bell) – Carlene had almost been relieved, she hadn't even tried to pretend that she hadn't done it and the torn bib packet was still in the van along with the empty turps bottle. Danny knew Carlene was a bit thick but he hadn't thought she could be that thick. She'd just gone with them, held up her hands to be handcuffed, kissed the kids and walked out. 'Bye Dan,' she said, as if she was just popping out to Safeway. It had been very early in the morning. The children were still in their pyjamas eating Frosties; Danny hadn't a clue what to do with them. 'Where's your nursery school, darling?' he asked Roxanne.

He tried calling his mother but she was done with helping. She had her own life to lead; she was a very merry fifty-two-year-old widow with a young DJ boyfriend and was off to Ibiza, thank you very much. Danny's sister lived in Stevenage, with an autistic seven-year-old, and his little brother was somewhere up in North London scoring crack pipes. He was on his own. Fortunately, the young woman police constable who had gently led Carlene to the black Maria had returned, still in uniform, that evening. Well, one thing usually leads to another and when Roxanne stumbled into Mummy and Daddy's bedroom at 6.00am the next day, she had been slightly surprised to see two dark heads looking sheepish on the pillows. Women like a man in trouble and by the end of the week they were queuing round the block to 'help'.

57

Revisiting the Scene of the Crime

I do not feel very well today: I have heartburn and I am very tired. I doubt whether I will ever have an affair again, this business has left me quite drained. I am forty-one years old, I daren't weigh myself, I have gone quite grey, my husband and family are in Wales and aren't really talking to me at the moment and my ex-lover's wife has burnt down my house. There, that's it in a nutshell. Any questions?

Last night they went to bed early again. I crept on to the landing when I heard them turn off the lights and listened at their door but they weren't making any of their rare nocturnal grunting noises, so I went downstairs and wiped a slice of bread around a greasy frying pan. If anyone had looked in, they would have seen me, in an Amnesty t-shirt that didn't cover my pubes. I wasn't sleepy, so I took a mac from the cupboard under the stairs, shoved a pair of Georgina's old trainers on my feet and after grabbing my handbag I let myself out of the front door. I knew how to immobilise the alarm, and anyway, it's not like I'm a criminal; I'm free to come and go. I have keys you know.

It was just gone eleven; people were coming out of the pub. I recognised a couple of them; the big red-haired girl who lives round the corner, who danced on top of our car one New Year's Eve with her bosoms out. And the lad who was with her, I'd seen him before, mooching about with his pink hair. I was way ahead of them and I just kept going, head down, tripping over the laces I couldn't tie up properly because they had knots in them. I wanted to see my house; I wanted to see how they were getting on.

It looked terrible. Its pink front all scorched to the roof, like a kid who'd blown off his face on Bonfire Night. The front door was corrugated over and there were signs up saying 'Danger Unsafe Property – Trespassers Will Be Prosecuted'. There was rubbish all over the front lawn; some of it was ours but other people had junked their unwanted stuff on top. There was a disembowelled washing-machine that I didn't recognise and a bag of wet baby clothes that never belonged to us. There were heaps of old milk cartons and soft drink cans that the workmen had just chucked down, and I was glad it wasn't daylight because it would have looked even worse.

All of a sudden it hit me what I'd lost; it was just a corner of a photo that reminded me. It had fallen out of the bottom of a soggy cardboard box: a fragment of a Christmas Day, all of us round the table at Jo's, Jed in a high-chair, everyone wearing paper hats and smiling, even Pandora. I remembered it was the year Jo cooked a goose instead of turkey; she never bothered again, terrible stuff goose, best left to nursery rhymes. So I just sat there, being careful of the broken glass and jagged wood and sticky-out nails, and I realised this was the worst thing that had ever happened to me, because up until now I'd been quite lucky. Whilst I was squatting there I had a wee; I only had on the t-shirt under the mac and so I just pissed like a lady dog and then I went back to Jo's.

I'm weeing all the time at the moment; as soon as I got indoors I needed to go again. Sometimes, when I have to go in the middle of the night, I do it in one of the empty wine bottles that I've hidden in Jo's boots. Three of them are quite full now and I really should chuck them down the sink.

I would like to visit my children in Wales but Chris isn't ready to see me yet and anyway, his mother won't have me in the house. How she must be loving this.

I miss my house and I miss my things; maybe that is why I have this feeling like an elephant has trodden on my heart and I have to keep burping to make myself feel as if I can breathe.

Of course she is going to get away with it. I have been warned: 'Mitigating circumstances,' my lawyer mumbles though his big, yellow bunny-rabbit teeth. He is about eleven years old and knows Jack shit. It seems these days that if you are suffering from post-natal depression and your husband is screwing someone else, then it is well within your rights to shove petrol-soaked rags through the mistress's letterbox, regardless of who might be lying innocently asleep upstairs. It's unbelievable, isn't it? Hey ho, never trust a woman who wears stonewashed denim, that's what I say.

So that is why I am here, in limbo land: I am in disgrace. Chris is very cross with me; I have begged his forgiveness but he has gone away to 'think about it'. No doubt his mother is dripping poison about me into my children's ears, colouring in the outline of the story Chris has told them with her venom. I suppose it's only fair; they have a right to know why they had to be dragged from their beds in the middle of the night and carried out of the window by firemen on long ladders. I remember the fire quite clearly. Jed was in seventh heaven; I can see him now in the arms of some huge helmeted man, being carried to safety, a big smirk on his face. Obviously, at that moment, he didn't know that it was all my fault.

Sinaed wasn't there that night; she'd gone back to Ireland for yet another clan wedding. She never came back, not when she heard why it had happened; her Catholic sensibilities were shaken to the core. Like I give a flying fuck what she thinks, self-righteous, ugly cow.

But it's facing the children again that truly bothers me. The last time I saw Pandora, she gave me a look that was full of pity and disgust. How many times have I looked at her like that? When she was six and I could no longer buy children's tights to fit her? When she was eleven and she started her periods? The moment she was born? Jed's reaction was somehow easier to deal with, it was so Jed-like; he just ran up to me after Chris had given them what I hoped was a watered-down account of the events, looked me straight in the eye, and said, 'My mother, the whore,' and slapped me smartly across the chops. It was as if he'd been rehearsing for that moment all of his life. Deep in my heart I know he will forgive me; he will grow up to recount the tale, revelling in the seedy drama of it. But I may have lost my daughter for ever. You can only push Pandora so far. It's like when she was bullied at school, forever coming home with gob on the back of her blazer, her trainers wet through from having been flushed down the toilet, putting up with it and putting up with it until one day, she finally cracked, punched the ringleader on the nose and tore out a lump of her hair. Apparently she was still holding a fistful of blond tresses when she was sent to the headmistress. From then on, there were no more wee-sodden Nikes. The school got in a trained counsellor to deal with the matter. Pandora and this Olivia girl were supposed to make up and shake hands but Pandora refused. She can be rather unforgiving.

When it first happened and the ash from my burnt house had hardly had time to settle, Jo was brilliant. She was on my side, she couldn't believe it, she reckoned that it was the work of some unbalanced psychopath. Now that she knows the truth, she has gone off me. Nigel thinks I'm a silly slag, and as for their children, they despise me. I am glad they have gone away, the bitch and the wanker. We all make mistakes, don't we? By the time I was forced to tell Jo the truth about me and Danny, the relationship had long passed its sell-by-date. It's funny how relationships end; with me and my plumber-lover, it happened very quickly. One day the spell got broken and, like magic, I turned into a frog.

Sometimes I dream about my home, the way it was: how the sun visited each room in turn, its graceful curves and surprising crannies, the vast-ceilinged rooms and its fifty-one wooden stairs. But when I wake up, I remember it all blistered and black, like a third-degree burns patient, saturated by hoses and totally ruined.

Everything has gone pear-shaped – especially me. I cannot bend down to put on my shoes: I am fatter than an American on an *Oprah Winfrey Show*.

It was hot last night and I had trouble sleeping. I just couldn't get comfortable and in the end I had one leg on top of the duvet and one underneath and my belly was slung sideways like a blancmange falling off a plate. My belly has a life of its own these days; it undulates and wobbles and every time I catch sight of it I am surprised by its size.

58

A Stalemate Situation

This morning she ate cold ravioli out of the tin. I try to persuade her to eat fruit, maybe some fresh veg. She is wearing odd clothes and there are always stains down the front. She has the telly on all day, all those talk shows, yap, yap, yap, and even though she wants the central heating on full-blast, she must have the windows wide open and the back door ajar. She says one moment she is hot, the next she is cold. I don't care any more.

As yet, we have not come to blows but it's getting perilously close. There is silent warfare going on.

When she first arrived, I couldn't do enough for her. I ran her baths using lashings of my best bath oil, that Jo Malone stuff from that special little shop in Chelsea. I made sure there were warm towels at the ready, cosied up the spare room, put in a portable colour telly, vases of fresh flowers. I would bring up trays of tempting little meals and hand squeeze her fresh oranges, making sure I removed the pips. I put things I knew she liked on my shopping list: dark chocolate, mangoes, smoked salmon, good brandy. I cleared cupboard space and made sure there were lavender bags in the drawers; not that she came with any clothes – so I told her to help herself to anything of ours, and she did.

Now that I am no longer Mother Teresa of SE5, I have taken to hiding things: the large bottle of L'Eau D'Issey, my Clinique skincare products, my one and only Chanel lipstick, little bits of costume jewellery and my Wolford silk tights that cost seventeen quid are under my bed in a box file marked 'Heating and Lighting'.

The other day I bought a cooked chicken. When I came home from work, she'd eaten the breasts and peeled the barbecued skin clean off. All Nigel and I were left with were the bones.

Years ago, when I first lived in a flat with three other girls, we had a shelf each for our provisions in the kitchen and left each other snotty little notes: 'Whoever nicked my tuna please replace it'. Now that I am a forty-year-old woman, I cannot be doing with all that nonsense. However, I will admit that my Fortnum's ginger thins have gone into the box file and occasionally Nigel and I eat them in secret. Sometimes we feel like children on Christmas morning opening a stocking too early, all greedy and a little guilty.

She went out last night; I watched her leave from the window. I suspected she might have been going to the pub but she went up the hill and not down. Anyway, it was gone eleven; she'd have missed last orders. She must have gone up to see the house; it's a terrible eyesore, like a broken tooth in a cheerleader's smile. Things seem to be moving very slowly. It obviously takes longer to mend a house than for a mere mortal to be driven insane. When the summer holidays are over and the kids have to go back to school, then Chris will have to come back and rent a flat or something. People do that all the time; their insurance will pay for it. They can't all come here, it's not as if the kids even like each other and can share rooms. In the past I have begged Georgina to be nicer to Pandora but she says she is a 'mongy spaz' and 'nobody likes her and she smells'. This is not entirely untrue, she does smell: of damp earth and blood, like a badgers' set, whilst Jed, of course, smells of Timotei and lily of the valley and for some strange reason, strawberry milkshake.

Anna smells too: of unwashed clothes, stale tobacco and alcohol. It's like having a lady tramp in the house.

These holidays are crawling by. We got a postcard from the kids today, so they were alive a couple of days ago at least. This is the first summer for many years that we haven't gone away on a proper family holiday. Nigel says that we'll go to Venice in the autumn. We went there on our honeymoon, only it was rather hot and the canals stank to high heaven under the open window of our bridal suite. At night the mosquitoes came in and bit me on the bum and the bites festered so I had huge pus-filled welts all over my backside. Oh, but I would kill to be in Venice, festering derriere or not. I want to be away from here, I want to be away from her. The court case will be in September; by then I would like to be in Harry's bar drinking peach bellinis.

She has taken photos out of our albums, pictures from her fortieth birthday party. 'See how happy I was,' she said. 'Chris gave me a mother-of-pearl trinket box and a pair of ruby studs. Danny gave me one up the shitter.' I'm glad to say that soon after that she went to bed and Nigel and I had another one of our 'What are we going to do?' conversations at the kitchen table.

We had a ham sandwich each and Nigel went to the cupboard to get some pickled onions but there was only vinegar left in the jar. My father pickled those onions; I was pissed off but Nigel was livid. That's when he said she would have to go, that she would have to get a bedsit, that for all he cared she could live in a cardboard box outside Waterloo Station because that's where she belonged. He said he would find her a box, give her a starter pack of Special Brew and drive her down there himself. I said we'd give it two weeks, and then I sucked the wine box dry. I was exhausted but before I could go to bed and forget everything, the phone rang. Nigel bolted; he knew it would be Chris.

These calls are a nightmare; it's all so difficult. I don't ever know what to say to him, we are both so embarrassed. He can't stay in Wales for ever, however much his mother would like him to; he has a job here, the kids have schools to go back to, he can't keep pussyfooting around. Personally I think he should sell the Pink House – preferably to people I would not want to get friendly with. I don't think I could ever set foot in the place again. Maybe it would be better if they moved away, it needn't be far: there are some nice big properties in Kennington, he could afford it – maybe I should call an estate agent? We didn't talk for long and I didn't say anything I really wanted to say.

There was a time when I couldn't imagine not seeing them. Our dining-room table has a middle section that has been permanently slotted in for the past ten years for their benefit; we have made space for them. I know that Jed doesn't like raisins, so when I made bread and butter pudding I left a special corner of it raisin-free. I have accommodated the Cunninghams for a decade now, and it's time other people took their places. I want normal people using my cutlery. Fuck Jed, from now on I shall make bread and butter pudding with raisins in all corners.

I will no longer have to attempt to make conversation with the dreary Pandora – like I gave a shit about her cello lessons. I will no longer have to turn a blind eye to the fact that their sexually deviant raisin-loathing child has once more borrowed Georgina's hair crimpers and is sitting down in my dining-room like a pre-pubescent, frizzy-haired Oscar Wilde. I want the lot of them out of my life.

Her mother doesn't really know, you know. I told Anna she should ring her, or at least write. She has lied: she told Sylvia that the house had been damaged by an electrical fire and that whilst Chris and the kids spend the summer in Wales, she is overseeing the repairs – huh. It's a good job Sylvia's not that fussed. What a crappy lot of mothers we have turned out to be. Recently I have realised that I don't know any particularly good ones; maybe I should get Georgina sterilised? Lord pity the child she ever brings into the world; if it doesn't match her handbag, she won't want to know.

A mother's love for her children is meant to be unconditional, but it isn't. We only really like them when they are either placid, pink-faced and asleep or achieving something, being mentioned in school assembly and getting gold stars. Most of the time they are frustrating and a bit annoying because they haven't turned out how we expected them to.

Anna's mother is as cold as ice. I met her once very soon after Jed was born when she came over to visit. It was more than nine years ago; I don't think she's been back since. She had the most beautiful hair and wore yellow linen trousers, which is nigh on impossible for most sixty-year-olds to get away with. She didn't bother speaking to me; I think she thought I was a lollipop lady who'd wandered into the house by accident.

My mother was a mass of contradictions. I think she found

her role as the wife of a high-ranking officer rather claustrophobic: the rules and the snobbery bored her, she was constantly expected to be on her best behaviour, which is why, I think, she started to drink. It was her little bit of rebellion. She couldn't stand having to have her hair done and being patronised at stuffy functions. Because she was cleverer than her role required, she would get very frustrated. She could be very naughty sometimes. 'I'm not going. I'm not wearing this stupid dress,' and she would tear at her beehive, hot tears spurting out of her eyes, whilst my brother and I kept silent under the kitchen table and my father hopped around looking anguished. On these occasions I would will her to open the drinks cabinet and get stuck in, then at least I would know that within a couple of hours she would be under the eiderdown, her stocking feet sticking out of the bottom, snoring her head off, docile at last. Now that she doesn't drink as much as she once did, she is very good at Scrabble and finishes the *Telegraph* cryptic crossword before elevenses. They still have elevenses, my parents; that is what they're like.

I have talked to my father a lot about 'the situation'. It's difficult because he is profoundly deaf and it's hard to shout the sordid details when Anna is in the next room. He is a stoical man, my father, he has had to be; he believes in sticking to your guns, he believes in loyalty, in seeing the job through. That is why he never left my mother and why I feel so guilty about wanting to get rid of Anna. My father has carried grown men with bullet wounds through the jungle, he has cut the heads off his enemies and carried them back to base in a rucksack because that is what his job entailed. We are all so wet these days. Maybe it's time we had another war to put things into perspective, and as I say that I almost laugh; it is impossible to imagine either Henry or Jed in combat. In the olden days women invested more time in their children but time became a luxury that even rich people like us couldn't afford and now it is too late. I blame Anna's mother for what Anna has become, even though it's more likely her father's fault, and I am horrified about what might befall our own offspring.

I dreamt about my daughter the other night, and in my dream she slowly and deliberately turned away from me. I am losing her daily. Henry and Georgina are no longer babies: in two years' time, Henry will be going to university or taking a year off. I am scared he might go to Australia and that someone will stab him on Bondi Beach; it has happened before. As for Georgie, soon she will want to go clubbing in the West End and the thought of it being three o'clock in the morning and her bed still empty fills me with dread. I miss my kids.

It's all so bloody ridiculous; just because she is estranged from hers, ours have had to be banished too. It's not fair, not bloody fair.

59

Nigel Loses It

Nigel Metcalf was fed up to the back teeth – literally; his jaw had been clenched so tightly for so long that his molars were killing him. How had Anna turned from wank-scenario sex-vixen into irritating fat cow? It was a mystery and one he didn't need in his house.

Nigel knew that in the past he had been as unthinking as Anna was now, as selfish as she had become, but it was a long time ago. Anyway he had an excuse: he had a dead sister. Anna hadn't lost anyone, not off the face of the earth; she hadn't had to go through what Nigel had. Okay, it was over twenty years ago, but you never forget the sight of your sister's coffin being dropped clumsily into the ground. It was the indignity of her burial that he couldn't forget: the mismatched pallbearers, the vicar presuming to call her Liz, which no one ever had, the stupid teddies which some of her O-level-challenged friends had placed by the grave – one of them held a tiny heart-shaped helium balloon between its furry paws. 'I love you,' it proclaimed.

No wonder he'd gone a bit off the rails. It was only now in his early middle age that he had started to go straight, cleaned up his act. Nigel no longer found himself staring into the mirror with hugely dilated pupils, checking for those tell-tale minuscule flecks of white powder suspended in the dribble of transparent snot that constantly ran out of the leaky tap of his nose. It had been easier than he'd imagined giving up the old Charlie; once he'd decided he was going to do it he tipped the contents of his last sachet down the toilet and flushed. There had been at least three lines' worth left but he had had enough. His dealer couldn't come to terms with it. 'Nige, my son, this is such good stuff, worthy of the finest nose in the land.' He wafted an open wrap of paper under Nigel's nose as if it contained an expensive Brie. 'Try a free sample.'

Phil the dealer had grown a long, grubby talon on the smallest finger of his right hand; he used it as a miniature shovel, piling it full of white powder as he offered Nigel a 'gratis toot'. There was something desperate about the act: Nigel was reminded of Jo valiantly trying to persuade a disinterested Georgina to eat when she was a baby, tempting her with little games. Any moment now, he expected Phil to start playing choo choo trains with the coke. Nigel turned his head away like an obstinate two-year-old.

'You know you like it, come on. You are the connoisseur of the old Bolivian marching powder. I cannot believe you can pass up this opportunity: two grammes for the price of one and call me mental, I'll chuck in a couple of Es.'

'No thanks, Phil,' said Nigel. 'Nice to have known you and all that.'

Phil had been a whizz kid before he turned to whizz; one of Thatcher's City boys, burnt-out at twenty-four. He still wore Church's brogues and red braces, but his suit was shiny and covered in stains. Phil only ever ate chocolate milk: his hands shook too much to be able to handle cutlery, he was better off with a straw.

Anna hadn't believed him when he'd told her he was off the coke. She'd cornered him just after she first arrived, backed him into the utility-room, refused to believe he had no little folded square about his person, literally started to rifle through his pockets until he had physically pushed her away. She was looking a mess. She stumbled over the laundry-basket and slipped; she was wearing a denim skirt and laddered grey pop socks. It was like a scene from *One Flew Over the Cuckoo's Nest*. 'I'm so unhappy, Nigel,' she said, sitting in a pile of dirty shirts and crusty-gusseted knickers.

'I know,' he replied, 'but who's fault is that?'

She had looked up at him almost sleepily at that point, as if she might just curl up in the basket and snooze amongst the fetid clothes. 'Don't play the goody-two-shoes with me, Mr Slag. I know where your willy's been.' She spoke slowly, staring directly at his flies, and as if she had the power of telekinesis Nigel felt his zipper grow hot enough to burn a hole in his underpants.

'I don't know what you're talking about,' he retorted, and he bent down so close to her that he could feel the warm fumes of the laundry-basket, 'and if I were you, I'd keep my filthy trap shut. I think you've caused enough trouble.' From that moment, they could never be friends again.

For the most part they avoided each other; he went out early and if she was in the living-room when he came home, then he would pretend to do paperwork in his study or simply take refuge in the bedroom.

Nigel was glad now that he had chosen Jo to be his wife. There had been many other girls a lot more attractive but she had turned out to be a sound investment. His wife was forty and so far she had not succumbed to mental neurosis, substance abuse or any one of those woman-cancers that ladies of her age seemed prone to. Yes, she had a temper, her tongue could be Sabatier sharp, she had crap legs and droopy tits, but she hadn't turned into a hysterical witch. He was grateful. Maybe he would buy her something really special for their next anniversary, like a diamond ring. She deserved it: the marital equivalent of the gold watch his father had received for years of long civil service. 'I love you,' Nigel said to his wife that night.

'It's about bloody time,' she replied, but she kissed him on the nose and they had a cuddle and made love face to face.

It was time Anna moved out. She was blighting his family home like a dirty paintbrush in a new box of watercolours; she was muddying it all up. Men are less sentimental than women; it's always blokes who will throw sacks of carpet-widdling puppies into rivers. With the exception of those unfortunate fools who have deep-rooted pacts with rubbish Third Division football teams and the poor saps who are obsessively smitten by clapped-out Jaguars, blokes on the whole are better at getting rid of the junk in their lives. Anna had become a great big bin liner of tatty memories; it was time she was chucked.

'It's you I'm thinking of,' he told Jo.

'I know, but what can I do?'

'Tell her.'

At least when the children had been there Anna had been

heavily outnumbered by Metcalfs, but now they were in Devon and it was just Jo and him against Anna.

Nigel was reminded of a video he'd seen starring Cameron Diaz as a kidnap victim who the kidnappers are trying to get rid of. Anna was like an unwanted hostage; the biggest shame being that she looked nothing like Cameron Diaz.

He had spoken to Chris a couple of times but only really by accident. He'd phoned once to say that he was popping to London to make storage arrangements for all the furniture and belongings which had survived the fire. 'Ah yes,' said Nigel. 'Good . . . and er, will you want to come by and see Anna? Would you rather Jo was here if you do?'

'No!' Chris almost laughed at the thought of possibly wanting to see his wife. 'To be honest, Nigel – and I know neither of us have ever been honest with each other, not really – I don't think I ever want to see Anna again. Obviously I shall maintain contact, let her know the children are all right, but that's as far as it goes.'

It was all rather uncomfortable.

'How's the weather?' Nigel inquired, the weather as a topic being like dry land to a sailor who's realised he's allergic to the sea.

'It's fine. Well, actually it's raining.'

'That's Wales for you.'

Chris sent Jo housekeeping money for Anna: seventy-five pounds a week for food and electricity. It was fair. He also sent Anna fifty pounds a week pocket money. She spent it on cigarettes and magazines.

It was such an invasion, she was always there: lurking, sniggering, falling down, weeing on the lavatory seat. Faced with the daily reality of this new Anna, he began to think that the old

Anna had been a fictional character whom he'd conjured up in his imagination. But he knew really that they were one and the same: the blue bird tattoo, now stretched across her fatty back, was inky proof, should a positive identification need to be made.

In truth, Nigel was slightly anal by nature: he liked his house tidy, shoe trees in his expensive loafers, CDs alphabetically arranged, ties graded by colour from light to dark. Living with Jo had knocked some of this precision out of him, after all, his wife was a borderline slob; but putting up with her untidyness was one thing, putting up with Anna's was another. She caused most of her devastation in the kitchen; whenever she made a cup of tea (twenty times a day, what else did she have to do?) instead of disposing of the tea bag down the waste disposal, she would carry it dripping over to the bin. She left the lids off jam jars or screwed them on so loosely that when you picked them up the jars would smash on the floor. Recently they had run out of coffee mugs and Jo had politely reminded Anna 'that if there are any in your room, would you mind bringing them down?' There were seventeen, all with various stages of penicillin growing inside them. It made him feel sick. Then there was her habit of kneeling, as if in obeisance, in front of the fridge, delving in with her unwashed fingers, tearing off little bits of ham, picking at cold pasta and leaving bite marks in the cheese.

Jo wasn't cooking as much as she used to; with the kids away and Anna in auto-stuff-mode it was a waste of time. She had made some buns last week but when she offered Nigel the tin, all that was left were twelve empty bun cases. How many straws does it take to break the camel's back? It was a bit like that children's game, Buckaroo, the one where you heap the poor donkey with various plastic shapes until it suddenly decides to snap, kicking up its back legs, bucking madly while plastic shapes fly through the air never to be found again. Nigel was as finely coiled as a buckaroo donkey; any moment now he might go.

It had been a hot day and when Nigel got home, Jo was in the garden deadheading roses. 'We could have a barbecue,' she suggested. 'I've a couple of chicken pieces in the freezer; be a love and get them out. Just bung them in the microwave on defrost for fifteen minutes, then I'll marinade them. We don't need to eat till nine.' Well, how nice and normal, thought Nigel, dutifully trotting off to the freezer. The chicken breasts were on the second shelf and a tub of ice-cream wobbled precariously on top of the polystyrene tray. As he withdrew the chicken, the ice-cream toppled out. Nigel instinctively moved his feet: he hadn't got shoes on and you can break a toe with a full tub of ice-cream. Too late. The tub bounced off his foot and rolled away painlessly; it was empty.

Well that was it, that was Nigel's buckaroo moment. 'Aaaaaaaaghhhh.' He hurled the frozen chicken at Georgina's old bike and went trumpeting up the stairs, holding the empty ice-cream tub high above his head, and because Anna hadn't bothered to close the freezer door properly, the last mouthful of melted ice-cream dripped forlornly on to his forehead and down his nose.

60

A Night on the Tiles

I suppose it was inevitable: Nigel's temper had been brewing for weeks. When he cracked, he really lost it; you should have seen him. He came barging into my room waving an empty tub of ice-cream at me, all spluttery and red. 'You selfish bitch. My Ben and Jerry's Cherry-Crunch Crumble: you know it's my favourite.' And I do, I know everything about him. I know about his dead sister and his affairs, his vanity, and verrucas. I know he is often constipated, I can hear him straining; I have seen him emerge from the lavatory on more than one occasion, his eyes bloodshot with the effort. He is literally full of shit.

I was in bed. I'd had rather too much sun and my skin felt tight and itchy. I rolled over and put my head under the pillow;

I didn't have to listen if I didn't want to. Next thing I knew, he'd started chucking stuff on top of me: all my clothes that lay in a heap on the floor he hurled at my head – 'You lazy cow' – my magazines – 'You stupid slag' – Henry's ghetto blaster that I'd sneaked down from his room – 'You're a user, you take and take' – shoes and plates and mugs containing dregs of tea, some of it trickling cold on to the nape of my neck. 'Well I've had it, you hear? I want you out. I don't give a toss where you go, you can get run over by a bus for all I care.'

'Blimey, Nigel,' I slurred at him; I'd been half asleep for heaven's sake. 'I do like a man with his dander up.'

'Fuck off,' he replied. He looked so cross that I started to laugh. That was when he hit me, smack wallop, across my face and in an instant I remembered all the other slaps I have received: the playful backhanders Danny would give me during our rough sex games, my son's premeditated reprimand and now this the latest one, the only one that really had any weight behind it. Nigel slapped me but I know he'd rather it had been a punch and it was all he could do to stop himself from really laying into me. At that moment he'd have liked to have split open my face and broken every bone in my body. It was quite exciting. I felt myself getting wet; I'd have fucked him then and there just to have made his life more terrible but he went stamping down the stairs, shouting, 'What more does a man have to take?'

The front door slammed after that and I lay there waiting for Jo to come up and apologise. I wanted her to come up immediately, to see me with all this crap everywhere. He'd emptied an ashtray on my head and I knew there was a satisfyingly large red mark on my cheek. To make it look worse, I dug my nails into the loose skin beneath my left eye and dragged them down my face, not too deep, I didn't want a scar, but I ripped the skin enough for it to show. Then I waited for Jo, fag butts and ash on my pillow, hot under the weight of all those shoes and back copies of *Tatler*. She took her time.

When she did eventually come up, she decided to play the bad cop. I wasn't expecting it; I had thought she might even give me a cuddle. I was so surprised. She was vile, she said some terrible things; I think she wanted me to cry, but I gave as good as I got. She was standing there with her arms folded, telling me off like I was some snivelling kid, all po-faced and meaning it, so I just started throwing things at her head. I was so angry and let down. 'Ow, Anna, stop it, stop it.' I think she was frightened; she was stuck against the door like a nervous knife-thrower's assistant, jumping and flinching every time I lifted my arm. She left the room when she realised I wasn't getting tired. I heard her run a bath and lock the door of the en suite.

I knew I was meant to apologise, but to be utterly truthful I'd have liked to have scratched off her stupid smug face. I can't stand this morally superior tone that she's adopted – and he's as bad, bloody Nigel the hypocrite. It's not as if he hasn't had his fingers in enough hairy pies in his time. Hairy pie, hairy pie; I was laughing and saying hairy pie to myself whilst I wrote 'sorry' on the back of an envelope, and my handwriting was as big and childish as I felt.

I read somewhere once that houseguests are like fish: they go off after three days. I have outstayed my welcome. When Maggie gets back from their place in Majorca, I shall go and stay with them. I don't care what the doctors say about her not having to be upset. I wish I'd bothered to make some different friends; I'm bored of my old ones.

She is jealous, of course, she always has been. Jo has never had a lover. She is a frigid, stuck-up bitch, who was only really any fun when she was pissed. Now that she doesn't drink like she used to, she has reverted back to the school prefect that she always was. Mr and Mrs Metcalf, I'm afraid, have become very dull.

I couldn't be bothered to tidy the bedroom; whilst I'd been lobbing things at Jo's head like I'd been aiming at cocoanuts, I'd trodden on a plate of congealed chips that had been lying around for a couple of days. I must have got tomato ketchup on my foot because there were splodges of the stuff all over the oatmeal-coloured carpet like spilt blood.

It was 8.30. I decided to go out: I'm a grown-up, I can go out at night if I want. I can stay out till morning time; no one can tell me what to do.

I put on some make-up. Georgina has loads of it and she hadn't taken much away with her, so I raided the little wicker basket where she keeps all her Superdrug slap. I put a glittery gel on my eyelids and cheeks, I used her blue mascara and tied my hair back in a velvet scrunchie and coloured my lips dark plum. She didn't have any foundation and I had a big spot on my chin, so I blacked it out with a felt-tip and from a distance it looked like a beauty spot. I sprayed myself all over with something that smelt like a mixture of teenager and boiled sweets and took twenty pounds from the Hello Kitty purse in her underwear drawer. Just the sight of that coloured nest of tiny knickers made me want to spit, so I did. Then I shut the drawer and tiptoed into Henry's room. Madam was still in the bath.

Despite Henry having been in Devon for over a fortnight, the room still smelt slightly briny – all that wanking I suppose. I'd found his money on a previous foray. Henry is a hoarder like his mum, while old tinkerbell-knickers spends money like water. Her father is a pushover. 'Go on, Dad, lend me a tenner,' and like a fool he hands over a note that no doubt has previously been rolled up in his nostril. Nigel's coke habit is something I have known about for years. When we were friends, I used to follow him to the bathroom; I had fingernails in those days and I'd scoop a talon full from his stash and shove it up my nose, whoosh, and the two of us would join our respective spouses all fired up and talking like game-show hosts. I knew he had a problem when he stopped sharing. Recently he seems to have given it up. I have searched his tie drawer, the linings of his suits, nothing. He is much duller for his abstinence, I used to have a laugh with Nigel; not any more, Scottish cunt.

Henry keeps his money in an old glasses' case. He is phobic about burglars and thinks this might fox them. He really is incredibly wet. I found the glasses' case under a pile of winter jumpers: there was also a packet of Durex and a picture of a girl in the same school uniform as Georgina's, flashing her tits. I doubt this was for Henry's benefit, especially as on closer inspection it turned out to be a photocopy. I took the Durex and twenty-five quid, and crumpled the picture into the toe of his football boots. Then I went to get changed.

I hadn't been out for a very long time. When you are married and you have children and you live in London, you don't. In the past, Chris liked going to restaurants; he has never been a pub man, he used to like coming home – ha. I swiped a pair of Jo's crinkly Ghost trousers from the laundry-basket – they were dark grey and had a small mustard stain on the knee – then I fannied about deciding what to wear on top. In the past I'd have gone for a little skimpy vest, but I looked too bulgy so I quickly ironed Nigel's best white linen shirt – badly – and wore that.

All the time I was getting ready, I was singing cheerful bits of songs to myself; the sort of songs that you heard on the waltzers when you were a teenager and the fair was in town. It is unbelievable that I was fifteen twenty-five years ago. 'Ooowee, chirpy chirpy cheep cheep.' I was drinking Cinzano and singing: it was that kind of night.

I shoved the money, the Durex and my keys into a silver mini-rucksack of Georgina's and slid my feet into a pair of her pink plastic sandals. As an ensemble it seemed to work: I have always been good with clothes. It was a lovely night; I didn't need a coat.

I saw Nigel with his head on his chest in the Saab. He was parked bang slap outside the house – wanker. I pretended not to notice him and crossed the road. As I walked past the pub, people were drinking at trestle tables on the pavement outside. The woman who lived next door to Jo was there with one of her disgusting pugs, talking to a man with grey hair. I half nodded but she didn't say anything, just looked a bit surprised. I didn't recognise any of the others; students mostly, all grubby toenails and baggy combat trousers, rings through their noses and Celtic tattoos round their skinny biceps. I marched right on by.

I could have ordered a taxi but I wasn't entirely sure where I was going. There were plenty of buses at the bottom of the road: I thought I'd get on the first one that came along. It was a number twelve, a proper double-decker. I hadn't been on a bus for a long time. I went directly up the stairs but there was a load of teenage black girls up there, with fancy hairdos and nails painted like cinema backdrops, all gold jewellery and hundred-quid trainers. As I retreated back down the steps, they all laughed. For a second I felt like going back up and ripping the shiny hoops out of their earlobes; instead I sat down by the luggage space and picked up a discarded copy of the *Sun*. There was a story about a family in the north-east who had died in a house fire: the mum and her boyfriend, the grandma and three little kids. There was a school photo of the kids: Stacey, Kelly and Shane, aged ten, eight and six respectively, all with slight squints. The mum was only twenty-eight. I never kept any school photos of my two, I find the photographer makes them brush their hair oddly and they don't look quite normal. Of course, Pandora hated having her photo taken, and who can blame her? It's bad enough suspecting that you look like a pig in a dress without having to deal with the photographic evidence. Jed, on the other hand, would primp and preen and smoulder at the camera, like a page three 'stunna'. I took him to have his photo taken for a passport when he was five; he made me put three lots of money in the Photo Me Booth in Sainsbury's before he was happy with the result.

The bus conductress told me it was one pound twenty to Piccadilly Circus. I thought it was as good a place as any to have a night out. I didn't want to stay local.

Down the Walworth Road we trundled, past the empty market and down towards the ridiculous Elephant and Castle shopping centre and further, towards Westminster Bridge and Big Ben. There were still a few Japanese tourists on the bridge; some of them got on the bus, all badly folded maps and tiny aching feet. I was quite excited, it had been months since I'd been Up West. Chris used to try to tempt me to go and to the opera. 'Fuck off,' I'd say. It's odd how you can be married to someone for so long and have so little in common. Jo once bought him a CD of the three fat tenors, an act of treachery if ever there was one.

Past Downing Street – those crappy little terraced houses. It's so typically British, isn't it, that our Prime Minister should live in a poxy two-up two-down, whilst the President of the United States gets the White House. It's embarrassing. Round Trafalgar Square: old Nelson on his podium, no doubt covered in pigeon poo! Up Haymarket, so called, I presume, because there used to be a hay market there. Did you know that according to some ancient law, it is still illegal for a London hackney carriage aka black cab to travel round London without a bale of hay? It's true. Nigel told us years ago, and we sat up all night making up other stupid ancient laws that might still be enforced. I came up with a law that insisted that every scout master is entitled to bugger at least one of his scouts with impunity. Jo didn't laugh much; Henry had recently enrolled, soft git. Jed, of course, refused to be a Cub. The only organisation he is a member of is the Boyzone fan club: he gets a lovely newsletter three times a year, badges and stickers, signed photos . . . Before I could think any more, we were at Piccadilly Circus and the sky had turned as dark as a bruise.

I wasn't quite sure where I was going to go. I thought I'd find a pub, then take myself out for dinner. I didn't worry about getting home, there were always loads of cabs whizzing round the West End. I was careful to keep Georgina's bag tightly by my side and I wasn't wearing any jewellery; my wedding ring had been too tight for some time. I walked from Piccadilly Circus through Leicester Square: it wasn't very nice. People were pissing in doorways and the place was full of tourists looking as if they'd made a horrible mistake and surely this couldn't be it? It had all the sophistication of a hot dog with extra fried onions. I felt excited; I had that fairground feeling again. A Scottish bloke with snot on his lapel started badgering me to let him do my portrait in charcoal. When I said no thanks, he got a bit insistent, so I told him I was a plain clothes cop and that my real name was WPC Collindale and that he'd better watch himself. I was in the mood for making things up.

I found a pub off the back of Shaftesbury Avenue, an Irish joint next to a theatre. There were photos of the actresses in those little glass boxes outside and I recognised a girl who'd been in the year below me at drama school, dressed up in a maid's outfit that she was obviously ten years too old for.

The pub was quite full. I got myself a pint of lager and a brandy and sat in a corner. I knew it wouldn't take long. Anyway, if the worst came to the worst, I had enough money to get myself pissed, have a slice of pizza and still have a few quid to get home. And if I wanted to get spectacularly smashed I could always get a night bus.

I'd almost finished the lager when the man sat down beside me. His eyes were red as if he'd been crying or drinking or probably both and he was unsteady on his feet, but he had a briefcase so I felt quite safe. I had a story ready in my head about how I was meant to meet a friend at the theatre, about how I'd been late and she must have gone in without me and that I was hoping she'd pop in the pub afterwards.

He asked if I wanted a drink; I said a pint of lager would be nice. I didn't ask for my brandy chaser, didn't want to frighten him off by being too expensive. He had grey hair but quite a lot of it, and he sold paper cups for vending machines – something like that. I can't say I was riveted. He was obviously divorced – he had that just-been-taken-to-the-cleaner's smell about him. His ex-wife and his child lived in the north-east and there was a new man in their lives. He showed me a photo, a younger him sitting on a chair with a baby in his lap. The wallpaper behind the chair was hideous. I decided to swap one sob story for another: I told him my husband had been killed in a motorway accident and that I was living with my sister in Norwood with my twin five-year-old daughters. That was another round in the bag. I didn't get out much, I told him, and anyway, I felt guilty if I enjoyed myself what with Graeme just a pile of ash in a little pot. His eyes filled up with tears. 'We were very much in love,' I embroidered, and I felt quite weepy myself. I made a few mistakes, I called 'Graeme' 'Gary' a couple of times, but by then we were ten sheets to the wind. At one stage I went to the ladies' and threw up. On the way back to my seat, I bought some more drinks and a packet of dry-roasted peanuts to take the smell of sick off my breath. At closing time, he suggested we went out for something to eat; it was a daft idea, neither of us was capable of lifting a fork to our lips. We had lost all sense of co-ordination, I'd forgotten his name and couldn't remember what I'd called myself. We were locked in this bubble of alcohol that refused to pop. We rolled out of the pub and I wished I'd brought a cardigan because I was shivering. He put his arm around me and we staggered down a side street like children doing a three-legged-race.

The hotel was called the Strand Imperial Palace, which was a lie because it wasn't on the Strand and it certainly wasn't a palace. Instead of chandeliers and marble floors, there was strip lighting and a nylon fag-burnt patterned carpet. I couldn't tell whether the pattern was intentional or not as I was having trouble focussing. We got into a very small lift and when the doors closed his face looked like an unripe tomato, all green and red. By the time we'd reached the third floor, I knew I'd made a mistake. His room was only a few doors down the corridor and its key hung from a massive metal knob, which made me giggle: I was a bit hysterical. It was a horrible room, just a single bed and a chair and the telly on a metal arm that came out of the wall – so that you could watch it in bed, I suppose. Oh hell, I thought, oh hell's bells. I think he felt all wrong about it too. Suddenly we were both very tired and we didn't know how to get rid of each other.

'We don't have to, you know,' he said.

'No, not a good idea,' I mumbled, and then I burst into tears. I have always found that when you don't know what else to do, cry. I have always cried quite prettily; I'm not a convulsing sobber, I don't go blotchy and my nose manages not to run. Tears simply roll out of my eyes, down my face and drip off my chin.

A weeping woman brings out the best in any man; it exposes any latent chivalry they may have. This one was no exception. 'Oh Christ, I'm sorry, I never meant . . . here,' and he offered me a small bottle of whisky. I have found recently with drinking that it only takes one sip to push me from pissed into black-out.

When I woke up it was light and I was in his single bed, but I still had my knickers on. The only things I'd taken off were Jo's trousers and Georgina's shoes. I was bursting for a pee. The man was asleep on the floor, just lying there on the carpet in his suit with a blanket pulled over his head; he'd obviously rolled up some towels to make a pillow. The only bits of him that I could really see were his feet: he'd taken off his shoes and socks and his toes were waxy and yellow. The room stank of farts and feet and whisky. I crept to the bathroom and wee-ed as quietly as I could; the wee went on for ever, a litre bottle full at least. His toothbrush looked mangy so I decided not to risk borrowing it; I didn't even wash my hands or flush, I just grabbed the trousers, the bag and the trainers and slipped out of the door. He was probably awake but pretending not to be, which was fine by me. I got dressed in the hallway and looked at my watch. It was twenty past seven.

61

Wine Bottles in the Wardrobe

I could hear the shouting – Nigel roaring at the top of his voice – then I heard him charge down the stairs and slam the front door and I knew he'd driven off because I heard the Saab squealing.

I hate Nigel taking the car out when he's angry; it frightens me. I always think he will do something silly: drive too fast and run over a child. But I didn't blame him. I sat for a long time trying to make sense of it all, weighing up the options, knowing there was only one solution.

I made up my mind to tell her. I chucked a brandy down my neck and like someone with lead implants in their calves, I pulled myself up the stairs.

I knocked but didn't wait for a response; it was my house after all, I could do what I liked. She was lying in bed; it looked like a wardrobe had fallen on her but I knew it couldn't have because ours are built in. Her face was a bit swollen on one side and there was an angry red scratch from her eye to her chin.

'Oh God, Jo,' she moaned, 'he hit me. Nigel hit me.'

'I don't blame him,' I said, 'if it hadn't have been him, it would have been me. We've had enough, Anna, we can't take it any more.'

As I spoke, I knew that the words sounded scripted, like a bad soap opera: but for my Home Counties cut-glass vowels, my received pronunciation, it could have been a scene out of *Eastenders*, it was farcical. She slipped immediately into the same schlock-telly gear; had I been a director, I'd have panned the camera on to her face for a close up, the wide-eyed moment of shock, the trembling bottom lip. God, she was better than she ever thought she'd been; the acting profession had let a diamond slip through their hands when they'd written off Anna. I, on the other hand, turned into a pantomime Mrs Danvers, gimlet-eyed and hard of mouth.

'You're putting everyone in the shit. We've tried and tried, Anna, but we can't cope with you any more.'

I meant it too. For years I have despised mothers who are not capable of controlling their teenage daughters: weak, chain-smoking, obese women with single-figure IQs, too feeble of brain to smell trouble round the corner, too willing to go whimpering off to social services. 'Take her away, put her into care.' But that's what I wanted to do with Anna: I wanted a professional, some-one who knew what they were doing, to come and take her away. She was spoiling everything for the rest of us. A hundred thoughts were going through my head as I read Anna the riot act. I kept thinking it was a shame that they didn't have some kind of Borstal for naughty forty-year-olds in need of a curfew and some old-fashioned discipline; I even had a mental image of her with her head shaved, at some boot camp doing pack drill.

Suddenly she started throwing stuff at me: CDs whizzed past my head, shoes ricocheted off the door behind me, she was pelting me with apple cores and empty boxes of Mini Rolls – it was ridiculous. She was like an overgrown toddler having an enormous tantrum. 'Shut up, shut up, shut up,' she kept shouting, and she was pulling at her hair, breaking off whole fistfuls at the root; at one point she bit her own shoulder. I ducked to avoid a mug hitting me in the teeth, left the room and closed the door. I didn't know what to do so I went and had a bath. I retrieved a bottle of Jo Malone amber and lavender bath oil that I'd hidden in the box file under the bed, and locked myself in the en suite. I was in there for hours. At some point she must have crept upstairs and pushed a note under the door. 'Sorry', it said, but I put it in the bin.

I lay in the bath for a very long time, topping it up with hot water whenever it felt chilly. I was up to my neck in thick, pale grey soapy water. I could hear her banging about the house. I knew she'd been in the kids' rooms; Georgina would go spare, privacy is very important to the teenager. While I was in the bath, I made some more decisions: we were going to get back to normal. I would talk seriously to Anna and as soon as she found alternative accommodation, I would book a flight to see my brother in Germany. Hanover is a very dull place and therefore ideal for my purposes. They are a very ordered race, the Deutsche, and I felt too emotionally frail for somewhere like Spain or Italy where the people get overexcited and wave their cutlery in the air. I was a bit surprised when I heard the front door slam again; she very rarely goes out. A few moments later, I heard Nigel coming in – it took several attempts before he managed to get the key in the door. I wrapped myself in a towel and stood on the landing watching him ricochet up the stairs.

'She's gone out,' I said.

'I know, halle-fucking-lujah, let's change the locks and have a party.' He had the remains of a small bottle of Scotch in his hand.

'Where have you been?'

He'd driven off, bought himself a tub of ice-cream from the garage down the road and the whisky from the off-licence, then he'd sat outside our house, drinking in the car, until he saw Anna come down the garden path and walk off down the road. Nigel said as she walked past, he'd locked the doors and ducked down. A fugitive from his own home.

Mind you, apparently caramel ice-cream and whisky are a winning combination, and there had been a very amusing comedy drama on Radio 4.

I made him get into my scuzzy old water and got him a fresh pair of pyjamas. I think he was quite glad to get into bed; he was asleep by 10.30, so I read for half an hour: *Northanger Abbey*. Normally I don't like to go to sleep without bolting the front door and setting the alarm, but with Anna still out I couldn't really do that. To be honest, I was so done in that if an intruder had broken in and shot us in our beds, I wouldn't really have cared. Just before I put out the light, I reached under the bed and delved into the 'Heating and Lighting' box file where I hid my special little treats from Anna; I'd a bar of Swiss chocolate from Marks and Spencer tucked away in there, but all that was left was the silver foil. That's when I started crying; I didn't dare wake Nigel, I had a horrible feeling he might have joined in.

When I went to sleep, I had a dream about the Pink House

looking all normal from the outside but inside the furniture and the walls were made of chocolate, which kept melting, and as it melted, it turned into blood. When I woke up in the middle of the night I'd started my period; if I'd had any energy left, I'd have had another cry.

I looked at my watch in the bathroom, it was ten minutes past one. I sorted myself out with a sanitary towel; sometimes I find them more comforting than tampons, it's like being a baby again, wearing a nappy. I felt sure she would be home by now, but when I looked over the banisters to check the front door it was still unbolted and the alarm wasn't winking its little red eye. I felt more annoyed than worried; she wasn't my daughter and these days she is certainly big enough to look after herself. I was just a little bothered, more about the safety of the house than anything else. I left the hall light on and went back into the bedroom and closed the door.

As soon as you become a mother you become a light sleeper. When Henry was very young he had a bad chest; one cough and I'd be out of that bed and in his room plugging in the vaporiser. You can't leave those things to nannies; it is all they can do not to blow smoke rings into the baby's face. Henry used to sleep-walk as well; I couldn't tell you how many times I have found him wandering around the landing, muttering: once we had quite a lucid conversation about alkalis and acids, indicators and neutralisers, before I managed to lead him firmly back to his bed. It is a sixth sense that we mothers acquire: the apron strings have ears, I am quite sure of that. So I was certain that I would wake up when Anna came home, and went back to bed feeling quite safe in my big pants, the sanitary towel firmly gripped between my legs.

As I nodded off, I remembered a feature I'd read in a magazine about a year ago about a man who had been unfaithful to his wife. Shagging his mistress in the marital bed – oh silly, silly, silly. So one day the wife comes home, and she notices that there is make-up on the pillows and a shrivelled pair of tights under the bed. 'What's going on?' she cries. 'Tell me the truth.' But of course he doesn't. He tells her that sometimes he feels the urge to dress up in her clothes, put on her make-up and pretend to be a woman. It is the only lie he can think of at the time. His wife, instead of throwing heavy objects at his head, calling him a 'weirdo pervert' and making him promise never to do it again, decides to be reasonable and calmly tells him that she will support his urges, these things being commoner than you would think. She has watched the American talk shows; there is nothing that's not normal any more. The husband is backed into a corner: if he tells his wife the real truth, she will leave and he will only ever see his children in McDonald's on Sunday afternoon. So he decides to live with his lie and every Wednesday night after that he is forced to dress up in women's clothing and let his wife apply his make-up properly and address him as Audrey. Together they sit and watch television and 'Audrey' pretends he's enjoying being in touch with his feminine side, when if the truth were told he'd rather impale himself on the nearest railings. Punishment comes in many different forms and wearing a shirtwaister from Debenhams is just one of them. They call it karma in India, don't they?

The next time I woke up, I expected it to be morning, but it wasn't, it was only quarter past two. Nigel was snoring gently. I didn't think I'd heard her come in, but I went to look anyway. The hall light was still on and I tiptoed down to check her room. It was a tip and it stank like a pet shop; I felt a bubble of rage rise in my throat. It was knee deep in clothes and she'd spilt blusher on the duvet; there were empty crisp packets and broken biscuits ground into the carpet and that yeasty smell of dirty knickers. Her pillow was ingrained with make-up and brown dribble patches and there was another smell that reminded me of when the children were small. When I closed my eyes for a second, I remembered what it was: when Henry was about four he went through a terrible bed-wetting stage and twice a week he'd appear in our bedroom, hot and crying, holding his pyjama bottoms, and I'd have to haul myself into his room and change the sheets, trying not to be furious with him. It was that same smell: Anna's room stank of wee. It wasn't the mattress, I checked, it was quite dry, but the smell was coming from somewhere and it seemed stronger in the corner of the room. I felt the carpet; apart from where it was still sticky with tomato ketchup that wasn't damp either. By now I was crawling around on my hands and knees. Suddenly it struck me, the wee smell was coming from the wardrobe. I opened the doors.

I am not a woman who shocks easily; remember, I have given birth, I have seen placenta. Living in London you see terrible things all the time: I have seen a tramp shit his trousers, I have seen crashed cars with blood on the windscreens, I have watched a lad come off his motorbike and the bone of his leg come poking through the ripped flesh of his knee – but nothing prepared me for the sight of half a dozen wine bottles filled to the brim with cloudy piss. I shut the wardrobe, and then I did a terrible thing. I flew downstairs faster than a witch on a broomstick and bolted the front door from the inside and set the burglar alarm. Whatever happened, I wasn't having her in this house again. Then I went back to bed and I slept like a dead person.

62

An Accident Waiting to Happen

The banished Metcalf children were halfway through their term in exile.

Georgina Metcalf had had quite enough of Devon; the countryside holds very little allure for a fourteen (going on twenty-seven)-year-old. 'The shops are crap,' she told Lucy Morris, who at eleven agreed with everything Georgina said. 'Yeah, crap,' she echoed, knowing full well that if her mother heard her say 'crap', she'd go ape.

Angela Morris wasn't sure that bringing Georgina away with them to Devon had been such a good idea after all. On paper it had seemed fine; her son Matthew was very friendly with the Metcalf boy. Henry was no problem, just permanently embarrassed, rather shy and wetter than a bank holiday weekend. Angela Morris's husband Grant had taken the two boys fishing, and Henry had almost fainted when they had pulled a live fish from the river and then proceeded to become completely hysterical when Grant had gutted it for lunch. The boy had refused to eat the fish and Grant had had to pop to a garage to buy him a Pot Noodle. Days later, he was still having nightmares: 'the fish, the fish'. Still, he had manners, even if he did sniff all the time. The girl was altogether a different proposition; she made Angela slightly nervous. Georgina was more sophisticated at fourteen than Angela was at forty-three. She'd arrived without Wellingtons, for heaven's sake, and refused to get out of bed till gone ten. Angela Morris was worried about the effect Georgina was having on Lucy; Lucy had always been such a good-natured girl – up until this holiday – and now she was copying this little minx and becoming more sullen and monosyllabic by the minute. It was like watching cream curdle.

Still, it was lovely to be back at The Orchards; the farmhouse was idyllic, real picture postcard stuff (if you lopped off the rather nasty 1970s extension). There was masses of space for the children: a field with a stream and a rope swing, and a separate barn where they could play ping-pong. But it didn't have satellite television and within minutes of arriving Georgina had complained to Angela, 'Your remote control's broken. It can only get five poxy channels.' Georgina was as peevish as a businessman who finds himself stuck in a two-star b and b rather than a Marriott.

'That's all we've got,' said Angela brightly. She was a cheerful woman and she expected everyone to make an effort. 'Go on, dear, why don't you run off and play.'

Angela Morris wore shorts because it was summer; she had a big bottom and very big knees and would have made a marvellous

Girl Guide captain. The farmhouse belonged to her parents, who lived in a bungalow nearby and rented out The Orchards throughout the year. Angela and her husband always 'bagsied' it for the whole of August; her parents, seeing as it was 'Angela', allowed her to rent it at an off-peak price.

Angela had lived in the farmhouse as a child; she was a country girl at heart and had the complexion to prove it. She found the fact that her old home was rented out to strangers mildly traumatic and flinched whenever she noticed the visitors' book lying on the table next to the payphone. The house was both familiar yet strange, the same but different. The rolling pin in the kitchen drawer was the one her mother had always used, ditto the weighing-scales and dented baking-tins. But there was a pared-down quality to the house that there hadn't been when she was a child. The pantry was empty save for a drum of damp salt and a chipped glass cruet. In the old days, the shelves had groaned with home-made jams and pickles, and the cake tin, with the picture of the Victorian lady in a bonnet on the lid, was always heavy when you picked it up. All the best bits of furniture had gone to the bungalow: the good glasses, the silver cutlery and nice china; in their absence, the farmhouse had been kitted out with car-boot sale knives and forks, factory seconds and a motley collection of chipped glasses, some of which looked suspiciously like garage freebies. Still, it was the paying guests who kept the place going, and Angela knew she should be grateful; it was just that every time they came, something else had got broken or gone missing and there was yet another stain on the carpet.

Whenever Angela arrived at the farmhouse, she would go round peeling off all the handwritten instructions that were Sellotaped around the place: it was her old home, she knew how to turn the immersion heater on, thank you very much.

Angela wanted her children to have some of the freedom that she had enjoyed as a youngster: climbing trees, chasing rabbits, going on long bike rides. In London, it was very difficult to let the children out of her sight; coming back to Devon was like falling into a sixties time warp, it was so much safer, as long as they all stuck together, as long as they were sensible. That Georgina had a mobile phone – ridiculous, thought Angela, but at the same time oddly comforting. The children were allowed to cycle into town; there was an assortment of clapped-out, rusty old bikes in the shed. 'They're all crap' (Georgina). It wasn't far, the first mile was private road, there was only one busy junction and then they were there. Angela didn't know what they wanted to do in town, but there was a record shop, a swimming pool and a cinema.

'Can you give us some money for a McDonald's, Mum?'

'I don't know why you can't take a picnic.'

Georgina's face at that! 'A picnic . . . like yeah, right.' Ooh, she was a madam, picky as well; wouldn't eat this, wouldn't eat that, just slunk about in that loose-limbed way. Little tie-dyed purple vest with her bra straps showing. Matthew fancied her but she was out of his league.

She was bullied into it, of course – letting them have a night out. She had a feeling that it wasn't a good idea; her husband Grant had gone back to London for a few days, she was on her own with them till the weekend. They wanted to go to see *Deep Blue Sea*; Lucy couldn't, she was a young-looking eleven and the film was a fifteen. She cried, of course. 'Not fair.'

'Oh shut it, Lucy,' said Georgina, and Lucy had run away and hidden in a tree for several hours.

'But you're only fourteen,' said Angela.

'So?' replied Georgina. 'Watch,' and she pushed her hair up

on top of her head, and larded her lips with a strawberry-coloured gloss. 'Go on, ask me how old I am.'

Angela did as she was told.

'Fifteen,' Georgina replied in a mock-cockney accent, 'wot, you want my birf certificate or somefink?' Angela had no doubt that the child would get away with it; she didn't even blink when she lied.

'Well?'

'I don't know. I'll think about it.'

But they were so determined that Angela could feel her resolve buckling. Georgina bribed Lucy to accept the situation with a couple of bindis, three quid and some fake tattoos. Gradually they wore her down until she agreed to a compromise: whilst the big ones went to the cinema, she would take Lucy to see her grandparents. 'Oh lucky me,' snarled the girl who used to like pretending to be a show jumper on an imaginary horse. After the film, Angela would meet them at nine o'clock in the square. If they weren't waiting on the steps of the town clock, she would kill them.

'Is that understood?'

'Yes, Mum' said Matthew.

'Thank you, Mrs Morris,' stuttered Henry

'Heil Hitler,' muttered Georgina.

Angela had misgivings before they even got in the car: if they were only going to the cinema, then why was Georgina tarted up like she was about to be playing a bit-part in a film about teenage prostitutes – jailbait leaning against lamppost? 'I'd take a cardi if I were you, Georgina. It might get nippy later,' Angela said, in her best tent-peg-and-mallet voice. And Georgina, to give her her credit, immediately tied a denim jacket around the place where one day she might eventually have hips. She wasn't being obedient, she was just avoiding any excuse for Angela to call off the trip.

Angela drove the BMW carefully. 'Can we have some music on?' The radio was tuned to Classic FM; they all groaned on cue. Teenagers are so predictable. She made sure that they all had their seatbelts buckled. 'Belt up will you, just BELT UP.' There was a note of hysteria in her voice; other people's children were such a responsibility.

She dropped off Matthew, Henry and Georgina by the traffic lights. 'And you've got Grannie's number?' 'Yeah yeah.' She felt a bit sick as she drove away; maybe she should have asked for the Metcalf mother's permission, oh ridiculous, between them they had a combined aged of forty-six.

'Cheer up, sweetie.' She tried to give Lucy's knee a squeeze.

'Gerrof.'

Her parents were frailer than the last time she'd seen them; she couldn't help but think that it wouldn't be long before all this – the bungalow, the furniture and the farmhouse – would be hers. Well, not all hers; Angela had two brothers.

'Would you like to go and see the ducks, dear?' Angela's mother asked Lucy.

'You must be fucking joking,' the flaxen-plaited one replied.

Angela felt quite faint. This was Georgina's influence; Lucy was possessed. Fortunately, her mother hadn't heard. 'Beg your pardon, dear.' She was struggling with a jar of beetroot.

Lucy looked at her mother and replied with the enthusiasm of an Angela Brazil heroine, 'Ooh, yes please, Grannie, that would be splendid fun.'

So they walked around the village duck pond and Lucy kept up the dutiful granddaughter act, gamely throwing old crusts at the 'quack quacks'. She was laying it on a bit thick: 'Oh,

Mummy, may I have an ice-cream? Oh please say yes.'

'Just wait till I get you in that car, young lady,' Angela hissed, when Lucy came skipping back with a ninety-nine.

'Oh thank you, lovely Mummy, you're the best mummy in the whole wide world.' She was taking the piss.

The temperature had reached the mid-eighties, but Angela's mother had cooked a 'nice hot meal'. Watching her mother's twisted hands serve the veg made Angela feel guilty: her father had his shirt open, and although he was tanned you could see the lilac scar of his triple bypass. God, oh God, oh God. She had half a glass of sweet German white wine.

'Can I have some?'

'No, Lucy.'

'Would you like some nice pop, darling?'

'Oh yeth, Grampy, a lovely glath of fithy pop. Can I have a thtraw?' lisped Lucy, clapping her hands like an overexcited three-year-old. She was really going over the top; Angela kicked her under the table.

'Ow,' winced Grannie.

They left at 8.40. 'What the hell are you playing at, Lucy?'

'Nuffink. Don' know wot yaw talkin' abaht.' She was doing the common voice again. Angela was a speech therapist; she really minded about glottal stops. Lucy was due to go to the same girls' school as Georgina that coming September. Angela was having serious doubts: if they all ended up like Georgina, she'd want a refund on the fees. They parked in Tesco's carpark and walked round to meet the others.

There was a small crowd gathered towards the bus depot end of the square. Instinctively, Angela started running. Her shorts, after such a large meal, were tight across her buttocks: it was like watching a sofa jogging. There was a lad sitting on the kerb with his head in his hands, blood pouring from a gash on his chin. A motorbike lay swerved across the road, its tail-lights smashed, and in the middle of the tarmac was Georgina, looking like a modern-day Degas with only one leg: the other was folded up behind her. Her eyes were closed and Matthew was kneeling over her. Henry was shouting at the boy on the kerb, 'You fucking twat. If you've killed my sister, I'll fucking have you.' His stutter had completely disappeared. 'Interesting,' thought Angela, ever the professional. Then: 'What the bloody hell is going on here?' Angela was highly trained and used her diaphragm to project – never mind the back of the stalls, she could have been heard in Cornwall: Angela was about to tear the boy with the cut face to pieces, using her vocal chords alone. He was crying, 'She asked. I said I ain't got me test. She told me to go faster.' It didn't take Angela long to fathom that he hadn't just knocked her over; Georgina had been riding on the back, 'WITHOUT A HELMET?' Angela bellowed. 'HOW COULD YOU BE SO STUPID!' Well, that was it. Lucy could go to the local comprehensive. She was damned if her child was going somewhere where for two grand a term, the girls turned out to be not just slags, but stupid slags.

An ambulance turned up at that point. Henry got in with Georgina and the boy with the lacerated chin. Angela decided to follow in the car. She didn't fancy sitting with Georgina; the last thing she wanted to do was hold her hand and make a big show of being nice. To be honest, she'd have liked to have broken the idiot girl's other leg. Lucy and Matthew followed their mother back to the carpark. Lucy was rather cheerful; she wasn't in trouble any more and now the emphasis of blame had shifted she reverted back to her normal voice. Angela would have been relieved had she even noticed. What the hell would

Jo Metcalf have to say about this? Her husband Nigel was a lawyer; maybe they would sue? Well, that was the school fees down the swanny; both of them would have to go to the local comprehensive.

There was a delivery van blocking their exit. Angela didn't swear as a rule but she made an exception on this occasion and a stream of choice Anglo-Saxon expletives poured out of her mouth and the inside of the windscreen was covered in a fine film of spittle.

By the time they got to the hospital, Georgina was already being X-rayed. The motorbike boy was still in casualty, bleeding into a bucket. 'How is she?' Angela asked Henry. 'Have you spoken to your mother?'

'N-no, um . . . ' Apparently Georgina had lost her mobile phone.

'I think she left it in the cinema. We were in McDonald's and she—' Matthew attempted to explain.

'McDonald's! But the film was only meant to be over at eight fifty-five. What were you doing mucking around in town?'

'I'm afraid we got chucked out for being a n-n-n-nuisance,' admitted Henry. 'There were these lads and w-w-w-well . . . it all got out of h-h-hand, and then Georgina went on the b-b-back of the b-bike and . . . '

'Yes, well, I think we'd better inform your parents,' and Angela frogmarched Henry to the payphone down the corridor. It was no good, they couldn't get through: when Anna had been in mid-frenzy earlier that same evening, she'd thrown the bedroom extension at Jo's cranium and consequently the line was permanently engaged.

They kept trying but deee, deee, deee was the only response.

It was one o'clock when they got back to The Orchards; Angela had to carry a sleeping Lucy out of the car. She sent them all straight to bed.

'Can we have some toast?' braved Matthew.

'Bugger off,' she roared.

Angela was so tired she accidentally knocked the visitors' book off the telephone table as she tried one last, unsuccessful time to get through to Jo. Bending down to pick up the red imitation leather book, she noticed that Georgina had penned an entry under 'visitor's comments'. 'Boring as shit' she had scribbled. Really, thought Angela, and she visualised writing 'I am a horrid little cow' on the virgin white plaster that now encased Georgina's right leg.

63

Full to Bursting

People seem to know when you have been a dirty stop-out; it's as if you give off a smell from the night before that needs loofahing off. Dirty girl, dirty girl.

I didn't have enough money left for a cab; thinking about it I should have nicked his wallet. Instead, I had to wait for a bus. Imagine, around me normal people were arriving for work. It was a lovely morning, but I knew my make-up had formed a crust around my ears like an old pie, and I wished I'd brought some sunglasses. I didn't even have enough cash for a packet of Nurofen. The hangover hadn't quite kicked in, but it was lurking: sand behind my eyes, my joints stiff and clumsy. In a doorway behind the bus stop, someone was sleeping in a filthy pale blue sleeping bag, just a snoring shaven head. I was quite tempted to lie down beside him. I was overtired. When I got back to Jo's, I would fry three eggs and eat them with beans on thickly buttered toast. I was very hungry.

A number one-seven-one lumbered along and I got on it; the top deck was almost deserted. It was going to be a perfect summer's day and the sun was shining as bright as acid as we trundled south across the river, landmarks to the left of me, landmarks to the right. All that architecture, all that effort; it was tiring just to look at it. The National Theatre, the Hayward, that daft new cinema that only shows 3-D films about monkeys and fish. I dozed for a while. When I woke up, we were circumnavigating the Elephant and Castle and I had dribble on my shoulder. I was hungrier than ever; I hoped there was some bacon in the fridge. I could see my breakfast on a plate in my head: eggs, bacon and beans. I added a couple of fat grilled mushrooms – yummy – and tomato ketchup – scrummy. I tried to concentrate on what I was going to be eating soon, trying to take my mind off my bladder, which was bursting at the seams. Because the bus was still quite empty, I was able to hold myself with my hand, pressing my fingers against where the wee comes out, like a five-year-old.

Eventually we got to my stop and I hobbled up the hill, clutching myself, willing the piss not to come torrenting out, but I knew that I wasn't going to make it. The wee started to leak between my fingers, hot and wet. Across the road there was an alleyway through to the churchyard, where the winos have their Tennent's mornings. I half ran to it; with every step there was more liquid. By the time I was able to pull down my pants, they were sodden – along with Jo's trousers. I leant back against the wall and let it go, a great yellow foaming river, streaming round the soles of

Georgina's trainers. At that moment a dog came snuffling round the corner and started to lap at it; it wasn't very dignified. I was mortified, sitting there with my bare bum out for all the tramps to see and a dog with a cataract eye sniffing and licking my piss off the pavement. I was relieved when I could pick myself up and pretend it hadn't happened. Maybe I would have a bath after breakfast.

I couldn't see the Saab, but Jo's car was still outside the house. That was a bummer. I was more or less counting on them both having left for work; I didn't want a scene before I had the chance to eat. I don't like eating in front of them, you have to remember to use cutlery and close your mouth. 'Manners, Anna, we aren't savages.' I tried to make up stories about where I'd been but I didn't have the strength. 'Anna, Anna, where have you been?' 'I've been to London to visit the Queen!' Bollocks to it. I figured I'd tell them the truth, that would shut them up. Sometimes honesty is the best policy – not often, it's just that sometimes the truth is so implausible no one believes you anyway. Jo would think I was joking out of spite.

'I picked up this strange bloke who smelt of failure and loneliness, and I went back to his hotel room and gave him a wank.' That last bit wasn't actually true, but it could have been. Then again, I thought to myself as I opened the gate, maybe they wouldn't even bother asking. For a second, I felt like a teenager who fears she might have pushed it too far, that this time Mummy and Daddy really would wash their hands of me. Then I remembered I'm a grown-up, I can do what I like; it's not as if they can stop my pocket money. Mind you, that said, things are a bit dodgy on the money front. Chris sends me a pittance and when I run out I have to go to the bank and ask in person for funds from the joint account. How embarrassing is that? No wonder I take money from Jo's purse, Nigel's inside pocket and Henry's sock drawer. Last week I nicked a fiver from stupid Sue's battered plastic wallet; always leave the underclasses short, that's what I say.

The front door was double locked; that was odd. I turned the key and let myself in; it was very quiet. 'Hello.' I raced to turn off the burglar alarm; you have to be quick, punch in the numbers before it starts wailing. 'Hellooo.' Again no reply. Maybe I'd been lucky; maybe whilst I was out, a murderer had crept through a window and stabbed them in their sleep. If they had, I'd leave it a couple of hours before informing the police: I needed some kip.

The coffee mugs on the kitchen table were still warm; they'd been alive and drinking Gold Blend quite recently then. The note was shoved under a jar of marmalade: 'Have gone to Devon, Georgina hurt, will call'. For some reason that tickled me, and I sat down and laughed for a while, hoping that she'd burnt her stupid face. See, luck runs out for everyone.

I took off the wee-stained things and chucked them in the laundry. I was humming while I put on an old t-shirt of Nigel's – it had been on top of the dirty washing pile but it didn't seem particularly smelly – then I went back to the kitchen to prepare myself a feast. There is nothing like being on your own sometimes. There was a twenty-pound note on the table for mop woman, but I decided to call her and tell her not to bother coming in till next week. I didn't need her snooping around, giving me the evil eye.

'Hello Sue, it's Anna. Jo's asked me to give you a ring, tell you not to bother coming in for the next few days. She and Nigel have gone for a weekend break to the country.'

'She never said anything to me.' (Cheeky bitch.)

'No, it was a surprise.'

'Well, shouldn't I be coming in anyway?' (Piss off.)

'No, they're having the hall painted, be a waste of your time.'

'But she never told me.' (So?)

'Why should she? It's none of your fucking business.'

'But—'

'But nothing, just fuck off.'

Then I put down the phone. I couldn't decide whether I'd buy one bottle of good champagne with that twenty, or three bottles of vaguely decent wine, though what with quantity over quality being my motto these days I knew, deep down, which it would be. I felt really rather cheerful as I got out the frying pan.

(Out of the frying pan into the fire.)

There were only two eggs, which was a bit annoying, but I found four rashers of bacon, a tin of sugar-free beans (Georgina's – still make you fart, mind) and, joy of joys, a cold pork sausage. I ate that whilst I prepared the rest. It was like some Japanese tea ceremony in praise of the God of Greasy Spoons. I did it properly: lard spitting in a pan, the grill on high, hot milk for my coffee – I was so excited, I needed another wee. At last, when it was all done and I was sitting down with my knife and fork, the phone went. I left it to the answer machine; it was Jo.

'We're on the motorway. Oh, Anna, Georgina's been hurt, she's in hospital, a motorbike accident. Please look after the house; be careful don't do anything silly.'

At that point I realised I'd left the grill pan on and the bacon grease was smoking. Ha. I cut up a bit of bacon and piled it on to some beany toast and dipped it into the runny yolk of an egg. Ahhh, bliss.

64

The Seven O'Clock Call

I got up at six – silly really – and went to check her room again, like she could have squeezed through the cat flap. Obviously she wasn't there. I picked up a few things from the floor: the phone, a bottle of Lea and Perrins. For a moment, I wondered if I should call the police, but I knew it would sound stupid: forty-one-year-old women are allowed to go missing and I knew she would be all right. Anna has always been a butter-side-up kind of woman; whilst the rest of us go through life snagging our tights and tripping over uneven paving stones, Anna is the kind of woman who can fry bacon without getting a spot of grease on her silk blouse. But then again, I thought, her luck has run out of late; what if something terrible had happened to her? What if she'd been run over and was lying in hospital with amnesia – and for a second I considered that this option might be a blessing. I went downstairs to put a wash on. Now that the kids are away, there is almost too little to do, just knickers really – my big, sensible lady's pants and Nigel's navy jockeys. I put it on half load and wished they were here and even more that I was there. Just because of bloody Anna, we won't be having a summer holiday. I was so fed up, I ate a big bowl of Alpen and two pieces of toast with masses of butter, and with every bite I was hating her more.

I have had much nicer friends in the past, normal women. She has always been a troublemaker.

The phone went at seven. It was a terrible line and I knew it was going to be bad news; it wasn't a normal time for anyone to be phoning. Immediately I thought that something terrible might have happened to my mother or my father and the guilt at not having visited them this summer hit me in the solar plexus. But when I heard the pips I knew it was someone calling from a payphone; bloody fucking Anna, I presumed, but it wasn't, it was Angela Morris and she sounded upset. 'Jo, it's Angela, don't panic, they're all right; it's just Georgina, she's in hospital – it happened last night. She's going to be okay, she's got concussion but they say it's only mild. But her leg, it's broken quite badly. We didn't know. There was a boy in town, she went on the back of his moped, I had no idea. Oh, Jo, I'm so sorry, if only it had been one of mine. Oh Christ, it's a nightmare.' And it was, it was a nightmare.

By 7.30, I had woken Nigel by screaming into his face, showered, thrown some clothes into a holdall and filled a plastic bag with biscuits, apples and a triple pack of pineapple juice cartons; it's quite a long way to Devon. I dithered over taking some rather nice chocolate but it seemed rather frivolous in the circumstances, so I popped in some rather nasty boiled sweets instead: it seemed more fitting, practical. You have to be practical in an emergency.

I am awful when my sugar levels drop and I knew if I was going to be doing any map reading, I was going to have to keep my wits about me. Nigel turns into a cliché when he's driving and I, despite being a Queen's Guide with prerequisite compass skills, am reduced to a gibbering idiot when it comes to motorway exits. I had the name of the hospital on the back of an envelope.

Nigel kept saying, 'We'll sue; sodding ridiculous.' He hadn't had time to shave properly and there were bits of bloody toilet tissue on his chin. I left a note for Anna – I don't know why – and some cash for Sue. I was trying not to cry.

Nigel drove with his mouth set hard, his lips pressed together tightly, looking like a grandma with a mouthful of pins. He was angrier than I was. 'What if she's scarred, what if my beautiful daughter has hurt her face? Did they say anything about her eyes?' Then I remembered that he had been through this before when his sister fell off the horse, and at first they thought it was nothing and 'She'll come round soon enough,' and all the time that no one had been really worrying, her brain had been bleeding, and even when they thought they could save her and his mother had been sent to get a hot drink from the canteen, she was dying. When they had got home from the hospital, there was a towel on the floor of the bedroom; it was still damp from her early-morning shower. It is terrible how I forget about Elizabeth, and all I could do was put my hand on his knee and promise him that it would all be all right. I couldn't think of anything else to say.

A lot of people seemed to be heading away on holiday: cars

full of suitcases and sun umbrellas – life goes on. We play out our individual dramas but everything else goes on as normal, so I put the radio on and Zoe Ball twittered like a bird. Nigel didn't speak, he just chewed at the skin around his nails; he yells at Henry when he does that. I just sat there, checking I had the envelope with the name and address of the hospital, hating myself for having let them go, and hating Anna because it was all her fault that they'd gone. She had made it impossible for my children to stay in their own house. It was the way she'd behaved around them: smoking at the breakfast table with her dressing gown not done up properly, her uddery breasts lolling around. The way she'd laughed that time she sat down and her vagina made a loud squelchy noise; we could have all pretended not to have heard it but no, she had to make a fuss: 'Ha ha, fanny farts, Jo. Don't you just love them?' and she'd gone on about going to a yoga class, and every time the teacher had lifted her leg, 'Her fanny would fart like Japanese fire crackers.' Poor Henry, the female sex should be a mystery to him; he knows too young that we are leaky and smelly. Anna has demonstrated this to him: once, about a month ago, when she had thrush, she opened the fridge door, put her hand into a pot of natural yoghurt and dolloped a load into her knickers. Henry had been eating a poached egg but he put down his knife and fork and exited the room gagging.

I phoned home several times once we got on the motorway; she didn't reply, I didn't know what else I could do. Every breath I took was hard work, as if all my energy were being spent trying to get to my Georgina. There was a stone pressing on my heart and I wished for all the world I hadn't shouted at her so much this summer. All those stupid rows: the make-up, the belly button ring, the lies about the black boy – none of it mattered. I wanted to get to her and wrap her up and never let her go. Love is a terrible thing, it hurts you so much; there is so much terror in having a family.

Georgina had never been in hospital before; thinking about it, she has never been seriously ill. Once I had to take her to out-patients because she put a dried pea up her nose and my nails weren't long enough to pick it out, but nothing serious; she has never known pain. Pain to Georgina is double maths on a Friday afternoon and not being able to get the skirt she wants in the colour she wants. 'Fucking Top Shop,' she rants. Georgina cannot handle pain: when she started her periods, she went to bed for three days with a hot water bottle. Apart from a few coughs and colds, she is hardly ever ill and when she is, she is mostly faking it. Georgina's feeble 'Camille' impressions tend to coincide with French tests and cross-country runs. Henry, on the other hand, is constantly off school: he suffers with his sinuses, his teeth need constant attention and I have taken him on several occasions to see a skin specialist. Poor Henry – he has to try so hard, life seems out to get him: he has broken his arm, a toe and his wrist. It's funny, I mentioned Henry's wrist to Anna recently and she said, 'He probably broke it wanking.' I was so cross, it was such an unnecessary thing to say. Bitch, bitch, bitch! Calm down, Jo. My fingers were so tightly curled into my palms that I looked as if I had leprosy – calm down.

Gloria was killed in a road traffic accident and Elizabeth was found lying in the road; we cannot lose another member of the family that way, it wouldn't be fair. Lightning cannot strike the same house three times. I'd rather we all went together. How do families pick up the pieces after a child's death? Nigel's parents never have, I know that. For a moment I imagined Christmas Day without Georgina, without that slightly disappointed face that she pulls when she opens presents she never asked for. 'Bloody book tokens.' 'Oh Christ, not slippers.' Once I bought her some hankies with her initials on them, just for a laugh; her face was like thunder till she realised they were a joke. Right now, I would buy her every hair mascara in the world, I would go with her and hold her hand whilst she had her tongue pierced, as long as she lived to scowl and sneer and slam her bedroom door. I would not even care whether she ever got a single GCSE.

Occasionally you need to be reminded of how much you love your children. When this is over, I am going to put my family first. Anna can take a running jump; I am going to cut the Cunninghams out of my life like the warts I once had removed from my hands. I'd forgotten that. When I was about fifteen I had warts, big ones. We tried everything: painted them with yellow ointment, buried lumps of meat in the garden – hopeless. In the end, I had them cut out. I have never missed them. That's what it shall be like without the Cunninghams.

Last night already seemed so long ago.

65

Dinner in Devon

The Metcalfs arrived at the hospital in Totnes just after lunch; a speed camera had caught Nigel doing a hundred on the A385. So what?

Georgina was in the children's ward. There was a female clown entertaining some of the smaller ones at the other end of the room; a number of them were in tears and the clown seemed rather bad-tempered. 'Will you stop pissing around, just shut up.' The white and red of her clown make-up had smeared around her mouth so that she looked as if she had recently bitten the head off a small woodland animal. Georgina was in the corner bed by the door.

'You've got to get me out of here. I keep expecting Gaby

bleedin' Roslin to turn up,' was the first thing she said. It had only been mild concussion; Georgina was back to her normal, shallow, self-centred self. Her parents were relieved: if Georgina was well enough to be nasty, she was well enough to leave hospital. The doctors agreed and the nurses, if truth be told, were glad to see the back of her; the girl had been a nightmare ever since she'd come round, asking for Pret A Manger sandwiches, getting nail varnish on the sheets, phoning up the hospital DJ and calling him a wanker. 'Yes Mr and Mrs Metcalf, you may certainly take your daughter home.'

Angela Morris arrived at this point. She was very flustered and apologetic; she wouldn't hear of them driving straight back to London, they must come to The Orchards, have supper and stay the night. All Georgina's stuff was at the farmhouse anyway and, of course, Henry was there. Suddenly Jo wanted to see Henry very badly. 'Well, all right. But we don't want to put you to any trouble.'

'Honestly,' Angela replied, her face straining with sincerity, 'I feel so ghastly about this whole situation, it might make me feel better if I at least gave you something to eat.'

The Metcalfs followed the Morris's BMW. It took half an hour to reach The Orchards and during this time Jo and Nigel quizzed Georgina on how she had been enjoying the holiday.

'It's been a living hell. Angela Morris is a bossy cow and she doesn't believe in fancy biscuits, just ginger nuts for Christ's sake, I mean like . . . ginger nuts!' Georgina was sitting with her back against the left-hand rear passenger door, her legs stretched out along the seat. 'They had to cut my best jeans, Mum. I'm so pissed off.'

'Don't worry, love, we'll get some more jeans.' For the time being, Georgina was wearing a pair of Matthew's combat trousers.

'He's a bloody idiot, that Matthew. When he laughs he goes all red and sweaty – jerk.'

'What's the girl like?'

'Pain in the arse. Mum, I lost my mobile. Anyway it was a crap mobile – can I have one of those really little ones you can get the Internet on?'

'We'll see, dear.' Jo didn't really want to think about buying Georgina an expensive new mobile, but she caught Nigel winking at his daughter through the rear-view mirror; she could wind him round her little finger. Suddenly Jo felt tired; she had a headache. 'Did you get your phone line cancelled?'

'Oh yeah, Mum, like that's the first thing I thought about when I came out of my coma!'

'You weren't in a coma, love.'

'Like you'd care.'

'All right, let's just leave it.' This wasn't how it was meant to be.

At least the weather was good. Suddenly Angela Morris pulled off the main road on to a private track, and they bumped along until the farmhouse came into view. 'It's rather attractive,' Jo said, and suddenly Henry loomed into view; he looked taller. 'Mum, Dad,' and he threw down a tennis racket and ran to meet them, so that was a nice moment.

It is difficult arriving at someone's house when it's not yet appropriate to drink alcohol: three o'clock is too late for a lunchtime drink and too early for an evening snifter. They would just have to drink tea, eat ginger nuts and make polite conversation for a couple of hours.

'My husband will be coming home this evening. He has to pop to London for work, but he likes to get back for the weekend.' Nigel went out for a walk with the boys, Lucy drew felt-tipped cartoons on Georgina's cast, whilst Angela and Jo chatted in the kitchen. They gave each other potted biographies: Angela mentioned that The Orchards belonged to her parents but she didn't say that it was rented out most of the time; neither did she give Jo any inkling of what she really thought of Georgina. 'Such a pretty girl.' Jo dished a little dirt on Anna, but left out the gorier details. 'Just a terribly sad situation.' Four pots of Earl Grey tea later, Jo had owned up to her miscarriage and Angela had admitted to a teenage eating disorder. Jo liked Angela's uncompromisingly large bottom, stuffed into the unflattering khaki shorts and Angela liked the way Jo got up and started peeling potatoes when supper was mentioned. Together they listened to the Archers; neither of them cared much for Ruth. Then Jo asked if she could use the phone and Angela said, of course, it's in the sitting room.

Jo was surprised to find that she needed change to make a call, but she had a few twenty pences in her purse. She repeated her own number in her head. Dr drr, dr drr. Anna didn't answer; Jo's own voice echoed back at her, 'Sorry, there's no one in to take your call right now, please leave your name and number and we'll get back to you.' 'Anna, Anna, it's me, Jo. Where are you?' She tried several times and then she remembered Sue. It was a Friday, Sue would have been in to clean; she felt a bit guilty about the state they'd left the house. She dialled her number, Sue picked up the phone almost immediately; she lived in a very small flat, after all. 'Sue, it's Jo. Was Anna home when you did our place today?'

'I didn't.'

'Sorry?'

'I didn't go over today.'

'But it's Friday. Are you ill?'

The pips went; Jo stuffed another forty pence into the slot.

'She told me you were decorating – in no uncertain terms. You know what she's like, Mrs Metcalf, you can't argue with her. Where are you? Are you not home yourself?'

'No, we're in Devon.'

'Yes, of course. She said you were having a weekend away. Is it lovely where you are?'

Pip, Pip, Pip.

'Yes, Sue.' The line went dead. Jo felt a bit sick. What the hell was the silly witch playing at?

Angela was cooking a chicken. 'Mash or roast?' she asked.

'Um, roast.' Oh well, there was nothing she could do about it now.

Grant arrived home in a taxi from the station; he was very tall and bald.

'So what do you do, Grant?' Jo asked.

'I'm a gynaecologist,' he replied, as if it were quite a normal thing for a grown man to do: probing the fleshy inner recesses of strange women, while they lay back on paper sheets with their goose-bumped legs akimbo.

'Oh my goodness,' said Jo, wondering whether he could tell just by looking at her that she was due for a smear test.

Grant carved the chicken; he was very precise, almost gentle. Jo found herself wondering what he was like in bed. Physically the Morrises were the opposite of each other: Angela short and pug-like, Grant elongated and pointed as a greyhound. The children seemed nice: uncomplicated, heterosexual and without cunning. It was almost like being on holiday, though Jo couldn't get over the nagging Anna doubt, that vague feeling of disquiet, rather like when you go out for the day and you can't for the life of you remember if you closed the bathroom window. She excused herself a couple of times and tried phoning home again. It was no good, Anna either hadn't returned from her nocturnal prowlings or she just wasn't answering the phone. Why not? Jo had another glass of wine to stop worrying and found herself fascinated by Grant's long, white fingers pulling apart an orange. She really must have that smear; she was reaching an age where one had to be conscientious about these things. Maybe Grant checked out Angela himself, at home with a torch?

Jo realised she was in danger of drinking too much and fetched herself some water. She didn't want to get loose-lipped; she didn't want the whole Anna saga to come tumbling out. It was too exhausting. Nigel seemed to be enjoying himself; he had that puffed-up look of self-importance that men get when other men are genuinely interested in their work.

Grant and Nigel talked a lot; the only thing they didn't discuss was Grant's occupation, after all, they were eating. Privately Nigel was fascinated: how many different vaginas had this man seen? Did they all feel different? Were some massively bigger than others? How did the Orientals compare to, say, the Nigerians? What was the strangest thing he'd ever found up a fanny? Did he ever smell his fingers afterwards?

Nigel realised he had better join Jo on the water.

66

And Then

As soon as I'd finished my breakfast, I started feeling quite dreadful. I wouldn't have been surprised if I had a massive coronary. My heart felt as big as a cow's.

Maybe it was the fifth slice of toast that finished me off. I had the most appalling indigestion: burp, fart, pardon! Every time I belched I could smell the beans. I could hardly walk I was so full, but I was determined to have a bath, so I pulled myself up three flights of stairs, hanging on to the banister rail and puffing like an old train.

The weighing scales in Jo and Nigel's en suite dared me to see how much I weighed, but I knew the little dial would register something in the region of forty-two stone so I resisted the temptation. I turned on the taps and went to rummage in Jo's box file for her posh bubble bath. As I knelt down I farted dramatically. 'Oh, do excuse me, that was a ripe one.' As I farted, I wee-ed a bit. 'Oops.' The fancy bottle of Jo Malone amber and lavender bath oil with its little ribbon round the neck was nearly empty. 'Selfish pig.' I hoped Georgina had severe brain damage, serve the sly little seven-and-a-half-stone cunt right.

I'd had a glass of sherry with my eggy beany feast; it seemed a good idea at the time, now I wasn't so sure. My breakfast was threatening an encore and it was the last thing I wanted to see again. I lay down on the carpet, trying to get my breathing back in sync. I ended up crouching on all fours, sniffing the clean, just-polished leather of a pair of Nigel's shoes. I found it oddly soothing. Time for a bath, Anna – bath, then sleep, merciful sleep. My back was aching; I must have slept funny in that lumpy single bed and the only position I was comfortable in was with my arse in the air and my face in Nigel's shoes. Come on, woman, I kept thinking, got to get up, mustn't flood the house,

Jo's answerphone message echoed in my head: 'Be careful, don't do anything silly.'

Yes miss, no miss, three bags full miss.

Then I got hiccups – shit! Hic, I held my breath: in – one, two, three, four; out – two, hic, three, four – but it made me dizzy. The last time I'd felt this bad, I'd eaten a dodgy falafel; it was just like food poisoning. Oh great, trust me: salmonella egg, mad cow bacon, mouldy mushroom. My ribs heaved and I was a little bit icky in Nigel's shoe. One of the beans was unbroken; when I get really hungry, I have a tendency to swallow without chewing. It used to drive my mother mad. 'Chew, Anna, chew.' I eyeballed the shoe of sick for a bit, but then I forced myself to get up and I staggered into the bathroom and did a Fosbury flop into the tub. It was better in there; so full I could almost float, my big belly sticking out, full of booze and grub. I stayed in that bath until the water was cold and the thick grey colour of mushroom soup and then I hauled myself out and sat on the toilet wrapped in one of Jo's best towels.

I decided to sleep in her bed: it would be nice to get between clean sheets, the ones on my bed were discoloured and limp. I could be the lady of the house for a few days; later I would dial myself a pizza and eat it up here, where it was comfortable and nice to be. I wouldn't even get up if I didn't feel like it; I could read books and watch the telly, it would be like being on holiday. I could do with a break; my adventure had tired me out.

When I stood up from the toilet, loads of water gushed down my legs: that's what happens when you have a bath and you are my age, the water floods your fanny and ten minutes later it just falls out. The towel was sopping wet. As I bent down to pick up another towel, I got this pain low and deep in my belly and I let out a noise like an ox trying to get up on four broken legs.

I was sweating when the pain stopped, but my throat was still making funny noises. I was grunting really, it sounded ridiculous, but when I tried to stop grunting, I couldn't breathe. So I grunted my way over to Jo's bed and lay down with a pillow between my legs, trying to make my back feel more normal, wondering whether last night, when I'd been really pissed, I'd been run over, because that's what it felt like. I have had hangovers before, but nothing like this one. I reckoned a stroke would have been less debilitating. I supposed the pain in my back was my kidneys protesting; I imagined them inside, shrivelled and brown, like little cartoon Mexicans dying of thirst in the desert. I couldn't decide whether I needed to be sick or have a shit, my stomach was seizing up as if a great big hand were squeezing it from the inside in an attempt to wring out the alcohol. I had this terrible dragging sensation as if my bowels had turned to liquid concrete and I found myself on all fours again, biting a pillow that smelt faintly of Jo's hair.

All in all it was most peculiar, but I expected it to pass; that soon I would feel better, not worse. How wrong can you be? There was a Braun alarm clock on the bedside table; every time I looked at it, it seemed to be stuck on ten o'clock. This couldn't go on for ever – but it did: wave after wave of pain and nausea until suddenly, in a moment of lucidity, I realised that I was going to have a baby. It was 10.55am.

I got the wet towels out of the bathroom; there wasn't time for newspaper and I knew things were about to get gory. It was a shame that Jo's towels were pale yellow; black or navy would have been more practical. For some reason I thought I should boil a kettle, but I couldn't remember why; anyway, there was no way I could get down those stairs, although the thought of slipping and falling down several flights held some appeal. I ruled out phoning an ambulance; I didn't want to answer any stupid questions, I didn't want to tell strange men in green pyjamas my name. A baby, having a baby – what an odd thing to be doing on a sunny Saturday morning!

I knew now that I was having contractions, those steel bands that grip you round the middle and take your breath away. It was hard to get hold of anything; Jo's bed doesn't have a headboard, and I was flailing around like a whale with appendicitis.

In the brief minutes between the contractions, I couldn't believe what was going on; it was if I was outside my body looking down on this moaning bulk. I was forty-one; these things do not happen to forty-one-year-old women, they happen to fourteen-year-old girls in council houses whilst their mums sit downstairs watching soap operas. They happen in school toilets up and down the country, not in the respectable homes of middle-aged people.

It was embarrassing. I was very shocked and I did have a bit of a cry, partly because it was so painful, partly because I was on my own and very frightened, but mostly because it was so silly.

We carried on like that for what seemed like hours – because it was: hours and bloody hours, me and my other self, normal Anna and the pig in breech-birth, one doing the talking and the other rolling round and bellowing. 'I wonder what it will be?' said the talking sensible head. 'I don't care,' the other one spat. I'd ripped a hole in Jo's duvet and feathers were coming out. 'You need to put a stitch in that,' the sane me reprimanded – as if! Obviously not only was I in the throes of labour, I was going mad too. The room took on a new perspective and I kept catching glimpses of things I'd never normally notice: the veneer on the bedside table, a cobweb on the ceiling, the bubbles in the glass of stale water on the floor.

I knew it wasn't going to be Chris's child, I just knew it. I was landing jam side down this time; it was as if someone had pulled a plug and my reservoir of good luck had drained clean away.

You'd think you'd faint; it's incredible how much pain you can endure without passing out. I wanted very badly to faint, but I couldn't.

I tried to breathe the way they tell you to at those classes, but I was panicking too much. I heard myself shouting for my mum, which was most peculiar.

I wondered if anyone had ever attempted a DIY Caesarean. People are always having to perform tracheotomies on planes, aren't they? With penknives and biros. There was a pair of nail scissors on the dressing table, but I knew I was being silly, and when the time came I would just have to push. I didn't even know how pregnant I was; what if I went through all this and something the size of a Beanie Baby dropped out? I tried to stay calm; when the contractions came I focused on the key in the door of the wardrobe as I'd read that concentrating on one specific thing can help control the pain. Bollocks; what I really wanted was for someone to hit me over the head with a hammer and put me out of my misery. Labour is bad enough at the best of times, but you must remember that I was going through all this with a stinking hangover.

67

Oh, Anna

We set off back to London in the morning; Georgina was desperate to come home. She lay across the back of the Saab with her crutches in the boot. Angela had lent us a couple of pillows to make sure she was really comfortable, which was kind. The Morrises were going to hang on to Henry till the end of the summer holidays; I promised to phone him the moment his GCSE results came through. When he hugged me I realised that he was taller than me and I found it oddly comforting. I missed him before we reached the end of the drive. He seemed to have grown up: his spots were better and there was a shadow of a moustache on his upper lip. We stopped off at a newsagent in Totnes and bought Georgina a pile of magazines and she filled in quizzes and did pop crosswords all the way home. We even allowed her to listen to Radio 1; it was ghastly. The fashionability of loutishness and all those daft tunes sounding like babies in a playpen. I made her cross by singing ga gag goo goo over some of the sillier ones. We still hadn't had our little talk, the one about getting on strange boy's motorbikes; the moment seemed to have gone. I suppose having a fractured leg was punishment enough. Georgina always gets away with it.

We stopped at a Little Chef for some lunch, the waiter (male, seventeen) took pity on Georgina's crippled state and brought her a complimentary knickerbocker glory; she has always been rewarded for her naughtiness. What can a mother do? All the while the sun shone like a holiday brochure; England looked like she used to when she was a girl, but I felt like Chicken Licken: soon everything was going to come crashing down on my head. It was that Andrew's liver salts feeling, like the evening before my A-levels, the seconds before the first scan; I felt as if I was counting down the minutes before I found out if something dreadful had happened. My flesh shivered away from my bones and it was all I could do to stop my teeth from chattering.

I just wanted to sit in that car for ever, never getting home. I'd have been quite happy to have spent the rest of my life in some motorway limbo. Inevitably, the journey went quickly; I don't think we hit a single red light. One moment we were in Devon, and the next Peckham was beckoning us in with her nasty little nicotine finger. It was a shock to be back in London, even though it had only been just over twenty-four hours since we left; it was as if Devon had been a dream and we were back to smack-in-the-face reality. At last we slowed down; crawling through Earl's Court I saw a man wee against a wall, I saw a boy throw a bottle at a dog and I saw the fattest woman you have ever seen: a whale in orthopaedic shoes, her legs all blistered and raw. Georgina screamed when she saw her. We had emerged from a Constable idyll into something by Hieronymus Bosch. We crossed over Chelsea Bridge and turned right at Vauxhall; Nigel locked the car doors and I closed my window, it wasn't so much for security as to block out the smell. South London whiffed as high as rotting meat.

They had started digging up the end of our road; there was a hole and an empty mechanical digger, but no workmen in sight. Brenda Donahue was walking up the hill; I wound down my window and said, 'Hello.' Raymond turned around and as he did so, the red ice-lolly he was sucking came away from the stick and landed on the pavement and Brenda had to stop him picking it up and eating it. People had their windows open and a girl was trying to sunbathe perched on a narrow balcony, whilst a man lifted a bag of charcoal out of the boot of his car and shouted, 'Did you remember the sausages?'

There was a silver Renault parked outside our house, so Nigel found a space further up the hill. We got Georgina sorted out with her crutches and she limped magnificently down to ours. I had the keys; Nigel carried the bags. I undid the Chub and turned the Yale but the door wouldn't open; it had been bolted from the inside. 'Hurry up, Mum, I need the loo.' Georgina tried to cross her good leg over the broken one; she could have fallen. I told her to sit down on the wall while I shouted Anna's name through the letterbox. 'Anna, ANNA!' Nigel was all for smashing a window, but the wooden shutters were pulled to. Then I remembered I had a key to the basement; I only use that entrance when I've been to the supermarket – the freezer is down there so it makes sense. It was just rather difficult for Georgina to negotiate the steps; they're very uneven. 'You stay here, I'll run up and open the front door.' I said. I didn't want to go in the house by myself, which was silly because I am a big strong woman and if it was in the process of being burgled by teenage boys I was more than capable of killing them. But Nigel came with me anyway. The lock to the basement is rather rusty; we need some re-pointing doing, it's all rather damp down there. We squeezed past the freezer and I made a mental note to nip up to Sainsbury's; like the young couple down the road, I was rather hooked on the sausages idea. There was still enough time to save the day.

The kitchen was in a terrible state: a big bluebottle buzzed around a fatty pan and there were empty eggshells dotted around the work surface, she hadn't closed the fridge door and a milk bottle was sitting sourly on the draining board. A pair of Georgina's shoes lay on the floor; she was home then. Nigel went up to let Georgina in and I started clearing up. My breakfast things from the previous day were still on the table, the cereal set hard around the bowl, and the answer machine registered five messages. I pressed the play button out of habit and heard my own slightly hysterical voice; I wiped the tape clean. The toilet flushed and Nigel came down to put the kettle on and open the back doors to the garden. In the distance I heard thunder and within seconds the sky had turned a contaminated yellow. Nothing in the garden moved; everything seemed to be waiting.

'I think I might have a bath,' I said to Nigel. He was sitting on his haunches with his head in his hands. He reminded me of when Henry was little and didn't know how to play hide and seek; he thought that if he just stood there with his eyes shut I wouldn't be able to see him. 'I'll leave the water in for you.' He didn't reply. I went up the stairs; Georgina was already on the phone in the sitting-room, talking to one of her friends. 'You've got to come and see me, I've been so bored.' I kept walking. 'Mum, can

Lydia come and stay the night?' 'Yes dear.' Who the hell was Lydia?

The door to the spare bedroom was shut; that meant the pig was in her stye. I kept moving; I was tired and hot and sticky and my house had too many stairs. I am too old for all this, I thought, and then the smell hit me: like a butcher's on a hot day, like that nosebleed Henry had that time, like the dead fox we once found at the bottom of the garden. The door to our bedroom was also shut; I noticed the cream paint had cracked a little, the whole damn house needed doing up. I pushed the door open and wished that I hadn't.

She was sitting in the middle of our bed. One of the curtains had been pulled down and the chair on Nigel's side had been knocked to the floor. Then I saw the blood and feathers and I thought, so that's why she's been too busy to answer the phone, she's been up here sacrificing chickens! There was so much blood, all over the sheets, bedspread and carpet; her legs stretched out in front of her were streaked with it. It was as if she'd taken a man-sized piece of raw liver into bed with her and had rolled around with it. She was holding something in her arms; it was wrapped in a t-shirt. I walked closer to the bed – my feet made me. Little scraps of black hair tufted out of the bundle. Anna's breast was hanging free of Nigel's pyjama top. She looked up at me and smiled. 'I don't know what's wrong with this baby, Jo; he won't suck at all.'

I put out my arms and she handed him over. The baby was perfect; he just wasn't alive.

'Oh, Anna, what have you done?'

She put her hand over her mouth and giggled. 'I'm afraid I didn't know what to do with the placenta, so I put it in your hat. Then I hid it under the bed.' She was really laughing now.

I gave her back the little stiff baby and looked out of the window that overlooked the garden. Nigel was standing there in the rain. I knocked on the glass; he looked up and waved. Then I went downstairs. All the time I was thinking, I must phone the Lydia girl's mother and tell her that tonight won't be convenient after all.